Helen shivered and heard a small moan lift from her
mouth. Every cell in her body stood at attention from
that one little touch. Her skin grew warm and her abdo-

BURNING ALIVE

ALIVE

THE SENTINEL WARS

SHANNON K. BUTCHER

AN ONYX BOOK

ONYX
Published by New American Library, a division of
Penguin Group (USA) Inc., 375 Hudson Street,
New York, New York 10014, USA
Penguin Group (Canada), 90 Eglinton Avenue East, Suite 700, Toronto,
Ontario M4P 2Y3, Canada (a division of Pearson Penguin Canada Inc.)
Penguin Books Ltd., 80 Strand, London WC2R 0RL, England
Penguin Ireland, 25 St. Stephen's Green, Dublin 2,
Ireland (a division of Penguin Books Ltd.)
Penguin Group (Australia), 250 Camberwell Road, Camberwell, Victoria 3124,
Australia (a division of Pearson Australia Group Pty. Ltd.)
Penguin Books India Pvt. Ltd., 11 Community Centre, Panchsheel Park,
New Delhi – 110 017, India
Penguin Group (NZ), 67 Apollo Drive, Rosedale, North Shore 0632,
New Zealand (a division of Pearson New Zealand Ltd.)
Penguin Books (South Africa) (Pty.) Ltd., 24 Sturdee Avenue,
Rosebank, Johannesburg 2196, South Africa

Penguin Books Ltd., Registered Offices:
80 Strand, London WC2R 0RL, England

First published by Onyx, an imprint of New American Library,
a division of Penguin Group (USA) Inc.

First Printing, May 2009
10 9 8 7 6 5 4 3

 REGISTERED TRADEMARK — MARCA REGISTRADA

Printed in the United States of America

PUBLISHER'S NOTE
This is a work of fiction. Names, characters, places, and incidents either are the
product of the author's imagination or are used fictitiously, and any resemblance
to actual persons, living or dead, business establishments, events, or locales is
entirely coincidental.

The publisher does not have any control over and does not assume any responsibility for author or third-party Web sites or their content.

For gamer nerds everywhere, especially those who grace our dining room table every Friday night. Stay out of tentacle range!

Acknowledgments

Thanks and hugs to Belles: Sara Attebury, Dyann Barr, Julie Fedynich, Sherry Foley, Liz Lafferty, and the newest Belle, Claire Ashgrove. Your ongoing support and boundless enthusiasm for this series are priceless.

I had the privilege of having two editors for this book, and I want to thank both Anne Bohner and Cindy Hwang, as well as my agent, Nephele Tempest, for their help on this project.

And finally, a big thank-you goes out to my beta readers, who keep me on my toes: Jayne L., Karen L., Pollyanna L., Cindy N., and Pricilla S.

Chapter 1

June 27, Olathe, Kansas

The man who was going to stand by and watch while Helen burned to death liked his coffee black.

Helen looked up from her menu and, across the little diner, she saw him sitting there, not twenty feet away. He was the man of her dreams—or more accurately, of her visions. Technically it was just one vision. Over and over. She was going up in flames while he watched. Smiling at her.

"See something you like?" asked Lexi, the diner's only waitress on duty. She'd been working at Gertie's Diner for only a couple of months now, but there was something about her that made Helen trust her enough to share things no other living person knew, including Helen's vision of her own death. "Cook's gone for the day, so all we have left is meat loaf, baked chicken, and pot roast. Pick your poison."

Across from Helen, her dinner companion, Miss Mabel, sat low in the red vinyl booth. Her age-hunched shoulders barely cleared the table. Her gnarled hands gripped the laminated menu, which wavered so much Helen wasn't sure how she could read it without getting motion sickness.

"How's the meat loaf?" asked Miss Mabel.

Lexi was a petite twenty-something with a killer body and a brain to match. What she was doing waiting tables in Olathe, Kansas, living in her car, was a total mystery to Helen—one Lexi refused to solve no matter how many times Helen asked. She'd offered to let Lexi stay with her until she found a place, but Lexi said she wouldn't bring trouble to Helen's doorstep when she clearly had enough of her own.

Lexi leaned down until her short, white-blond spikes threatened to poke Miss Mabel in the eye. "You'd be safer eating two-day-old roadkill, which is what I'm guessing Paulo used to make the meat loaf. He left early when I started asking questions about it. Smart man."

Miss Mabel blanched a little. "Definitely no meat loaf. I'll take the pot roast."

Lexi winked and wrote it down on her pad of order slips. "How 'bout you, Helen? What can I get you today?"

Helen tried to focus on her menu as she held it up to shield her face so Vision Man couldn't see her. Her hands trembled, making the words blur. She was already on the verge of panic. If he caught her watching him, she was sure she'd lose it completely.

Helen wanted to scream at Lexi to throw the pot of scalding coffee into his lap and run away. Instead, she fought her rising panic for a chance to learn something about him in the hope of escaping the vision. She sank lower in her seat and tried to pretend that everything was fine, which she did with flying colors. Helen had a lot of practice at pretending everything was fine.

"I'm not sure," said Helen to stall for more time, hoping her hands would stop shaking so hard she could read the menu. Against her better judgment, she eased the menu aside so she could take a quick peek. Maybe she'd imagined it was him.

Nope. It was Vision Man. In the flesh.

He listened to what one of the men sitting across from him was saying while he sipped his coffee. One thick arm was sprawled out across the back of the booth and she could see some sort of tattoo peeking out from under Vision Man's T-shirt sleeve. Strands of hair, maybe? Vines? She couldn't be sure at this distance and she didn't think staring long enough to figure it out was a smart move. She did not want him to notice her staring. She didn't want him to notice her, period.

He had thick brown hair that was just getting long enough to show off a bit of curl. And that was the only thing about him that looked soft. He had high, almost sharp cheekbones with deep hollows beneath. His mouth was pressed into a hard, flat line as he listened to his friend, his expression grim, almost angry. The muscles in his jaw bunched as if he was grinding his teeth, and Helen had the distinct impression that he was in pain. Lots of pain.

Good. It served him right for watching her die. Not that he'd committed that particular crime yet, but he would. She knew it like she knew the sun would set in a few minutes. There was nothing fake or distorted about her vision. She'd tried for years to find some flaw, some speck of doubt that what she saw was real. Tried and failed. And now she knew that her time was nearly up. The man in her vision was this man, not an older version of him.

Helen was going to die soon. Maybe tonight.

Grief and fear swelled up in her chest and she fought them down. Focused on her breathing and relaxing each little muscle starting at her fingertips. She'd learned the technique from her therapist, who was convinced she was suffering from some sort of delusion. All she had to do was face it and it would go away. Well, she was facing it now and it wasn't going anywhere. Fifty thousand dollars and many years later, she was still just as deluded, but at least she could keep the fear at bay. Breathing and relaxing was the only way she knew to control the panic. The only way to keep herself from screaming in terror.

Burning alive. What a fucking gruesome fate.

She'd tried to prepare herself for this, but she'd obviously failed. It was too soon. She wasn't ready to die yet. There was still so much work left to be done. So many people who needed her help.

"You okay?" asked Lexi, her pale forehead puckering with a frown. She glanced over her shoulder to where Helen kept trying not to look. Vision Man and two others sat drinking coffee and eating pie as though they had all the time in the world. Man, wouldn't that be nice.

"Those guys bothering you?" asked Lexi, sounding more worried from Helen's lack of response.

"Uh, no." Just breathe. That's all she had to do. Breathe in. Breathe out. "I'll have the pot roast, too."

Lexi turned back around. "Now I know something's wrong. You never eat red meat."

"Yeah, well, you can't live forever," said Helen.

Lexi's petite body stilled and Helen could almost hear the wheels in her head turn. "Holy shit! That's him, isn't it?" asked Lexi in a near whisper.

Helen wished for the millionth time that she'd just kept her mouth shut, or that Lexi wasn't quite so intuitive. Lexi should have been a bartender or an interrogator instead of a waitress, the way she was able to get a woman to spill her guts.

Miss Mabel's scarlet lips turned down in a disapproving frown. "I thought I'd quit hearing talk like that when I retired from teaching high school."

"Sorry, Miss Mabel," said Lexi, patting the older woman's hand. "Pie's on me tonight as payment for my potty mouth."

"Forget the pie, tell me about the man." Miss Mabel twisted her bent body around in her seat so she could see where Lexi had been looking. Not that the men were hard to spot, seeing as how they were the only other customers in the diner tonight—well after the dinner rush.

Helen felt a frantic bubble of fear rise up inside her. "Don't look!"

"You never told me you had a boyfriend," said Miss Mabel as if it was the crime of the century—a huge betrayal of their friendship that she'd kept a secret.

"He's not my boyfriend. Stop looking!" She was begging, on the verge of panic. What if he noticed them looking? What if he walked over here right now and looked at her with that half smile on his face—the one he wore when he watched her die? This could be her last few minutes on earth and the only solace she could find was that her will was updated and all the money she'd inherited from her mother would go to help pediatric burn victims.

Lexi—bless her—shifted her slim hips so that they were between the men and Miss Mabel's wide, obvious gaze. Helen knew that if the men did bother to look over here, one glance at Lexi's ass would be enough distraction for any red-blooded man to forget what he'd just been thinking.

Miss Mabel struggled to get her frail spine to cooperate, but couldn't manage to outmaneuver Lexi—not with her waitress reflexes. The old woman gave a frustrated sigh. "You either tell me what's going on or I get my walker and go over there and find out for myself."

Lexi gave Helen an apologetic grimace. "I should have kept my mouth shut. If you want, I'll kick them out."

"That wouldn't really help the whole trying-not-to-get-noticed thing I'm working on here," said Helen.

"Why don't you want those men to notice you? Are they stalkers? Should I call the police?" asked Miss Mabel. "I knew I should have bought one of those cell phones."

"No," said Helen, trying to think fast enough to outwit a woman who had taught public school for thirty years. "He's just a guy I have a crush on. I don't want him to know."

"Why not? You're a lovely girl and you should just go right over there and ask him out. That is how it's done these days, and if I'm not too old to know that, then neither are you."

"I can't do that." Helen slid down deeper in the booth seat and lifted the menu up to shield her face again.

"Well, then, I will. You need a man, Helen. I'm not going to let you end up old and childless like me." And with that declaration, Miss Mabel reached for her walker at the end of the booth, positioning it so she could stand.

Helen had to get Miss Mabel to stop before Vision Man saw her. Maybe if Helen got out of here unnoticed, there would still be time before she died. Even if it was only a few more days, or even hours, Helen wanted every one of them.

"You can't. He's married." The lie slipped out so smoothly it surprised Helen. It was the first time in her life she'd ever lied to a teacher, and already her stomach was turning sour.

Miss Mabel's head whipped around faster than Helen would have thought possible, considering her frail neck and the weight of the giant bun she wore held up by a single yellow number-two pencil. "You're lusting after a *married man*?" She whispered it as if just saying the words was a sin. "Oh, honey, don't you know that can only end badly?"

Thank you, God. Miss Mabel swallowed the lie. "I know," said Helen, hanging her head, still strategically placed behind the menu. "That's why I'm staying away from him. I can't help the way I feel about him, but I can keep my distance."

"See that you do," said Miss Mabel, slipping into her lecturing voice. "Maybe we should just go now and have dinner elsewhere."

Hallelujah! "Good idea. We can go anywhere you like," Helen told Miss Mabel. They always went out to eat on Tuesday night, and Helen couldn't stand to disappoint her, not even if her world was spiraling toward its end. She'd spent the past ten years trying to do something meaningful with her life. She wasn't smart enough to find a cure for cancer and she wasn't strong enough to join the military or brave enough to join the police or firefighters, but she made a difference to a few dozen shut-ins, bringing them food and company or just getting them out of the house for a few hours. It wasn't much to her, but it was to them. She saw it in their eyes every time she showed up at their front doors and every time she left. For some of those people, she was all they had and that was enough for her. It had to be.

"I think it's too late to escape," said Lexi. "He's looking this way."

Helen lowered the menu enough to peek over it and

sure enough, Lexi was right. Vision Man was looking right at her.

Drake saw the pretty young woman trying to hide from him. Under normal circumstances, he wouldn't have looked twice at a human—pretty or not—but something about her tugged at his attention. Every time he looked at her, some of the grinding pressure inside him eased. The fact that she was trying not to get noticed only added to his curiosity.

"Have either of you ever seen the woman with the braids before?" he asked his buddies, Thomas and Zach.

Thomas swiveled his head around, leaning so he could see past Zach. He shrugged one massive shoulder. "Not that I can remember."

"Sorry, man," said Zach, an appreciative grin on his dark face.

"You're looking at the waitress," scolded Drake.

"Yes, I am."

Unapologetic as ever, Zach rubbed a hand over his jaw and watched the waitress with the name tag that read LEXI wiggle her behind.

Drake thought about calling Zach on how easily he was distracted, but he knew it wouldn't do any good. Besides, nothing important ever got by Zach. He could look at all the women he wanted and if things went to hell, he'd still have his sword in his hand faster than any of the three men at the table. Which was good, considering their mission.

He, Zach, and Thomas were hot on the trail of the Synestryn demons that had taken Kevin's sword after they'd slaughtered him, and the last thing he needed right now was a distraction. This suburban Kansas town was crawling with demons. Literally. Or at least it would be once the sun set.

Drake checked his watch. Eight thirty-two. Nine minutes to sunset. Then Logan would show up and they all could get back to work. That left him eight minutes to figure out who this woman was and why she was hiding from him.

Drake got up and went to do just that.

The waitress stepped in his path as if she could actually stop him. How cute. He doubted there was a whole five feet of her unless he included those ridiculous blond spikes sticking out from her head.

"Can I get you some more coffee?" she asked with a cheerful, fake smile.

"No. My friends could use a refill, though." Zach had been eyeing the waitress all night, and as far as Drake was concerned, he could have her. She was just a little scrap of a woman—too fragile for any of the really fun stuff.

The shy brunette on the other hand . . . she had potential. He'd seen her come into the diner with the old lady, being so careful to help her walk without damaging the older woman's pride. She was all soft curves and glowing warmth. Her light brown hair fell forward over her shoulders in twin braids, drawing his eye right to her breasts. As if he needed any help finding those. She filled out her tank top and then some, which he dutifully noticed. She was a couple of inches taller than average, and all that extra height was in her legs—long, curvy, bare under the cuffs of her khaki shorts. All of her was curvy and soft and feminine and Drake hated that he'd noticed.

He had more important things to think about—like killing off a slew of demons—and it was hard enough to keep his focus on his work when the pain was getting worse every day. He sure as hell didn't need some soft, curvy distraction.

The waitress hadn't taken the hint and she was still barring his path. Not a good idea considering he never let anything get in the way of something he wanted—certainly not something that weighed about as much as a week's worth of laundry.

"How 'bout some more pie?" she asked.

"No, thanks." He picked her up under her arms, like a child, and set her aside.

"Hey!" he heard her sputter behind him, and almost expected her to jump on his back.

"I got her," said Zach, his voice deep and satisfied with the task of keeping Lexi at bay.

Drake glanced over his shoulder and saw the waitress staring at Zach as if he were about to eat her whole. Maybe he was. Zach was into human women. As often as possible.

Drake felt a half smile tug at his mouth. "I just bet you do."

The brunette had given up hiding behind the menu and had started to gather her purse and sunglasses to leave. Not bloody likely. At least not until he was ready to let her leave.

Drake covered the distance between them and placed one hand on the back of the booth and the other on the table, caging her in. She'd scooted to the edge of the seat, but with Drake standing in her path, she had nowhere to go. He leaned down, letting her know with his body language that she was trapped.

He liked her face, the smooth curve of her cheek, the fullness of her mouth. She'd stayed out in the sun too long today and her nose and the top of her cheeks were pink. She wasn't drop-dead gorgeous, but she was lovely. From here, it was easy to see fear brighten her hazel eyes, bringing out chips of gold and green.

She was afraid of him. He had no idea why, and he sure as hell didn't like it.

"Please let me go," she said. Her voice was quiet. Soft, like the rest of her, and it stroked over his senses like a caress.

A weightless warmth shimmered through him, washing away decades of tension and torment. For the first time in more than a century, Drake was no longer in agonizing pain. He let out a slow breath of relief. The ever-expanding pressure of the power he housed no longer beat at his insides, seeking an exit, trying to pound its way through flesh and bone. Every rioting bit of energy inside him quieted at the sound of her voice as if listening.

Without the pain that had been his constant companion for more years than most people lived, a wave of dizzying relief threatened to buckle his knees. He gripped the seat and table to keep himself upright, but he couldn't keep his eyes from closing, just for a moment. The joy of simply not hurting was so intense it was nearly its own kind of pain. He wasn't sure how long it took him to regain his senses, but when he did, she was staring at him, wide eyed and trembling.

"Who are you?" he demanded.

She blinked twice as if shocked by the question. "Please. Just let me go. I don't want to die."

Die? What the hell? "I'm not going to hurt you," he told her, his tone a little more gruff than he'd intended. He'd spent his too-long life defending humans from the Synestryn at great personal cost. There was no way she could have known that, but it still pissed him off that she would jump to the conclusion that he was here to hurt her.

What he really wanted was to touch her and see if she felt as soft as she looked. All those smooth, womanly curves were driving him a little crazy. And crazy was the only explanation for what he was feeling—this uncontrollable need to touch a woman he didn't even know. A human woman. Maybe she was blooded—a descendant of the Solarc—and that's why his reaction to her was so strong. He'd never experienced anything like it before even with a blooded human, and he wasn't entirely sure he liked it. The pain-free part was nice, really nice, but nothing that good came without a price.

"I need to get Miss Mabel home. It's getting late." Her mouth quivered a bit and damn if he didn't want to bend down and kiss her to make it stop.

This was insane. Drake pulled in a deep, steadying breath, but only managed to fill his lungs with her scent. Lilacs. She smelled like lilacs.

Drake didn't have a freaking chance of resisting her. He was a goner, completely over-the-edge insane. He leaned down until his nose was tucked into the curve of her neck, and breathed her in. There was nothing he could have done to stop himself, and the fact that she didn't flinch away only made him that much crazier.

The silky strands of her braid teased his nose and the supple band of the luceria around his neck hummed happily, sending a shiver shooting down his back. He felt something shift inside him. Deep and hard, almost painful. This woman had changed him somehow, with her mere presence, and he would never be the same again.

Whoever she was, he was keeping her.

*   *   *

Helen didn't dare move. Not with Vision Man standing so close, nearly touching her. She felt his warm breath spread out over her neck, swirl up around her ear.

He was purring—a low, deep sound of satisfaction—and that purr resonated inside her.

All she could see was the side of his thick neck where it joined his shoulder, the curl of his dark hair, and a section of the necklace he wore—some sort of iridescent choker about a quarter inch wide. Every color imaginable swirled inside the supple band as the lights of the diner played off its surface. She felt the urge to touch it to see if it was as slippery as it looked, if it was warm from his skin.

Instead, she hugged her purse more tightly against her chest, holding still, praying he'd move away from her before she lost her head and stroked her finger over the band.

She was breathing too fast, making herself dizzy. She closed her eyes to block out the sight of him so she could calm herself, but instead the vision flashed in her head, driving everything else away.

He was standing a few feet away. It was dark all around them and the only reason she could even see his face was that the fire that consumed her body reflected off the sharp angles of his cheeks, the shadowed ledge of his jaw, the strong tendons in his neck, the wide span of his shoulders. Mirrored flames danced in his golden brown eyes and a proud half smile tilted his mouth. She could smell her flesh burning, could feel the heat consume her. The pain of her blistered skin as it blackened was too much to bear. She screamed, begging death to come claim her.

Reality snapped back into place, washing the vision away. Helen sucked in a desperate breath. She wasn't dead. At least not yet. The bright lights of the diner seared her retinas, and the smell of burning flesh was replaced by that of onions and french fries. A draft from the air vent overhead cooled her skin, making her shiver.

She forced her body to relax, to remember where she was. *Just breathe*.

Her lungs expanded, pulling in the scent of the man who had her trapped. Soap. Coffee. Clean male skin. He smelled nice. Safe. And if that wasn't the most ridiculous thing she'd ever thought, then she didn't know what was. If there was one person on the planet who wasn't safe for her to be near, it was him, no matter how he smelled.

He was still only a scant inch away, giving off that low purr that resonated in her chest. Helen wasn't sure if she wanted to push him away or stroke her finger over the intriguing curve of that choker he wore. Something about it tugged at her memories, though she was sure she'd never seen anything like it before.

He hadn't been wearing it in her vision. The realization dawned on her. His throat had been bare. His shirt had been different—not the black cotton he wore now, but lighter. Tan. With some kind of tree printed on it.

The details of her vision didn't match what was happening right now, which meant she was safe, at least for the moment.

Some of the panic drained out of her, making her feel weak, boneless. She knew she should push him away or scream or do something. Even if he wasn't here to watch her die tonight, he was still too damn close.

He leaned a fraction of an inch closer and wrapped his long fingers around one of her braids. On his finger he wore a ring that matched his necklace and it flashed in an intriguing pattern of swirling colors that made her want to stare. An insistent tug on her braid tipped her head back and she was sure she'd felt his lips brush along her neck, her cheek.

Helen shivered and heard a small moan lift from her mouth. Every cell in her body stood at attention from that one little touch. Her skin grew warm and her abdomen tightened against a jolt of heat. She wanted something she couldn't name. Needed it. It wasn't just desire. It went deeper than that. Bone deep. Soul deep. He had something that belonged to her and she wanted it. Even if it killed her.

His lips slid over her cheek, barely touching. Maybe not even touching, just stirring the fine hairs along her skin. Whatever he was doing, it was wonderful, fear or not. She felt as if she was being filled up with energy. She felt more alive than she ever had before. All from a barely there touch from the man who would watch her die.

Freaking irony.

From somewhere far off, Drake heard the old woman gasp in shock and he struggled to pull himself back to reality. By the time he'd made the long, long journey to the here-and-now, his fingers had wrapped themselves around one of the brunette's braids so that her head was tilted back to the optimum angle for a slow, deep kiss. Perfect.

He would have done just that if it hadn't been for the way she was clutching her purse against her chest like a shield. She was still afraid of him. *Shit.*

"Give me your name," he ordered her, not caring how rough his voice sounded. He needed her name. Hell, he needed a lot more of her than just that, but with the audience they had, he was going to have to settle for that small piece.

"Helen Day."

God, he loved the sound of her voice, so soft and sweet. He closed his eyes again, letting the sound of her, the smell of her, sink into him. He could spend half a year just listening to her talk, letting the gentle sweep of her voice soothe him.

He was way too wrapped up in how he could make the small space between them even smaller when he heard a warning shout from Thomas half a second too late. Miss Mabel's walker slammed down over his head, sending pain screaming over his skull.

"Go back to your wife, you ... you man-whore!" shouted the old woman, raising her walker for another strike.

Whore? *Wife?* Drake had no idea what she was talking about, but he didn't stand there long enough to ask. He could already feel a lump swelling up on the back of his skull. The old woman might look frail, but she packed one heck of a wallop.

Drake reached for Miss Mabel, intending to carefully take the aluminum weapon from her hands before she hurt herself. Or him.

He was too late. Thomas was already on the case and had taken the old lady into his burly arms, holding her carefully despite her struggles.

Helen stood up, pushing her way around Drake to get to the old lady. "Let her go!"

Thomas ignored her, still holding on to the old woman, trying to calm her down with soothing words. "I'm not going to hurt you, ma'am. None of us are going to hurt any of you. Isn't that right, Zach?"

Five feet away, Zach had Lexi pinned against the

countertop by the cash register, nearly bent over backward. She was fighting him, pounding and clawing at
him, but Zach accepted her blows, grinning like they
tickled.

"Hey, she's the one trying to hurt me. I just want to
talk." Zach's voice dipped lower and his grin widened.
"But I'm willing to play if you want, honey. I don't mind
if you like it rough."

Lexi growled and lashed out at Zach with her fists.

From the corner of his eye, Drake saw Helen start to
make a dash toward Thomas and the old woman, but
Drake was faster. He snagged her by looping an arm
around her waist and pulling her up against his chest. It
was a mistake. As soon as he had her soft, curvy body
against his, his brain started to shut down. From a vague,
fuzzy distance, he could feel her fighting to free herself,
pushing and pulling at his arm. He could hear her frightened voice calling her friends' names. He could sense
the panic inside her, the frantic strength that increased
with every swift beat of her heart. He just couldn't seem
to figure out what it all meant or what he should do. All
he knew was he couldn't let her go. He needed her.

This whole situation had gone completely out of control, but he just didn't care. He had Helen in his arms,
reluctant as she was, and he didn't hurt anymore. For the
first time in decades, he felt *good*. It was such a shock
that it left him reeling, staring stupidly at the part between her silky, dark braids. He wanted to bend down
and kiss the smooth skin at the nape of her neck so bad
it made him shake.

Drake had bent to do just that when his grip failed
and Helen slipped out of his grasp.

Pain slammed into him with a tangible force that
drove him to his knees right there on the chipped tile

floor. Power flooded him and ripped through his veins, hammering his bones with pounding agony. He was sure every one of them had been broken, that his organs had been pulverized. Nothing else could explain so much pain. He couldn't stand. Couldn't see. Couldn't breathe.

The power he housed inside his body had grown slowly, steadily, over the course of years. The pressure had increased over decades, giving him a chance to get used to the pain it caused. But now it all came flooding back inside him in the space of an instant and his brain couldn't adjust. His body couldn't function. At the gray edges of his mind, he heard himself scream, a terrible, high-pitched noise. He knew he was dying, but right now that was a good thing. It would all be over soon, but it couldn't be soon enough.

Helen wasn't sure what she'd done to Vision Man to send him to his knees, but she didn't stop to worry about it. Miss Mabel was still trying to get away from the big bruiser who held her, and it looked as though she was running out of steam.

Lexi, on the other hand, was holding her own against the third man. He'd pushed her down so that she was almost lying on the counter near the cash register. "Stop fighting me before you hurt yourself," he told her.

Lexi knocked the toothpick dispenser to the floor, making it spew toothpicks everywhere. She got one knee between them and pushed, but it didn't work.

The man simply pressed his body down harder onto hers until she had no room to maneuver. "Are you done yet?"

Her hand fumbled over the counter until she found the metal stand used to collect order tickets and jammed the sharp spike into her captor's arm.

He looked down at the metal sticking out of his skin and smiled. Actually smiled. "Good shot, woman." He sounded as if he was proud of Lexi, which was completely insane, but at least Lexi was still able to fight.

Miss Mabel wasn't, and Helen wasn't sure how she was going to get her free. The man who held her was huge. Tall, wide, muscular. He probably outweighed her and Miss Mabel put together.

"Let her go," demanded Helen, racking her brain for what to do now. Pick up a chair and hit him? No, she might hit Miss Mabel. Throw a sugar shaker at his head? She might be able to hit him without hitting her friend.

Helen was out of ideas, so she went with the best one she had. She grabbed for the closest sugar shaker, but before she could throw it, the giant stepped forward and simply handed Miss Mabel to Helen. She wasn't sure what had changed his mind, but she didn't question her good fortune. She gladly took over the job of supporting Miss Mabel. He was careful with her frail body, gentle. He took his time making the transfer and then when she was clear, he shot to the floor, where Vision Man was writhing.

"Zach!" he shouted. "Need a little help here with Drake when you're done playing with the girl."

The man who had pinned Lexi—Zach—let her go, ripped the spike out of his arm, and set it back on the counter, bloody tickets still in place. Lexi had barely regained her feet before he was also at Vision Man's side. Zach turned to Helen, glaring at her. His pale green eyes stood out in stark contrast against his brown skin, almost looking as if they were lit from within. "What did you do to Drake?"

Helen held Miss Mabel a little tighter, turning her toward the exit. They were getting out of here as fast as possible. "Nothing. He was the one attacking *me*."

"He didn't do anything more than try to talk to you. You were the one who freaked out. What did you do to him?" he demanded.

Vision Man—Drake, they'd called him—was still convulsing on the floor, his body bowing in a powerful arc. He'd been screaming a moment ago, but now he made these horrible choking sounds, as though he couldn't breathe. The veins in his neck and temples stood out and something odd was happening to the shimmery choker he wore. The colors in it were seething, swirling in a mix of reds, oranges, and yellows. Thin tendrils of smoke drifted up from the necklace and a matching ring on his left hand. Helen could smell the scent of burning flesh—just like in her vision.

The man who had held Miss Mabel checked his watch, his expression grim. "Three minutes until sunset. Logan isn't going to make it in time to save him."

Zach stood up and took a step toward Helen. Lexi had recovered her mobility and found a giant knife somewhere behind the counter. And she held it like she knew what she was doing.

Could this night get any weirder?

Zach must have seen Lexi moving toward him, because he turned and pointed a thick finger in her direction. "Stay out of this. It doesn't concern you."

"The hell it doesn't. They're my friends."

"And Drake is mine." Zach turned to Helen. "Let the old woman go and come here." It wasn't a request and Helen was certain that if she didn't do as he said, someone was going to get hurt when he *made* her do it, probably Miss Mabel.

This was it. Helen was fairly certain that she'd reached the end of the line. She wasn't about to take Miss Mabel with her, so she settled the frail woman down on a seat and gave her what she hoped was a brave smile.

Miss Mabel clutched Helen's arm with weak, gnarled fingers. "Don't go, honey."

"I'll be fine," she lied. Helen turned back toward Zach and took a step forward.

The big guy was holding Drake down so he didn't hurt himself thrashing around, but it didn't look like an easy job. Drake was strong—his arms and legs thick with muscle. She could see all that strength tighten his body against the convulsions. The big guy took an elbow in the stomach for his effort, letting out a pained grunt. Zach had a hold on Drake's legs, but he didn't take his eyes off Helen. She was sure that if she didn't keep moving toward him he'd come for her.

Man, she didn't want to be here right now. She didn't want to be in the middle of this mess, completely confused as to what was happening and totally freaked out to be getting closer to a man who made her feel better with an almost touch than all the real touches from all the other men in her life put together.

"He's going to be fine," she told them, taking another half step forward.

"How do you know?" asked Zach.

Great. Now she'd gone and backed herself in a corner. She couldn't exactly tell them that she knew he'd be fine because he had to live long enough to watch *her* die. "I just do."

Another half step and she was close enough that Zach reached out his long arm and grabbed her by the wrist. "Whatever you did, undo it."

"I didn't do anything! I swear. All I did was push his arm away and he fell over."

Zach's heavy brow wrinkled for a second; then those pale green eyes of his went wide as if he'd just figured out what had gone wrong. "Come here," he demanded, tugging her down to the floor until her hand was pressed flat against Drake's stomach—his bare, hard, warm stomach that should have been completely covered by his T-shirt, but wasn't. All that writhing had worked it up over his ribs and she could see half of a large tattoo running up over his left side. It was a tree, inked in lifelike colors and perfect detail. Every swirled knothole, every twist of the tree's roots were so realistic she was sure she could almost feel the rough texture of the bark beneath her fingertips. Fine tendrils of roots spread down over his stomach and disappeared beneath the belt on his jeans. She refused to think about where they led.

Her fingers touched his skin, and it didn't take two full seconds for Drake to relax. Both men looked at her in shock, then looked at each other, sharing some secret guy-speak. She had no clue what was going on, and at this point she wasn't sure she wanted to know. All she wanted was to take Miss Mabel back home and crawl into a deep, hot bath for about a week. She was fairly certain she couldn't burn alive in a bathtub, and it was the only time she ever truly relaxed.

"You're coming with us," said the big guy. His bright blue eyes scanned Drake's body, concern pulling at his brows.

"No, I'm not," said Helen.

Zach let go of Helen's wrist and stood up. She should have pulled away and headed for the door, but something stopped her. Something was happening beneath her hand. Drake's skin heated and she was flooded with that odd rush of energy she'd felt before. It filled her up inside, like a warm light, finding all the cold, dark little cracks and holes inside her. There was a faint buzzing sensation and the taste of honey in her mouth, the smell of rain in her nose. She felt light. Buoyant.

This wasn't right. It felt incredibly good, but it wasn't right. This wasn't supposed to happen. Couldn't be real.

She started to pull her fingers away, but Drake's hand caught hers before she finished lifting them from his skin. His fingers wrapped around her wrist and she could feel that disturbing hum of energy sinking into her where each of his lean fingers met her skin.

He sat up, looking alert and coherent, and she felt the soft knit of his shirt pool against her wrist. He held her hand in place and leaned forward until there was barely two inches between them. "I'm not letting you get away again. Not until we figure out what this thing between us is."

It was a vow. She could feel the power of it settle around the two of them, shutting out the rest of the world.

This wasn't real. This wasn't happening. A lot of strange things had happened to her throughout her life, but this was way off the weird chart. "There is no *thing* between us."

He gave her that half smile from her vision. "There is now."

Behind him, just inside the window that led to the diner's kitchen, orange flames erupted, spewing up like a geyser.

Fire. The smell of burning skin.

Helen's world collapsed down to a pinpoint of panic she couldn't escape. It sucked her in and robbed her of oxygen. She couldn't even remember how to breathe.

Chapter 2

Zach liked a little spice in his women, but this was ridiculous. He'd seen the sexy little waitress sneak around the counter with that knife. After the stunt she'd pulled with that damn skewer, Zach didn't doubt for a second that she'd use it. He knew she would. The trickle of blood running down his arm was proof of that.

"You wanna play, little girl?" Zach asked her, stalking closer. She was so damn beautiful he just wanted to eat her up. Her big brown eyes were dark, like bittersweet chocolate, which he guessed fit her personality well. She'd been all sugar and smiles when she'd taken their order and brought them their dinner, but as soon as she thought her friends were in danger, all that sugar had blown away, leaving the real woman behind. Ferocious. Lovely. That dainty pointed chin of hers wasn't fooling him. She was all spirit and backbone and he loved it.

Lexi wasn't very big, but that wasn't her fault. She was built with quality in mind, not quantity, and that spiky, bad-girl hair and the brief flash of the tattoo she had spiraling down from the small of her back was really working for him. Zach wasn't sure exactly what the image was—he just had an impression of sinuous curves—but it didn't matter. He liked that she was tough enough to take the pain, that she was willing to make that small sacrifice for something she found beautiful. This vicious streak she was showing now was just an added bonus.

Now, if he could get her to put down the knife, they could have a nice, long talk, and maybe after his work was done, she'd let him see just how far below her low-rise jeans that tattoo went.

From the corner of his eye, Zach saw the little old lady had recovered her walker and was headed for the telephone. The last thing they needed was for her to call in a bunch of human police to muck things up. The seizure thing Drake had done was enough fun for one night.

Drake was sitting up now, which was a good sign, but sunset was in less than a minute, and once that happened, things could go from ugly to fucking ugly in a heartbeat. Those demons were likely champing at the bit to get out of their dank hidey-holes and start hunting. The scent of blood running down Zach's arm was going to ensure that this was one of the first places they stopped.

Lexi was circling to his left, toward the old woman—likely to protect her. As if any of the Sentinels would ever hurt some old lady. Of course, she couldn't know that.

"Put down the knife, honey. There's been enough bloodshed for tonight."

"I'll tell you when I've shed enough blood," she spat.

Zach wanted to kiss that violent mouth of hers. He'd thought she was pretty before when she'd been Lexi the Waitress, but now that she was Lexi the Avenger, she was glorious. Stunning.

He moved forward, keeping his eye on the knife as he gathered up small specks of energy from the air. The added power hurt like hell, but he needed it to mark her.

He couldn't let her go, not without being sure he had a way to keep tabs on her. One little touch and he'd leave behind a tag that he'd be able to follow anywhere. All he had to do was get close enough to touch her without getting sliced open. Logan wouldn't appreciate having to patch him up before the night had really even started.

Lexi didn't back up. Didn't give an inch. The knife gleamed in her grip and Zach felt himself smile. What a woman.

He stepped closer, counting the seconds it would take the old lady to reach the phone. Maybe fifteen. It was plenty to disarm Lexi and leave his mark.

Zack lunged toward her, ducking her knife as it sliced at him a split second too late to do any damage. He grabbed her wrist to keep the knife at bay, and pinned her body against his, her back to his chest. Under the arm he had braced across her body to hold her still, he could feel the rapid rise and fall of her chest and the frantic pounding of her heart.

For a brief second, Zach hesitated. She was afraid of him. She didn't want this.

He let go of the energy he'd gathered and felt a searing rush of power jolt through his hand into the tip of his forefinger, which was pressed tight against Lexi's upper arm.

She sucked in a terrified breath and went still.

Zach opened his mouth to reassure her, but before he could get a single word out, a giant column of fire blasted up out of the kitchen and barreled through the ceiling, blowing a hole in the roof.

They were out of time. The demons were here, and they were pissed.

"Change of plans," shouted Thomas. Drake could barely hear him over the sound of dishes exploding from the heat of the fire in the diner's kitchen. As fast as the fire was spreading, there was no way it was natural fire.

Some of the demons they hunted had the power to call fire. They used it to create panic, make their prey run so they could herd them into clusters or ambush them as they fled.

The Synestryn that had caused this fire would be closing in on them, maybe even lurking outside, waiting for the last sliver of sunlight to fade.

Drake had to get the women to safety. Especially Helen.

He pulled Helen tight against him, making sure her head was down to protect her from flying debris. Once she'd seen the fire, she'd frozen up with a look of stark terror on her face. She was pale, shaking, and no longer resisting him. Not a good sign.

Thomas was still by Drake's side even though Lexi was waving a knife around, looking like some sort of tiny commando, and Miss Mabel was inching toward the telephone.

"We're getting out of here," yelled Thomas. "Logan will have to catch up. Can you walk?"

"No problem," said Drake. Whatever had happened when his internal lights went out had been bad, he was fine now. Better than fine. He was ready to take on the whole freaking nest of Synestryn by himself and recover Kevin's sword single-handedly if necessary.

Helen's wrist was still in his grip and he sure as hell wasn't letting go. That tidal wave of agony that had washed over him when she pushed him away had been an efficient teacher. It was not a lesson he needed to learn a second time.

"You take her," said Thomas. "I'll get the old lady and we'll let Zach deal with Rambette."

Drake nodded and pushed himself to his feet, pulling Helen up with him. She was still unresponsive, her eyes glued to the fire.

She'd dropped her purse at some point, which he stopped to grab along with Miss Mabel's. No sense in leaving behind obvious traces of the women at the scene of what might well be ruled arson. Fires like this one were often mistakenly reported as arson because no one could figure out how they started. He guessed there probably wasn't a little box to check beside the word *magic* on most fire inspectors' reports.

Drake lifted Helen's compliant body up into his arms and headed for their Chevy Tahoe.

The last rays of sunlight flickered between long shadows, preventing the demons that had started the fire from attacking for a few more seconds.

It took several of those seconds to get her loaded into the far backseat of the SUV and fasten a seat belt around her middle. Never once did he stop touching her skin, which was no hardship at all.

By the time he was done with that, Thomas had packed Miss Mabel into the front seat and her walker in back, but Zach was nowhere to be found.

Flames had already broken through the roof and the back wall of the diner. A small crowd of onlookers was forming across the street.

Sirens whined in the distance, and when they got here, Drake and his buddies needed to be long gone. Dealing with the authorities was not something they had time for tonight. Kevin's sword was still out there, able to do serious harm if any humans stumbled across it—able to do a hell of a lot more harm in the hands of one of the Synestryn.

"Where's Zach?" asked Thomas, scanning the small parking lot.

Tires squealed on the asphalt and Drake saw Zach running after an old Honda with Lexi behind the wheel. Zach was fast, but not that fast, and he didn't stand a chance of catching up with her bat-out-of-hell routine. It took Zach about ten more seconds to realize he wasn't going to catch her and he changed paths and sprinted back toward the SUV.

"We've got to catch up with her," Zach said, breathing hard.

"You leave that poor girl alone," ordered Miss Mabel. "You boys have done enough damage for one night. Setting the diner on fire. What were you thinking?"

That fire hadn't exactly been part of their plan—they'd planned on being out of the diner before the demons awoke—but no one bothered to explain that part to her. The sirens grew louder and Thomas was already behind the wheel, starting the engine. Zach slipped inside and slammed the door shut. Hard. "Did you see which way she went?" he asked.

"East. I'll try to find her." Thomas moved the vehicle into traffic and got caught at the first light.

"Shit!" bellowed Zach. "Blow through the intersection."

"You mean drive right over this nice young couple in the itty-bitty convertible in front of us?" asked Thomas, peering at Zach in the rearview mirror.

"If that's what it takes."

"I think not. We'll find her, Zach. Chill."

Zach pounded the seat next to him in frustration. "I can't believe she got away."

Drake had a hard time believing it, too, but right now his top priority was Helen and finding out why she hadn't said a word or offered any resistance since the moment she'd seen those flames. Not a good sign at all.

*   *   *

Lexi gripped the steering wheel so hard her hands cramped. She hated leaving Helen and Miss Mabel behind, but there was nothing she could do for them now. She should have known better than to let herself get close enough to care what happened to any of the regulars of Gertie's Diner. She should have learned her lesson by now. Caring that much about anyone was foolish.

Helen and Miss Mabel were gone. The Sentinels had them, and once they had someone, they never let go. Her mother had drilled that lesson into her since before she was old enough to walk.

She'd come close to being taken right along with them. Too damn close. Zach had overwhelmed her with his size, which was something she could handle. But he'd also overwhelmed her with his personality. He was a disturbing mix of charming humor and deadly hunter and she hadn't been prepared for the swift change in his demeanor. She also hadn't been prepared for the way he looked at her. The way he smiled at her.

He had seemed like a harmless flirt all through dinner, which was why she hadn't let the men's tattoos and collars alarm her. As long as they thought she was human, she was safe, so she played the part. Even flirted back, taken his phone number when he'd offered it.

Staying had been a mistake.

When he attacked her, she knew he'd figured out her secret. She fought back as hard as she could, but he was too strong. She stabbed him and he grinned. Who the hell did something like that? Only a lunatic. That's who.

A lunatic whose mark tingled on her arm. She had to do something about that as soon as possible.

Damn him. She loved that job. Loved the people she got to see every day. It was almost like having a family,

and Zach had stolen that all away from her just by showing up and barging into her life.

Lexi let out an enraged scream, making the windows
on her old Honda vibrate. She hated this—hated being
afraid, hated being alone, hated having to rebuild her life
every few months—but it was time to move on. Again.
The damage was done and she was no longer safe here.
Everything she owned was in this beat-up old car. She
was leaving a week's pay behind, but that was something
she'd have to deal with. She had enough money squir-
reled away to keep moving for a couple of weeks, which
was exactly what she was going to do.

Her mother had warned her that she could never let
the Sentinels find her. They were dangerous men who
enslaved women, forced them to do unspeakable evil.
Her mom had never been completely sane, but on the
days she was lucid, this was the one thing she drilled into
Lexi's head over and over, and Lexi took that warning to
heart. She knew what would happen to her if they ever
learned of her secret—if they ever learned she wasn't
entirely human.

She'd have to get a new name, alter her appearance,
and find a new town. It was getting harder and harder
to change her identity, and the papers cost more every time, but there was no help for it. She was free and
she'd stay that way or die trying. She couldn't let herself
fall into the hands of the enemy. The lives of too many
women—special women like her—were at stake.

Helen couldn't even scream. She was too terrified
to pull in enough air. Seeing that pillar of flame while
Drake wore that half smile on his face . . . It was so much
like her vision that she just shut down, waiting for the
blistering end to come.

But it hadn't come. And although there were similarities between reality and her vision, it wasn't exactly the same. She could see too much of her surroundings, it was bright inside, not dark, and the fire was behind Drake, not engulfing her. That was the biggest difference—the one that really mattered. She wasn't burning alive.

Breathe. Just breathe. That's all she had to do.

She couldn't open her eyes yet. She could feel the vibration of a car beneath her thighs and the slight swaying of her body as they turned corners. Someone was holding her. She could feel the heavy weight of a man's warm arm around her shoulders. Strong fingers drew comforting circles over her bare arm. Her head was tucked against his shoulder and she could smell smoke clinging to his shirt, a subtle hint of soap clinging to his skin. Streamers of energy that felt like warm bubbling water trickled into her flesh where his other hand circled her wrist.

Drake. Drake was holding on to her, keeping her from flying apart. He'd carried her out of that burning building. He hadn't watched her die.

Maybe her vision was wrong. Or maybe it just wasn't time for her to die yet. Either way, she was grateful to still be alive.

"Turn here," she heard a man say, and forced her eyes open enough to take in her surroundings. She was in the back of some big SUV, and even through the heavily tinted windows, she could see the western sky was a deep orangey pink. Miss Mabel was safe and sound in the front seat and Zach was all but crawling into the driver's lap, helping him steer the car.

"Welcome back," said Drake. Her head was down and there was no way he could have seen her open her eyes, but he knew she was coherent again.

Helen sat up straight, which he let her do, and then

tried to scoot over and put a couple of inches between them, which he didn't let her do. He kept his arm firmly about her shoulders, holding her right up against his body. His very warm, very firm, very manly body.

"Here, Thomas! Turn here!" shouted Zach. He was frantic about something, but Helen couldn't bring herself to wonder what he was frantic about. She had worse problems, like how she was going to get Miss Mabel out of this mess and back home to the safety of her crocheted doilies and giant antique book collection.

"You okay?" he asked, leaning a little closer to her ear so she could hear him over Zach's bellowed directions.

Helen swallowed, hoping her voice wouldn't come out in a childish squeak. "I will be once you take me back to my car."

"No can do. Firefighters and police are probably already crawling all over the diner. Who knows how long it will take them to put the fire out?"

Fire. Right. They could have her car. She wasn't going anywhere near fire, not while he was around. "Home, then. You can take Miss Mabel and me home."

"Damn it! I've lost her." Zach ran a frustrated hand through his long, wavy hair, dragging half of it out of the ponytail band that held it in place.

"I thought you said you put a marker on her," said the driver, Thomas.

Her? Lexi. Oh no.

"I did," grated Zach. "I thought it was a strong one, too, but apparently not. How could she have slipped away so easily? It just doesn't make any sense."

"Tell me Lexi made it out of the fire," said Helen, looking up into Drake's shadowed face.

"She did. And the cook was already gone for the day, which was lucky for him."

"It wasn't luck, just laziness," griped Helen. Paulo always left early, making Lexi clean up the diner by herself most nights.

"She not only got out," said Zach with the distinct sound of grating teeth. "She also got away. Do you know where she lives?" he asked Helen.

"I have no idea." Which wasn't exactly the truth. She knew Lexi lived in her car, just not where that car was. "And even if I did, I wouldn't tell you." Which was the exact truth.

"I think I've had enough adventure for one day," said Miss Mabel. "I'm ready to go home."

Helen was in full agreement about the adventure part. "I'd really like to know what the hell is going on. Who are you guys and what do you want from us?"

"We're the good guys," said Drake. "We want to keep you safe. That's all."

"Then let us out here. We can take care of ourselves."

"Not a chance," said Drake. "Not until we figure out why you have this effect on me. Besides, it's dark out. You're not safe running around once the sun's down."

"Fine. At least let Miss Mabel go."

"I'm not leaving you with these ruffians," said Miss Mabel. "We're sticking together. I'm keeping my eye on these boys."

"We need to get back to work," said Thomas. He was calm where Zach was frantic, moving the giant vehicle through traffic with expert ease. His wide shoulders stuck out on either side of the driver's seat and his head was only inches from the SUV's headliner. "Logan should be finished feeding by now and he'll need to know where to meet up with us."

"My house," said Miss Mabel. "Have him meet you at my house."

Oh no. Helen was not going to let these men know where Miss Mabel lived. She was a mostly defenseless old woman and these men pegged the weird-o-meter. Not a good combination. "I don't think that's a good idea. Just take us to the mall. Someplace public. Miss Mabel and I can catch a bus or a taxi."

"Don't want the big, bad wolves knowing where you live?" asked Drake. She felt his words slide along her temple in a warm wave that contrasted with the chilly hint of mockery in his tone.

"I'm not an idiot," she told him.

"No, but you are a mystery. One I'm going to need some time to solve."

"We don't have a lot of time, here, Drake," said Thomas. "We have a job to do and only about eight and a half hours to do it in."

She felt Drake's body tense up all along her left side. His arm gripped her harder and his fingers tightened on her wrist like he didn't want to let go. And that only made Helen more nervous. Even with those lovely streamers of energy that flowed into her everywhere his bare skin touched hers, she wasn't sure she liked where his possessive body language was going.

"I realize that," said Drake, "but I also realize that I'm not going to survive another attack like that last one, so we'd better find someplace to do a little testing. And for that, we need Logan. Miss Mabel's house is as good a place for that as any."

"No," said Helen, a little too quickly. "Go to my house instead. It's closer." She was a lot better equipped to handle these men than Miss Mabel was, even if that didn't mean much. At least Miss Mabel's home of thirty years would be safe. Maybe Helen would ask to move in with her after all of this was over.

"Fine. Which way?" asked Thomas.

Helen gave him directions, praying she wasn't making the biggest mistake of her life.

Drake couldn't stop touching Helen. He wasn't sure if it was because he was afraid that the pain would return if he did, or if it was because her skin was so incredibly soft everywhere he touched. Either way, he was useless in a fight unless he found a way to detach himself from her. And fighting was definitely on tonight's agenda. It wasn't going to be easy making the break, but he had no choice. They had to get that sword back, and if they didn't do it by sunrise, the whole demon nest would relocate and there was no telling when they'd find another lead to its location.

Kevin had been a fierce, proud warrior. He'd died with honor and Drake owed it to him to recover the sword and hang it in the Hall of the Fallen. To do that, he was going to need both hands.

He kept a careful hold on Helen's wrist, unwilling to break contact until absolutely necessary. Maybe Logan would know what to do to fix this mess. All the Sanguinar, including Logan, had freaky-strong abilities when it came to healing. They knew how to fix damn near anything that went wrong with the bodies of humans and Sentinels alike. If anyone knew what to do to separate him from Helen without pain, it would be Logan or one of the other Sanguinar.

They pulled into Helen's driveway and piled out of the van. It was a nice neighborhood. Older, but well maintained, and although he was sure that most of the trees had been chopped down when this development was built, the new trees had time to grow back up, serving to shade the houses from the blazing Kansas sun during the day. In the growing dark, those same trees left deep pockets of shadow along the sidewalk and between the homes.

Zach had been bleeding, thanks to Lexi. Not a lot, but enough to bring every Synestryn within a mile radius right to Helen's front door. Until Logan patched him up, Zach was a walking bull's-eye, making everyone near him a target.

Including Helen.

He glanced at her as they made their way up the concrete steps to her front door. The curve of her cheek glowed pink in the fading sunlight and he could just make out a cluster of freckles on her left shoulder. Her arms were smooth and feminine—pretty, but not nearly strong enough to fight off the demons headed this way. She was too soft to face down the Synestryn, and if her reaction to that fire was any clue, she was too fragile as well. Part of him wished he'd never even seen her, but the rest of him was doing a ridiculous happy dance, reveling in his pain-free state. He didn't know what he was going to do with her any more than he knew what she was doing to him.

Thomas carried Miss Mabel up to the front door of Helen's raised ranch, rather than make her go up the stairs with the walker. She'd griped about it, swatting ineffectively at his muscular arms, but Thomas just ignored her.

Zach was keeping watch over the group, guarding their backs, scanning the shadows for demons or any of the other Synestryn nasties that wanted a piece of them.

Helen stood under the yellow glow of her front porch light, rummaged through her purse one-handed, because Drake was not going to let her wrist go. His stubbornness earned him a disgruntled frown from her, but he was man enough to take it.

"It's not going to kill you to give me ten seconds to find my keys," she told him.

"It might. You want to take that chance?"

She actually paused a moment as if considering it as an option. A brief flash of grief dulled her hazel eyes for a split second, then was gone, leaving behind bleak acceptance in its wake. "Fine," she said, and shoved her purse against his ribs. "You can at least hold it while I dig."

Drake stared at the top of her bent head. Her brown hair was glossy in the glow of the porch light, and although her twin braids were getting a bit fuzzy from wear, they still drove him crazy, taunting him.

Handles. That's all he could think when he saw them. The woman had braided handles into her hair, just begging a man to grab them and guide her head where he wanted it to go. Surely she had to realize that. Surely she had to know that between those braids and her soft, full mouth, there was only one place his mind could go. A wonderful, bad, bad place where she was naked and begging him to do all kinds of wicked, delightful things. And he'd do every one of them before he let her go. Twice. But right now all he really wanted to do was grab hold of those handles, tilt her head back, and kiss her until he forgot all about his dead friend and the lost sword and Zach's bloody arm, which was calling in every nearby demon to come have a bite from the Theronai buffet.

"Found them," she said, jangling her keys.

Thank God. At least now they'd have a door to put between them and the demons. It wouldn't last long if an attack came, but it was better than standing out here in the open.

Helen unlocked the door and they all spilled inside

with Zach bringing up the rear. Thomas carried Miss Mabel up the half flight of stairs leading to the living room and set her down. He held her steady until she'd taken a solid grip on her walker, which made him a braver man than Drake. That walker was a dangerous weapon in her hands—for which the throbbing lump on the back of his head spoke eloquently—and Thomas was still close enough to be a giant target.

Helen flipped on the lights, revealing a neat, sparse living room. It was done in neutral shades—lots of tan, beige, and gray. The walls were bare and a few sealed moving boxes were stacked in one corner. Helen had either just moved in or was getting ready to move out. He couldn't tell which.

A couple of library books sat on the glass coffee table. Both of them dealing with spontaneous human combustion. Hell of a topic, and one he would definitely have to ask her about as soon as they got a spare moment. A pair of running shoes stood in the middle of the floor as if they'd been taken off right there. Multiple fire extinguishers stood in bizarre readiness, three in the living room alone—two sitting on the hearth of a fireplace that had been completely filled with bricks. Another extinguisher sat by the front door and he could see a fifth one on the kitchen counter.

Apparently, Helen really didn't like fire.

"Thank you for seeing us home," she said. "I don't want to keep you." A polite dismissal. One she made staring pointedly at the fingers he had clutched around her wrist.

"Nice try," said Drake, and just to be contrary, he slid his thumb along the silky inside of her wrist. She was so soft, so warm. Drake wasn't much for female attachments, but Helen was one he was getting used to, fast.

He looked at Thomas, who was still hovering like a mother hen over Miss Mabel, watching her as though he was afraid she'd fall over any minute. The way she was swaying, maybe that wasn't such a stupid move after all.

"We need Logan," said Drake. Without him, this night was going straight to hell with two humans along for the ride. They couldn't let that happen. As one of the Sentinel races, the Theronai's sole purpose in life—their entire reason for being—was to protect humans and to guard the gateway into the Solarc's kingdom, keeping the Synestryn away from both. They needed to get out of here and away from Helen and Miss Mabel before the demons showed up. And there was no question about that part. They *would* show up.

Thomas pulled out his cell phone. "Logan. We need you to meet us at 17804 East Sunflower Lane." His bright blue eyes zeroed in on Drake, right to where he was stroking Helen's wrist, and his expression turned grim. "Yeah, we got a problem. And Zach is bleeding, so make it fast."

Uh-oh. That demanding tone wasn't going to go over so well with Logan. He was not a man to push around. None of the Sanguinar were. There was currently peace between the Theronai and the Sanguinar because they each had something the other needed, but that peace was tenuous at best and Thomas knew better than to be anything less than diplomatic. Kevin's death must have gotten to him more than Drake thought.

Thomas had been closer to Kevin than any of them. All that anger made Thomas one hell of a deadly asset in a fight. Since taking on this mission, the man had been a killing machine. The four of them had blasted through three Synestryn nests in the past week, which had to be some kind of record, and Thomas had been leading the charge every time.

But when it came to getting something from one of the Sanguinar, finesse was the only way to go.

Thomas was apparently hearing all about his insolence, if the tight bunching of his jaw was any sign. "No, of course I didn't mean it like that, Logan." His knuckles turned white as his grip tightened on the phone. "*Please*, make it fast," he grated out, barely audible.

Zach peered out of the window between two slats in the miniblinds. His hand was pressed tight over his bleeding arm. "How close is he?" he asked Thomas.

Thomas slid the phone back into his pocket and shifted the hilt of his sword so it was clear of his clothing. All of the men carried swords, but thanks to a little hocus-pocus, they were hard to see as long as they were sheathed.

"Five minutes," said Thomas.

Zach shook his head. "Too long. I'm going to take off, draw them away from here."

"That's not a good idea," argued Drake. "We're going to need you."

"Not if all the beasties are following me. It will give Logan some time to figure out whatever it is you've got going on there." He waved toward Helen.

Drake did not want Zach going out there alone. He was one badass Theronai, but he wasn't invincible. "You're just doing this so you can go after the girl."

Zach shot him a vibrant green glare. "You wanna throw that particular stone, Drake?"

Shit. Zach was right. If Helen had gotten away, he would have wanted to go after her, too. Assuming he was able to even walk, which he doubted. "Just be careful."

"Always. Keys, Thomas."

Thomas tossed the Tahoe's keys across the room and Zach was out of the driveway in fifteen seconds.

Thomas looked out through the blinds and spat out a caustic word, which made Miss Mabel shoot him a dirty look. "He put the windows down," said Thomas.

So the demons could smell the blood and follow him. "I don't like it any more than you do, but there wasn't much of a choice left. He couldn't stay here and risk the women."

"One of whom is standing right here," said Helen. "Will you at least tell us what the hell is going on? Why did Zach just run off and why does it matter that he had the window down?"

Oh, hell. How was he going to explain all of this to her? There was way too much to cover for her to even begin to understand what they were up against. She was human. Protected. She wasn't even allowed to know the Sentinels existed. One of them was going to have to scrub her memories and Miss Mabel's before they could leave. The less they knew, the less there was to erase, and the easier it would be on them. "Don't worry about it."

"You won't let go of me. We almost burned up in a fire. Lexi is out there alone and now Zach is, too. Something is coming this way, but apparently it's too horrible to even speak of. Please tell me you did *not* just tell me not to worry."

He was in trouble. He could hear it in her tone—the anger, the fear. What bothered him wasn't that she was afraid so much as the fact that he really didn't want her to be afraid. He should have been able to distance himself from her enough to keep her safe without all this emotional involvement. If he couldn't keep a clear head, she'd be a lot more than afraid; she'd be dead. Zach might have lured the majority of the demons away, but he wouldn't have gotten them all. They were like cock-roaches. There were always more lurking in the dark.

"Okay," he said, taking a deep breath, "I know all of this is bizarre to you, but I need you to trust me."

Helen looked at him as if he'd just told her she was his long-lost half uncle. "Trust you? You've got to be kidding."

"No. I'm not. You have no idea what's going on here and there's no time to explain it. Ergo, trust me."

"That's it," she said, throwing up her free hand. "We're done here. I'm calling the police."

Helen headed toward the kitchen and he trailed behind, keeping his grip solid. She could call the National Guard for all he cared. It wasn't going to change anything. He wasn't letting her go. "It would be better if you didn't try to get them involved," he told her.

"Better for you, maybe." She turned on the kitchen lights and took a step toward the phone, but Drake just stood his ground. She got to the end of the tether he'd made of his arm, and that was as far as she could go. She stumbled, having expected him to continue to follow her.

"Ouch!" She rubbed her shoulder.

Her pain was the last straw. He wasn't going to let it happen again. Drake collected her body and pressed it up against the kitchen wall so she had no choice but to pay attention. They had some things to straighten out, and now was as good a time as any.

Chapter 3

Helen couldn't breathe. Not because Drake's body was so tight against hers that she couldn't pull in a breath, but because he was so tight against hers she could feel his heat sinking into her through their clothing, along with something else. Something delicious and powerful. Those strange wriggling streamers of energy flooded her, making her head spin and her eyes drift shut.

It felt good and that scared the hell out of her.

Trust me.

Yeah, right. She wasn't a genius, but she knew better than to fall for that one. The only problem was that even though her mind was on board with the not-trusting-him thing, her body wasn't. Whatever it was he was doing to her was shorting out her system, making her feel all syrupy inside. Being this close to him felt like sliding into a hot bath on a cold night. It gave her shivers and she just wanted to sink into him until she was in over her head. Way over.

This couldn't be good for her. Whoever he was, he wasn't normal. He was going to watch her die, for heaven's sake. How could she be falling for this kind of seduction?

Helen forced her eyes open and instantly wished she hadn't. He was staring down at her mouth, licking his lips like he was thinking about kissing her. As soon as she saw the thought cross his face, she was doing a little thinking in that direction as well. Okay, maybe more than a little.

Kissing him sounded lovely.

Above them, a clock ticked off the seconds and he didn't move. Didn't so much as flinch. He just stared at her mouth.

She had a point to make—something she was going to say or do—but for the life of her, she couldn't remember what it was. It didn't seem relevant any longer. The only thing that seemed to hold any importance at all was whether or not she could get him to come just a little closer. Whether or not he'd give her enough space to go up on her tiptoes and reach his mouth because he wasn't making the first move nearly fast enough to suit her.

His eye twitched; then his jaw tightened and his warm gaze went from her eyes to her mouth and back again. "We are not going to do this," he said, though he sounded like he was trying to convince himself.

"We're not?" she asked him, sounding disappointed and out of breath.

"No, you're not," said a low, cultured voice. Someone new. "At least not until we know more about your ... situation."

"Your timing sucks, Logan," said Drake. His body shifted away from her a scant inch, allowing Helen space to draw in a deep breath. It didn't help. Her head was still spinning and she was still thinking about how Drake's mouth would have felt against hers. She hadn't been kissed in a long time. Way too long for her tastes, and he had a nice mouth. Firm and wide with just the tiniest hint of softness.

"Drake, would you care to introduce me to your friend?" asked the new man.

"Not really," said Drake, still not taking his eyes off her, "but I guess I don't have much of a choice, do I?"

"From what I'm told, no. You don't."

Drake backed up a half step, but didn't go any farther. His thumb slid over her bare shoulder, stroking her as if he had the right to do so. And she didn't want him to stop. She didn't even care that they had an audience, which should have been its own giant warning bell.

She heard the man clear his throat and finally managed to pull herself away from Drake enough to look at the newcomer.

He was gorgeous. Drop-dead, perfume-model gorgeous. He was taller than Drake by a couple of inches, only thinner, almost gaunt, but he made gaunt look good. His facial features were so perfect, so symmetrical and balanced that they had to be surgically altered. No one was that pretty without a lot of help. He had thick black hair that fell just over the open collar of his shirt. A silky wave draped artfully across his forehead, barely shielding one silvery blue eye. His skin was pale and flawless, making him look inhuman in his perfection.

Helen wished she was half that pretty.

"Well, hell," muttered Drake. "Do you do that to all the human women?"

"No. Usually they've already started taking off their clothes by now. She's beginning to hurt my feelings."

"We need to get you a paper bag or a giant scar or something."

"Yeah," said the man, his tone dry. "I'll get right to work on that."

Helen had to blink a couple of times before she could stop staring and felt her face warm with embarrassment. There was nowhere to look that wasn't filled with either man pretty or man manly, so she decided she was better off looking at the kitchen floor.

"Helen, this is Logan," said Drake. "He's here to help."

Well, she definitely needed help. That was for sure. "I'd say, 'Nice to meet you,' but I'd be lying."

"I get that a lot," said Logan.

"Can we hurry things along here?" asked Drake. "We may be having visitors any time now and I'd like to be able to deal with them when they get here."

"Visitors?" asked Helen.

"Have you told her?" Logan asked Drake.

"Told me what?"

Drake ignored her question, addressing Logan. "The less she knows, the better."

"Excuse me?" said Helen. "I really wish you wouldn't talk about me like I wasn't standing right here."

Drake clenched his jaw in frustration and she felt his fingers tighten around her arms. He leaned forward until she had to tilt her head back to look him in the eye. There was something truly frightening lurking there—some dark knowledge or power she couldn't even begin to understand. And she wasn't sure she wanted to.

His voice was a low rumble that wouldn't carry into the next room where Miss Mabel was. "I get that this whole situation is confusing to you, but I really am trying to do what's best for both of you. We're up against some serious time constraints, not to mention the bad things that may be coming to your door at any minute, and if you prefer to live the rest of your life without me as a permanent attachment, then you'll cooperate and let Logan do his job."

A lot of weird stuff had happened tonight, but she was beginning to think that it was just the tip of the iceberg.

All she really wanted was for him to leave her in peace so she could go back to her normal life and try to pretend none of this had ever happened. If that meant cooperating with pretty-boy, then she really didn't see any other option. "Okay. I'll be good."

"Excellent," said Logan. He rolled his shoulders, making the leather of his long coat creak.

A coat? In this heat? Something was wrong with that picture, but she figured it was the least of her concerns.

"Did Thomas tell you what happened?" asked Drake.

"Only vaguely. I'd rather see for myself, if you don't mind."

Helen didn't know what Logan meant, but Drake definitely looked like he minded. "Can't I just tell you?"

"You could. You could also skew the facts or leave something out that you didn't think was important. And there is that whole time issue we have right now. My way is faster."

Drake sighed. "Fine. We'll do it your way."

"Is that okay with you?" Logan asked her.

"I have no idea what you're talking about."

Drake's thumb slid over her arm in a soothing arc. "He wants to see your memories of tonight so he can figure out what's happening to us."

See her memories? "How is that even possible?"

"It just is," said Drake. "Tick-tock."

"I promise it won't hurt," said Logan. "And it will just take a moment."

Having someone poke around inside her head was near the top of her list of things she did not want to happen. Right below being permanently attached to Drake, which was right below being burned alive. "Whatever. Let's just get this over with."

"We're going to need a quiet room," said Logan.

"My bedroom is at the end of the hall. Will that work?"

Logan nodded.

Helen led both men down the hall into her room. She could feel the weight of Drake's presence at her back, the strong shackle of his fingers about her wrist. She'd spent plenty of time thinking about what it would be like to lead some handsome man to her bed, but she'd never imagined anything like this. Even if she had time for dating right now, which she didn't, she never would have brought a man like Drake home. He was far too . . . predatory for her tastes. She needed a nice, sedate man. An accountant, maybe.

Helen turned every light in the bedroom on. She was not going to sit in the dark with these two strangers, no matter how attractive they were. With any luck at all, Logan would fix whatever was wrong and they'd all go away. At least for a while. She needed more time before Drake came back into her life to watch her die. Just a few days. She didn't think it was too much to ask.

Logan shut the door behind them and looked around the room.

Helen loved this space more than any other in the house. She'd decorated it herself using a palette of cool ocean blues and greens. There was no clutter because she hadn't lived here long enough to collect it, and the blond oak furniture was all streamlined and understated. She'd used the insurance money she'd collected when her last house burned down to buy a few high-quality pieces and she loved every one of them. She really hoped that the unexplainable fires that haunted her all her life wouldn't destroy this piece of solace she loved so much.

"Are you ready?" asked Logan.

"As I'll ever be," said Drake. "Helen?"

She was never going to be ready for whatever they were going to do, but the sooner it was done, the sooner she would be rid of them. "Let's just get this over with."

Drake sat on the edge of her bed, tugging her down beside him. He stroked the side of her face with a barely there glide of his fingers. She couldn't handle his gentleness, not when she knew how things would end between them.

She covered his hand to stop his caress, but instead, she only managed to press his hand against her cheek. Her skin tingled and streamers of what she could only describe as electricity were winding their way down her body, through her chest and stomach, down her legs until they disappeared through her toes.

Drake offered her a reassuring smile. "It'll be okay. I promise."

Helen closed her eyes, fighting the sting of tears. He had no idea what he was going to do to her. She could see it in his face, in the earnestness of his expression. He'd never hurt her on purpose. He was going to watch her die, but she couldn't believe he would be the one to kill her.

Logan reached up and placed an elegant, long-fingered hand on Drake's head, then did the same thing to Helen. She felt a jolt of something she couldn't name and then suddenly, she was back in Gertie's Diner helping Miss Mabel into her seat.

Thomas wasn't exactly sure what he was going to do with Miss Mabel. She kept eyeing the front door like she thought she might actually be able to outrun him. The last thing he wanted was for her to hurt herself doing something stupid.

"You never did get to eat tonight. Are you hungry?" he asked her, hoping to help her relax and quit thinking about escape.

"I suppose I am."

"Do you think Helen would mind if we rummaged through her fridge?"

"I'm sure she wouldn't. The woman doesn't have a selfish thought in her head."

Thomas checked outside again, hoping none of the Synestryn had found them here. If Zach had spilled so much as one drop of blood on the driveway, this place would be swarming with them soon.

"What are you looking for?" she asked him. "You're making me nervous with all that fidgeting."

Fidgeting? It sounded like something a two-year-old would do. Thomas tried not to be offended. "I'm just making sure we weren't followed."

"By whom?"

Not whom. What. Dealing with humans was such a pain in the ass. He would so much rather just go kill something. Tonight was supposed to be a prime-time killing spree, too. This area was crawling with demons, though no one had figured out why yet. And Thomas didn't particularly care. He was nearly out of time and he wanted to make sure he made the most of what he had left.

The wind shifted outside and he felt the last leaf on his lifemark—the image of an ancient tree stamped into his flesh—sway over the skin on his chest. One leaf left. Once it was gone, his soul would die and his ability to distinguish right from wrong would fade. He'd no longer care about the people he loved. He'd no longer love.

Part of him longed for it. No love meant no grief,

and the grief he carried for Kevin kept gnawing at him, eating him from the inside out. He was so fucking tired of hurting. Tired of watching his brothers die. As soon as they found Kevin's sword, he was going to leave the Theronai before he could hurt any of them. He'd find the biggest, baddest nest of Synestryn he could and dive in headfirst.

But before he could do that, he had to make sure they found Kevin's sword, and before they could do that, they had to make sure Helen and Miss Mabel were safe. His vow to protect humans demanded no less.

"Listen," he said, trying to hold on to his patience, despite the pain and grief gnawing at his insides. "This is really a lot more complicated than it seems. Why don't we just go have a sandwich or something, okay?"

"Don't you get all snippy with me, young man."

Young man. Thomas couldn't help but smile. He might look like he was around thirty, but he'd passed his five hundredth birthday a few years ago. "No, ma'am. No snippy here. Come on."

He helped her up off the couch and got her settled behind her walker. She was so frail, he worried about hurting her every time he got close. Every move he made with her was carefully controlled, slow and methodical. It took them a few minutes to get into the kitchen, and Thomas tried to hide his impatience. He had no idea how long Logan and Drake would take, but the longer they did, the more dangerous things were going to get.

Thomas sat Miss Mabel at the kitchen table and peeked inside Helen's fridge. She had several stacks of sealed trays with clear lids. Inside each one was a full meal, though it would probably take three or four of them to fill him up. It looked like more than two dozen trays and each of them was labeled with dates and contents on a strip of masking tape. Boy, this chick was organized. "What do you want? Chicken and noodles, beef Stroganoff, or spaghetti with meatballs?"

"We can't eat those," she said. "Those are tomorrow's meals."

Thomas peered at her over the refrigerator door. "There's no way the two of you could eat all this food in one day."

"Not just us. Helen takes food all over town, bringing it to people like me who have trouble making it on their own."

"So she brings you food?"

"Every day. And we go out at least once a week. I'd like to go more often, but she's all booked up. Tonight was our night out, which you boys completely ruined."

Again, Thomas had to struggle not to smile. Miss Mabel was cute when she was disgruntled. "Sorry about that. I didn't mean to spoil your fun."

"I don't know what's going on back there with Helen, but I don't like it one bit."

"Don't worry about them. They'll take good care of her."

Miss Mabel snorted. "All you men have done since we saw you is push us around. You made Lexi run away, for heaven's sake. I don't trust you one bit. I don't care how handsome you are."

"You think I'm handsome, do you?" His flirting tone made her blush.

"That's not what I meant."

"My apologies, then, for misinterpreting you."

She pushed herself up from her chair and he could see her shaking with the effort it cost her. The poor thing had worn herself out with all this excitement tonight.

"I'm going to go check on Helen," she said.

Thomas shut the fridge and stepped in her path. "That's not a good idea. I promise you she'll be fine. Just give them some time to figure things out, okay?"

"She's my friend," said Miss Mabel. The woman didn't even come up to his sternum and she was bent under the strain of age, but there was a fierceness in her eyes that told Thomas that she'd do whatever it took to keep Helen safe.

"Have you heard any screams?" he asked her.

"No."

"Any crashing noises or anything else that leads you to believe they're hurting her?"

"No, but that doesn't mean—"

"She's safe. Let Logan finish his work and you and I will just sit right here and have a nice peanut butter sandwich."

"You're an insolent man. You know that, don't you?"

"Yes, ma'am. I've been told that a time or two."

She stared up at him for a long moment as if debating what to do. "I don't like this," she said.

"I know."

"And I think you all are up to no good."

What else was new? "Yes, ma'am."

"If you hurt her I'll make you pay. I may be old, but that doesn't mean I can't make you suffer."

"Damn right. You've got the AARP on your side."

"Stop being insolent! I spent thirty years teaching school and I know all the best ways to punish naughty boys."

"Now you're just trying to scare me."

She tilted her head back and he wondered how that bun stayed up. It looked as if the only thing holding it up was a single pencil, but that seemed like an architectural impossibility. "You're beyond hope, aren't you?"

"Absolutely. A walking lost cause."

Her glare softened and she looked at him with something nearing pity. If she'd been a man, he would have decked her for looking at him like that. But she wasn't and all he could do was stand there and take it. "You really think that, don't you? That you're a lost cause?"

He didn't just think it, he knew it, but that was still no reason to pity him.

Thomas couldn't stand the way she was looking at him, so he turned away and stalked back across the kitchen. Maybe a giant helping of peanut butter would shut her up.

He slapped together a pile of sandwiches and all but slammed them down on the table.

She looked expectantly at the empty chair across from her, then back at him and just stared until he sat down with her at the table. She waited until he'd reached for a sandwich before saying, "You forgot the milk."

Logan loved walking through people's memories. Maybe it was the voyeur in him, or maybe it was some sort of power trip, but whatever it was, he didn't get to do it nearly often enough.

His body was in Helen's house, but his consciousness was at a little restaurant called Gertie's Diner. Logan took the memories from both Drake and Helen and superimposed them on top of one another until time synched up.

When he'd first learned how to walk memories, it had been hard to adjust to the weightless sensation and the skewed reality different people saw. Although many people saw things the same way, others didn't. Colors were the worst. While some people saw the sky as blue, others saw it as purple or green, only they'd learned to call it blue because that's what they'd been taught it was called. Every time he walked in the memories of some-one like that, it always made him nauseated.

Maybe it was his perception that was wrong, but he'd never once let anyone walk his memories, so there was no way to know. He'd rather die not knowing than risk letting someone dig into his mind as he was doing to Drake and Helen. He had too many secrets to keep.

If any of the Theronai learned what his people were doing to the blooded humans, it would be the end of his race.

Logan shoved the unpleasant thought away and fo-cused on his job. He sped the couple's memories for-ward until he saw Drake rise from his seat in the nearly empty diner. Helen was trying to hide behind a menu. She was afraid of Drake, though Logan knew from be-ing in her mind that she'd never met him before.

Logan froze Drake's progress across the tile floor and concentrated on Helen. He reached deeper into her mind, searching for the source of that fear, seeking out some thin tendril of it that he could follow backward in time until he reached the origin.

Her mind was cluttered with worry, fear. She was terrified of fire. She'd lived through two house fires and had lost her mother to the first one. He saw the faces of many elderly humans—some who were dying, some already dead. Those who remained were the center of many of her worries, but there was one worry that didn't fit. One that went deeper, that veered away from those faces.

He followed it, letting his mind snake along the path,

watching the movie of her life replaying backward at
lightning speed. He saw her grow younger, felt knowledge slip away from her. She lost the ability to do simple
math, the ability to read, the ability to speak, and yet the
tendril continued.

She was tiny now, unable to even roll over in her crib.
The world looked huge through her eyes, and the center
of it was a woman's face. Her mother.

Logan stopped, unwilling to go back any further. He
had no idea where this tendril would lead, but nothing
he saw through her memories now would mean anything. There would be no frame of reference for her
to understand what was happening, which meant he
wouldn't either. She had no worldly experience and
wouldn't be able to interpret anything into information
he could use.

With a thought, Logan was back in Gertie's Diner.
He let time roll forward, watching Drake's seemingly
unavoidable attraction to Helen. He felt Drake's desire
for her—something beyond mere sex. He wanted something from her even he didn't understand.

Logan still felt Helen's fear, but lacing with it was
something new. Something pleasurable. Drake was sending streams of power into her without even realizing he
was doing it. Usually, releasing power was impossible for
the Theronai once it was stored within them. That's why
they all suffered as they aged. They were like walking bat-
teries, storing more and more energy until it killed them,
consuming them from the inside out. The only outlet was
through their luceria—the necklace and ring combination they wore. Before most of the female Theronai had
been slaughtered, each one would choose a man as her
partner in battle. She would take his luceria and wear it,
linking them together. The necklace served as a conduit,

channeling the male's power into her where she could use it to destroy the Synestryn. A bonded pair of Theronai was a humbling sight to behold.

Logan had never seen anything quite like this power transfer before. Even if Drake could funnel off some of his power into Helen, doing so would have injured or possibly killed any human woman. This was supposed to be impossible.

Obviously that assumption had been wrong, because there was no mistaking what was happening. He could feel it happen from both Drake's and Helen's points of view. She was absorbing his power and she certainly wasn't dead. In fact, she was enjoying it.

Logan felt the spark of a theory forming, but it seemed too ridiculous to even consider. He needed more information.

He moved the memories forward, saw Drake all but kiss Helen, both of them enthralled by their connection. The older lady hit Drake with her walker, which made Logan smile. Something was happening between Zach and a little blond woman, but there wasn't enough information from either of their memories to put together what it was. Drake grabbed Helen. She fought back and finally freed herself. Drake collapsed in pain and Logan quickly pulled away from the sensation before it could overwhelm him. Logan tuned the pain out and concentrated on Helen. Drake was nearly unconscious and Logan needed her eyes.

He waited until she turned around to look at Drake and stopped the image there. Helen was frantic, worried for someone named Lexi and the old woman—Miss Mabel. He brushed past her fear, trying only to see what she saw without the taint of emotion.

Logan studied Drake through her eyes. He was frozen in a painful convulsion, his body arching up off the floor. Curls of smoke rose up from his hand and neck where he wore both parts of the luceria.

Logan squinted at the image, trying to figure out what was bothering him about it. Besides the obvious smoking flesh.

Then he saw it. Just barely. Helen didn't know what his luceria was supposed to look like and Logan never paid attention to colors in memories because so many people saw them differently. Because of that, he nearly missed the subtle difference. Instead of being a silvery, iridescent band, the luceria was a mixture of reds and yellows.

The only time a luceria changed color was when it came in contact with a female Theronai.

Helen? No way. She couldn't be. Nearly all their women had been killed more than a hundred years before she was born, and those who remained were carefully guarded. The notion that one could be walking around unprotected seemed ludicrous.

Logan was stunned to stillness for a moment before he managed to pull himself together. If it was true and Helen was a Theronai, then he had to have proof. He needed her blood.

No way was Drake going to let that happen. Logan knew all too well how protective the Theronai were of their women. Even if Drake didn't know she was a Theronai, his instincts would still be there—guard and protect, his life for hers.

Logan was going to have to find a way to separate them and not just so Drake could have both hands free for his sword. He needed to get Helen alone because that was the only shot he'd have to get a taste of her blood.

*   *   *

Helen stared at the soothing blue wall in front of her, trying to shed the sickening disorientation that spun in her head. Whatever Logan had done to her, she did not want him to do it ever again.

"How do you feel?" asked Logan, looking at Helen with those too-pretty silvery blue eyes that almost seemed to glow.

She closed her eyes, trying to block out the light in hopes that it would help her spinning head. "Like I just got off one too many roller-coaster rides."

"That will pass in a moment. And you, Drake?"

"I'm fine," he said, but it sounded like a lie, making her think he probably felt about as bad as she did. "Did you figure out what's going on?"

"Perhaps."

Helen felt Drake's fingers tighten on her wrist for a moment. "Vague answers are a really unhealthy idea for you right now. Cut the mysterious shit and tell me what's going on."

"I have a theory, but that's all. Whatever it is that's going on between you, this is the first time I've ever encountered it."

She heard Drake's irritated sigh and slanted a narrow glance at him. She really wished she hadn't turned on quite so many lights now. The brightness was killing her.

"Turn out the lights," Drake told Logan as if reading her mind. Then again, maybe his head was feeling the same way.

Logan flipped off the overhead and both lamps, leaving only the rectangle of light from the bathroom doorway.

"Better?" Drake asked, looking at Helen. He was doing that gentle fingertip caress thing along the inside of her wrist that made it hard for her to think about anything else but the feel of his bare skin gliding over hers. A little shiver rode along her spine and settled low in her abdomen.

She swallowed, which didn't loosen up her voice, then cleared her throat. "Yeah. Thanks."

Drake gave her a nod and a wink. "Let's have it, Logan. What do we need to do?"

Logan propped his perfect butt on the edge of her dresser and crossed his lean arms over his chest. "I think it's the way you broke contact last time that was the problem."

"What do you mean?" asked Drake.

"Helen was afraid. Frantic. She was fighting to get away and you were fighting not to let that happen. I think that it was the violence of the separation, or maybe the fact that you didn't both want it, that was the problem."

"So what do we do?" asked Helen.

"Take it slower. Ease the two of you apart. Make sure it's what you both want."

"It is," she told them. "I mean, I'm sorry that I hurt you last time, but we really have to fix this." Before either one of them had to use the bathroom. Wouldn't that be fun?

"She's right. We've been here fifteen minutes already. Zach will only be able to hold them off for so long."

Helen felt her shoulders tense. "Hold who off? What are you talking about?"

Drake's mouth flattened and he looked away as though he wished he had just kept it shut.

"You may as well tell her," said Logan.

Drake sounded angry, but Helen had no idea why. "The less she knows, the easier the mind wipe will be on her."

Mind wipe? That didn't sound good. In fact, it sounded distinctly *not* good. "What is that?"

"Can you feel her starting to panic?" asked Logan. "If we don't explain what's going on, she's going to go over the edge and that won't be good for any of us. We have to tell her."

Helen was pretty sure she wasn't going to like what she heard, but she was also sure that not knowing had to be worse than knowing, even if it was terrible.

Drake spat out a single, violent word and scrubbed a hand over his face in frustration. "Fine. We'll tell her, but I swear to God that if you aren't careful with her memories, I'll make sure *you* remember it for a long, long time."

Logan smiled at Drake as if he were two years old and he'd just done something cute. "I'll be gentle with her. I swear it."

O-kay. This was sounding worse by the second. Exactly what were they going to do to her memories and why was Drake so worried Logan wouldn't be gentle? Even worse, what would happen to her if he wasn't? This whole situation was way too messed up to be real.

"She's panicking," said Logan.

"I realize that," said Drake from between clenched teeth.

"I can put her to sleep for you, if you like."

"No!" shouted Helen, trying not to freak out. Drake was stroking her wrist as if to calm her, but it wasn't working. Not even those tingling streamers flowing into her were doing any good right now. "No one is doing anything else to me until you tell me what's going on."

"Okay," agreed Drake a little too quickly. "I'll tell you. Just relax, okay?"

Relax? Not freaking likely. "Spit it out. Apparently

we don't have a lot of time before they get here. Whoever *they* are."

Drake pulled in a deep breath that stretched the fabric of his shirt, showing off more muscle than Helen had realized he had. Oh, man, she was so far in over her head she was never going to get out of this.

"Our friend Kevin was killed a few days ago. We're going after his killers."

As revelations went, that was a doozy. He'd lost a friend and she was too wrapped up in her own problems to even think about the ones he was dealing with. Some of the tension drained out of her. "Are you sure that's wise? I mean, shouldn't the police be the ones to do that?"

"Not in this case."

"Why not?"

He took another deep breath and paused as though he really didn't want to tell her more. "Because those killers aren't human. They're monsters called the Synestryn."

He was serious. Helen sat there, waiting for the punch line, but it didn't come. She looked from Drake to Logan and both of them wore deadly serious expressions. This wasn't a joke. "Monsters?"

"Demons, if you prefer the term."

"Yeah. Not so much," she said, still trying to absorb what he was saying.

"These monsters killed Kevin and took something from him—something we must get back. That's why we're following them."

"I thought they were following you."

"Only when Zach started bleeding."

"What?" she asked, frowning in confusion.

Drake's wide jaw bunched up under the pressure of

his clenched teeth. He looked at Logan like he was hoping to find an escape. "I'm really making a mess of this. She doesn't need to know this part."

"Yes, she does," said Helen before Logan could answer for her. She turned Drake's face back to her so she was sure she had his attention. "Why are the, um, monsters following you?"

He stared at her for a long second and she could feel his hesitation, see regret glowing in his golden brown eyes. "They followed us once Zach started bleeding because they like to . . . eat us."

Oh God. That was too disgusting to even contemplate. This had to be some sort of sick joke. But no one was laughing. "You're telling me that you are being chased by man-eating monsters and you *brought them to my house*?" How could they? Miss Mabel was a defenseless old woman who wouldn't even be able to run away if she had to.

"They're not man-eating," said Drake in a tone that was supposed to be reassuring.

As if she could possibly be reassured by anything after that kind of news. "What?"

"They don't eat humans."

"But you just said—"

"I said they eat us. As in Thomas and Logan and Zach. And me."

The line of logic he left for her to follow was a short one. "You're not human?"

Drake shook his head slowly.

She had to get out of here. Had to get away from all this insanity. She'd left Miss Mabel out there alone with Thomas. Who wasn't human.

Helen suffered through the first rush of fear and forced herself to remain calm because she knew it wouldn't be the last. She had to stay calm. Miss Mabel needed her. She tried to pull her wrist away, jerking it hard, but Drake's grip held.

"Don't do this, Helen," he said in a calm tone. "Don't fight me again. I won't hurt you."

She didn't stop to figure out whether or not he was telling the truth. Not while he held her captive. She felt herself panicking. Her breathing sped, then faltered. Her heart pumped hard and fast, one beat crammed on top of the next. Sweat broke out on her skin and her mind funneled down to one single goal. Escape. She'd freaked out enough times before to know what it felt like. Every time things got bad and it was vital for her to stay calm, she panicked. Every time the vision hit her, she panicked. Every time she saw so much as a candle flame, she panicked.

Now Drake was trying to prevent her escape and she didn't care if she hurt him again. She needed to get away. Right now.

Chapter 4

"She's still panicking," said Logan.

Drake felt her fear. The queasy, oily emotion trickled through his skin where his fingers held tight to her flailing wrist. "No shit. Tell me something I don't know, like what to do about it."

Helen's hazel eyes were wide, her pupils shrunken down to tiny dots. Her skin had gone pale and clammy and he could feel the wild beat of her blood pumping through her wrist.

Her fear made him sick. He'd finally found someone who made his pain go away and he terrified her. Not that he could blame her. She was human and had no experience with his world. Why did he ever think he could tell her what he did without terrifying her?

She wrenched her arm away, trying to break free, and Drake drove her down to the bed, pinning her with his body. She was going to hurt herself if she kept this up and Drake would not allow that to happen.

He let go of her wrist, but made sure that he still had contact with her bare skin. It wasn't hard. In her summer shorts and tank top, there was a lot of bare skin available, all of it incredibly soft and warm. She felt so good beneath him. He wished like hell he'd gotten her there under different circumstances.

Helen tried to claw at his face, so he gathered her hands and pushed them between their bodies, holding them there. As soon as she realized she was trapped, she stopped fighting and went limp.

"She's human—not capable of dealing with this, Drake. You've got to let me put her to sleep," said Logan. He was right there on the bed with them, concern marring his too-pretty face.

Like hell Drake was going to let him muck about in her mind again. She was already suffering from the first time. "Back off. I'll handle this."

Helen made a frightened sound—half panting, half whimper, and completely heartbreaking. "Shhh," he told her, leaning his mouth close to her ear. "You're fine. I'm going to let go of you now. Just relax."

She made no reaction—nothing to indicate that she'd heard him. She just stared chanting in a low breathless whisper, "Breathe. Just breathe."

"That's right, honey. Just breathe. You're fine." It was a lie. She was way past fine, but if the lie worked, he'd use it. He looked up at Logan. "You sure this easing away slowly thing is going to work?"

"No. I'm not."

Great. Just what Drake wanted to hear. The Sanguinar—the most gifted healers among the Sentinel races, the guys who had all the answers when it came to fixing what ailed you—wasn't sure. Shit.

Drake lowered his voice to a whisper and stroked the stray hairs back from Helen's face. "You're okay now. You're safe." Her braids were a complete mess and her skin was too pale, but she was still lovely and having her

curvy body under his on a bed—even one he was sharing with a leech—was just about more than he could
stand. He wished that things had started out differently
between them, that he could have had a chance with her,
even for a brief fling. He wasn't prone to having rela-
tionships with humans because it was just not worth the
worry that they'd get hurt, but for Helen, he would have
made an exception. He would have made sure she didn't
get hurt.

Yeah, as if he could really pull that off.

Drake felt her calming down, just a little. He stroked
the fine tendrils of hair that had escaped her braids back
from her forehead. Her skin was clammy, but he didn't
care. She still felt better under his hand than any other
woman he'd ever had.

Slowly, her breathing evened out and her chest shook
with a silent sob. Not a single tear fell even though he
could feel how terrified she was.

She opened her eyes and looked up at him. Bright
green shards glowed in her hazel eyes and despite the
dimness of the room, her pupils were tiny. He could feel
her pulling herself together, shoving away the panic and
forcing herself to face reality. As far as he was concerned,
it was about the bravest thing he'd seen in a long time.

"Better?" he asked her.

She gave a twitchy nod.

"All right," he told her. "I'm going to move away now.
Just relax, don't fight me and this will all be over soon."

"Please, Drake." Her voice broke on a sob. "I can't
do this."

"You don't have to do anything. Just breathe."

She closed her eyes and pulled in a deep breath. She'd
heard him and it was all he could ask for.

Drake shifted his weight, rolling off her body so that

he was lying next to her. She didn't try to run away, which was a good sign. He slid his palm from her hand up her arm, over her shoulder, and back down. He could feel the subtle vibration of energy flowing into her through his skin. It was vaguely erotic, the way she took his power into her body. She might have fought his touch, but she didn't resist this flow of energy between them. He could tell it made her feel good, made her warm, made her tingle. Oh yeah, definitely erotic.

Her eyes were still closed and he couldn't help but run his fingers over her face. He closed his eyes and just felt the fine texture of her skin, the delicate structure of her bones, the gentle curve of her cheek. The skin on her eyelids intrigued him, but not nearly as much as her lips. They were smooth, damp from her tongue, and so full and warm he had to hold perfectly still for a moment until the urge to kiss her subsided.

Helen pulled in a breath and his eyes were drawn to the soft swell of her breasts above her tank top. Her clothing wasn't revealing, but there was enough of her that she couldn't be completely contained. Without permission, his fingers quested lower, over her jaw, down her throat, and drew small circles along her collarbone.

Her hands clenched into fists at her sides and her breathing sped. He felt a rush of desire flood the connection between them, though he couldn't tell if it was his or hers or a combination of both. Whatever it was, Drake couldn't resist one light touch—just a single delicate glide of one fingertip over the top swell of her breast. Power sparked between them, arching through his body into hers.

She sucked in a breath, her nipples tightened, and Drake felt himself harden in response. He hadn't imagined that. She wanted this almost as much as he did.

Drake was ready to give her more than just a fingertip caress when he felt Logan's hand on his shoulder reminding him where he was. And that they had an audience.

With a gusty sigh of frustration, Drake pushed away his plans of seduction and focused on the job at hand—getting the two of them apart rather than closer together. What a suck plan that was. Too bad it was necessary.

Drake steeled himself for the pain he knew was coming at any moment. He moved his touch to safer territory and traced a single finger back down her arm, along the baby-soft skin of her inner arm, over her palm until only the tip of his finger touched the tip of hers. That was all the contact there was between them and Drake could feel a current flowing through that single point. He could feel every ridge of her fingerprint where they rasped against his. Heat spread out from that point until he was sure that a spark would ignite.

Helen blinked several times and looked up at him, then to the point where their fingertips touched—where the invisible sparks of energy were sinking into her. "What is that?" she asked him.

"I'm not sure." What he was sure of was he didn't want to pull away. That crushing avalanche of pain was waiting for him.

He took a deep breath, held it, and separated that last point of contact. The pressure came back in a giant wave, filling him until he was sure his skin would split open. It wasn't as bad as it was before, but it was a long way from good.

Drake gritted his teeth and a pained growl rumbled out of his chest. He gripped the bedspread in both fists and tried not to fight the pain, tried to embrace it. Accept it.

"Don't fight it," he heard Logan say from somewhere beyond the pain. "You can do this."

Drake wasn't sure. At least he wasn't sure he wanted to.

"You've got to do something," said Helen. Her voice was so sweet and clear, and just the sound of it helped him focus.

"There's nothing I can do. I'm sorry."

Drake thought about begging Logan to knock him out, but then he wouldn't be of much use to anyone in a fight. He had to beat this thing. He'd lived with pain for decades. He was tough. He could take it.

"I can't let him suffer like this," said Helen.

"I'll be okay," said Drake. "Just give me a minute." God, was that his voice? It sounded like his vocal cords had been shredded.

"I have to do something." She sounded as though she might be crying and Drake forced his eyes open. He couldn't let her cry.

"If he doesn't recover in a moment, then you can touch him. Be patient." That was Logan. Calm, sure, not at all upset by Drake's pain. Then again, he was the closest thing they had to a real doctor and if pain freaked him out, he was in the wrong line of work.

Logan had a hand on Helen's shoulder, keeping her from reaching out to Drake. It made Drake want to kill him for touching her. It gave him something to fight for. He forced himself to accept the pain. No one else was ever going to touch Helen. Only him.

It seemed to take forever, but he started to become accustomed to the pressure. It still hurt like a son of a bitch, but at least he wasn't writhing on the floor wishing he'd die.

"See?' said Logan. "He's already recovering."

Recovering. Hell of a way to put it. He felt like he'd

been forced to swallow a truck, but at least that truck was no longer on fire. As a recovery, it sucked, but it sure beat the pants off last time.

Drake let his breathing slow before he tried to move. When he looked at Helen, her hazel eyes were bright with unshed tears and she reached out to touch his face.

Logan's hand shot out faster than a lightning strike and grabbed her wrist. He shoved his body between them to serve as a barrier. "Don't touch him. He'd have to go through all of that again and I'm not sure his body could take it right now."

"I promise it couldn't," panted Drake.

"Sorry. I don't know what I did to hurt you, but I'm sorry. Whatever it was, I didn't mean . . ."

Drake still hadn't caught his breath and he hated looking weak in front of her. "It wasn't your fault."

"I should go check on Miss Mabel now."

"Wait a minute," said Logan. "I need to make sure you're okay, too."

Something in Logan's tone bothered Drake, but he wasn't at the top of his game right now and he couldn't figure out what it was. The Sanguinar stood up and followed Helen to where she stood with her hand on the door. Drake could see her body shaking a bit, but that wasn't completely unexpected, considering what she'd been through tonight.

"I'm fine."

"Just let me look you over. It will only take a moment."

"No!" She backed away from Logan, her eyes widening with fear.

Damn, Drake hated seeing that look on her face. He pushed himself up from the bed, surprised that his legs held him up. Barely. "Let her go, Logan. Let her go check on her friend."

"This is important," said the Sanguinar. "She's not okay."

"Yes, I am. I'm just worried about Miss Mabel."

Drake had to shove his hands into his jeans' pockets to keep from reaching out for her. He wanted to pull her into his arms and tell her everything would be fine over and over until it was true. Which would be never. One of them still had to erase the memories of tonight from her mind—at least the parts that involved anything that could endanger her or give her nightmares. That process alone was no fun, and since he couldn't touch her, he wasn't going to be the one to do it. The thought of Logan's hands on her made Drake want to reach for his sword.

Logan turned around and glared at Drake. Prettyboy didn't have a chance at intimidating him, no matter how powerful he might be. Drake was able to stand toe-to-toe with Thomas without backing down and that was no small feat. Thomas knew a thing or two about intimidation.

"She's not okay," Logan ground out, barely above a whisper. It was as though he didn't want Helen to hear. "Something is wrong with her. I really should figure out what it is."

Drake felt anxiety slither in his belly. If he'd done anything to hurt Helen he'd never forgive himself. Everything that had happened to her from the moment he walked over to her in the diner was his fault. He could have stayed in his seat. He could have ignored the pull she had on him. But he hadn't. He'd dragged her into his world and he was now responsible for her.

"What do you want to do?" Drake asked him.

"She needs to come with us," said Logan. "Back to the compound."

"You know what that means." Once she went there, she'd stay there. Her normal life would be over.

"Yes, but there's no other choice."

"Stop talking about me like I'm not here, damn it! What is it with you guys? You act like I'm some kid who can't make up her own mind."

Dealing with humans was so unnecessarily complicated. "You're right. I'm sorry," said Drake. He looked at Logan, who didn't look at all apologetic. "We're sorry."

Helen rolled her eyes, slipped out the bedroom door, and slammed it shut behind her.

Drake's head pounded, his bones ached, and his stomach twisted with guilt. He'd handled this whole night so badly and he wasn't sure how he was going to fix it.

He wasn't left much time to ponder the problem, though, because a few seconds later, he heard the sound of glass shattering in the living room followed by the distinctive snarl of Synestryn demons.

A heartbeat later, Helen screamed.

Chapter 5

Helen's front window blasted into the living room. A splinter of glass sliced across her cheek, but she barely noticed. Her attention was fixed on the monster standing in the middle of her living room. It was vaguely wolflike, but twice as big. Its muzzle was all wrong, though. It had the wide jaw of a shark and was filled with rows of serrated teeth. Where its eyes should have been were empty black holes surrounded by singed flesh, as if they'd been burned out of its head with a hot poker. Rust-colored fur covered its body and it shook off bits of broken glass like a dog did raindrops.

Blood trickled down her cheek and the thing swiveled its head around and stared at her with those empty black holes. Even without eyes, she was sure it could see her.

Helen screamed.

She was still standing partly in the hall and saw Thomas rush by from the kitchen with a gleaming sword in his hands. His big body blocked her from the monster's sight, giving her a chance to pull herself together.

"Out of the way!" shouted Drake from behind her, and she pressed herself against the wall to allow him and Logan room to pass.

Drake also wielded a sword—a big heavy one that

had to have been longer than her arm. He leapt past her just as a second monster jumped in through the shattered window. Drake stepped to his right so that he was between it and her. The thing stared past him, looking right at her with empty sockets. It bared its shark teeth and let out a rattling hiss that froze her in place.

"Time to go," ordered Logan. He grabbed her arm and started tugging her down the stairs toward the front door.

"Miss Mabel! We can't leave her behind."

Helen jerked away from his grasp and saw Miss Mabel rising unsteadily from a kitchen chair. She ran to the older woman's side to help her up. There was a door leading out to the deck, but it was a whole flight of stairs down to the backyard. Miss Mabel would never make it in time and Helen wasn't strong enough to carry her.

Before she could yell for help, another monster slammed into the glass of the back door, trying to break it, and it no longer mattered. They were trapped.

Logan was there by her side again. "I'll get her. You get yourself out of here."

Helen nodded. Logan lifted Miss Mabel into his arms, surprising her with his strength. He was too thin to lift her that easily, but Helen wasn't complaining.

The monster flung its body against the glass again, and this time the frame around the door splintered. The door banged open and the monster stepped inside on silent paws.

"Go. Now!" shouted Logan.

Helen picked up one of the nearby fire extinguishers and pulled the pin. "You first."

"Like hell," said Logan. "Drake! Kitchen!" he bellowed.

The monster sniffed the air, and once again she was

on the receiving end of an eyeless stare. It was only eight feet away and looked like it wanted to come closer.

Helen aimed the fire extinguisher and pulled the trigger. Yellow powder spewed out, hitting the thing right in the face. It let out a roar of pain, opening its shark mouth wide.

Drake ran into the kitchen and she saw something oily and black dripping down the blade of his sword. He stepped in front of them, facing the monster. His shoulders were wide, the muscles in his back and arms coiled and ready to strike. He wasn't frightened or breathing hard like she was. In fact, he looked like this was just another normal day for him. Get up. Go to work. Kill some monsters. Go home. No big thing.

The monster prowled forward but Drake held his ground. "Get her out of here."

Logan had no free hands to grab her, but Miss Mabel did. She clutched the strap of Helen's tank top in her bony hand and didn't let go so that Helen had to either follow along or risk hurting Miss Mabel. Logan headed for the front door, but through the narrow sidelight windows, Helen could see at least three more of the monsters sniffing around, looking for a way in.

They weren't going to make it out of here. No way.

"We'll go out through the garage," Logan told her. "My van is just outside and the keys are in the ignition. If you can get out, don't wait for the rest of us. Just go."

"I won't leave you all behind." Helen grabbed her purse from the table by the door.

"We know how to take care of ourselves. If you stay, you'll just get in the way."

Before she had a chance to respond, the wooden door that led into her garage shuddered under the weight of an assault. They weren't getting out this way, either.

"Any more exits?" asked Logan.

"Just through the bedroom windows."

"How far up are they?"

"Eight or ten feet, maybe."

Logan glanced down at Miss Mabel. "That's not going to work."

"Don't you dare stay behind for me," said Miss Mabel. "I've had a good run. Just give me one of those fire extinguishers and I'll hold them off so you can get out."

Helen's heart broke a little in the face of Miss Mabel's selfless courage. She thought that because she was old, her life was of less value than the others'. For all Helen knew, Miss Mabel had a lot more years to live than she did. "Not going to happen," replied Helen. "We're all going to get out of here."

"New plan," said Logan. "You two will hole up in the bathroom until we can clear a path."

There were no windows in her hall bathroom—no way for the monsters to get in except for the door. It sounded like a good idea to her. Helen nodded, slung her purse strap over her neck, and picked up a fire extinguisher.

As they passed by the front door, one of the monsters lunged into it. The thin metal sheath around the insulating core buckled, leaving a lump in the door about waist high. Helen yelped and scrambled up the stairs, nearly running into Thomas, who was holding off one of the beasts.

Three furry bodies lay crumpled on her carpet, leaking black blood. A fourth monster leapt for Thomas's throat and he sliced at it with his heavy blade. He scored a thin line along its chest, but the thing kept coming. Drake had killed another two monsters in the kitchen and a third one scrambled over the pile of his fallen brothers in order to swipe a claw at Drake's face.

Helen's throat closed down on a scream and her body went tight. *Please, God, don't let him get hurt.*

Drake dodged the strike, his sword flashed, and the monster's severed paw hit the kitchen wall, bouncing off. Oily blood sprayed across Helen's oak cabinets and it was all she could do not to vomit. She would never be able to cook in this kitchen again. Hell, she'd never be able to walk into this house again. Assuming she was able to get out of it alive.

The monster Drake had maimed let out a scream that sounded almost human. Chills raced over her limbs and her body froze in place. Which was probably for the best because at that moment Thomas took a long step back. He ducked below a furry body, shoved his sword into its belly, and stood up, hurling it over her head and down the hall with a massive burst of strength. He came only inches from knocking her over.

The monster lay sprawled in the hall, unmoving, soaking the carpet with its blood and . . . something else leaking out of its wounded abdomen.

Now all five of them were gathered at the top of the stairs where the hall, living room, and kitchen all met. There were monsters pounding at the front door, nearly through it, and more were climbing in the broken back door and front window, crawling over the dead bodies.

"We need an exit," said Logan in a calm, even tone.

"Working on it," said Thomas.

Drake kept his eyes on the approaching monster who was struggling to climb over the slippery bodies of the dead. "We've got maybe two minutes until the Handlers show up. Then things are going to get ugly."

Get ugly? She didn't know what he was looking at, but from where she was standing, surrounded by dead monsters leaking black blood all over her carpet and kitchen, she'd never seen anything uglier. She didn't even want to think about something uglier.

She felt panic start to set in now that she wasn't moving, and she had to fight it down with a force of will. She couldn't afford to lose it until she got Miss Mabel away safely.

"Van's in front," said Logan. "We won't make it out on foot with humans along."

"Thomas?" asked Drake.

"I'm on it," replied Thomas.

"How long do you need?" asked Drake.

Helen had no idea what they were talking about, but she didn't stop them to ask questions. The metal sheet on the inside of the front door was ripping open a little more with every thud. She could see a wide set of furry jaws snapping at her through the crack. No way was she going to distract them from making sure those shark teeth didn't get to her and Miss Mabel.

Thomas stepped forward to meet the monster that had just made it over the pile, hissing and pawing at the furry bodies. "Sixty seconds," was the answer to Drake's question.

"You got them." With that, Drake and Thomas both whirled into action, their powerful bodies making quick work of the remaining monsters. She'd never seen anything so beautiful, so deadly, as the two of them wielding their swords.

With one hand, Drake lifted Helen's kitchen table over the pile of dead bodies and used it to cover the hole where the back door used to be. He braced his left hand against it, holding it in place while he kept his sword in his right hand, ready to strike. He looked at Helen and gave her a reassuring smile and a wink. "Follow Logan out. He'll get you to the van."

"I don't want to leave you."

"You're not. I'll be right behind you. Now go!"

Helen felt a tug on her shirt—Miss Mabel's fingers around the strap of her tank top again—and followed along behind Logan. Thomas had gone berserk and was slashing through monster after monster as if he were cutting down wheat. As soon as one came scrambling through the window, he sliced it open or sent it flying. Sweat darkened his hair and made his shirt cling to his back.

Logan led her over the dead bodies and she tried not to think about the feel of the fur on her bare leg or the squish of blood under her feet. Thomas was through the front window and Helen briefly wondered whether her neighbors were watching this whole show. Not that she cared. As long as they all got out of this alive, she'd figure out something to tell them. Attack by wild dogs, maybe. She wasn't going to continue to live here, anyway. Not after tonight. Let the neighbors think what they want.

Logan cleared the remaining shards of glass away from the window frame with his booted foot and hopped down. She wasn't sure how Thomas did it, but he managed to keep his sword between them and every monster that came after them. And there were a lot. She didn't stop to count, but Thomas had already killed a bunch and there were at least four more coming for them. They'd abandoned the idea of getting in the front door as soon as they'd seen Thomas jump out into the front yard. For a big guy, he was fast and he used that bulk to push forward, clearing them a path to the van sitting in her driveway.

Miss Mabel had lost her hold on Helen's shirt somewhere along the way and she and Logan were a few feet in front of her. Helen jumped out of the window and

looked over her shoulder, hoping to see Drake right behind her. Instead, she saw his body fly out of the kitchen,
followed closely by her kitchen table. He hit the railing
at the top of the stairs, nearly spilling over it. His body
crumpled to the floor and the kitchen table slammed
into him, pinning him there. Then nothing moved. He
didn't get up.

Frantic, Helen lifted herself back up into the window,
feeling a bit of glass slice into her palms, and scrambled
over the bodies to reach him. He was big, but she could
drag him out. It was only a few feet. She could do it.

Helen shoved the table off him and he let out a
groan. His eyes fluttered open and he shook his head
as if to clear it. It only took a couple of seconds for him
to become coherent again, and when he did, he looked
pissed.

He opened his mouth to say something to her, but
then his gaze slid past her and Helen turned her head to
see what he was looking at.

It was tall, easily seven feet tall. It walked upright like
a human, but it wasn't even close to being human. The
thing's head was too large, missing a nose and lips to
cover the openings in its skull. Pointed teeth gleamed
and dripped saliva. Its legs bent the wrong way. Its skin
was snow white, completely hairless, and for clothing,
it wore a cloak made out of the rust-colored fur of the
monsters. In one hand it held a whip made from fine
chain links and in the other it held a red-hot metal rod
three feet long. Little wisps of flames danced up from
the tip of the rod.

Fire. *Oh God, no.*

She felt her muscles lock up with terror. The thing
stepped forward on oddly jointed legs, appearing to be
in no hurry.

Drake shifted his grip on his sword and pushed himself to his knees. She heard him stifle a gasp of pain and
wanted to reach out to him, but couldn't. She couldn't
move. Couldn't think.

The thing cracked the whip, hitting the railing next
to Drake's shoulder. The wood burst into flames and
even from three feet away, Helen could still feel the
deadly heat. The railing needed no time to catch fire; it
just went up in a blaze, spreading faster than normal fire
ever could. But then, this was not normal.

Drake was still trying to gain his feet. The thigh of his
jeans was soaked with blood and she could see a sharp
spike of bone sticking partially through the tough fabric.
His leg was badly broken. There was no way he was going to be able to stand on it, much less fight.

She wanted to tell him that, but her throat was closed
tight—too tight to speak, too tight to breathe.

The thing lifted the glowing rod and pointed it toward Helen.

"No!" shouted Drake. Somewhere, he found the
strength to jump to his feet and lunge at the thing. His
sword sliced high, taking off the arm that held the rod.

Fire erupted from the place where its arm used to
be. Drake threw his body over hers, knocking her to the
ground beneath him.

Helen felt a blast of heat and sound, but could see
nothing. Her face was buried in the greasy fur of one
of the dead monsters and the heavy animal stench of it
made her sick. She could feel the cold squish of blood
under her knees and Drake's heavy weight atop her.

Drake's body stiffened and he let out a deep groan
of pain that got louder and louder until it turned into a
scream. Then he fell silent and limp atop her.

The heat abated and Drake's weight disappeared.

Helen pushed herself up to scramble to her feet. All she wanted was to shove her shoulder under Drake's and help him get out of here, broken leg or not.

But it was too late.

Logan had been the one who picked him up off her, and now she could see the burns running down the right side of Drake's body. His hair and some of his clothes had been burned away, revealing blistered flesh beneath. Some beyond blistered to blackened.

Logan's too-pretty face became a mask of grief and pain, and Helen knew then that even if Drake was alive, he wouldn't be for long.

Drake had used his body to shield her from that fire and now he was going to die.

Logan had to get Helen out of here before another Handler showed up or before the fire near the stairway started burning out of control. Drake had killed the Handler, though Logan had no idea how he'd gotten close enough to manage that. Handlers were frail, but they rarely got closer than they needed to strike out with their whip. That was usually close enough for them to kill something. Even if it wasn't, the fire their bodies bled when injured burned hot enough and fast enough to take down anything unlucky enough to be in its path.

Thomas made sure the Handler was dead while Logan pulled Drake off Helen. He didn't like leaving Miss Mabel in the van unprotected, but Helen was the one who was important here. He had to figure out how she'd been able to absorb Drake's power. It could be the key to stopping the slow death of all the Sentinel races. The key to winning the Synestryn war.

Logan took in Drake's injuries in a sweeping glance.

The broken leg and ribs were no problem, but the burns . . . Drake wasn't going to make it, not even if Logan put every ounce of his dwindling reserves into healing the Theronai. He just didn't have the strength. He'd fed tonight, but the bloodline had been weak and it hadn't even managed to ease his gnawing hunger, much less fuel his magic. Walking Helen's and Drake's memories had taken enough out of him that it was as if he hadn't fed at all.

It was so fucking unfair that Logan wanted to howl. To have the ability to heal his ally but not the strength made him furious—made him want to lash out and drain every blooded human he could find. Take their power and leave their corpses to rot. Why should he even care anymore what happened to the humans?

Thomas's wide shoulders blocked out the overhead light, forcing Logan to look up. This was the part he hated most—admitting his weakness, crushing Drake's friends with the weight of grief. Living with that weight himself.

"How bad is it?" asked Thomas, his deep voice thick with rage.

Logan just shook his head. "I can ease his pain. It won't last long."

"No," said Helen. Her voice was thin and high and breathless. Almost panicked. "He's not going to die."

Denial. It always happened and Logan hated every fucking second of it. "I'm sorry, Helen."

"You don't understand. He can't die. He has to watch *me* die."

Logan had no idea what she was talking about, but something in her words tugged at a memory.

"We don't have time for this now," said Thomas. "We have to get out of here."

Logan picked up Drake's heavy body, being careful to avoid getting cut by Drake's sword. The flames had seared his fist closed, locking the weapon in his grip. Thomas took Helen by the arm. Behind them, Helen's house was swiftly being engulfed by flames. Thankfully, she was too worried over Drake to really notice. A small favor.

Sirens screamed in the distance. The human authorities were coming. It was time to go.

They laid Drake in the back of the van on a clean white blanket. He didn't even groan. The stench of burning flesh stung Logan's nose and made his empty stomach twist with nausea.

Helen scrambled in behind him and reached for Drake, but Logan stopped her. "Don't touch him. He has enough pain as it is."

Helen swallowed hard and nodded. Tears welled up and slid down her dirty cheek.

Chapter 6

The van swayed as it turned a corner, knocking Helen's head against the metal wall.

"Careful," said Logan. "It's going to be a bumpy ride."

Helen didn't even feel the impact. She was numb. Overloaded. She couldn't take this all in. The monsters, her house burning down. Again. Drake's horrible burns. It was all too much and something inside her had just shut down. She felt as if she were moving through cotton, every motion slow, never really feeling anything. The only thing that stood out among all the fuzziness was her certainty that Drake would live. She held on to that, knowing it was the only thing keeping her going right now. And she had to keep going. Miss Mabel still needed her to focus, to get her home safely.

"Will they be able to help him at the hospital?" she asked Logan.

His skin had lost all its color and he looked gaunter than before. He was still beautiful, but there was a fragileness about him now that hadn't been there before. He looked tired. Frail. Even his voice sounded weak. "We're not going to a hospital."

"We have to. He needs help."

"They can't help him, Helen. Thomas knows where to go."

Helen thought about arguing, but bit her tongue. She was out of her league here. She was floundering around trying to figure out what was happening to her normal, tidy world. Nothing was the same anymore and likely never would be again.

"How's it going back there?" asked Thomas. He was driving the van a little too fast, but his big hands held control of the wheel without effort.

"Not great. How much longer?" asked Logan.

"We'll be off the highway in five minutes. It's another fifteen to the house. I've put in a call for help and we should have some Gerai showing up within the hour."

"He's not going to last that long," said Logan. His voice was even, but there was a mask of anger on his face that he didn't bother to hide from her.

"What's a Gerai?" asked Helen. "Medicine? A doctor?"

Logan pressed his elegant hand against Drake's brow. The side of his face was burned beyond recognition, and if he did survive, the scars would be horrific.

Which didn't synch up with her vision at all. For the first time in her life, Helen was beginning to doubt that the vision was real. She wanted to be relieved by that hope, but not if it meant that Drake was going to suffer. She just wished she'd known what he'd been doing when he knocked her down. She would have stopped him. She wasn't sure how, but maybe she could have found a way.

"No," replied Logan. "A Gerai is a special kind of person who can donate blood to help Drake. Though I'm not sure that even that will help at this point."

"I'll donate if it will help. How can I tell if I'm one of these Gerai?"

Logan looked up at her, and something frightening flashed through those silvery blue eyes. For a second, he no longer looked beautiful. He looked deadly. Hungry.

The look was gone so quickly, she almost convinced herself she'd imagined it. Almost.

Logan shot a furtive glance toward Thomas, then down at Drake, as if he was checking to see whether anyone was watching him. He spoke in a low whisper that was barely loud enough to hear over the sound of the van. "You would share your blood?"

"Will it help?"

"Absolutely."

"How?"

"I am able to use the power in your blood to heal."

"How?"

"It's what I do. I'm not human, remember?"

Right. Not human. And she'd offered him her blood.

Logan licked his lips and pulled his hand away from Drake's head. There was plenty of room in the back of the van, but suddenly it seemed much smaller. Logan leaned forward with a predatory gleam in his eyes and reached his hand toward Helen.

Drake's good hand shot out and gripped Logan's wrist. "Don't," he ordered Logan, the single word mangled by his ruined lips.

Helen gasped, not expecting Drake to be alert enough to move. Pain twisted his face, or maybe it was rage. She couldn't be sure, but one thing was clear: Drake did not want Logan to touch her.

"She offered," said Logan. "It's my right."

"Not today it isn't." Drake's words were slurred as his mouth tried to move against the tightness of the burns.

"I need her blood. You'll die unless I'm strong enough to save you."

"Then I die. I won't have her obligated to you." Drake's eyes squeezed shut and he gasped for breath.

"You're not quite so demanding without me dulling your pain, are you?"

Drake made horrible choking noises and she could see him struggling to breathe. Whatever Logan was doing, it was killing Drake.

"Stop it! Stop hurting him."

"What's going on back there?" asked Thomas, glancing over his shoulder.

Logan ignored him and looked at her again. There was no longer any question about whether or not she'd seen something odd in his face. She had. He wasn't human. Not even close. Logan was something else. Something frightening and powerful and hungry. "You can help him, Helen. All I need is a little of your blood."

"No," ground out Drake between choking gasps.

"What the hell is going on?" bellowed Thomas.

"Helen, are you okay?" asked Miss Mabel.

"He'll die without your help," said Logan. "He'll suffer horribly and then he'll die."

Helen was not going to let that happen. "You can have as much blood as you need."

A triumphant light glowed in Logan's eyes. "Swear it."

"No," gasped Drake, barely audible. He was dying. Getting weaker by the second.

"I swear it." Helen felt the power of her vow wrap around her, become part of her. A sliver of her free will shriveled up and turned to ash. She had no idea what she'd just done, but whatever had just happened had changed her life forever.

Logan smiled a cold, inhuman smile. So beautiful. She couldn't help but stare.

She felt herself relax and start to drift. She could no longer remember why she'd been so upset. All she knew was that the world went away and the only thing that remained was Logan's beautiful face. Those haunting silvery eyes that almost seemed to glow.

"Close your eyes," he told her, reaching out for her.

Right before she obeyed, she saw sharp, white fangs lengthen from between his parted lips.

Drake couldn't move. He could barely breathe. He wasn't sure whether it was something Logan had done to him or if it was because of his injuries, but it didn't matter anymore. He couldn't save Helen. She'd given her blood oath to the Sanguinar and was bound to it for the rest of her life.

Drake choked on his rage, struggling against the weakness and pain that held his body down. All he could do was watch as Logan lowered his head to Helen's neck—her beautiful, soft neck that smelled like lilacs— and sank his fangs deep. Helen didn't even flinch. Her body was limp in Logan's arms, unable to fight. Not that she would have had a chance. Her vow had made sure of that. For the rest of her life, Logan would be able to feed from her whenever he wanted.

Drake heard a pitiful mewling sound and realized it was coming from himself. He couldn't stand to watch, but he couldn't look away, either. All he could do was bear witness to Logan's treachery and pray that he would stop before it was too late.

"That's it," said Thomas, his voice tight with worry. "I'm pulling over." The van slowed, but not nearly fast enough to make a difference.

Logan pulled away from Helen's neck, and a second later the wound closed as if it had never been there. Not even a pink spot remained. He laid her limp body gently on the floor of the van and smoothed her hair back from her face. His touch was loving in its tenderness and it made Drake's stomach give a sickening twist.

Logan turned to Drake and he could see something was different about him. Logan was no longer as pale or as gaunt as before and he wore an expression of victory. Conquest.

Thomas was in the back of the van with them now, but it was too late. There was nothing he could do to help Helen. The damage was already done.

Drake tried to warn Thomas that Logan had betrayed them, but he couldn't speak.

"What's wrong with her?" asked Thomas.

"She fainted. Everything's fine. Just drive."

"How's Drake?"

"Awake. Suffering. Leave me to tend him. Your job is to get us to the Gerai before it's too late."

Thomas hesitated as if sensing something was wrong. He pressed a blunt finger against Helen's wrist, checking for a pulse. "Did you know she was bleeding?" He held up Helen's hand and across the palm were several deep cuts. Glass was still embedded in one of them.

"I'll tend her. Go." Logan's voice was steady and even.

Drake struggled to speak. His eyes were wide and he was silently begging Thomas to understand what was wrong. Those damn choking noises came out, but nothing else. Nothing coherent.

Thomas laid her hand back down over her stomach and gave Drake a pained look. "You've got to do something for his pain."

"I will."

Thomas squeezed Drake's hand. Whether it was to reassure him or to tell him good-bye, Drake wasn't sure. A moment later, Thomas was gone and the van started moving again.

"I'm going to heal you now," he told Drake, "but before I do, I want you to listen. I know that as soon as your body is whole once again, you're more likely to kill me than thank me."

At least Logan knew the score. Now Drake had no obligation to warn him that he was going to kill him for taking Helen's blood.

"Helen is one of ours," whispered Logan in a reverent voice. "I don't know how it is possible, but I believe she is a Theronai. Your Theronai, should you choose to claim her."

Drake struggled to accept what Logan had just said. It didn't make any sense and between the searing pain of the burns and his broken bones, he couldn't think clearly enough to figure it out.

"We need her," continued Logan. "And she needs you. Who knows if any of the other Theronai would be compatible with her? Neither Thomas nor Zach is or they would have known it tonight like you did. They would have been drawn to her in some way. She needs you to bring her into our world, but if you try to kill me, you won't survive. I'll make sure of it. Before I'm done healing you, you will be peace-bound."

No! Drake struggled, but the movement only managed to make the broken ends of his ribs grate together. A wave of pain swept over him and he had to struggle to stay conscious.

Peace-bound to a Sanguinar who had hurt Helen. He couldn't stand the mere thought. The Sanguinar had been known to put a kind of self-destruct mechanism into the people they healed as a guarantee that their patients wouldn't try to kill them after they were well. War among the Sentinel races had been common for centuries, and the Sanguinar needed the insurance. Still, it hadn't been done in years. Human bloodlines had grown too weak and none of the Sanguinar were strong enough to wield that kind of magic any longer.

Maybe he was just bluffing so Drake wouldn't try to kill him the second he had the chance.

"You think I'm not strong enough, but you're wrong. Helen's blood is nearly pure. I don't know how that's possible, but it is. I am no longer the weakling you've come to know."

Drake forced himself to look up into the Sanguinar's too-beautiful face.

Oh, hell. It was true. Drake could see it in Logan's triumphant expression. He could see the power glowing behind his pale eyes.

Logan smiled, his beauty too intense for Drake to stare at for very long. He looked away and prayed that whatever power Logan had, he wouldn't use it to harm any humans. There was nothing any of the Theronai could do to stop a Sanguinar at full strength. Not even the Slayers had that kind of power and they were virtual killing machines.

"I think we understand each other," said Logan, satisfaction ringing in his voice. He ripped open the remains of Drake's shirt, sending bits of charred cotton into the air. Logan placed his hands on Drake's chest and closed his eyes.

A cool rush of power swept over Drake, as gentle as a breeze, and in the blink of an eye, the burns were gone, his leg was whole, his ribs no longer crushed. Drake had never seen anything or felt anything like it before. He'd been healed by the Sanguinar plenty of times, but it was never like this. Healing hurt. All the pain of recovery was shoved into a short interval of time, increasing its intensity. Usually, the Sanguinar didn't have enough power to both heal and prevent pain. The Theronai had learned to accept the pain as part of the price for recovery, and Drake had expected the worst, considering the extent of his burns.

Not only did the healing not hurt; it felt good. Soothing, like cool water lapping gently over his skin.

Drake looked up at Logan. The Sanguinar sat back on his heels. "Would you like to take a swing now just so you know the measures I've put in place are real?"

Drake shoved himself upright. Taking a swing would have been fun, but even thinking about it made his head throb. Whatever physical harm he did to Logan would come back to him greatly magnified. A punch to that pretty jaw might cost Drake all his teeth, or even break his neck. He'd had enough pain for one night and he needed to take care of Helen—make sure the Sanguinar had done no lasting damage.

"Fix Helen's hands, her face," ordered Drake. "You owe her at least that much." As soon as Logan complied, Drake was going to have Thomas come back here and beat the hell out of him. Drake couldn't touch him, but Thomas sure as hell could. Hard.

It took Logan only a few seconds to pull the glass from her wounds and knit her skin back together. Even the blood evaporated, leaving nothing but smooth, pink skin.

Drake ached to touch her—to check her for injury—but held back. There were too many odd things happening between them and he had to figure out what to do before he touched her again. Once he did that, he knew his thinking would be skewed and rationality would fly right out the window. She felt too good under his hands. Too right.

"Wake her up."

Logan reached for her, but let his hand fall. "No. Do it yourself."

"I'll have to touch her."

Logan smiled. "I know."

That was it. Drake was done dealing with Logan. It was time for Thomas to lend a helping fist. "Thomas, pull over. Now."

Thomas spared one quick glance over his shoulder, saw Drake awake and lucid, and the van screeched to a halt.

Logan wasn't going to wait around long enough for Drake to tell Thomas what he'd done. Drake wouldn't be able to hurt him, but Thomas was another matter entirely.

Before Thomas had completely stopped the van, Logan jumped out the back doors and sprinted into the trees skirting the rural Kansas road. His body was humming with power and even at a dead run, he wasn't breathing hard. He dialed Tynan, hoping his cell phone's signal was strong enough out here to stay connected.

"Yes," answered Tynan, his voice smooth and deep. He'd lost his accent years ago and not even a hint of it remained to give away his foreign birth in a country that no longer existed.

Logan's feet pounded over the ground. The air was warm and smelled like freshly tilled earth and prairie grass. "I need you to pick me up immediately. I'm on foot."

"Aren't you with Drake?"

"Not anymore. I had to leave. My company was no longer welcome."

Thankfully, Tynan didn't question him further. As leader of the Sanguinar, he had the right, but Tynan was a man who favored action as well as protecting those of his own race. "I can have someone out your way in an hour. We have plenty of men in the area."

"No," said Logan. "It needs to be you."

"I'm farther away. It will take me at least six hours to reach you."

Damn. That was putting it too close to dawn for Logan's taste. "Where are you?"

"Just north of Dallas."

"Project Lullaby?" asked Logan.

"Yes."

"You'll definitely want to meet me, then. Update me on our progress so I can help."

"I thought you said you weren't able to help—weren't strong enough," said Tynan with a hint of irritation. "That's why you were assigned to hunt with the Theronai."

"Things have changed." What an understatement that was. His whole world had shifted. For the first time in two centuries he was no longer starving. No longer weak. He wanted to howl out his triumph, but that would only give away his location.

"What's changed? Exactly?"

"Not on the phone. Meet me at Dabyr as soon as you can." The Theronai Nicholas liked his gadgets and it wouldn't surprise Logan at all to find out that he used them to listen to phone conversations when it suited him.

"This had better be worth my time," said Tynan.

"It is."

*   *   *

"Do you want me to go after him?" asked Thomas.

Drake watched Logan disappear into the trees, moving faster than he'd ever seen any Sanguinar run. Catching up with him wouldn't be easy and there were still two women to look after—one unconscious and the other without her walker to help her get around. "No. Let him go. He'll turn up eventually."

"What happened? You look like you never got blasted by the Handler. Even your hair has grown back."

"Logan did it. Right after he tricked Helen into a blood oath and fed from her."

Thomas let out a low whistle. "She's blooded?"

"Not just blooded. Logan says she's one of ours. A Theronai." Drake still couldn't believe Helen was one of his kind. It didn't seem possible even though it did explain a lot about the way he was drawn to her. The way he felt compelled to touch her no matter how much pulling away hurt. He had to shove his hands deep into his pockets to keep from doing just that.

Thomas stood still for a moment as if absorbing the words, then looked down at Helen's prone body. One of her braids had lost the band securing it and it had unraveled most of the way up. Her face was smeared with soot as were her bare arms. Oily black patches darkened her knees and the hem of her shorts. Synestryn blood. They'd have to wash it off her as soon as possible, though Drake suspected that if it had left any taint in her body, Logan would have neutralized it.

"If she's one of ours . . . You were drawn to her. You can bond to her."

Drake nodded.

"Do you think that I might be able to, too?"

The desperate hope lighting Thomas's eyes made

Drake's chest tighten. Thomas was older than Drake. He'd had more years to gather power into his body, more years to suffer under the excruciating strain of containing it, like a balloon forced to hold too much air, stretched to the point of breaking. Even so, Thomas had never once complained, never once ignored his duty because it was too painful to go on.

Thomas had already touched Helen several times tonight, and if he felt anything odd, he'd never said so. Drake understood now what Logan meant when he said that Helen needed him. So far, Drake was the only one of the Theronai who could join with Helen and bring her into their world—show her her rightful place. Only the men she was capable of uniting with would be drawn to her. The power between a bonded pair of Theronai had to be compatible. That unexplainable, almost magnetic attraction was nature's way of letting them know which partners could make effective use of their power. If Thomas had felt it, he wouldn't be questioning it now. He'd already know.

Thomas reached out a wide, blunt-fingered hand slowly as if afraid he'd hurt her and placed it on her forehead. Drake wanted to stop him. He didn't like the thought of any other man touching her, but he held himself still. Silent.

Thomas needed to know the truth, and the only way to do that was to feel it for himself.

Thomas felt nothing when he touched Helen. No pull, no spark, no heat. Nothing but cool, smooth skin.

Helen could never be his.

He had one leaf left, only days until it fell and his soul shriveled, and for the first time in more than two centuries a female Theronai had walked into their lives. This was the thing they all prayed for. It was the only thing that kept the Theronai going despite the pain, despite the constant battles and bloodshed. That single, precious hope that one day they'd find a woman who could save them and help them fight. He'd found the woman, but there wasn't a thing she could do to save him.

He wasn't sure whether he should laugh or cry or just give up entirely—will his body to fly apart under the strain of holding too much energy and end his suffering.

Thomas closed his eyes and turned away from Drake, not wanting to share his failure with anyone. He refused to cry. Refused to wallow in self-pity. He'd known for a long time that he was nearing the end. This changed nothing. At least not for him.

Drake could claim her. At least Thomas could take some comfort in the fact that his friend would no longer suffer. Not a lot, but some.

Thomas cleared his throat. "We're only a couple miles from the farmhouse where we're supposed to meet the Gerai. We should get going."

"Thomas." Drake had reached for him, but Thomas saw it coming and stepped aside.

"Forget it. I'm fine."

"How much time do you have left?" Drake's chest was bare with only the shreds of his tattered shirt hanging from his shoulders. There were at least a dozen leaves left clinging to Drake's tree.

Beneath his own shirt, Thomas could feel the minuscule weight of the last leaf clinging to his lifemark. He pressed his hand against it as if he could help it hold on just a little longer. He could live for years even after it was gone, but he'd be doing so without his soul. Good. Evil. Soon it would all be the same to him. Whatever got the job done.

Thomas was not going to let that happen. He would not become like the things he hunted. "Enough time to find Kevin's sword. Let's go."

Drake hadn't moved. He was still standing beside Thomas, watching him. "She might not be the only one. What if there are others like her out there? You have to hold on."

"I will," Thomas lied. "Stop worrying about me. Helen's the one we need to worry about now."

Drake nodded. "I need to get her cleaned up. Burn her clothes." They were smeared with blood, both red and black. All of it was dangerous to leave behind. The scent would draw demons from miles away. Which was just one more reason to get moving.

"You shouldn't be touching her, at least not until you know you can stop without hurting yourself. If the Synestryn come again, she'll need you to be able to fight."

"I'll be able."

"You sure as hell weren't able to fight when you were on the diner floor, convulsing."

"It's better now."

"Yeah, because you're not touching her, moron." Thomas hated the sound of anger in his voice. He loved Drake like a brother. It wasn't Drake's fault that Helen couldn't save him.

"I'm sorry, Thomas."

"Forget it." Thomas looked at Helen lying so still in the back of the van. She was a miracle, just not his. The less time he spent thinking about that—looking at her—the better. "Let's just get out of here."

Drake managed to keep his hands off Helen for the rest of the drive, but by the time they got to the isolated farmhouse, his knuckles ached from keeping his fists so tight.

The Gerai had already arrived and were waiting for them outside. Two young men and a girl who couldn't have been out of high school sat on the steps leading to the covered porch. They were all armed in the manner of humans—each carrying a pistol as well as a shotgun. The girl had her pale hair hidden beneath a baseball hat, and her watchful eyes peered out from beneath the brim. The two men who were with her looked to be in their early twenties, both stocky and sharing enough facial features to identify them as brothers.

Drake stepped out of the van, keeping his hand near his sword while he surveyed the area for signs of Synestryn.

"It's safe," said the girl. She stood and held out her hand in an incongruously masculine gesture. "I'm Carmen and these are my cousins Slade and Vance. We live one county over, so we thought we'd come help. Alexander contacted us."

Alexander the Broody. A Sanguinar. Great. Just what this night needed. Another fucking bloodsucker.

Drake shook her hand, checking to make sure she wore the ring of the Gerai. It was a simple silver band etched with a single leaf. One ring was given to each of the blooded humans who vowed to aid the Sentinels. They were sworn to offer help whenever necessary, and it wasn't uncommon for entire families to swear their loyalty. They were also bound to secrecy. More often than not, the Gerai were humans who had been saved from the Synestryn, at least at some point in their ancestry. The more Athanasian blood a human had running through his veins, the harder it was to wipe his memories. Sometimes recruiting him was easier than scrubbing his mind.

Camen's ring gave off a subtle hum of power that any

of the Sentinels could sense. It only worked for the one for which it had been created, so if someone stole a ring, it would be useless to help them pose as a Gerai. She was the genuine article, young as she was.

Maybe Drake was just getting old.

The two brothers stepped down and offered their hands as well. Both checked out.

"I'm Drake. Thomas is the big guy. Miss Mabel is in the front seat. We lost her walker, so we'll need one of you boys to help her get inside. Carefully."

"I'm on it," said Slade, hopping down off the steps. He wasn't very tall, but he had the solid build of a man who'd grown up with hard labor. Considering that this was farm country, that was likely the case.

Carmen felt under the porch railing until she found the hidden key that would let them in.

"Wait," said Thomas. "Let me check it out first."

Carmen tipped her head back until she could see him from under the hat. "I'm telling you the place is safe. I can always sense the Synestryn when they're nearby. And they're not."

"I'm sure you can, little girl. I'm also sure that I'm not letting you lead the way into a dark house without so much as a pocketknife to protect yourself."

She patted her shotgun. "I've got Hazel."

Thomas peered down at her weapon and lifted a dark brow. "They did teach you that most demons out there can't be killed without a sword or magic, right?"

"Sure. I also know that if Hazel knocks them down first, you'll have a lot easier time chopping them to bits."

Thomas grunted. "Just stay behind me and keep Hazel pointed in some direction other than my back."

Carmen accepted the order like a good little soldier and handed Thomas the key.

"Vance," said Drake. "Grab whatever gear is in the back and bring it in so we can inventory it."

"Don't you know what's in your own van?" he asked.

Drake opened the back doors of Logan's van. There were no windows back here and a heavy curtain could be pulled to block out the light from the front windows. The bastard was going to have fun finding shelter before the sun came up.

The thought made Drake smile. "Not my van. Bring in the sheet she's lying on, too. There's blood on it and we need to burn it."

Helen hadn't moved. And she was pale. Drake wanted to kill Logan, but just the thought gave him a violent headache.

"I'll carry her," offered Vance.

Drake should have agreed, but the sound of interest warming Vance's voice changed his mind. He'd take the pain of releasing her again if he had to, but he wasn't letting some human he didn't know touch her.

"Like hell," said Drake.

He lifted her into his arms and the second his skin touched hers, he was flooded with a sense of completion— all the empty spots filled up, easing an ache he didn't even realize he had. He pulled her against his bare chest, closed his eyes, and let his power soak into her, let her sweep away the pressure that had already built itself back up to painful levels. Less than a half hour without touching her and he hurt. How in the world was he ever going to let her go?

He wasn't. That was the simple truth. He was going to claim her. He'd never be able to wait long enough to take her back to the compound and figure out if any of the other Theronai were able to bond with her. He was going to claim her for his own and to hell with the consequences. He wasn't going to put Helen on display and let all the other Theronai touch her. He'd found her and he was keeping her for himself. That part was easy. The hard part was going to be convincing her she wanted to be kept.

Chapter 7

"Time to wake up, sleepyhead."

Helen felt Drake's voice in her head as much as she heard it in her ears. It was an odd sensation, a sort of resonating echo that vibrated her brain. She could feel his touch inside her as well as outside, gentle fingertips stroking her face and arms, gentle thoughts stroking her mind.

"Come on. We've got to get you cleaned up. Out of these clothes."

She felt a tug at her waistband and the pop of the button being released. He was taking off her shorts.

That got her synapses firing. She jerked awake, her arms failing out to bat his hands away. She forced her heavy lids open and found herself in a bathroom, sitting in his lap. His hard thighs were warm under her bottom and one thick arm was wrapped around her, just under her breasts, keeping her from sliding onto the floor.

The bathroom was big, old, a little shabby, but clean. A giant claw-foot tub was filled with water and she could hear the faint pop of thousands of bubbles along the water's surface. The air was steamy and smelled like lavender.

Helen stared at the water in longing. She was safe

in the water, and as the memories of the night flooded back to her, what she truly wanted was to feel safe. To know Miss Mabel and Lexi were safe. That Drake was safe, not horribly burned and dying.

But if he was dying, then how was he holding her in his lap? Confused, Helen looked up at Drake. He was whole—not a burn or scar in sight. Even his hair had grown back.

Was she dreaming this? Or had the attack been the dream? Her head was still clouded from sleep and she couldn't seem to make sense of what was going on.

"Shhh." He slid a hand over her hair as if to calm her. "Don't try to sort things out yet. You were really out of it, thanks to Logan. Give yourself a chance to wake up first."

"You were burned."

"Yes, but I'm okay now. It wasn't as bad as it looked."

"Liar." It had probably been a hell of a lot worse than it looked. At least for him. Helen had done a fair amount of research on burns, thanks to her vision, and she knew that they were one of the most painful injuries possible.

"We'll talk later. Right now we need to get this blood cleaned off."

Helen looked down at herself and cringed. She was filthy. There were smears of blood on her clothes and skin and what looked like oil. What looked like, but wasn't. It was blood from those monsters.

She had their blood on her. It was too disgusting for words.

Helen felt a wave of nausea roll through her. She tried to fight it. She clenched her teeth and breathed through her nose.

Drake lifted her up into his arms and stood, then

let her feet drop to the ground. She could see now that he'd been sitting on the lid of the toilet, which he raised, along with the seat. "You're all right," he told her. "Just breathe."

She was. She was breathing and Drake was breathing with her, and slowly it started to work. She felt Drake's rough thumb sliding along the inside of her arm, sending tendrils of comforting energy rushing through her. Her stomach settled enough that she was confident she wouldn't puke, at least. And she was standing on her own two feet, which was an improvement as well. Drake still held her close and he still had his forearm wrapped around her, but he wasn't holding her up. She was doing that all by herself. Thank God.

Helen needed to get clean. That was the next rational thought that went through her head. She wanted every bit of this . . . stuff—which she was not going to name—off her. "I'm fine now," she told him. "Just give me a few minutes to bathe."

He lifted her arm to show her his long fingers wrapped around her wrist. "Sorry. We're connected again. Don't worry. I'll be a good boy and close my eyes."

"Can't you pull away again? Like you did before?"

"I could, but it would hurt. You don't want me to hurt, do you?"

He was playing her, trying to make her feel guilty. And it was working.

Helen turned around and glared up at him. The sharp angles of his face were highlighted by the harsh light of the bare lightbulb over the sink. His shirt was gone and she could see the tattoo on his chest clearly now. It was a tree that ran all along his left side. The roots snaked down below his belt and the branches reached up until some of them stretched over his shoulder and partly down his left arm. The branches were mostly bare with only a few leaves left and the artwork was so perfectly lifelike that she imagined she could see the leaves sway with every breath he took. Amazing.

Beautiful.

Without realizing what she was doing, Helen reached out and ran her finger over the branches, down the trunk until it turned into thick roots. Heat and power sizzled beneath her fingertip and she felt herself growing stronger, more awake, with every second.

Drake's stomach tightened until she could see ridges of muscle standing out, and his hand flattened over hers, trapping it against his muscles. Nice.

"If you go any lower, you won't be the only one getting naked, sweetheart."

For one insane moment, it sounded like a great idea—getting to see all that manly flesh naked, up close and personal. And then she remembered where she was. Who he was. She was getting the hots for a man who was worse than merely wrong for her. He'd be there when she died. Soon.

Helen's face heated along with the rest of her and she had to suppress a shiver. He was staring down at her and she could swear those golden brown eyes of his were glowing from within. His gaze took in her blush, followed it down her neck and lower, where she could feel her nipples draw tight.

The muscles in his jaw bunched and his nostrils widened as he breathed in deep. "You sure do know how to tempt a man," he told her in a rough voice. "And I'm more than happy to climb into that tub with you and make sure you're clean all over, but we can't wait any longer to get you out of those clothes."

Oh, man. That all sounded good, every insane bit of

it. It had been a long time since she'd felt like this for a
man. Maybe she never had felt quite like this. Even so,
she wasn't about to let herself get involved with the man
who was going to watch her die. Somehow that thought
made the whole vision more horrible—put a spin on it
that she'd never thought of before. It was one thing to
have a stranger watch her die. It was completely different if the person standing there was one she cared about,
one who was supposed to care about her.

A knock sounded on the door and Thomas's voice
drifted through the thick wood. "I got a fire going. We
need to burn her clothes now."

Helen felt her body tense at the mention of fire. She'd
had more than enough of that for one night. The fire
in the diner, then another in her home. Drake's burned
body. It was too much, so she just stopped thinking
about it.

It took Helen a moment to clear her head and recap
what he'd just said. Burn her clothes?

The blood. It drew the monsters to them.

Helen no longer cared that she had an audience.
She shucked her shorts and tugged her tank top over
her head and handed them to Drake. She'd knocked his
hand away in her haste and he'd gasped in pain before
he recaptured her wrist. "Sorry," she told him with a grimace. "Didn't mean to hurt you."

He nodded in acknowledgment, opened the door a
crack, and shoved the clothes out.

Helen looked down at her bra, panties, and socks, checking for signs of blood. "I don't see any blood, do you?"

She wasn't a fashionably skinny woman, and even
though she was as covered as she would have been in a
bathing suit, she still felt naked. Exposed. Clothing hid
a lot of sins, and heaven knew her body had plenty of

those to hide. She wished like crazy that she'd actually started that exercise program she'd promised herself she would on New Year's Eve.

Drake's jaw did that bunching up thing as he stared down at her. His hands found her waist and settled there, gripping and releasing like he was stuck on a loop, trying to decide what to do. He was staring at her breasts, her hips, her legs. Sure, she'd asked him to check for blood, but what he was doing was more than just a casual glance. She knew that her sturdy bra and modest panties kept her covered, but that didn't stop him from finding a way to make her feel naked.

Helen had never seen anyone look at her like this before, not even the men with whom she'd shared her bed, few as they were. Drake was looking at her like his life depended on it, like his whole world was right there and that nothing else mattered.

"God, you're beautiful."

Of all the things she'd expected to hear him say, that was not even on the list. She was stunned speechless by his ludicrous statement. Sure, she was no hunchback, but she'd seen enough TV to know the kind of women guys really wanted and she was nowhere close.

"Um," was all she managed to get out.

"Anything else?" asked Thomas from the other side of the door, sounding impatient.

Drake's eyes blazed with hope.

Helen fought the urge to cover herself with her arms. "Did you see any blood?" she asked him again.

"Turn around," he ordered in a sinfully thick tone.

Helen did and squeezed her eyes shut in the hopes that it would make this whole embarrassing situation go away. She was sure she could feel Drake staring at her ass. As if he could miss it.

"Your clothes are fine," he said with a distinct note of disappointment. Then, louder, to the door, "That's all, Thomas. Thanks."

So, there she stood with her back to him and she could see his face in the bathroom mirror. He was still looking down at her with an expression that she would have called lust in any other circumstances, or had he been looking at some other woman. But he was looking at her and he kept looking and didn't stop. Helen felt a blush covering her skin, or maybe it was just the warm, humid air that had her heating up.

He still had a loose hold on her left wrist and he used it to pull her back against his bare chest. Oh, baby. She was filled with a rush of warmth, a whole swarm of those tingling streamers of energy that made her body sing. He pressed his hand over her ribs and held her tighter. She could see his tan fingers splayed out across her paler skin in the mirror. Her wrist was pinned at the small of her back, trapped between their bodies. His hold was too intimate. Too possessive.

And, man, did she like it. She didn't want to move.

She watched him in the mirror as he lowered his head until his mouth just barely brushed her neck. He didn't move, didn't kiss her, just breathed in deep.

He mumbled something against her skin.

"What?" It was hardly a whisper, but he heard it all the same.

He looked up, just lifting his face enough to look at her in the mirror. He smiled then, a dark, sensual smile that told her he knew she'd been watching. "You smell like lilacs. I've always liked lilacs."

What could she possibly say to that? "Uh, thanks."

As responses went, that was a ten on the lame-o-meter.

He just chuckled and she felt the deep sound reverberate in her chest. He pulled away a little, but his hands stayed on her, scattering her thoughts.

"We should stop before I forget all about why we're in here."

"In where?" she asked, dumbfounded.

"In the bathroom. For a bath."

"Oh, right." She'd forgotten, but then she had an excuse. A gorgeous man was looking at her like she was a Victoria's Secret model who held the key to the meaning of life. She'd never had that happen before and she wasn't quite sure how to react. "You should go, then, so I can get undressed."

"Not going to happen. I've spent enough time hurting tonight. But I did promise not to look. Unless you want me to." That was an offer that not even she could miss.

"No. Looking is definitely a bad idea."

"Sounds like a great idea to me, but I promise to play nice." He closed his eyes, but kept her wrist captive.

"I'm going to have a hard time getting undressed without my hand."

"I'm happy to help."

"Gee. Thanks. What a guy."

He laughed. "Okay, okay. Here." He put his hands on her waist again, wearing a pleased smile. "Now your hands are free."

"You're enjoying this, aren't you?"

"Not nearly as much as I would be with my eyes open, but you're worth the sacrifice."

Helen shook her head, but couldn't help the smile that curved her mouth. She liked this side of Drake, this teasing, playful side that she never would have guessed existed.

She made quick work of the rest of her clothing,

grabbed a towel, and led Drake the few steps it took them to reach the tub. She stepped into the warm water. It was perfect and she let out a small sigh.

"No fair," he told her. "Noises like that make me want to look."

"Don't you dare."

"Spoilsport."

"Pervert," she shot back.

Drake laughed and tightened his hold on her.

Helen pried his hands from her waist and held on to them as she lowered herself into the water. The tub was deep and she sank down in all the way to her neck. Pure bubbly bliss.

She couldn't help but groan in pleasure.

"You're killing me with those noises, Helen. Have some pity."

"Sorry." She was covered from neck to toe with bubbles, so she said, "Just have a seat and I'll be done as fast as I can."

Drake sat down on the floor with his back to the tub and draped her fingers over his bare shoulder. "You'll just have to keep a hold on me for a change."

Helen stared at her hand. On his shoulder. No big thing, right? She was a grown woman and had touched plenty of men's shoulders in her lifetime. Even some naked ones. Sure, never any quite so wide or well sculpted as Drake's, and certainly none with intricately tattooed branches etched into them, but that didn't mean she had any reason to be staring, unable to move or even blink. It was just a shoulder. It wasn't even a naughty part.

Which brought up a whole new set of images in her head. Naughty parts, indeed. Naked Drake naughty parts. Yum.

I'm losing it. It was a statement of fact at this point.

Or perhaps *lost it* would have been closer to the truth. Past tense. No turning back. No hope.

"I don't hear any splashing back there," he said. "Need some help?"

Lots of help. Of the psychiatric variety. More than he could give. "I'm fine." It came out as a squeak and Helen winced.

"You don't sound fine." He started to turn his head.

Helen freaked and covered her sudsy breasts with her arms. "Don't look!"

Drake let out a pained gasp and doubled over.

Shit. She'd let go of him. "Sorry," she yelped, and she scrambled to sit up enough to reach him. Water sloshed over the side of the tub, making a mess of the floor. She pressed a dripping hand against his lower back—the closest thing to her—and Drake pulled in a deep breath.

"Son of a bitch!"

"I'm so sorry, Drake." She stroked his spine, hoping to ease his pain.

He was breathing hard and a fine sweat had broken out over his back. It took him a couple of minutes to pull himself together, but Helen didn't try to hurry him. She felt bad enough as it was forgetting that he needed her to stay in contact. After he'd put his body between her and a fire-wielding monster, remembering that one little thing should have been the least she could do. She felt horrible that she'd forgotten.

"I'm okay now," he said, but it sounded like a lie. He was still stiff, holding his arms around his middle as if his stomach hurt.

He leaned back and Helen petted him for a minute, making slow, sweeping passes over his bare back. That seemed to help him relax, so she let her hand slide up his spine until it settled at the nape of his neck. His dark hair fell over part of her hand and she could feel the slippery width of the iridescent choker he wore. There was no clasp that she could detect and she wondered how he got it off.

"I'm going to reach in that water and take hold of your ankle, and I swear to God if you pull your hand away or freak out again I'm going to climb into that tub with you and make sure that enough of our skin is touching so there's no chance of another mistake. Got it?"

Oh yeah. She got that image in all its wet, slippery detail. It would be a tight squeeze to get him to fit in the tub with her, but she was fairly sure that they could get creative enough to manage it. "I won't freak out."

Without turning around, he reached his hand back and found her ankle deep in the warm water. His fingers curled around it and only then did he let out a relieved sigh.

"You think you can make this quick? This whole having you naked thing is a little harder on me than I thought it would be."

She was not going to ask how hard. No. Not even with an opening like that. Instead, she threw herself into the washing process, scrubbed herself from head to toe, and was done in less than three minutes flat. Her hair was still dripping into her face when she reached for the towel she'd laid by the tub. Part of it had been soaked by the water that she'd sloshed out of the tub, but she didn't care. She also had no idea where her elastic hair bands had gone, but if she could find a brush, she would count herself fortunate.

Helen unstopped the tub and rose a little awkwardly to her feet. She was careful not to dislodge Drake's hand while she did a quick job of drying off. Everything from the knees down was still dripping, but the rest of her was good. When the towel was securely around her torso, she said, "Okay. I'm covered."

"Pity," he replied.

She smirked and offered Drake her hand. He gallantly helped her out of the slippery tub, then laced his fingers through hers.

"What now?" she asked. "Other than the part where I stop being naked. Obviously."

He looked like she'd punched him in the gut. "I am not going to survive you, woman."

The vision of her death reared up for a split second, the flames and Drake's smiling face blocking out all else. A moment later, she was back in the bathroom, damp and naked, but safe. She felt a tremor run through her limbs and she tried to give Drake a playful smile. She was pretty sure it came out as more of a grimace. "Actually, I'm fairly certain you'll survive me just fine."

He was looking at her funny, his head bent down so he was eye level with her. "What's that supposed to mean? And what was that I just felt—that spike of fear?"

"Nothing. Just forget it."

"Like hell I will. It's not the first time I felt it, either. What was that?"

"It's really no big deal."

"Anything that makes you that afraid that fast is a big deal. It's my job to kill things that scare you like that. Tell me what it is and I'll go kill it for you."

He was serious. He really, literally, meant he would kill something for her. She wasn't sure whether to be disgusted or flattered. He really knew how to throw a woman for a loop with a caveman statement like that.

"How about we just find me something to wear instead?" she suggested.

"Now you're just trying to distract me, reminding me that you're all wet and naked under that towel."

Oh yeah, as if she really thought a man like him could be swayed by the thought of her not-so-hot body. How ridiculous. "Is it working?" she teased, giving him the opening to laugh it off.

He didn't. In fact, he backed her up until she was flush against the door. His body crowded hers and he held both her wrists against the door, just above her head. "The distraction would work better if you took the towel off."

He was giving her that hungry stare again—the one that made her wonder just what it was he was looking at because it sure as hell wasn't her. No way. Men did not look at Helen like that. Not like they wanted to devour her.

"Wh-what are you doing?" she asked only because she really wasn't sure.

"Wanting you. Needing you."

"Yeah, right," she scoffed.

"You don't believe me?" he asked, silky smooth. His hips pressed forward, tight against her, and she could feel the unmistakable ridge of his erection hard against her belly.

Words failed her. Breathing failed her, too. She just stared at him with a deer-in-the-headlights look because she couldn't do anything else.

His gaze shifted to her mouth and lingered as his head bent down, drifting closer and closer. Helen knew he was going to kiss her and there was nothing she could do to convince herself to make him stop.

Chapter 8

Drake was dying to kiss her. He wanted more than just a kiss, but the kissing part was no longer an option. She was just going to have to let him have a taste. After, she could kick and scream and rant, but right now she was just going to have to deal. He was going to kiss her and that was that, just like he'd been longing to do since the moment he'd gotten close enough to see her mouth—that soft, full mouth of hers that was now parted on a shocked gasp. She was looking at him like she didn't really believe he'd do it, and that kind of challenge was just too much for him to resist.

He bent his head and saw her eyes flutter shut in acceptance. The thrill of victory raced through him, but he didn't let it make him hurry. Not this. He kissed her, just a little, just a soft press of his lips on hers. Almost chaste. It shouldn't have been enough to even warm him up—wouldn't have been with any other woman—but instead, lust boiled through him until he felt singed, heated from the inside out as if he were burning alive and loving every second of it.

She made a soft sound of wonder, which parted her lips, and Drake took advantage of the opening. He slid the tip of his tongue along her upper lip, getting a tiny taste of her.

Dear, sweet, merciful heaven, she tasted good. His stomach tightened and he tried to remind himself to be careful. Go slowly. Enjoy the ride. In theory, it was a good idea, but in reality, with her body softening against his and her lips parting wider in invitation, restraint just wasn't feasible. He needed more of her. All she had to give.

He threaded his fingers through her wet hair and tipped her head back like he'd been longing to do all night. Too bad those wicked braids were gone, because he was just sure that tugging on them would make him hotter than hellfire. She complied eagerly, going where he led until the angle was perfect for him to tease her mouth open, to give him room to taste her deeper, to sink into her and let his senses just soak her in.

Sparks of power jolted through him and were absorbed by her wherever bare skin touched bare skin. The rush of sensation made him dizzy, greedy for more. He didn't want any barrier between them—no space, no clothing, nothing.

Her fingers curled over his naked shoulder and held on to him like she thought he might try to get away. Not bloody likely. She made lovely little desperate noises that had him halfway to insane with need. All he could think about was what she'd sound like once he had her spread out naked and open and slid inside her, filling her up. What would those streamers of energy feel like there? Would she be able to stand the intensity? Would he? Or would they both just career over the edge into pleasure and never come back? He was more than ready to find out.

Helen's fingers dug into his shoulder and she lifted up

on tiptoe, pressing their bodies tighter. The towel between them pissed Drake off, so he ripped it away, exposing her bare breasts to his chest. She was so soft, her breasts molding to the hard contours of his chest as if she'd been made to do just that. It was perfect. The way she fit against him, the way she smelled, the way she tasted. All of her was perfect and he couldn't get enough.

His hands slid down her spine until he could cup her soft bottom, all naked and warm under his grip. He could die now and be happy that he'd gotten just this much of her. He wanted more, but even this—just the feel of her body against his, the sweet play of her tongue over his—was satisfying on some deep, visceral level he'd never known before. All the pressure he carried seemed to drain away, making him feel stronger, like he could do anything if it meant that he'd get another moment to hold her in his arms.

Helen pulled away from his mouth and pressed a line of kisses over his jaw and down his neck until she reached his luceria. The wet, hot path her mouth and tongue traced over his skin made him shiver and clutch her bottom tighter until he was sure she could feel how hard he was for her. Helen sighed and wiggled her hips, teasing him.

Oh yeah, he could definitely die happy knowing she wanted him, too.

Her tongue slid under the luceria, and that contact made both the necklace and matching ring hum in response. Power and desire both surged up inside him, mingling together until he couldn't tell the difference between the two. Some instinctive part of him urged him to let go of that power, to send it flooding into Helen. Somehow, that power belonged to her and he'd only been holding on to it long enough to find her.

Drake wasn't sure what he was doing, but he followed his instincts and willed that tidal wave of energy to leave him. It streaked through his body, gathering in power, concentrating itself into a single bolt that flowed along the trunk of his lifemark, down his left arm, and into the iridescent ring.

Helen gasped and jerked away from his necklace as if she'd been shocked. She held a shaking hand to her mouth and looked up at him with dark, heavy-lidded eyes. "What was that?"

"I don't know," he said, hoping that whatever it was, it hadn't disgusted or hurt her.

A shiver shook her and he felt her thighs press together and her nipples bead up against his chest. She gave him a look so full of desire that it nearly melted the metal button on his jeans. "Can you do it again?"

Drake let out a low groan. "Oh yeah. Anything for you, sweetheart."

She gave him a slow, sultry smile that had his guts twisting into knots of need.

The bathroom door rattled under the weight of a heavy fist pounding against it. "Are you coming out sometime this century, or should I just go after Kevin's sword without you?" asked Thomas.

Drake closed his eyes in frustration and struggled to regain a toehold on sanity. It took a bit too long, but finally, he found enough of himself to gather a coherent thought. Thomas was right. As much as Drake was enjoying this, he still had a job to do. "We'll be out in a sec. Can you find something for Helen to wear?" Just asking the question was like ripping off his own arm. He wanted her to stay naked way too much.

She looked like she just realized that she was standing there naked, pressed up against him from knees to chest, and tried to pull away and cover herself. Drake wasn't ready to let that happen. Not yet. He kept one hand on her curvy bottom and the other between her shoulder blades. She wasn't going anywhere until he let her.

"I'm not going to let you get shy on me now," he told her. "As soon as I'm done with this job, you and I are going to pick up right here and finish what we've started. I want you to remember where we left off. You naked. Me nearly so. Burn this image into your head because this is right where I want you when I come back."

A deep blush crept up her neck and over her face. "This is not happening."

Drake gave her bottom a light squeeze. "Feels like it's happening to me."

"I assure you it's a mistake. A temporary lapse in judgment on my part. It won't happen again."

"You liked it."

"Yes, well, that was part of the lapse."

"You'll like it again," he promised her.

She closed her eyes and dropped her head to his chest. "Only if I'm stupid enough to get undressed while you're around. I think it's time for us to part ways. Permanently this time."

"You don't mean that." She couldn't mean it. Drake couldn't stand the idea of being the only one left out there dangling in lust-land. He needed her right there with him, wanting him as much as he wanted her.

"I've never meant anything more in my life." She was serious. All the softness had drained out of her and she was rigid in his arms. Frightened.

Well, hell. So much for his plans to pick this up later.

He hated seeing her like this and wished they could just go back to the place where she was asking him to make her feel good again. But from the way she was closing herself off more by the second—naked in his arms or not—he didn't think that was going to happen. Shit.

And he had to find Kevin's sword. He couldn't very well do that with her hanging on to him. She might get hurt if she came with him, and if he didn't go, Thomas *would* get hurt.

It was time to bite the bullet. Time to pull away from her and take the pain like a man. "Hold still," he ordered her, sounding more gruff than he'd intended.

He closed his eyes, shoved aside his lust, ignored his damn hard-on, and took a step back. No way was he going to look at her nude body and not combust. Not a chance in hell. So he kept his eyes shut tight and slid his fingertips over her arms, easing away slowly as Logan had taught him. When the only thing keeping them in contact was the tip of his finger on the back of her hand, he pulled in a deep breath and jerked it away.

Pain ripped through him and he felt as though he were going to blow apart into a million flaming pieces. A cold knot of agony gripped his stomach and he had to struggle to stay upright. He could feel the skin under his luceria and ring burn and blister and he had to grit his teeth against the compulsion to reach for her, to force her to make the pain stop.

Drake held on to his control by a thin thread and accepted the pain, let it become a part of him until it defined his existence. All he felt was pain. Scalding, burning, pounding pain. Nothing else.

Slowly, his body adjusted and his mind started to function again. When he opened his eyes, Helen was staring at him, gripping the soggy towel to her chest. Her arm was outstretched like she'd been reaching for him, but her hand was clenched into a tight fist. Her hazel eyes

were wide with chips of golden green highlighting her
worry for him.

"I'm sorry," she said. "I never meant for you to hurt
like that. If I knew another way ..."

"I know." And somehow, knowing that she cared
made it hurt less.

Helen splashed some cold water on her face in the
hopes that it would clear her head. What had she been
thinking letting Drake kiss her like that? And more im-
portantly, what had she been thinking when she kissed
him back? And oh, man, had she kissed him back. Open
mouth, mating tongues, naked skin on naked skin. Just
thinking about it made her toes curl.

She wasn't going to survive another attack of lust like
that one. Not a chance. Her only option was to keep her
distance and hope that she'd never see him again until
the day she died.

Helen pulled the oversized T-shirt Thomas had
shoved into the bathroom over her head and slipped the
running shorts on. The sloppy look wasn't exactly run-
way chic, but it was definitely better than bloody clothes
or a too-thin towel. Definitely not better than feeling
Drake's naked, oh so manly chest rubbing against her
nipples.

She was not going to go there. Not if she wanted to
keep her distance from Drake.

Now that she was decent, Helen slipped out of the
bathroom to see about getting them to take her and
Miss Mabel to a hotel tonight so that tomorrow she
could start to clean up the remains of her life. She was
going to need to find someone who could bring meals to
the people she fed until she could figure out what had
happened to her car. And then she was going to have

to face the fire inspector and the insurance company. Again. That was going to be all kinds of fun.

With a weary sigh, Helen left the bathroom and went down the narrow hall. She stopped at the doorway to a bedroom where Miss Mabel was sleeping. The room was dark, but light from the hallway spilled across the bed and the small hump that Miss Mabel's body made under the faded quilt. She looked pale and fragile and Helen wanted to kick herself for dragging the poor old woman into this mess. So much for being a caretaker. Now Miss Mabel couldn't even get herself around, which was going to grate on her sense of independence and remind her just how frail she really was. Helen hated it that she'd caused that to happen.

She was going to have to get Miss Mabel back on her own two feet as quickly as possible to prevent any further insults to her pride.

Helen heard voices down the hall and went to join them. She entered a kitchen that hadn't been redecorated since 1965. The faded orange and yellow wallpaper had been here almost long enough to be back in style, but nothing would have brought the garish green tile back into fashion. A worn harvest table ran the length of one wall and although it was scratched and dented, it looked sturdy enough to stick around for another forty years of hard use.

Drake lounged against one wall near the table, talking to Thomas, and as soon as she walked into the room, he fell silent and his eyes locked onto her. She saw his relaxed expression change—his eyes darkened to a rich brown and his jaw bunched. She wasn't sure whether his look was due to anger or desire or a little of both, but whatever it was, it was making her want to stay on this side of the room, far enough away to be out of his reach.

Thomas stood from the table and the map that he had spread out in front of him. He regarded her with an even stare, but something about the way he looked at her was different. There was something sad in his blue eyes—some kind of grief she didn't understand. He nodded his head in greeting and held his hand out toward an empty seat. "Want some coffee?"

"She probably wants dinner," said Drake. "Hers got interrupted."

Interrupted. That was one way to put it.

"I'm on it," said one of the two young men who looked almost identical. He had a heavy brow and flattish nose, but his smile was kind enough that it made him appealing. He opened a cabinet and peered in. "Want to pick something?" he asked her.

Helen stared blindly at the rows of canned goods and grabbed something at random.

"Pickled beets?" he asked her, curling a lip in disgust.

Eeew. No. "Sorry." She read the labels this time and picked a can of ready-made pasta.

"Better," said the man. "I'm Slade, by the way. My brother's Vance and that's Carmen." He nodded his head toward a teenage girl who was sitting on the counter, swinging her thin legs while she watched Thomas. Helen recognized the look on the young woman's face—the one that proclaimed her teenage hormones to be rampaging through her.

Thomas was completely oblivious of Carmen's gaze. Unsuspecting prey.

"I'm Helen," she responded.

"So, pretty weird, huh?" asked Slade in a friendly manner that had her relaxing just a bit. "All this magic and monsters stuff?"

"Uh, yeah. Weird." Understatement of the century.

"I know. I mean, I've known about this stuff since I was a kid—our whole family has worked for the Sentinels for generations—but the first time you see it, it's like *whoa*, you know?"

Boy, did she ever. "Sentinels?"

Slade nodded toward Drake and Thomas. "You know. Those guys."

"And what do you do for them? Besides donating blood."

Slade shrugged. "Lots of stuff. We take care of their property, keep watch out for the Synestryn. Report anything odd. That kind of thing."

"What's a Synestryn?"

He grinned and waggled his eyebrows. "Monsters. Demons. Beasties. The things that creep around in the dark and eat—"

"Helen," said Drake from across the room, interrupting Slade's increasingly disturbing list. "You should come sit down. You've got a decision to make."

Uh-oh, that didn't sound good. "What decision?" She slid onto the bench beside Thomas, and Drake's mouth tightened. Her chosen seat probably wasn't making Carmen any happier, either.

"You can either come with Thomas and me or we'll have the Gerai take you to our home."

Helen had been thinking more along the lines of getting a hotel room, so this threw her for a bit of a loop. "I'll take what's behind door number three."

"There is no door number three," said Drake, his expression hard, unyielding.

"Sure there is. It's the one where you take me and Miss Mabel back to Olathe and we live happily ever after."

"Miss Mabel can go back as soon as we've ensured her safety. You, on the other hand, can't."

"Yeah, see, here's the thing. I'm what they call a *grown-up*." She made air quotes with her fingers just to piss him off. "Which means I get to make my own decisions. If you're not willing to drive me back into town, then I'll happily call a cab."

Drake took a step forward, then stopped, curling his hands into fists at his sides. "I would have thought you'd seen enough tonight to drive all the stupid right out of you, but apparently, I was wrong."

"It's not stupid for me to want to go home."

"You have no home. All you have is a pile of ash and blackened rubble."

Helen flinched at the words, feeling a sick twisting in the pit of her stomach. He was right, and she knew it, but that didn't make dealing with it any easier. She'd come to love her new home and now it was gone.

"Don't be such an insensitive ass, Drake," scolded Thomas. "I realize what you've got at stake here, but this is not the way to go about getting Helen's agreement."

"What agreement?" she asked. "I don't know anything about any agreement."

The microwave pinged and Slade set a bowl of steaming ravioli in front of her. Helen ate some because she needed the food more than she wanted it.

Drake shoved a wide hand through his hair in frustration. He'd found dry jeans and a clean shirt somewhere, which Helen had to admit was a damn shame. He looked good shirtless, even when she was mad at him. "You're going to need some help putting your life back together," he said as if it was the beginning of a speech he'd practiced in front of the mirror. "And I want to help you do that."

"I appreciate the offer, but I'll be fine. I have obligations. I need to get back to town so I can make arrangements for tomorrow's meals and visits."

"You can't go back to town," said Slade from behind her. "You're wanted as a 'person of interest' in connection to the fires tonight."

"I'm what?" She hadn't meant to bellow it, but that was just too damn bad.

Slade's friendly smile fell off his face, leaving a blunt cliff of flat features. "I heard it on the news. They found your car at the diner. Then when your house burned down . . . I guess the police thought they should find you. The reporter said that it wasn't the first fire connected with your name. I mean, they didn't say it or anything, but they made it sound like you're wanted for arson."

Well, wasn't that just the whipped cream on the pile of shit her day had been. There was no way she'd be able to explain to the police what had happened without getting charged with arson or thrown in a loony bin. Or both. Definitely both if the way her life was going was any indication.

Helen suddenly felt too tired to move. She slumped over and propped her head on her palms, staring into the steaming bowl of kid food. A warm, strong hand settled on her back and she knew instantly it wasn't Drake's.

"Get your hands off her, Thomas," growled Drake. She could almost hear the sound of grating teeth in his words.

"Screw you. The woman needs comfort."

Helen needed a lot more than that, but she kept her mouth shut. She didn't have enough energy to gripe at them. She barely had enough energy to care that her whole world had been turned upside down. If it weren't for all those people counting on her, she might have just found a nice, comfy spot on the floor and escaped her problems in the oblivion of sleep.

But she did have those people counting on her, so she forced herself to think. To care. To pull herself back together so that she could fulfill her responsibilities. "Will one of you loan me a car or not?"

"Not," said Drake. "But I will make sure that the people you take care of are safe."

Helen looked up. "How? I thought you had some sword to go after or something. Do you really think you'll have a few hours to spend preparing and delivering meals to elderly shut-ins?"

"Slade and Vance can do that tomorrow, right?" He looked pointedly at the two young men, who were both nodding and grinning, eager to help.

"Me, too," said Carmen.

"Are you even old enough to drive?" asked Thomas, slanting her a skeptical look.

Carmen shot him a hormone-filled, lust-glazed look. "I'm eighteen, old enough for whatever service you might need me to provide, Theronai."

Oh yeah. Carmen was way into Thomas, but none of the men seemed to notice it.

"Good," said Drake. "You can help, too, then."

Carmen smiled a slow, sexy smile and Thomas's eyes narrowed in confusion as he looked at her. He tilted his head from one side to the other like a dog trying to understand a new word. A split second later, Thomas's eyes widened in shock and a blush crept up his thick neck.

Thomas had figured it out. Finally. At least he'd figured out that Carmen had a crush on him. Whether or not he'd figured out what to do about it was another story entirely.

Thomas turned back to his map slowly and stared at it as if it held the meaning of life.

"What about Miss Mabel?" asked Helen. "She needs a new walker and to go home."

"She needs more than that," said Thomas, clutching on to the topic like a lifeline. "She's going to need the memories of tonight wiped from her mind."

"You're going to *what*?" demanded Helen. She shot to her feet.

"Uh, sorry," said Thomas, looking between her and Drake and back again. "I thought you knew."

"That you were going to screw with my friend's mind? I think I would have remembered that one. Unless you've done something to my memories, too." Just the thought of it made her sick. It was such an intimate violation, and nothing in her experience gave her any way to justify such a horrible thing.

"No one's altered your memories," assured Drake.

"Yeah, like I can trust you to tell the truth. How can anyone trust a group of people who can *erase memories*? That's like trusting a bunch of pedophiles to run a day care."

Drake circled the table, his mouth flat with anger, but before he could reach her, Thomas shoved Helen behind his big body. "You told me not to let you touch her again. Remember the pain?"

Drake spat out a hissing curse, backed up a step and shoved his hands into his pockets. When he spoke, his words were clipped and precise with rage. "Do not compare what we do to deviants like that. You have no idea of the sacrifices we've made to keep people like Miss Mabel safe. I've watched hundreds of people I love die in order to protect humans. Hundreds."

Helen had nothing to say to that. She'd spoken in anger, but maybe she'd judged too quickly. He was right that she had no idea about what his life was like. How could she? Everything she'd seen tonight was completely out of the realm of reality for her.

This was all getting out of hand and if she wanted to take care of Miss Mabel, she was going to have to swallow her pride, accept her ignorance, and face the truth: She needed Drake's cooperation. "I'm sorry that I compared you to a pervert, but I can't let you hurt Miss Mabel. I can't let you mess with her mind."

He pulled in a deep breath and let it out slowly as if expelling his frustration. "It's important, Helen. We have to take away her memories of the Synestryn and ourselves. She can't know about any of us. It wouldn't be safe for her."

"Why? Because she's too old to deal with it?"

"No, because the memory of those demons leaves behind a psychic imprint—a sort of beacon that has the potential to draw more Synestryn to her. They don't want humans to know they exist. It's easier to move around and feed from humans if they aren't being hunted by them. Once a human knows about the Synestryn, they sense it and try to kill that human before they can spread the word that monsters are real. Even one little memory can act as a lure, and if one of the Synestryn found Miss Mabel, she'd never survive."

Fear slid through Helen and she felt her legs start to give out on her. She reached for the table to steady herself, and Thomas—gallant man that he was—grabbed her arm and helped lower her to the seat. "You're saying that just knowing that those monsters exist can make them come after you?"

"Exactly."

"How fucked up is that?"

Behind her, one of the guys snickered.

"This isn't a joke," warned Drake with a stern reprimand. "The longer we wait to remove her memories, the deeper we'll have to dig and the harder it will be on her. And even though she would hit me again if she heard me say it, she is frail. She's going to need someone to watch out for her for a few days. She'll be disoriented, dizzy."

Poor Miss Mabel. "Are you sure this is necessary?"

"I'm sorry," said Drake, sounding sincere.

Helen wished he wouldn't be compassionate like that. At least if he was an asshole she would understand why he'd stand by and watch her die while he did nothing. All this kindness confused her to the point that she wanted him to take her in his arms and tell her it was all some sick joke. They'd planted this vision in her head. It wasn't real.

Wishful thinking wasn't going to get her anywhere, so she pushed it aside and focused on what she needed to do. "I'll stay with Miss Mabel until she's better. Not having a house will give me a good excuse to stay at her place for a while so I won't hurt her pride."

"You can't stay with her. You have to come with us."

"This is the part where you don't get to pick," she told Drake. "Take my memories, too, if you must, but there's no way I'm going anywhere with you."

"Please don't make me force you, Helen."

"So you're admitting you will force me? In front of all these witnesses?" She pointed to where the young people stood behind her.

"They're not witnesses, they're Gerai. They're loyal to us."

Helen turned to look at them, convinced she'd see a look of horror on their faces at what Drake was suggesting. Stealing memories, abduction. Instead, they each stood still, watching Drake as if waiting for instructions. "Is this true?" she asked them. "Would you really let him kidnap me?"

The oldest one crossed his arms over his chest. Without the smile warming his features, he looked cold, almost sinister. "We do what the Theronai say. That's our job."

He wasn't lying. They would. Including Drake and Thomas, there were five of them and only one of her and she had Miss Mabel to protect as well. There was no way she could beat those kinds of odds.

"I don't like this," said Thomas. "She should have a choice."

Drake lifted a dark brow. "Would you feel the same way if she could bond with you?"

Thomas's mouth tightened and his blue eyes flashed with anger. "She should have a choice," he repeated, this time through clenched teeth.

"She has as much of a choice as we did. She is a Theronai. She has to take her rightful place."

"*She* doesn't even know what the hell you're talking about," said Helen. "What is a Theronai and why do you think I am one?"

Drake's golden gaze met hers and held on. "You know that feeling you get when we touch?"

Boy, did she. "Yeah."

"That's how I know what you are. Logan sensed it as well. You're like me and Thomas. We are Theronai. We fight the Synestryn—those monsters—protecting humans from them."

"And you think I'm one, too?" she asked, not bothering to hide her incredulity.

"I know you are," said Drake.

"But I thought all the female Theronai had been killed two hundred years ago," said Carmen.

"They were," replied Drake. "I don't know how Helen got here, but that's one of the things we're going to figure out."

Helen pushed to her feet, tired of being talked about when they should have been talking to her. "Excuse me, but I got here in the normal way. Some guy knocked my mom up and ta da, here I am. No big mystery there."

"But you shouldn't exist," said Drake.

"Then maybe I don't. Maybe I'm just a big ol' figment of your imagination, in which case, you shouldn't care whether or not I go with Miss Mabel."

Drake let out an exasperated breath. "That's it. I'm done trying to reason with you. I'm going to lay this out for you nice and neat so there won't be any confusion."

Helen did not like the way this was sounding at all. Nor did she like the way Drake was prowling closer to where she stood. She took a step nearer to Thomas.

"You don't want to do this, Drake," warned Thomas.

"Yes, I do. We're running out of time and unless we find that nest tonight, it may be weeks before we pick up the trail again. Do you really want Kevin's sword out there that long? Assuming we're able to find it at all."

"You know I don't, but this isn't the way to deal with her. We'll take her back to Dabyr and let Joseph straighten this out."

"Joseph would go straight to the Sanguinar. I'm not letting another one of those bloodsuckers near her. Not after what Logan did."

Helen had to agree with him there. She didn't want any bloodsuckers—whoever or whatever they were—near her, either. Some fragile memory flickered through her head. Something about her offering to give blood.

Thomas placed a thick arm in front of Helen as if he was preparing to shove her behind him again. "You don't have a right to do this."

"I'm claiming my right," said Drake, but he wasn't talking to Thomas, he was looking at her—giving her this hungry stare that had her wondering just exactly what he meant to claim.

Drake took a predatory step forward and Thomas pushed Helen back just as far. "You can't. There might be other Theronai who are compatible with her who need her more."

"I found her. I'm keeping her."

"Okay," said Helen. "No one's keeping me and that's final. This caveman routine has gone on long enough. Someone is going to start answering questions or I'm out of here right now, even if I have to carry Miss Mabel."

"We don't have time," said Drake.

"Make time."

Thomas said, "She has a right to know what she's getting into."

Drake's jaw clenched. "We both know it would take years for her to know everything."

"How about we start with some basics?" said Helen. "What exactly do you want me to do?"

"Help us find our dead friend's lost sword."

"Why? What's so important about it?"

"It's dangerous," said Drake.

"Dangerous in ways other than the obvious?"

"If a human stumbles across it, it would raise all kinds of inconvenient questions about its origin—questions that would get innocent people killed. And if a Synestryn found it, they could shatter the blade and release the twisted souls of countless evil creatures—those Kevin killed in his six and a half centuries of battle. The scales are already tipped too far in favor of the Synestryn. Losing the sum of Kevin's life's work would be devastating."

Six and a half centuries of battle? "You make it sound like you're at war," said Helen.

"We are."

"And yet no one knows? That seems hard to believe."

"That's because we're doing our job well—hiding the war from humans as best we can."

"If you hide the war from humans, then what do you think a puny human like me could possibly do to find a sword that you big, manly men can't?"

Drake's mouth twisted like he didn't want to say the words. "We think you're special."

Helen held back a snort of disbelief by sheer force of will. "Special how?"

"That feeling you get when we touch? I think it means you have . . . powers."

This time the snort broke through. "Really. Don't you think I'd know if that was true?"

"Maybe. Maybe not. If I'm wrong, you go on your merry way with my promise to guard and protect Miss Mabel and all the people you care about."

After what she'd seen Drake do with a sword, that was more than merely a tempting offer. Even so, she had to ask, "And if you're right?"

"You promise to stay with me."

This possessive side of Drake was a little scary and a lot overwhelming. She'd never had a man act like this over her and she wasn't sure how to handle it. What she was sure of was that she wanted all of her friends to be safe. If she wasn't there to care for them, no one would be. Her days were numbered now that she'd met Drake, anyway. Her vision would come to pass soon. This was her chance to see that everyone she loved was protected. Maybe her only chance. She owed it to all of them not to let it slip by.

"How long?" she asked. "How long do I have to stay with you?"

A golden flash of triumph lit Drake's eyes, but he hid it quickly. "Until we find Kevin's sword."

"We may never find it," argued Thomas. "You can't bind her to you for that long."

"I can and I will. If we don't find his sword, we're going to need her more than ever, so that's the deal. Take it or leave it."

Helen was sure she was stepping into something she knew little about, but she also knew that if there was a man alive who could protect the people she loved, it would be Drake. She'd seen him fight. She'd felt him throw his body in front of hers and take the blast of fire from that monster. He was fearless and she wanted to have him on her side, caring for her friends. "I want you to promise that you'll take care of everyone on my list, even if something happens to me. You'll keep them safe for as long as they live."

"I won't let anything happen to you," said Drake.

Except he would. He was going to let her burn. "That's my one and only condition. Take it or leave it." Shooting the words back at him felt good, but the feeling didn't last long.

"Done." The second he said it, Helen felt the weight of her promise settle over her shoulders. Whatever had happened wasn't normal or like anything she'd ever experienced, but it was powerful. Binding. Unbreakable.

Chapter 9

The smile of male satisfaction on Drake's face made him even more attractive to Helen. As if he needed any help in that department.

"To seal the deal, you must wear my luceria."

"I can't watch you do this," said Thomas, and he stormed out of the kitchen.

Carmen went after him, but no one seemed to mind that a teenage girl was headed out into the dark to follow a grown man she had the hots for. Drake didn't even spare her a glance. His eyes were fixed on Helen.

"Wear your what?"

"My necklace. We've made a binding pact and the luceria is a sign of that pact to all other Theronai."

"So they won't try to steal you away," said Slade.

"Silence," barked Drake.

Both young men flinched and looked contrite.

"I don't think I understand. Is me wearing the necklace really important?"

"Absolutely."

Helen sighed and held her hand out. "Fine. Give it to me."

"You have to come take it off."

She remembered feeling the slippery length of the luceria when he'd kissed her, and there had been no clasp. Besides, she really didn't want to get any closer to Drake while he wore that heated, hungry look. "I don't know how to take it off."

"All you have to do is touch it. Think about wearing it around your throat and it will fall into your hand."

It didn't sound likely to her, but then again, a lot of what had happened tonight wasn't likely. She took a timid step closer and stalled. She wasn't a coward, but something about the way Drake watched her made her feel hunted.

"Come here, Helen."

"You're not supposed to touch me, remember?"

"We won't have to worry about that once you're wearing my luceria."

"It doesn't really go with my outfit."

"You're scared."

"Hell yes, I'm scared. My world has been turned upside down tonight. I don't understand half of what I've seen and now I've made a promise to a man who is going to watch me ..."

"What, Helen? What am I going to watch you do?"

"Nothing."

"You might as well tell me."

"No, thanks."

"I'll be able to know anything I want to about you as soon as we're bonded, anyway."

"There will be no bonding. None. I only promised to help you find the sword."

"And to do that, you have to join with me. It's the only way."

Drake flicked a menacing stare to the two young men who were watching with rapt attention. "Leave us."

Slade and Vance scurried to obey, leaving Helen and Drake alone in the kitchen.

"I don't want you to be afraid of me," Drake told her as he stalked closer. "It will only make this process more difficult for you."

"You know what would make this process easier on me? Not doing it." Helen backed up until she ran into the counter. The beginnings of panic skittered through her along with the thrill of something else. Something darker and more exciting.

"That's not an option." Drake took two steps and closed the distance. He gripped the counter on either side of her, locking her between his arms, but not one part of him touched her. "I need you and I'm not letting you get away. Touch the luceria, Helen."

Her eyes shifted to his throat and the iridescent band that encircled it. Shimmering color wavered over it, like rainbows over a soap bubble. She stared, fascinated by the swimming ribbons of color. Part of her wanted to touch it, but the saner part of her warned her of danger. Drake hadn't told her everything. She was sure of it.

"Go ahead, Helen," he urged in a low, seductive tone. "You don't have to be afraid. I'd never let anything hurt you."

He sounded like he meant it. She knew better, but that sincerity ringing in his voice was her undoing. She reached a single finger toward the band and let the pad of her finger graze the surface.

Drake let out a low moan of pleasure and his eyes darkened, became unfocused. "That's right. Now, imagine it opening, see yourself wearing it."

Helen did, and the sinuous weight of it slid from around his neck. She caught it before it could fall. The heat of his body radiated from the band, soaking into her palm.

Helen suppressed a shiver of pleasure.

The colors had frozen in place as if they needed Drake's touch to fuel them. He held out his left hand, showing her the matching ring he wore. The colors in it were also still.

"See," he told her. "Whatever happens to one part of the luceria, happens to both. It's a connection between us, binding us together."

He turned his hand over, silently asking her to give him the necklace. Helen let it fall into his hand, being careful not to touch him. He found the loose ends and gave her a look so full of reverent hope that it nearly brought tears to her eyes.

"Lift your hair for me."

Helen's hands shook, but she did as he asked. His arms reached around her and he leaned down so that his eyes were level with hers. They glowed with a brilliant, hopeful light. "As long as you wear this you'll never be lost. You'll never be powerless. You'll never be alone."

She heard the ends of the luceria lock together with a muted click, and her body was frozen in place. She could hear and see, but she couldn't move.

Drake made a sword appear out of thin air and knelt in front of her. He tugged his shirt up, sliced a shallow cut over his heart, and said, "My life for yours." Then he rose to his feet, pressed his finger into the blood that welled from the cut, and touched it to the luceria.

She had no idea what he was doing and she was pretty sure that she didn't want to be any part of more bleeding—hers or his. She tried to tell him that, but nothing came out. Her mouth wouldn't move to form the words.

Helen felt the band shrink until it fit close to her skin. It grew warm and vibrated. That warmth trickled into her, growing until she could feel a cascade of heat fill her up. All the dark, empty places inside her—her fear, her loneliness, her worry—all vanished until there was nothing left but a glowing flush of energy suffusing her. Every cell in her body vibrated in time with the luceria. It hummed happily around her neck, pulsing with a living energy she could sense was much larger than anything she'd ever known existed.

Colors filled her vision, a swirling mass of reds and oranges with bursts of yellow sparkling in between. She was blinded by the beauty. She could feel herself falling, but it didn't matter. She wasn't worried. There was no place for worry inside her now.

She felt Drake's hands grip her upper arms and hold her steady. Streamers of power shot into her where each of his long fingers touched her skin. She heard herself gasp at the new sensation, felt the sudden breath fill her starved lungs. Only then did she realize she'd forgotten to breathe.

Drake said something, but the words sounded muted and far off. The roar of power in her ears sounded like a waterfall and blocked out all else. She felt him give her a little shake and some of his desperation filtered into her through the luceria. She had no idea how it happened, but she knew that she was feeling what he felt. She just couldn't figure out why he was worried.

The swirling colors in her vision cleared, but she didn't see the outdated kitchen she stood in. Instead, she saw a grassy field surrounded by high hills. Everything was green but the sky. It was a brilliant blue that was so intense it stung her eyes. A group of boys played on the grass, wooden swords in their hands clashing against each other while an older man stood by offering instructions.

One of the boys was Drake, as a child. He laughed as he fought, excitement glittering in his golden brown eyes. He lunged with his wooden practice weapon, missed his target, and took a heavy blow to the ribs for his mistake.

Helen felt his ribs crack, felt the searing pain shoot through his body. Before she had time to pull in a pained breath, the sensation was gone. Her vision shifted to another time and place.

Mountains shot up toward a cold winter sky lit only by the glowing moon. Drake and three other men stood in a narrow gap between giant slabs of stone. From that gap poured dozens of monsters. They were huge, ten-foot-long insectoids with shining black bodies and giant, snapping claws. The men sliced at the monsters, but their swords skittered off the hard exoskeletons, leaving only scratches behind.

One of the men whose fiery red hair shone bright under the moon shouted something in a language Helen couldn't understand. Drake shouted back an acknowledgment and burst into a frenetic flurry of movements. His sword gleamed in the moonlight until it was nearly a blur of motion. He let out a rough, primal roar and drove one of the monsters toward the man who had shouted. The redheaded man crouched low, found an opening, and shoved his sword into a space between the jointed segments of the monster's body.

Black blood frothed from the creature and it crumpled to the ground dead. A victorious smile curved Drake's face and he jumped on top of the dead body to face the next monster. His partner was there beside him, ready to try their ploy again. He pointed his sword toward one of the things. Drake gave a nod. The redheaded man suddenly stiffened and looked down to where the tip of a black claw was sticking out of his chest. From the deep shadows of the craggy mountainside came one of the monsters that no one had seen. It had stabbed one of its six legs completely through Drake's partner.

Drake let out an enraged bellow and jumped down to face the thing that had his friend. But it was too late. The redhead slumped, his body going limp in death.

Furious grief slammed into Helen as she shared Drake's emotions. That man had been his friend for years. They'd waged countless battles together and now he was gone. The first of Drake's friends to die.

But not the last.

The grief she felt coming from him was connected to countless other moments from Drake's life. Countless faces. With each beat of her heart a new face appeared from his memory. She saw face after face—all the loved ones Drake had lost to the Synestryn. The pulsing vision seemed to go on forever. Men, women, children. No one was spared. Some of them had died in battle, but most of them had simply been killed while they slept. They'd done nothing to deserve their deaths. They existed and that was enough of a reason for the Synestryn to destroy them.

A sob tore at Helen's chest, forcing the breath from her lungs. So much death. So much suffering. She had no idea how he could stand living under the weight of it and she was frantic to find her way back to him in the here and now so that she could hold him. Comfort him.

No one should have to suffer that kind of pain alone.

Helen fought against the grip the vision had on her. She squeezed her eyes shut, but nothing could block out the parade of the dead flashing in her mind. She willed it to stop, begging whatever power controlled this vision to have mercy.

Finally, the images began to slow until the last one appeared and held fast in her mind. Kevin. The man whose sword Drake sought. He was handsome in an almost boyish way with messy blond hair and deep green eyes. He looked like he was about twenty, but she sensed he was much older than that. Like Drake.

She'd never known him, but she could feel the deep, grinding ache of loss Drake felt over his death, the sense of guilt that Drake hadn't been able to save him—that he hadn't taken Kevin's place.

Just the thought that Drake wished it had been him who had died was enough to give Helen the strength to find her way back to him. She reached for the power that filled her and followed it back to the source. Drake.

It took her a moment to clear her mind of what she'd seen, to force herself to focus on the garish green tile and outdated wallpaper of the farmhouse kitchen. She was breathing hard. Sweating. Shaking.

"How can you stand it?" she asked him. Her voice was hoarse, making her wonder if she'd been screaming.

"Stand what, sweetheart? What did you see?" Drake's face was tight with worry and he smoothed his wide hand over her hair as if trying to convince himself she was okay.

Helen swallowed around the ache in her throat. "You've lost so many people."

His jaw bunched and she felt his fingers tighten around her hair. "But I'm not going to lose you."

Helen blinked, trying to make her fuzzy brain understand what he was saying. It didn't make any sense. She'd already promised she'd go with him and help him find the sword. "What?"

"The luceria gives us glimpses into each other so that we can start to learn to work together. It helps us understand each other, and now I understand something about you."

Helen had no idea what part of her life the luceria had chosen to show him, but whatever it was, it pissed him off. She could see it in the angry set of his mouth and the rigid way he held his body. Even though his touches were gentle, he was feeling anything but. "What do you understand?"

"You think I'm going to watch you die."

Chapter 10

Thomas stared up at the night sky, struggling with the jealousy that plagued him and left a bitter taste at the back of his throat. He'd never been a jealous man before. Didn't want to be now. He wanted to be happy for Drake. He'd found a woman who could save his life. End his suffering. That was something worth celebrating.

But instead of feeling like celebrating, Thomas felt like lashing out at Drake. He wanted to beat his friend into the ground and take Helen for himself. It didn't even matter that she couldn't help him. Part of him wanted to make her try—wanted to force her to be something she wasn't. His salvation.

Thomas's chest ached with the weight of his jealousy and he rubbed a wide hand against it in an effort to ease the pain. It did no good, of course. Nothing could help him now. Even if there were other women out there like Helen, Thomas didn't have enough time left to find one. His time was up as of five minutes ago when he felt the last leaf fall from his lifemark and his soul began to die. He could feel it shriveling, leaving a bleak, empty numbness behind. All he had left to look forward to now was losing himself in the gray swamp of soulless amorality.

He heard the slight rustle of grass behind him and

turned to see Carmen striding toward him with purposeful steps. She'd taken off her baseball hat and her pale hair shone bright under the moonlight.

Enough of himself remained for him to worry about her being easily seen, even in the dark. His hand strayed to his sword, making sure it was ready if any of the Synestryn found them out here alone. He would make sure she was protected.

That thought eased him a bit. At least he wasn't completely self-centered. Yet.

"What are you doing out here?" he asked her. "It isn't safe."

"I was worried about you," she told him.

God, she was young, barely even a woman, but with all the lovely trappings. She had that glow of youth about her—a sort of freshness that helped him remember why it was he'd fought his entire life to keep others safe. Her whole life was ahead of her, full of choices and promise.

He wished he could say the same for himself.

"I'm fine. I just wanted to be alone," he told her.

She sat down beside him, sharing space on the fallen tree he'd found under the old oaks behind the house. "I don't think it's good for you to be alone right now."

Thomas slanted her a questioning look. "Oh yeah? And what do you know about it? You're just a kid."

"I told you, I'm eighteen. Not just a kid. Besides, you're old enough that even Miss Mabel is just a kid to you. Get over yourself already."

Get over himself? "Is that any way for you to be speaking to a Theronai? You're supposed to show respect. Obedience."

She shrugged and it brought his attention to the slim line of her arms. She was slim everywhere, but in the kind of proportion that left Thomas staring a bit too long.

"Give me an order that isn't stupid and I'll follow it."

"Here's one. Go back inside."

She snorted. "Try again, He-Man."

He-Man? Wasn't that a cartoon?

Thomas was starting to feel more than a little offended by her casual attitude when she hopped up and stood behind him.

"What are you doing?" he asked, frowning at her.

"You're all tense. I'm going to rub your back."

Danger. He sensed danger, but he wasn't sure why. She was just a little girl. A blooded human, but still human. Her fingers settled on his shoulders and pushed deep into tired muscles. It felt good. He couldn't remember the last time something had felt good. He'd been fighting for too many days without a break. Ever since Kevin died. He couldn't rest while his friend's sword was lost, and until now, he hadn't realized what a toll it had taken on his body. He ached from head to toe, inside and out. He was used to pain—constant, intense pain—but what Carmen was doing to him felt nice.

He let out a deep groan of contentment.

"Glad you like it," she said as she leaned closer. He could feel the swell of her breasts against his back and that feeling of danger increased.

She stroked her hands over the nape of his neck in a slow, gentle caress and he realized what that alarm was all about. She wanted his attention. Not the way a student wanted approval from a teacher, which he could have handled, and would gladly have provided, but the way a woman wanted a man's attention.

Thomas shoved himself up to his feet and backed away from her in shock, nearly stumbling.

She smiled and it wasn't the smile of a girl. Oh no. That smile was full of womanly desire and very grown-up hunger. "What's the matter?" she asked. "Don't you want me?"

Thomas's mouth opened, then closed again. What was there to say to something like that? He'd never even considered the idea. Want her? She was just a kid. Noble, honorable men like him didn't want little girls.

She came forward, matching his horrified retreat step for step. Her hips swayed and her breasts jiggled and she forced him to think about what it would be like to just give in. Let her make him feel good for a little longer. Let her touch more than just his back. Let her take him into her sweet body and lose himself in feelings of the flesh.

So what if he had sex with her? She clearly wanted it and was technically an adult by modern-day standards. He deserved a little fun before he died. Better to take a woman now than when there was nothing left of his former self to hold his baser instincts at bay. He could still be gentle now.

Couldn't he?

The thought made his stomach twist with disgust. What if he couldn't? What if he gave in to his lust and it took over? He had no idea what would happen to him now that his leaves were all gone. He was strong enough that he could easily hurt her.

"No," he told her, using every bit of conviction he could muster.

Carmen's pursuit stalled and she looked up at him with the hurt of rejection shining in her eyes. "You don't want me."

"It's not that."

"It must be. I've listened to the human women talk. You can't spread disease and you can't get me pregnant, so the only thing stopping you must be the fact that you don't want me. Unless you've already got some human woman on the side and you're worried about cheating."

"I don't. You're too young."

"I'm old enough to know when I want to have sex. And I do. With you." She settled a slender hand on his chest and let it slide down slowly.

Thomas's stomach tightened and he bit back a groan of need. "It's not that simple."

"It is if you want it to be."

He felt his control slipping. She was offering him a chance to escape his life, if only for a little while, and he wanted to take it. After centuries of service he deserved a little happiness, even if it was only fleeting.

Thomas cupped her shoulders in his hands, unsure whether to push her away or pull her closer. She looked small standing next to him. Felt small under his fingers. He'd always liked that about women—how they could feel so delicate and yet be so strong at the same time. It was a wonder that never ceased to amaze him.

"I know you hurt," she said in a low, soft voice. "Let me make you feel good."

He found the strength to ask, "Why?"

"Because I can. Because I want to."

His resolve was crumbling by the second. She was saying all the right things to put his nagging conscience at ease. He wasn't forcing her. Hell, he wasn't even trying to seduce her. She was doing this all of her own free will.

Carmen looped her hands around his neck and nestled her body against his. He could feel her heartbeat against his ribs, see the flush of excitement creeping up her cheeks. "I know exactly how to make you feel good."

Something about that bothered him. He closed his

eyes, blocking out the alluring sight of her so he could concentrate on what was wrong. "How do you know? You're too young."

She laughed. "You don't know anything about today's youth, do you? Did you think I was a virgin or something?"

Actually, the thought had crossed his mind, but he kept it to himself.

"Oh, man, that's priceless. I started sleeping with boys when I was thirteen."

"Thirteen?" He sounded disgusted, but he couldn't help it. She'd been just a baby then. "What the hell were you doing having sex at thirteen?"

Carmen's body stiffened and she dropped her hands and took a step back. "You sound like my uncle. Jeez."

Not her father, her uncle. "Where the hell was your father while his baby girl was out having sex?"

"You're kidding, right? I offer to have sex with you and you want to talk about my father? Fuck you." She rolled her eyes and started to walk away.

Thomas stopped her. He wrapped one hand around her arm and she had no choice but to come to a halt. "Tell me," he ordered, using his official Theronai voice—the one that usually had Gerai hopping to do his bidding.

He saw her consider her options—try to get away or answer him. "Fine. You want to know? I'll tell you. My dear old dad started raping me when I was eight. When I was ten, Mom found out and tried to stop him. He killed her for her effort and went to prison. Poetic justice came a-callin' and he ended up dying after being gang-raped himself. Isn't that a pretty story? I put it on the Christmas card every year."

Thomas was stunned speechless. What was there to say to something like that? Her life—her short life—had been destroyed by the man who was supposed to protect her, and here he was upset by the fact that after living for nearly four hundred years, he was dying. God, what a selfish ass he was.

"Come here," he whispered, and pulled Carmen into his arms. He held her tight, refusing to let her go when she struggled against him. Slowly, she stopped fighting and let him hold her. He could only imagine how alone she felt in the world. She'd been abused, terrorized, orphaned. Apparently her uncle had taken her in, but he could never replace her father. And nothing would make up for the betrayal she'd suffered at his hands.

Thomas wished that her father hadn't died, because he would have loved killing the man himself. Slowly.

She sniffed, the sound muffled by his chest. "I'm not going to have sex with you now, so just forget it."

He pulled back enough so that he could tip her chin up and make her look at him. "You have more to offer the world than just sex. You're a Gerai. You're important."

She snorted. "That's what my uncle says, but he's a fool. I hardly have any power at all other than being able to tell when the Synestryn are near, and a lot of us can do that. Slade and Vance both found their gifts, but I don't have one."

"That's not true. You just haven't found it yet. Give it time."

A haunted look took hold of her features and he could see her bottom lip tremble slightly before she controlled it. "I don't have any more time. My uncle says I have to move out by the end of the summer."

"You should go to college. The Sentinels will pay for your tuition."

"I was never good enough in school to go to college."

"Do you have a job?"

She shook her head. "There aren't enough jobs in the area to go around. My friend moved to Kansas City and got a job dancing. She said I could come work with her."

Dancing? "You mean stripping?" The thought of her degrading herself further like that made him sick.

"It's not as bad as you make it sound. The tips are good and no one gets to touch the dancers."

Like hell she was going to take her clothes off for money.

Thomas took her by the hand and dragged her back to Logan's van. It took him a few minutes of searching, but he finally found a little notebook shoved under one of the seats. He scribbled a note on it and signed his name, then pulled out his sword.

Carmen took a long step back, but he couldn't blame her. The lethal gleam of his blade was a blatant menace, just the way he liked it. He sliced a small cut on the tip of his finger and pressed the bloody spot over his signature. Any Sanguinar would be able to authenticate the mark as his.

He folded the paper and handed it to her. "I want you to promise me two things."

"Why would I do that?"

"Because if you do, I'm going to make sure that you have a safe place to live for the rest of your life and something meaningful to do with it. Do you understand?"

Carmen nodded, but looked skeptical. Not that he could blame her. Her life wasn't exactly a bounty of good fortune and kindness.

"One, don't read the note until after you give it to a man named Joseph Rayd."

Her eyes widened. "But he's the leader of the Sentinels. I'd never be able to meet him."

Her statement just proved to Thomas how little value she placed on herself. "He'll see you. Just tell him about the note."

"Okay. I can do that. I've always wondered what he looked like, anyway. What else?"

The first one was easy but the last one wasn't going to be. He took a deep breath, expecting her to throw a fit. "Promise me you won't have sex again until you fall in love."

She let out a harsh bark of laughter. "You had me going for a minute there. Sorry, but that ain't gonna happen."

Thomas couldn't let this go. He was compelled to find a way to protect her—to give her a chance to heal. "It's your choice. Make it happen. Swear you will."

"That's a stupid thing to ask of me. I won't do it."

"Then you're already lost and nothing anyone can do will help. You value yourself so little that you're willing to throw away one of the most precious gifts you have to give."

"I'm good, but not that good."

He captured her chin and held it in his hand so she had to look at him—had to see that he spoke the truth. "Yes. You. Are. You're too young to know your own worth and too hurt to even see that you can't. Promise me, Carmen."

She was silent for so long Thomas thought he'd lost her. But then he saw a sheen of tears glitter in her eyes and he knew that he'd gotten through, maybe just a little, but it was going to have to be enough. He wasn't sure whether what he was doing would help, but he had to try.

"I promise," she said.

Thomas felt the power of her vow surround them like a tingling blanket and she gasped, having felt it, too.

She looked around as if she expected to see something jump out at her. "What was that?"

"You're bound to your word. It's one of the powers we Sentinels possess. When you make us a promise, it sticks."

"I did that when I became a Gerai, but it wasn't so ... intense."

"It's a big promise."

"So no sex until I fall in love, huh?" She sounded almost relieved.

"That's right."

She swallowed nervously, looking uncertain and achingly young. "Do you think that you and I could ever, you know, fall in love?" Such a small voice for such a big question. It made his heart break to hear so much yearning in her words.

Thomas didn't let any of the crushing grief he felt come through in his voice or expression. He didn't give away even the barest hint that he was slowly becoming a monster or that he was already planning his death to keep that eventuality from happening. Instead, he smoothed his knuckles over her cheek and told her the rest of the truth. "Falling in love with you—having you love me back—would make me the luckiest man on earth. And whoever you choose to give your heart to will feel the same way."

Lexi pulled off the highway at Wichita after two in the morning. She needed gas and caffeine and a tattoo parlor. In that order.

It took her five minutes to get the first two, but the last one was going to be more of a challenge. She'd spent too many hours zigzagging across the state, hoping to throw off anyone who might be following her. Because

of that, she was still a long way from the Oklahoma border where a slew of tattoo parlors had grown up out of
necessity.

Oklahoma had been the last state in the nation to
legalize tattooing, and because of that, for years, drunk
teens had to drive just over the border into Kansas,
Texas, or Arkansas to get inked. The laws of supply and
demand dictated that there would be someone there
waiting to take their money, and she knew many of those
someones by their kick-ass reputations alone. She knew
only three artists on the border who were good enough
to cover up the mark Zach had left on her arm. The one
he could use to track her.

But Lexi wasn't going to make it that far. She didn't
want to wait another hour to cover the damn thing up,
and even if she did, she wasn't sure the parlors would
be open once she got there. She was going to have to
find a local artist and hope that he was good enough to
mask Zach's tracer. The frowny face she'd drawn over
his fingerprint with a Sharpie wasn't going to do more
than slow him down, if that.

Lexi turned on her cell phone and checked for calls
from Helen. She'd left three messages since ditching
town and had even called the police to report her possible abduction. Lexi wished she could do more, but
even if she did figure out where the Sentinels had taken
Helen and Miss Mabel, she wouldn't be able to do anything about it. She was no match for that kind of power.
Her mother's journal was detailed when it came to the
things the Sentinels could do to her.

She was dialing the artist who had masked the birthmark on her back to see whether he knew any talented
locals when her cell phone rang. Unknown caller. For
half a second, Lexi debated letting it roll over to voice

mail, but what if it was Helen? What if she was calling for help?

Lexi took a deep breath and pressed the TALK button. "Hello?"

A deep, rich voice filled the line. "Hello, honey."

Zach. Oh God. She was so screwed.

Lexi's hand started to shake around the phone and she had to swallow twice before she could speak. There was no way he should have been able to track down her prepaid phone number. "How did you get this number?"

"I stole it from Helen's cell phone. But that's not really what you want to know, is it?" His voice was deep and lazy and it made a shiver course over her skin. "What you really want to know is, where am I?"

He was taunting her. She could hear the teasing smile in his voice. She could see it in her head—that same smile he'd worn when she stabbed him. The one that said no matter what she did to him, he would never stop chasing her.

She tried to sound bored, nonchalant. "I don't care where you are."

"Yes, you do. You want to know if I've found you yet."

"If you had, you wouldn't be talking to me over the phone."

"True enough. I'm glad I don't have to explain how things are to you."

"Don't try to follow me," she told him.

He laughed, a rich, sinful sound that vibrated along her nerves and made her squirm in her seat. This could not be happening. She would not let him get to her like this. Her mother had warned her that this was what they did—charmed their way into your life, took over, and left you lying in the ruins, left you to clean up the remains of your life, assuming they even let you live.

"I'm not just trying, honey. I'm succeeding. I imagine you're getting pretty tired by now. All that adrenaline has had time to wear off and you're starting to fade. You have to sleep soon. I don't. I can go for days without rest. It would be a lot easier on both of us if you just tell me where you are."

For one heart-stopping moment, she actually considered giving in. She was so tired of running. All she wanted to do was stop. Rest. She hadn't lived in the same place for more than six months since she was seventeen. Not since the night the Sentinels came for her mother.

Lexi leaned her head against the steering wheel. He was right. She was tired, but not tired enough to let them do to her what they'd done to her mother. Not even close. "Omaha," she lied.

Zach chuckled. "Come on, honey. You don't have to be afraid of me."

"Said the spider to the fly."

"As much as I'd like to wrap you in silk and eat you up, that's not what I have in mind." He paused and she heard him pull in a deep breath. "I need you." Those three words were deadly serious without even a hint of teasing.

He'd said that to her before when she was fighting him off in the diner, when he'd had her pinned on the counter, before she'd stabbed him. He'd looked at her with those pale green eyes that glowed so bright in contrast to his dark skin. Leopard eyes. He stared right into her and told her just that. He needed her. He was so earnest and pleading that she almost gave in then, too.

It was just as her mom had said. The Sentinels were masters of seduction. Zach knew exactly what to say.

Lexi had never been needed before. Not by anyone. Maybe it wouldn't be so bad after all to let him find her. "You're too big and strong to need anyone. You're just trying to trick me."

"I'm pleased you noticed the big, strong man thing, but you're wrong. You have no idea how wrong. Just meet me. Let me show you how much I need you."

Oh no. There was no way she was going to let him get that close. "Nice try, but I have a lot of miles to put between the two of us, so we're done here."

"Don't run, Lexi. I'd never hurt you."

There he went again, saying just the right thing with just the right amount of sincerity to make her question her decision. She hated that he could do that to her so easily. She was stronger than that. She didn't let men sway her confidence. "Lies. All of it."

"Not one word was a lie. Meet me and I'll prove it. Please."

Lexi's chest tightened. She couldn't stand this any longer. She needed to get off the phone before he drove her over the edge and convinced her to simply give up. She couldn't do that. She'd promised her mom she wouldn't. "I'm sorry. Don't call back. I won't pick up."

Lexi ended the call and dropped the phone out of the car window so she wouldn't be tempted to make herself a liar and answer when he called back. Because she knew he *would* call back. He wasn't going to stop looking for her until he found her. Her days of living in one place for six months were over. She was going to have to live on the run if she wanted to stay free.

For the first time in her life, she wondered whether her freedom was worth the price.

Chapter 11

Drake couldn't take his eyes off Helen. He stared at the luceria around her throat and wanted to howl with joy. She was his. She'd saved him. Already he could feel something happening along the branches of his life-mark. A sparkling sensation pricked over his skin, like millions of popping bubbles.

He pulled his shirt off, needing to see the proof that their union had worked. Before their eyes, new buds formed on the branches, then unfurled into baby leaves. The pale green color of new growth was beautiful, and the perfect shine of each tiny leaf was testimony to the miracle Helen had given him.

"Wow," she breathed, tracing a finger delicately over the intricate lines of the tree. Drake's body tightened with longing. "What is that?"

"It's called a lifemark. It's kind of like a visual gauge of my soul's health. I was born with it, only at the time it was just a seed. As I grew, so did the tree, until I was about eighty and the power inside me had grown too strong. The tree started to die and the leaves began to fall and have been falling ever since. Until now."

"What power?"

"I'm like a magnet, attracting stray scraps of energy

from my surroundings. Tiny sparks in the air, heat from the earth, light from the sun. It all flows into me, building up over the years. I can't stop it, and eventually, without a means of escape, that power will kill me."

He could see the confusion in Helen's eyes and he wanted to explain everything to her, but first, he had to put her mind at ease. He'd seen her vision when they'd bonded. It was the only thing about her the luceria had chosen to show him.

It was dark where they were. So dark he couldn't see anything beyond the sphere of light the fire cast. She was dressed all in black except for the fiery red splash of color around her neck—the luceria. Her hair was in twin braids, as it had been earlier tonight. Her arms were spread wide, almost as if she was bound, but he could see no chains or ropes holding her. Flames engulfed her, reaching up from her feet until they rose ten feet into the air. Her face was a mask of pain and she screamed, a desperate, high-pitched scream that made every hair on his body rise in protest. Yet in the vision, he stood there. Doing nothing. He watched as the flames blackened her clothes and blistered her skin. He watched as she stared at him with terror and agony widening her hazel eyes.

Drake didn't want to believe Helen's vision. If he hadn't seen it himself, he wouldn't have believed it. He simply wasn't capable of watching a woman die without doing something to stop it. Was he?

At least he now knew why she'd been so afraid of him from the moment she saw him. He hated it, but at least it made sense now. He cupped her face in his hands, reveling in the feel of her soft skin against his sword-roughened palms. "Your vision is not going to happen, Helen. I would never stand by and watch you die. Never."

"I want to believe you."

"Then do. I know people—powerful people—who can help us sort this out. I'll take you to them tonight."

Thomas had pushed the kitchen door open in time to hear that last comment. "No, you won't. We're going after Kevin's sword. Right now."

Carmen darted into the kitchen and headed straight for the bathroom. Her eyes were red as if she'd been crying.

Drake frowned at Thomas, fighting the urge to ask what had happened. It was none of his business, but whatever it was, it had upset Thomas. He looked different. Harder.

Thomas's eyes settled on the luceria around Helen's throat and his jaw clenched. He drew his sword, knelt down, and scored a thin line over his heart without bothering to remove his shirt. He uttered the customary "My life for yours," before rising to his feet. Blood trickled down his chest, soaking into the thin cotton shirt he wore, but Thomas paid it no heed.

"I wish you wouldn't do that," said Helen.

"Sorry," said Drake. "It's our custom."

"It's a violent custom."

"We're a violent people," said Thomas as he cleaned the blood off his sword with a paper towel.

"Isn't that blood going to draw the monsters to us?"

"Yes," growled Thomas. "It is."

"Then why do you do it? Seems kind of stupid to bleed all over the place when you know it will make the monsters come."

Drake took her hand. "It's proof of our dedication. Our courage. Not only are we willing to bleed for you; we're also ready and able to fight off whatever danger may come without fear. It's symbolic of our commitment to you and our willingness to risk our lives on your behalf."

"Guess Hallmark doesn't make a greeting card for that, huh?"

Thomas scowled at her. "We'd better get moving."

"Where are we going?" asked Helen.

"I'm taking you to see Sibyl."

"The hell you are," said Thomas. "She's coming with us to find Kevin's sword."

The idea of dragging Helen into battle made Drake's hands shake. He knew it was silly, that she was now more able to protect herself in battle than he was, but that didn't mean she knew it. "She's not ready. She doesn't even know how to use my power yet."

"We don't have time to wait. The trail will dissipate at dawn."

"What trail?" asked Helen. Her fingers were gripped tight around his arm and even without the aid of the luceria linking them, he would have been able to feel her fear. She'd had too much thrown at her tonight and it was beginning to take its toll.

Thomas stepped close and Drake could see the difference in Thomas more clearly now. There was no warmth left in those bright blue eyes. No humor. All that was left was cold, lethal intent. "Thomas? Are you okay, man?"

Thomas turned his back, heading down the hall without a backward glance. "I'm leaving to find Kevin's sword in ten minutes. With or without you."

That wasn't good. Without Zach around, he'd be on his own, and as tough as Thomas was, he was no match for an entire nest of demons.

"What's wrong with him?" asked Helen.

"A lot of things." Not the least of which was he was dying. He hadn't taken off his shirt when he'd offered his oath to Helen. That was a bad sign. One of the first signs that a Theronai was nearing the end. Drake wondered how many leaves he had left.

Not many if he didn't want Drake to see.

"What can we do?"

Drake had to swallow hard to ease the tightness in his throat. He and Thomas had been friends for decades. In fact, they were more like brothers than friends. All of the Theronai were dying slowly, but if Thomas's lifemark was nearly bare, then that process would speed up. And there was no way to know how much. Each man was different. Drake could only hope that Thomas would be one of the lucky ones and that he'd have at least a few more years left. "Nothing. There's nothing either of us can do for him now."

Helen gasped and pressed a hand to her chest. "Oh God. He's dying. I can feel you grieving for him."

Drake cursed. He'd forgotten that the link they shared allowed emotions to filter through. He was going to have to be more careful with her and make sure he kept his emotions under tight control.

He pulled in a deep breath and focused on clearing his mind. "I'm sorry. Is that better?"

She nodded, but he could still see his grief haunting her face.

"I've got a lot of things to teach you and not much time to do it. Are you up for that?"

"Do I have a choice?"

"If you want, I'll take you to my home. We'll have all the time we need there."

"And Thomas would be on his own."

Drake nodded.

She was afraid. He could feel it coming through their link—could see in the way her eyes changed colors, leaning toward green as they did every time she got scared. She was afraid of what was happening to her, afraid for Miss Mabel, afraid of the unknown, but she was also afraid for Thomas.

"We can't let him go alone, Drake. We can't let him die."

He couldn't resist the urge to pull her to him, to enfold her in his arms and hold her close. She felt so good there. Perfect. He still couldn't believe he'd been lucky enough to find her. Her capacity to care what happened to others humbled him and made him want to shelter her. Instead, he was going to have to throw her headlong into his world and show her her true potential.

Drake kept a tight hold on his thoughts so she wouldn't feel them. He didn't want her to know that even if they did go with Thomas, there was nothing they could do to save him. The only person who could do that would be another woman like Helen. Assuming another female Theronai even existed.

He had to believe it was true. The thought of watching his friends die in hideous pain one by one was not something he could stomach. As much as he hated it, the Sanguinar already had a sample of her blood. They were probably already analyzing her ancestry to learn where she came from. If there were more women like her, the Sanguinar would probably be the first to find them.

What a scary thought that was. Talk about lambs to the slaughter.

Helen stiffened in his arms. His control on his thoughts was slipping and he slammed the barrier back in place. There would be time enough for grim thoughts like that after they found Kevin's sword.

"We should get moving," she said.

His fingers slid through her silky hair and he wished that there was time to take her to one of the empty bedrooms upstairs and kiss her until they were both too wild to stop and forgot all about the Synestryn. Hell, he would have been satisfied with simply having enough time to share a conversation with her so he could explain to her how their union worked.

"Are you sure you want to go with Thomas?" he asked her.

"Yes. He needs us."

"Okay, then. We'll go, but you're going to have to trust me. If we'd known you were a Theronai, you would have been learning about your abilities and what you could do with them from the time you were first able to speak. You didn't have any of that training and all we're going to have is the time it takes for Thomas to track down the nest of Synestryn."

"What are you talking about? What power?"

Hell, this was going to take forever to explain. How could he take her from not even knowing that magic was real to being able to wield it all in one evening? It didn't seem possible.

He took her hand. "Come with me. It's going to be easier—quicker—to show you than tell you."

Drake led her outside, well away from the vehicles and the house. "Okay, see that stump over there?" he asked, pointing across the field.

"No. It's too dark."

Right. He forgot. She didn't even know how to pull enough power from him to see in the dark. "Okay, first things first. Here's how it works. Inside me is this reservoir of energy, but I can't do much with it. All I can do is store it. You, on the other hand, are able to pull that energy out of me and use it, but you can't store any on your own. It's like a checks and balances system so that no one person ever wields too much power."

"Power to do what?"

"Whatever you like. I could tell you what I've seen women do before, but it would only bias you against your own instincts and possibilities. Every woman has her own unique set of skills—things she's better at than others."

"You may need to bias me, then, because I have no clue what you mean."

Drake refused to get frustrated. She'd saved his life; the least he could do was give her his patience. "We'll start small. Tell me something you can see."

She pointed to a rock twenty feet away. A little too close for comfort, but it would have to do.

"Okay, I want you to picture the rock lifting off the ground. I'm going to touch my ring to your necklace to strengthen the link and make it easier for you to draw power from me."

"I don't even know where to start doing something like that." Drake could feel her confusion and uncertainty. He was pushing her too fast. Expecting too much from her.

Damn it. This was not the way it was supposed to be. Their bonding was supposed to be easy. Natural. Maybe it would be best if he took her to the compound and went with Thomas himself.

"No. I won't let you go alone."

Drake felt a little burst of excitement go through him. "You heard that thought?"

She frowned. "I don't know if 'heard' is the right word, but yeah. I knew what you were thinking."

"That's good. Try to do it again, only this time, I'm going to show you what I need you to do, okay?"

She nodded and Drake closed his eyes, trying to picture in his mind what he needed from her. He pictured his power as a light, a glowing pool of energy inside him. He placed his hand on her throat so that his ring made firm contact with the necklace. Immediately, he felt the flow of energy rush out of him. That light poured into her through the luceria until her skin glowed with the force of it.

He heard her make a shocked sound, but didn't open his eyes. Instead, he visualized taking her hand in his and stretching it out toward the rock. He sent the light streaking out from her hand until it engulfed the rock; then slowly, he lifted her hand, making the rock float up inside the light.

Drake opened his eyes to see if she understood. Not only did she understand, but she was doing it. There was no glowing light, but her hand was held out and the rock hovered three feet off the ground.

"You did it," he whispered, not wanting to break her concentration. Her bottom lip was held tight between her teeth and she shook with effort. A fine sweat broke out along her hairline, and her chest—her lovely, womanly chest—was rising and falling in rapid succession, playing havoc with his concentration.

Her arm lowered until the rock returned to the ground, and even though she was out of breath, she looked at him with an excited light in her eyes. Her mouth curved in a proud smile and let out a giggly little laugh. "I can use magic!"

Between the happiness shining in her features and the warmth of her joy filling him through their link, Drake couldn't help but laugh along with her. "You sure can."

"That is the coolest thing ever." She twirled around in a circle and for the first time since he'd met her, physical

separation didn't hurt. He no longer had to touch her to
be free from his pain. The link of the luceria was apparently enough of a connection. He wasn't sure whether
he was relieved because it was a lot more convenient, or
he missed having the excuse to touch her.

He'd just have to come up with another excuse because he sure wasn't going to stop touching her.

"I want to try something else," she said.

"Like what?"

"I don't know. What can I do?"

"I honestly have no idea. You're going to have to figure that out for yourself. Each woman is different and
has her own strengths and weaknesses."

"How many more women like me are there?"

"Not many."

"Can I meet them?'

"You'll get to meet Gilda as soon as we go back to
my home."

That beautiful smile of hers made his breath catch in
his throat. She was such a precious gift and he had no
idea how to thank her for saving him.

"I know how," she told him, as if answering his
thoughts. She slid her hands over his shoulders and
pulled his head down to hers. Her mouth settled over
his in a tender kiss, and the gentle touch of her soft lips
drove all other thoughts from his head.

Tender wasn't enough for him. Not by a long shot.
He wanted more. He wrapped his arms around her and
pulled her close so that there was no space between
them. The scent of lilac bubble bath filled his nose, and
beneath that soothing smell was the much more exciting scent of warm, happy woman. He teased her lips
open with his tongue until she granted him access to her
mouth. Drake wasted no time claiming the space as his

own, learning every slick contour and sharp edge. He tasted her sigh of pleasure and offered her one of his own.

His skin heated until the warm summer air felt cool brushing against him. His blood was pounding through him, hot and greedy for more of her. He let her feel his lust, forced it though the link so that she had no choice but to feel it. He wanted her to know how much he desired her. He wanted to let his own need magnify hers. He wanted her desperate for him. He craved it.

She let out a needy whimper and her whole body softened in his arms.

A heady rush of victory slammed into him, making him grip her harder to keep from being swept away by the force of it. Losing himself in her was so easy, felt so right. She was warm, willing, eager, and his for the taking. And taking was exactly what he had in mind.

He wanted to feel her naked in his arms again, only this time, he wanted to finish exploring her body and giving her pleasure. He wanted to taste every smooth inch of her until she was quivering in his arms, begging him for completion. The soft curve of her breasts against his chest teased him and the feel of her bottom filling his hands drove him wild.

He was hard, aching for her, arching against her so that she could feel just how hard she made him. He was ready to take her right there on the grass, under the stars. She would have let him, too, but some sliver of sanity held him back.

He pulled away from their kiss and sucked in a deep breath of midnight air. Crickets sang around them, heedless of the battle he waged to hold himself in check.

Her mouth moved on to new territory, leaving a hot line of kisses down his neck. Her fingers tangled in his hair and if he wasn't careful, he was going to be bald trying to separate them.

As much as he wanted her, there wasn't time for the kind of thorough loving he had in mind, and even if there was, both he and Thomas had bled giving her their oath. The scent of their blood would no doubt draw Synestryn from whichever dark holes they hid in.

"We have to stop before we can't," he told her. His breathing was harsh and his body shook in resentment that he had to let her go.

She went still and he realized too late that he'd let too much of his thoughts flow through their link. He knew the Synestryn would come for them and he hadn't bothered to hide that knowledge from her. She'd felt his anxiety and it had doubled inside her, washing away all traces of lust.

Helen pushed away, but didn't meet his gaze. "I can't believe I'm doing this. Kissing you while we wait for monsters to show up. Wishing we'd do a lot more than just kissing while there's a house full of people not twenty yards away. What was I thinking?"

"Neither of us was doing much thinking."

"Yeah, well, at least you had enough sense to stop." She pushed her hair away from her face with a trembling hand. "I'm sorry I got carried away."

She was embarrassed. He didn't need the link between them to figure that out. The fetching blush staining her cheeks was evidence enough. "Don't ever be sorry for that. I love it that you got carried away. Makes me feel all manly."

A hint of a grin played at the corner of her mouth and she glanced down at his groin where his erection was straining at the fly of his jeans. "If you were any manlier, you'd scare me away."

"If you don't stop talking about it, it won't go away."

"And that would be bad because . . . ?"

There was only one way this conversation could go and it was down to the grass with both of them naked and loving it. "We'd better get back to the van. I wouldn't put it past Thomas to try to leave without us."

"Where are we going?"

"We found a trail leading to the nest where we think the Synestryn took Kevin's sword. It's outside Spring Hill, not far from here."

"And we're going to follow it and take the sword back, right?"

"Exactly. If we're lucky, the Synestryn will be out hunting and we won't have to fight the whole nest of them to get the sword back."

"You said it was invisible. How are you going to find it?"

"It's only invisible when it's being worn. Gilda imbued all our swords with that power so we could carry them without interference from human authorities."

"Is that why it looks like your sword just appears out of nowhere?" she asked.

"Yeah. Want to feel it?"

She arched a dark brow. "Please tell me you did not just ask me to feel your sword."

Drake let out a laugh. It felt good to laugh and he couldn't remember the last time he'd enjoyed such a simple pleasure. Months, maybe years.

He caught her hand and laced his fingers through hers as they walked over the grass to the van. Thomas was helping load Miss Mabel into Slade's beat-up pickup truck while Carmen was speaking in a quiet voice to Vance. He didn't look happy, but he gave her a hard hug and watched her as she drove away in her own rattletrap.

"I'm going to say good-bye to Miss Mabel," said Helen.

He almost told her to make it quick, but held back. It wouldn't hurt them to wait an extra minute for Helen to reassure herself as well as the old woman that everything was going to be fine. She was going to need her mind free of distractions for the next few hours.

Drake followed Thomas back into the farmhouse, where he gathered up an armload of the gear they'd taken out of Logan's van. His friend didn't even meet his gaze when he said, "Change your shirt before you get us all killed."

O-kay. So much for no hard feelings. "Don't give up yet, Thomas. There's still time for us to find another woman like Helen. She can't be the only one."

"I know how much you love to play cheerleader, but I'm not buying in to your shit. Just lay off."

"So . . . what? I get lucky and you can't even be my friend anymore? Is that it?"

Thomas stopped dead in his tracks and let everything in his arms fall to the ground. And the man could carry a lot in those huge arms of his.

He turned around slowly, wearing a look Drake had never seen on his face before. Hopelessness. Despair. "I want to be happy for you, Drake, but it's too late for that."

"The hell it is. We're like brothers. As soon as we find Kevin's sword, Helen and I will help you hunt for another female Theronai. I know she will want to do that for you."

"What part of 'it's too late' do you not get?" Thomas gritted his teeth in an obvious effort to control himself, and when he spoke again, Drake saw a glimpse of the man he remembered. Gentle. Kind. Patient. His voice was a quiet whisper of defeat and he pressed his hand over his lifemark as if it ached. "I'm out of time. I can already feel the change coming over me. It's happening faster than I thought and I can't control it."

"No," said Drake, refusing to believe it was true. "You can't give up yet. Helen changes everything."

"For you, yes. Not for me."

"Promise me you'll hold on until we can find your Helen."

"No."

"Damn it! Promise me!"

Thomas said nothing. He picked up the supplies he'd dropped and left the farmhouse in silence. With every angry step, Drake could see more of the gentle man Thomas had been slowly slipping away.

Thomas was out of time and there was nothing anyone could do to stop it.

Chapter 12

Zach wanted to scream. No, screaming wouldn't have done anything to ease his rage. He wanted to rip the SUV apart with his bare hands and hurl each chunk into a lake. That might take the edge off.

Lexi was gone. Not gone and he'd find her later. She was gone gone. Really gone. Not a trace of her remained.

He'd marked her with a bloodmark—sort of a biological tracking device—that he should have been able to locate halfway across the planet, and he knew she hadn't gotten that far. Even if she'd hopped a plane, he should have been able to at least sense the direction that she'd gone in.

He'd pulled the Tahoe over along the edge of a deserted Kansas highway as soon as he realized he couldn't feel the subtle tug coming from her any longer. He could keep heading south, but that would only do him so much good. Once he hit ocean, he'd have to stop.

The night wind swept through the open window, bringing with it the sound of crickets. He hadn't bothered to wash the blood off his arm, though he had tossed his shirt out the window a few hours back on another equally deserted stretch of road. There wasn't much blood left to attract any snarlies, and even if they did come, he was itching for a fight. Hell, it might even help him burn off some of this anxious tension that was growing in him more by the second.

How had she slipped free so easily? It didn't seem possible.

Zach dialed Nicholas, hoping to make some progress another way.

"Heya, Zach," answered Nicholas, sounding just friendly enough to piss Zach off more.

"I need you to put out all you geeky little feelers on a waitress named Lexi."

"I'm fine. How are you?"

"Cut the shit, man. This is serious."

"Your snarl is my command. Lexi who?"

"How should I know? All I got was the name on her name tag."

"Ever think she might have borrowed the tag from another waitress?"

Zach was not going to admit to being that stupid. Not a chance. "Just help me out. Please." Ouch, that near begging had hurt.

"Wow. You must be desperate to go pulling out the 'p' word."

"Pussy," grumbled Zach under his breath.

"Yep. That's the Zach I know and love. Always the charmer. Okay, what else can you give me?"

"What else? I already gave you her name."

"I'm good, but even I am going to need a little more than that."

"She drove an old Honda Civic."

"License plate?"

"I was a little too busy chasing it on foot to notice."

"I would have paid money to see that race."

"Don't make me come back and hurt you, man."

"Yeah, yeah. You're all big and tough and mean and I'm shaking in my boots. What color?"

"She's a blonde. With these melted chocolate brown eyes and—"

"The car, shit-for-brains. What color was the car?"

"Oh. Uh. Rust orange. Primer gray. Maybe a little blue in there somewhere."

"Blue. Check. Do you remember what state the plate was from?"

"Kansas."

"That'll help. Anything else you can give me? Any other names people called her? Maybe she just happened to write her phone number on a napkin and slip it to you."

"Phone number!" Zach scrolled through his call log until he found the number Thomas had ripped off Helen's cell phone for him. It was listed there in his outgoing call log about twenty times, so it wasn't hard to spot. He read the number to Nicholas.

After a few clicking keystrokes, Nicholas said, "Prepaid. No name. Pays with cash. This isn't going to help any. Sorry, man."

"I've got to find her."

"Why? Does she owe you money?" asked Nicholas.

"Funny."

"I do try."

Zach held on to his panic. Panicking would not do anyone any good. "Okay. Hypothetical question. If you place a bloodmark on someone and a few hours later they disappear, what does that mean?"

"You put a marker on her and she disappeared? That's not even possible. Not even if she died."

"I would have said the same thing a half hour ago."

Nicholas gave a low whistle. "You need to call Logan in on this. Or Tynan. I'm good with the electronic tracers, but if you put a bloodmark on her and she slipped it, I have no clue how to help you."

"Can you at least work your mojo to see if you can find her through her credit cards or something?"

"I can try. All we have is her car model, maybe the color, the state it was registered in, and a name she put on a name tag. None of that is solid, man, but I'll do what I can."

"Thanks."

Zach ended the call and set the phone down before he shattered it on the inside of the windshield. He didn't think Thomas would appreciate having his ride screwed up like that.

He rolled up the window and flipped on the air-conditioning. His choices were to keep following her not knowing which way to go, or help his buddies kick some ass.

Not a hard choice. Lexi was gone and he was in one heck of an ass-kicking mood.

When Drake said "nest" Helen pictured a big pile of sticks and leaves sitting on the ground somewhere. Like a giant gerbil's nest or something.

She had not pictured the gaping black maw of a forgotten mine shaft out in the middle of nowhere. That meal replacement bar she'd eaten during the drive was considering its chances for escape so it wouldn't have to go down there with her.

"You're not claustrophobic, are you?" asked Drake.

"I am now," she said, unable to imagine going down into that black hole.

Thomas turned off the van, leaving the keys in the ignition. For a fast getaway, no doubt. That did little to ease Helen's growing anxiety.

Thomas eyed her with something bordering on disgust. "If she's going to be a liability, she can damn well stay in the van."

Being a liability sounded pretty darn good right now, even if it was the coward's way out.

"You'll do fine," soothed Drake. He slid his hand over her hair—which she'd put back into braids to keep it out of her eyes. It felt good having his wide palm touch her. She was starting to get used to having him around, touching her like he had the right to. It was nice. Comforting. And right now she could use every scrap of comfort she could find.

"Tell me again what we're going to do." Maybe the plan would sound better the third time she heard it.

Thomas rolled his eyes and got out of the van, slamming the door shut behind him.

Helen felt like a foolish child. Drake had already told her what to expect. Twice. But if he was as frustrated by her anxiety as Thomas was, it didn't show. Instead, he took her hands in his and stroked her palms with his thumbs. "I'll go in first, you in the middle, and Thomas will bring up the rear. Most of the Synestryn will be out hunting for another hour or two, so we'll have plenty of time to find Kevin's sword. We'll get it and sneak back out. No sweat."

"And are you sure it's here?"

"As sure as we can be."

They'd used some electronic gadget that was a cross between a GPS gadget and a blood glucose monitor. Drake had taken a sample of black blood he'd brought with him in a little vial and put a drop of it into the machine. A map appeared on a small color display, showing the location of the mine. Less than an hour southwest of Olathe.

"How does that thing work, anyway?"

"I have no idea how it works. It's something Nicholas and one of the Sanguinar came up with. Major magic is built into it as well as some killer electronics. But I can tell you what it does. We put a drop of Synestryn blood into it and it tracks down the monster that it came from."

"You're saying that you know there's one of those monsters in that mine?"

"Afraid so."

"Okay, I have to ask. How did you get the blood? I doubt the thing sat down and rolled up its sleeve."

Drake's face twisted in a grimace. "I'm not sure you want to know."

"I'm sure that not knowing is only going to make my imagination go crazy, which will scare me more."

Drake sighed and unzipped a duffel bag. He pulled out three clear plastic face shields, like the kind sometimes used in surgery. "The Theronai who was with Kevin when he was killed was poisoned. We're still not sure if he's going to live." He said it like that was supposed to mean something to her.

"I still don't get it. Was there blood on him or something?"

"He was poisoned with Synestryn blood. It was injected into his body through the monster's fangs."

She pictured a giant snake, and that image was now number three of her Most Disgusting Things Ever list.

Drake continued. "One of the Sanguinar managed to extract enough of the blood from Torr for us to hunt the thing down, but it will only be good for about twenty-four hours. We're down to less than two of that now."

Drake handed her one of the face shields. "Wear this. Some of them spit. And when I say spit, I mean acid."

No, *that* was number three. "This is getting grosser by the minute."

"If you don't want to do this, just say the word. I won't force you."

Staying behind was a serious temptation. Helen was no hero. She'd only slow them down no matter how many rocks she could lift. "Would it be safe for me to stay here? I mean, I wouldn't get swarmed by a bunch of those things running away from you big sword-wielding, manly men, would I?"

His mouth twitched with a grin, but it was gone a second later. "You'd be perfectly safe because I'd be right here with you. No way am I letting you hang here alone. Too many things could go wrong. Including getting overrun by a swarm of Synestryn."

"But Thomas needs you to go help him."

"Thomas knows the risks. You don't. Besides, we both swore an oath to you and we meant it."

"You mean that 'my life for yours' thing?"

"Exactly."

"You actually meant that?"

"Every word."

She stared at him for a long moment, hoping to see some hint that he was joking. He wasn't. He was deadly serious. And he was waiting for her decision.

"I don't want to go. I also know that if something happened to Thomas because you weren't there to help him, I'd never forgive myself. So we go."

Drake's lips curled in a proud smile. "You're one hell of a woman. I'm glad I found you first."

He pulled her close and gave her a quick kiss on the mouth, which drove all the nasty thoughts out of her head so fast it spun. She loved his mouth—smooth and firm and warm—even if it was only against hers for a brief second. That quick kiss still did more for her than an hour of sex from most of the other men she'd been with. She wasn't sure whether that made her lucky or pitiful. But she did know that if getting through this mine alive was what she had to do to get more of his mouth on hers, then she'd find a way to become Superwoman. Whatever it took, she wanted more of Drake and his luscious kiss.

He pushed open the back doors of the van, dragging the duffel bag with him. Thomas was crouched near the opening of the mine, peering at the ground. His sword was in his hands, gleaming with lethal intent under the moonlight.

Drake handed him one of the face masks and fastened his own in place. "Any idea what's down there?" he asked Thomas.

"At least three sgath. Four, maybe five haest. No malkaia that I can detect, thank God."

"Any anguis?"

"No."

"Good. It'll be hard enough to breathe down there without them sucking up all the oxygen."

Helen did not want to know what that meant. Going underground to fight monsters was bad enough. Doing it while worrying about having enough oxygen was terrifying. "Are you two sure this is necessary? I mean, if all those monsters' souls are released, won't they just go to hell?"

Thomas took a threatening step forward and Drake shoved his body in the way of the bigger man's progress. "She doesn't understand. It's not her fault. She was raised human."

"I *am* human," said Helen. And she was sticking by her story. No way was she going to let these guys tell her otherwise, not while she was already dealing with heading into a dank monster nest.

Thomas growled and she could see a flicker of something frightening and wild glowing in his blue eyes. Something definitely not human.

Drake was a big man, but Thomas was freaking huge. Drake had to lean all his weight against Thomas to keep him from coming forward, and even then, he skidded over the ground a couple of feet before coming to a stop. "Let it go, Thomas. Focus on the job."

Helen took several frightened steps back.

"She should have more respect," growled Thomas.

"She will once she understands. Back off. You don't want to do this."

Thomas's body shuddered and his eyes fell shut. When he opened them again, that inhuman wildness was gone and he offered Helen an apologetic grimace. "Sorry. I'm not . . . myself."

"We're running out of time," said Drake. "We need to get moving."

"I'm ready," said Thomas.

Both men turned to her with expectant looks. Helen fought the urge to get back in the van and drive away. It would have been easier than taking that first step forward. "I'm ready, too." What a huge lie that was.

"All right, then. Let's move," said Thomas.

Drake took Helen's hand and gave it a quick squeeze. "You'll be great. Just listen to your instincts and trust me. If I say duck or run, don't waste time asking questions. Just do it. Okay?"

Helen nodded, feeling numb inside.

Drake pulled her face shield into place and handed

her a small flashlight. "You may need this. At least until you figure out how to see in the dark."

"I can do that?"

Drake nodded. "You sure can. I wish there was more time to teach you. I'm sorry for that."

So was she, but she kept it to herself. She had to focus on being brave enough not to throw up. Putting one foot in front of the other was taking all her concentration.

They entered the mine and followed a man-made tunnel that sloped down at a steady angle. The light in her hands showed her where to put her feet and she kept the fingers of her left hand looped around Drake's belt so she didn't fall behind. She was not going to be left alone in a place like this. Just the thought was enough to send fear skittering through her nervous system.

"Deep breaths, Helen." Drake's voice was calm and confident and it helped her pull herself back under control.

The ground under them was a mixture of loose dirt and rocks and black stuff she did not spend any time thinking about. A musky animal scent filled the air along with something she couldn't identify. Something rotten, stagnant, and oppressive.

After about fifty feet, they came to an intersection. Drake checked the monster finder and turned left. Behind her, she heard a scraping noise and looked back. Thomas was carving an arrow in the dirt with his boot pointing back the way they'd come.

Smart man.

"Will you be able to see this?" he asked her.

Helen nodded.

"I'll leave one at every turn. If you have to get out alone, at least you'll know the way."

She didn't even want to think about why she would

have to leave alone. Being flanked by two competent, sword-wielding badasses was one thing; running around down here by herself was completely different. Completely frightening.

Drake reached behind and squeezed the hand curled around his belt. "Just hang on, Helen. You're doing great."

"I don't feel great."

"I know. We'll get out of here in a few minutes. We're almost there."

Drake slowed and veered to the side so that his body was pressed up against one wall. Helen followed suit, as did Thomas behind her. Instinctively, she flipped off the flashlight, fearing it would give their position away. Darkness swallowed her and she felt a bubble of panic break open inside her. She stomped on the need to flee and focused on breathing through her mouth.

Just breathe. She could almost hear Drake's voice brush against her mind in a soothing caress, and the luceria grew warm against her throat.

She needed to see. The blackness was smothering her, sparking a primal fear that she couldn't control. If only they'd had more time and he'd been able to teach her how to see in the dark. He'd said she could do it. She needed to figure out how.

A ribbon of energy hovered between them, an invisible connection running from his ring to her necklace. She tugged on that ribbon, pulling some of his power into herself in an effort to figure out how to make it do her bidding. Her eyes were the problem, so she redirected some of the power into them.

Instantly, the world flashed into bright focus. She could see the tunnel they were in with perfect clarity. Every sparkle of mineral that had been broken to form the soil shone like glitter along the walls and floor. The grainy texture of the rocks littering the ground stood out in stark relief. She zoomed in on one until she could see each individual crack and bump and hollow. It was like looking under a microscope. Amazing.

She was so distracted by her newfound talent that she was startled by the tug of Drake's belt at her fingers. She stumbled into his back and felt Thomas's big hand wrap around her arm to steady her. "Sorry," she whispered.

Up ahead, something skittered in response to the noise.

Oh, crap. This was not good.

Drake reached back and pressed her against the wall, flattening his own body as well. In a voice so quiet she could barely hear, he said, "Two haest, feeding. South wall."

Helen had no idea which way south was. Or what a haest was.

"I'll go in alone," whispered Thomas. "I can handle two."

Drake shook his head and she could see the grim set of his mouth with her newly perfect vision. "There are more tunnels branching off. Those two may not be alone."

"Do you see the sword?" asked Thomas.

"No."

"Let me look," said Helen, before the words could filter through her brain.

"Like hell," said Drake.

"I did something to my eyes. I can see perfectly now."

Drake was silent for a moment as if deciding.

"If she's tapped in to your power, she could be stronger than the two of us put together," said Thomas. "Let her try."

Helen wasn't sure about that, but with a silent curse on his lips, Drake stepped back to give her room to slide into his position at the opening of the tunnel.

Her heart was pounding in her chest and her breathing was too fast, but she found the courage to lean forward just enough to see. It was an open area that was about three times as wide as the tunnel and fifty feet across. Large sections of the walls had been scraped away with metal tools. She could see tiny metal flecks still clinging to some of the rock. Ancient timbers braced the ceiling, but they were so eroded by termite damage that she didn't think they were holding up much of anything. The floor was covered with bits of fur, bone, and dried leaves. Piles of the stuff stood in mounds near the walls. She could see things moving underneath the refuse—small, furry things with spines—things one would never see displayed in a petting zoo.

She repressed a shudder of revulsion, but not for long. Along what she had to guess was the south wall were two giant mosquito-looking creatures, as tall as a man. They each had two yard-long fangs protruding from their heads. The other ends of the fangs were shoved into the belly of a dead cow. Through the semitransparent tubes, she could see them pump something black into the cow until its hide expanded to the point of bursting. One made a clicking sound, which was returned by the second one. Then in unison, they started sucking something back out of the cow—a mix of blood and bits of muscle and bone. The cow's stomach collapsed until it looked starved and the two things started the process all over again.

Helen's stomach spun in a nauseating roll.

Her Most Disgusting Things Ever list had a new number one.

She closed her eyes, cursing her perfect vision for a moment before she forced herself to look into the opening again. She scanned the room, telling herself to focus on looking for something shiny. Several pieces of quartz caught her eye, as did an empty beer bottle, a scrap of aluminum foil, and the glass eyes of a doll's head. No body. Just the head. Creepy.

She felt Drake's hand on her neck as if he was going to pull her back, but instead, his ring touched her necklace and she felt a surge of power. Since she'd been channeling his power to her eyes, that's where that surge went, and for a moment she could see through everything. She could see the cow's skeleton, the thick plates of the monsters' bodies, the spiky bones of the scurrying ratlike things hiding in the mounds of organic rubbish. She could even see several veins of minerals running through the walls of the mine.

Buried under one of the mounds of refuse was the unmistakable shape of a sword. The tip of it had been sticking out, but it was coated with dried blood and not at all shiny, so she hadn't seen it before.

Helen ducked back into the tunnel and forced herself to keep her voice quiet through a sheer act of will. She was humming with energy and excitement and the thrill of finding the lost treasure. "It's in there," she told them. "Under one of those piles of fur and stuff. On the far wall. Middle pile."

Drake gave her a proud smile and his eyes strayed to her mouth. He was thinking about kissing her and she loved that about him. Nothing like having a hot man wanting to kiss her to distract her from all the disgusting things in the world.

"I'll take the haest," said Thomas. "You get the sword."

Drake nodded. "Don't take them on unless you have to. They've just fed. They'll be strong."

"What do I do?" asked Helen. She was all pumped up on victory and adrenaline and the thrill of knowing they'd be out of here soon.

"Stay here. Warn us if you see something we don't."

She could do that.

"Keep a close eye behind you, too."

Some of the thrill wore off with those words, reminding her that they weren't out of the woods yet.

Drake turned to Thomas. "On your go."

Thomas straightened his face shield and gripped his heavy blade with both hands. "Go."

Both men moved into the opening on silent feet, crossing the distance quickly. Thomas stayed close to Drake, keeping a watchful eye on the two mosquito-like creatures they'd called haest. Drake moved directly toward the sword.

Helen looked over her shoulder every three seconds, but nothing was there.

Drake saw the blackened tip of the sword and nudged it with the toe of his boot. The mound exploded in a flurry of movement as spiny rat things scurried out in every direction.

The haest heard the sound and turned their fanged heads around toward the noise.

Thomas smiled and stepped forward, squaring his heavy shoulders for attack.

Drake bent down to pick up the sword.

Something resembling a puddle of tar dropped from the ceiling, engulfing the mound of garbage and the sword inside it. Drake hissed and jerked his hand back. Helen could feel her own hand burning where the tar had touched him.

"Kajmelas!" Drake shouted the warning, but it was too late. A second tar-thing dropped from above and slithered over the ground toward Helen.

Helen stared at it, trying to figure out what to do. Her legs felt heavy and her brain spat out terrified commands to flee, but she'd been hearing those all night and tried to fight them. She wasn't sure whether she was supposed to do that now, too. The time it took her to figure it out made the decision moot.

A thick, oily tentacle shot toward her.

She jumped back. Both men charged it, but Thomas was closer to her than Drake. He lunged toward her on powerful legs and pushed Helen back. She stumbled and landed on her butt.

The thing hit Thomas instead of her. It wrapped a slimy tentacle around his legs. Thomas screamed in pain and slashed at the thing with his sword. It did no good. His blade sliced right through it, only to have the cut close up as if it had never been there.

The black stuff oozed up Thomas's body, covering him inch by inch. Thomas was still screaming in ragged cries of agony.

Helen felt Drake's panic—something she'd never felt from him before. It set off the beginnings of her own panic and she had to struggle to remain coherent.

Drake took a step toward Thomas and the sludge thing shot a tentacle out toward his legs. The two mosquito monsters made a series of excited clicking sounds and skittered over the dirt floor on skinny insect legs.

Drake was caught between them.

Helen tried to scream at him to run, but her lungs had seized up and all that came out was a thready squeak.

Drake held his position until the last second and jumped out of the way. The mosquito monsters slammed into the sludge thing, which promptly began eating them. They made frantic clicking noises and struggled to get free of the sticky beast, but they were no match for the slow advance of the oily mound.

Drake spared one quick glance to see that his plan had worked and rushed to Thomas's side.

Helen didn't know what to do or how to help. Her mind raced for a way to save Thomas, but she could think of none.

Helen felt that wavering tendril of power floating between them and tentatively pulled at it. Energy flooded her, but she had no idea what to do.

The second mound of sludge had absorbed the two mosquito monsters, leaving behind only the spindly insectoid legs. Now it was looking for a new target.

Drake was closest and the thing headed right for him in a flowing mound of slime.

She had to stop it. She had no clue what she was doing, but she couldn't just stand there. She had to do something.

She shouted a warning in her mind, but if Drake heard her, he didn't respond. He was too busy pounding at the thing eating Thomas.

Helen pulled more power from Drake. Too much. She had to concentrate to keep herself from doubling over in pain. The energy flowed into her in an agonizing rush. It stretched her insides until she thought her ribs would explode out of her chest. Her body heated until her eyes and mouth went dry. It was hard to think with all that pain. Hard to breathe. She had to get rid of the power before it killed her.

She sent up a quick prayer that she was doing this right and focused on the sludge thing headed for Drake. She pushed the energy out of her and built an invisible wall around it. She made the air thicken, forced the molecules tighter together until a semitransparent cylinder surrounded the thing.

Helen didn't know what would happen if she relaxed, so she held her focus, drawing more power from Drake to keep the barrier in place.

She was breathing hard and her vision grayed around the edges. The luceria buzzed and heated until she was sure blisters would form under the band.

She couldn't see Drake any longer, but she could feel his desperation to save Thomas.

Chapter 13

Drake's sword did no good against the kajmela, so he dropped it and picked up a heavy stick from the ground. Thomas's screams rose an octave until they were shrill and sickening. He wasn't going to last much longer.

Thomas had turned his sword around, holding it by the blade and using the hilt in an effort to pound the thing away from him. His hands were slick with his own blood where the sword had sliced through his palms. As strong as Thomas's arms were, the hilt was of little use against the thing eating him whole.

They needed fire. It was the only thing that could kill a kajmela, and Helen was the only one who could make it.

He felt Helen tugging at his power, but still there was no fire. Not even a spark.

Drake swung the stick at the kajmela and a big blob of sludge disconnected from the mass and hit the far wall. He hit it again and again, tearing chunks of the kajmela off, but there were always more to fill in the holes.

They needed fire, damn it. Why wasn't Helen using his power to give them fire?

Because she had no clue that's what she was supposed to do. He suddenly remembered she'd never been taught. He only hoped there was enough time left to teach her now.

Thomas was covered up to his chest now and the thing had constricted around him until he could no longer pull in enough breath to scream. The acidic Synestryn dissolved flesh wherever it touched, causing Thomas to bleed heavily everywhere kajmela and human skin met.

Drake kept batting away, frantic to save his friend even though he knew it was futile.

Thomas's struggles ceased and Drake could see that Thomas had accepted his fate. He was going to die.

While he continued battling the kajmela, Drake formed a mental image of what he wanted Helen to do and sent it through their already crowded link. He could feel her revulsion at the idea, so he pushed harder— demanded that she listen to him.

"Take my sword," he said to Drake. "I don't want it to hurt anyone." His voice was ragged from screaming and shallow from lack of breath.

The kajmela inched higher until it was nearly at Thomas's throat. Thomas gritted his teeth against the pain and tossed his bloody sword to Drake. Drake let it clang to the ground. Once Drake took Thomas's sword, his friend would give up. He'd be as good as dead.

Drake beat the kajmela, taking out all his fury on the thing. This wasn't the way it was supposed to end for Thomas. He was supposed to live. He was supposed to find his own Theronai. He was supposed to end his life peacefully years from now when every last Synestryn was driven from the earth.

He wasn't supposed to die suffering in a dark cave, knowing it was going to happen.

"Go, Drake," he gasped.

"I won't leave you." Drake's chest bellowed for air. Sweat covered his body. He pounded the kajmela mercilessly until nearly half of it was smeared over the rock wall.

"I'm dead either way. My lifemark is bare. Go. Take my sword."

"No!" Drake let out an enraged bellow and beat at the kajmela. The stick broke off in his hands.

"Save . . . Helen."

Helen. She was still siphoning off more power than was safe and still there was no fire. Finally, he figured out what she was doing with it. She was holding off the other kajmela so it wouldn't kill him. She was protecting his back, but she wouldn't be able to do it for much longer.

Drake knew what he had to do and hated every second of it. He looked Thomas straight in the eye, memorizing every pained line of his friend's face. He picked up Thomas's sword, making sure he saw Drake had it safe in his keeping. Thomas's sword would never hurt anyone. "I love you, Thomas. You'll never be forgotten."

Thomas couldn't speak. The kajmela had filled his mouth. A tear slid from Thomas's bright blue eye before it, too, was consumed by oily black sludge.

When nothing of Thomas was left, Drake turned away, pushed aside the grinding pain of his grief, and focused on what he had to do. Get Kevin's sword and get out of here while they still could.

He grabbed his sword from the ground, shoved it in the scabbard, and went to Helen's side. She was breathing hard and shaking. Her skin had a sickly gray cast to it that scared the hell out of him.

"Release it now," he told her. His voice was rough and strained with grief.

She didn't respond. Drake settled his left hand at the

nape of her neck, connecting the two parts of the luceria. "Let it go, Helen. You need to let it go."

She shuddered and sagged against his side. The wall around the kajmela dissipated and the thing oozed toward them. It was bigger now. Faster. Somewhere inside that mass was Kevin's sword. The only way to get it out was to burn the kajmela to ash.

Helen stood there too shocked to move. Her body was weak and trembling and if it hadn't been for Drake's support, she would have sunk to the ground.

Drake turned to her, his face a mask of tortured grief. "You need to call fire," he told her.

Helen didn't understand. She didn't understand any of what was happening.

"You have to burn it off Kevin's sword. Now, while there's still time."

Helen felt her necklace heat and saw a split-second image of what Drake wanted her to do. She saw herself standing in the tunnel, fire spewing from her fingertips. The tar thing heading toward them, bursting into flames.

Drake wanted her to make fire come out of her body? No freaking way. Drake had nearly died by fire. Her mother *had* died by fire. Her house had burned down three times. The diner caught fire while everyone was in it. She was going to burn alive in darkness much like this and Drake was going to watch it happen.

How could he ask that of her?

"We need Kevin's sword."

She felt Drake's quiet desperation pounding at her. He was crushed under a mountain of grief and guilt, and somehow, recovering the sword was still at the top of his list of priorities.

The sludge thing oozed forward and melted into the one that had eaten Thomas. The two became one—a much bigger one. Drake pulled her back down the tunnel as the thing slowly advanced on them.

"Please try, Helen. We need that sword," he said in an even voice.

Helen lifted her hand and closed her eyes. She didn't want to do this, but she had no choice but to try. She sure as hell didn't want to have to come back here later.

She pulled on the ribbon of power, gathered it inside herself, keeping the frightening image that Drake had given her in her mind. Fire flowing from her hand. He thought she could do that. He was insane, but he had faith in her.

The power inside her built and heated. Her ribs ached as if being pushed out from within. The pain grew until she started to sweat and shake with the force of it. Sweat burned off her skin, rising up in wisps of steam that smelled like fear. As the power inside her built, so did the heat. She couldn't stand it, yet no fire flowed from her hand. Her insides had to be blistered. It was too much heat. She was going to erupt into flames. Be consumed by them. She was going to die. This was how it was going to happen.

Something inside her broke, some panicked, childish part of her she couldn't control. She couldn't do it. She couldn't bring herself to use his power that way. A deep-seated sense of self-preservation entangled with a primal fear of fire made it impossible.

She felt herself scramble away and shut down, felt her too-hot body grow cold and numb and saw her vision recede into a gray mist. She could still hear Drake urging her on, but she couldn't do it. She couldn't call fire. Not fire.

* * *

Drake felt Helen's mind go blank with terror and shut down. Her fear of fire had won. The sword was lost.

It was time to get out of there before the two of them were as well.

He tugged at Helen's hand, but she didn't move. He reached out to her mind and found her cowering in terror.

He scooped her up and hauled ass out of the mine.

The pale light of dawn showed him the entrance. Even if the kajmela had followed him, they wouldn't come outside with sunrise so near.

Wind blew across his face, drying his tears of grief. Thomas was gone. Helen was unresponsive and Kevin's sword was still lost.

He'd failed everyone.

Helen started to regain coherence a little at a time. She felt Drake settle her in the front seat of the van and buckle her in. The door slammed. Another opened and slammed shut. She heard the engine start.

They were leaving. The monsters were behind them. She hadn't died in a fire.

Thomas was dead. Helen couldn't stop that thought from repeating in her mind. She was alive, but Thomas was dead. It didn't seem right somehow—like someone had made a giant mistake and would come back any minute and fix it. They'd all go back into the mine and do it right this time.

But the minutes ticked by and that didn't happen.

The van rocked as they made their way over the rutted country road. The mine was more than a mile behind them, but she could still feel the oppressive evil of that place, smell the rotten odor of it clinging to her skin.

Thomas was dead and they didn't even have Kevin's sword to show for his sacrifice. That part was her fault and her failure made her sick.

Drake sat silently as he drove, his hands tight on the wheel. The back of his right hand was blistered and swollen where a tar monster had touched him, but he didn't seem to notice. His attention was fixed on the gravel road.

Helen's insides burned, though whether from physical injury or from emotional overload she wasn't sure.

Drake turned onto a paved road, heading east. The sun hadn't broken the horizon, but the sky was growing lighter. Even though it stung her eyes, Helen welcomed the light. Instinctively, she knew that darkness such as they'd faced in that mine wouldn't be able to tolerate the purity of sunlight.

"We're not going far," said Drake. His voice was rough and harsh in the silence of the van.

Helen nodded, not trusting herself to speak. She was afraid that even one word would send her into tears and she'd never be able to stop crying. As much as she wished she could let go and give in to the tears, Drake needed her. She could feel how much he was suffering. His grief dwarfed hers, flowing over their connection in shuddering waves of agony. He'd loved Thomas like a brother and she'd only known him for one night. She wanted to be strong for Drake, to find a way to help ease his pain, and if she cried, she'd be useless. Again.

There was nothing she could do to make up for her cowardice, but maybe she could offer Drake some small measure of comfort. It was the only thing she could think to do to honor Thomas.

Assuming Drake would even want comfort from the woman who had failed so completely.

"It wasn't your fault."

He gave her a hard stare. All the warmth in his golden brown eyes was gone.

Helen swallowed past the clog of tears in her throat. Her eyes burned against the need to cry. "I should have called . . . done what you asked." She couldn't even say the word *fire*.

"I shouldn't have asked that of you without first teaching you what you needed to know. It's a mistake I won't repeat. We're going to find a place to rest for a couple hours. Then I'm taking you home. Once you meet Gilda, you'll have a much better understanding of what you can do."

"She's the woman you told me about. The woman like me."

"Yeah. And we'll see Sibyl, too. She'll know what to do about your vision of your own death."

Helen gave an involuntary shudder at the reminder. "What do you think she can do? Make me forget it?"

"No. But she might be able to tell you it isn't real. Maybe it was something that was planted in you to prevent you from reaching your full potential."

"You think that someone put that vision in my head?"

"It's possible. Sibyl will know."

There was something he wasn't telling her. She could see it in the way he refused to glance her way, feel his guilt tingling along their link. "What?" she asked him. "What are you hiding?"

"Fucking luceria," he grated out. "It's nothing. Just try to get some rest. We'll be somewhere safe in a few minutes."

"It's not nothing. What are you hiding? Spit it out."

He was silent for a few minutes, his jaw bunching and

relaxing repeatedly. "Logan said there was something wrong with you. I think this is what he meant."

"Something is wrong with me? Why didn't you say anything?" She couldn't believe their arrogance in thinking they had the right to hide things from her. "Damn it, Drake, I have a right to know that kind of thing."

His mouth twisted into a sneer of disgust. "I've told you everything I know. Besides, you can't always believe everything Logan says. He'd twist the truth or even flat-out lie if it served his agenda."

"So there might not be anything wrong?"

"I wish I knew. What I can tell you is that we'll figure it out and get through it together."

She let out a weary sigh. "I'm sick of feeling like I'm two steps behind everyone else."

"Helen. There is no 'everyone else' anymore. It's just you and me now."

He was right. They were on their own and that was a frightening reality. Drake was strong and capable, but she wasn't. She feared she would never be.

What if what happened to Thomas happened to Drake? They'd both given her that stupid oath—their lives for hers. Thomas's oath had cost him his life. She couldn't let Drake do the same.

"Stop it," he ordered. "Things have gone badly to-night, but it will be okay."

"How can you possibly know that? Can you see the future?"

"No, but I remember the past. As much as I loved Thomas, my grief for him will fade with time. I know because it's happened dozens of times before. It hurts like a son of a bitch now, but in time, the pain will fade. The grief will diminish and life will go on. We don't have the luxury of shutting down and wallowing in our grief. We have a job to do."

"Kevin's sword," she guessed.

"Yes. We still have to find it. Hang it next to Thomas's in the Hall of the Fallen."

"Is that what you do? When one of you dies, I mean?"

Drake nodded and swallowed hard, blinking several times. "It's how we honor them. How we remember them."

She looked back into the empty van. No light shone in back there—there were no windows—but she could still see the gleam of Thomas's sword where Drake had laid it. Thomas's blood was all over it as well as some of that black goop from the monster that had killed him. It bothered her that his sword was lying on the floor of the van. It seemed somehow disrespectful of the man who had wielded it. The man who had saved her life.

Helen went into the back of the van, found a clean sheet stowed in a duffel bag, and wrapped the sword up in it, being careful not to get any of the blood or black stuff on her. She tucked it inside the duffel bag and zipped it closed.

It felt like shoveling dirt in over his grave. So final.

"We'll find Kevin's sword," she told Drake. She hadn't known Kevin, but if Thomas and Drake were willing to risk their lives to get his weapon back, then he had to have been one hell of a man. He deserved to be honored in line with their traditions.

"Are you saying you're still willing to help me?" asked Drake, shooting a quick glance over his shoulder.

"I made you a promise. I intend to keep it or die trying." She knew which one of those was more likely, but kept that to herself.

Chapter 14

Drake needed a little time to pull himself together before he faced Gilda and the rest of the Theronai with the news of Thomas's death. Bad news could wait. At least that's what he told himself as a means to justify putting it off.

It was another three hours' drive to the compound, but there was a Sentinel house less than ten minutes away, just outside Carbondale, Kansas. He'd take Helen there and give her a chance to rest, too. She'd been up all night and fatigue and the strain of using magic had made her eyes bloodshot and slumped her shoulders.

He shouldn't have pushed her so hard. He realized that now, but it was too late to do anything but give her time to sleep. As it was, he was barely holding himself together. He was no good to anyone like this—raging inside to the point that he wanted to scream and lash out at the world for taking Thomas from him.

His emotions were nearly overwhelming and he needed some time to meditate and ground himself. He needed to shove his grief and anger into the earth and let it absorb them deep into the stones so that they couldn't hurt anyone. It was a tool all the Theronai learned from the time they were young as a means of dealing with the pain of their steadily growing power. Those men who couldn't master the technique didn't make it past their hundredth birthday.

Drake thought that when he found his lady he would no longer need that skill, but he could see now how wrong he'd been.

He pulled into the driveway of the small brick home. It sat on a few acres of land that had been recently mowed. No one lived here, but one of the duties of the Gerai—the blooded humans who aided the Sentinels in the war—was to keep these places of refuge safe. That meant giving them the appearance of being lived in so humans would leave them alone. Many Gerai earned their living by spending a few days in houses all over the country, making sure their neighbors knew that they traveled for business, or were enjoying their retirement seeing the country. Whatever story they used, they made sure it stuck and that the surrounding neighbors didn't get nosy enough to go poking around into Sentinel business. The last thing the Sentinels needed was extra attention.

Drake had been to this particular house before. It had been clean and well stocked with fresh produce and meat, rather than the typical nonperishable foods he usually found in Sentinel houses. It had been a long time since his last meal and he hoped that whoever cared for this place was still as conscientious as before. Despite his grief and sorrow, his body couldn't keep going without fuel, and he *had* to keep going.

"We'll get some rest here," he told Helen, forcing his voice to come out steady and calm. "Then I'll take you to my home."

Helen gave a weary nod and slid out of the van. Drake found the key taped to the back of the porch light and unlocked the door. Rather than the stale smell of disuse,

the house smelled of wildflowers and fresh-baked bread.
His stomach rumbled in appreciation.

"You hungry?" he asked Helen.

She nodded. "Not really. I'm about to fall over."

"Let's see if there's something quick in here."

Drake opened the fridge and found a giant bowl of
salad and a casserole dish with a note taped to the top
that gave heating instructions for the lasagna. Whoever
stocked this house deserved a raise and a promotion.

He set the salad on the counter and slid the lasagna in
the oven, following the carefully written instructions. It
didn't take long to find plates and forks and the loaf of
still-warm bread sitting on the counter.

"I feel like I'm invading someone's home," said
Helen.

"You're not. The Sentinels own the property and pay
people to keep it up. It's here so we have a safe place to
rest."

"Good policy." He could hear her weariness rasping
her voice.

Helen washed her hands and dished up some of the
salad for both of them.

"We've had a lot of years to get it right. I still remember when the only comforts we had were whatever our
horses could carry."

Helen stilled in the process of filling his bowl with
lettuce. "How old are you?"

"Old," he said. "Really old."

"You're starting to freak me out a little."

"Which is why I'm not going to tell you exactly how
old. You're exhausted. We'll eat now and I'll answer
questions after you've slept."

The fact that she didn't argue proved just how tired
she was.

The rising sun streamed in through the kitchen windows and he could clearly see the lines of strain around her mouth. Her borrowed clothes were dirty and hanging on her frame. She sat slumped, looking fragile. At the end of her strength. Defeated.

He knew what that was like and it made him want to pull her into his arms and make all the bad things go away. He wanted to find a way to show her the good parts of his life. Convince her that it wasn't all fighting and blood and death. He wanted to teach her what they could be together—a powerful force to drive the Synestryn back into their own black world and save the human race from destruction. But he feared that once she learned that there were other men she could choose, she would look upon their time together as tainted. She'd want a fresh start with a man who would be more careful with her. One who would ease her into their world and show her the joy it was to be a Theronai.

When she found out that she could have some other man, he might lose her. The thought made his hands curl into fists and he knew that he would prevent that from happening with every breath in his body. She was his and he was keeping her. He would find a way to make up for the pain and terror she'd suffered tonight. He'd take the time to train her so that she was confident in her power. With any luck at all, they'd never find Kevin's sword and she'd be bound to him forever.

Drake stilled as the thought entered his mind, taking root. He couldn't do that to her. He couldn't do that to Kevin. He took his oath to protect humans seriously, and allowing Kevin's sword to roam free in Synestryn hands was in direct violation of that oath. None of the Synestryn they'd seen in the mine had hands to wield the sword, but eventually, one that did would claim it as his own. Or worse yet, one of the Synestryn powerful enough to use magic would find it, use its power to fuel his magic. A demon that strong could release all the dark souls that had been slain by Kevin's blade and countless humans would die as those souls took over their bodies.

Drake couldn't let that happen. Not even if it meant a lifetime free of pain and a woman by his side. The idea was tempting, but not worth what betraying his oath would cost him.

He shoved the grim thoughts away and looked at Helen. Her head was propped on her outstretched arm and she was asleep.

He'd pushed her too hard. It was time to make up for bad behavior.

"Helen," he said quietly, and waited for her to open her eyes before he picked her up. He didn't want to scare her anymore. He wanted her adrenaline to stay nice and low so she could sleep. Then they would talk.

She gave him a startled look, but then subsided and laid her head against his chest. Holding her felt so good he didn't want to put her down. He didn't know how he was going to find the strength to tell her everything. The secrets he'd kept from her would drive her away from him once she knew the truth.

"Do you want to eat before you sleep?" he asked her.

She shook her head, and her silky braid rubbed against his arm. "Too tired."

Drake carried her into one of the bedrooms and set her on the king-sized bed. Most of the Sentinel houses had big beds because the Sentinels tended to be big men. This one happened to be draped in a rich royal blue, and matching, light-blocking shades covered the windows to allow for easy sleep during the day.

Helen rubbed her eyes and yawned.

"The closet and drawers are full of clean clothes labeled with sizes and the bathroom should be stocked with shampoo, new toothbrushes, toothpaste, that kind of thing. If you need anything, let me know."

"Where will you be?"

Drake pointed to the door directly across the hall. "In there." *Unless you'd like me to stay here.* He barely kept himself from saying the words. He wanted to hold her close, to give her comfort and take his own in return. He was confident enough in his manhood to admit he needed a good dose of comfort right now. Things were all messed up.

Thomas was dead.

His chest ached for his lost friend and the burden his death would bring upon all those who had loved him. So many people had loved him.

Helen stood and wrapped her arms around his body. Until then, he'd forgotten about their link. He still wasn't used to it. He'd let his feelings go unchecked and she'd felt his need for comfort.

She snuggled her cheek against his chest and stroked her fingers down his back in a soothing motion. She didn't say any mundane words of comfort or empty words of sympathy. She just held him and let him know he was not alone. It was more than he deserved, but he wasn't going to let her stop.

He held her against him and breathed in the scent of her hair. Lavender. From her bath last night.

The memory of her naked in the tub—naked in his arms—came rushing back to him in all its inappropriateness. He felt his body harden and he shifted to shield her from his untimely lust, while at the same time, he shielded his thoughts from it as well. He had no business thinking about what his body wanted at a time like this. And even if he did, Helen was too tired for the kind of loving he wanted to give her.

Drake pulled himself away, feeling like he was leaving a chunk of his soul behind with the effort it took. "Get a shower if you want. Try to sleep if you can. I've got to make some calls, so I'll be awake for a while if you need anything."

"Are we safe here?"

Such an innocent question, but it made his heart break a little. He'd put her through too much fear and pain and he knew there was only more to come.

"Yes. We're safe during the day. We'll be home before nightfall and that place is a fortress. Nothing gets in that we don't want to get in."

"Promise?"

"I promise."

Helen woke hours later to a feeling that something was wrong. She opened her eyes, but stayed still, listening. It took her a minute to remember her surroundings. It took her twice as long to remember why she was here and the events that led up to this point.

It all came rushing back and Helen had to stifle a groan. So much pain and blood and death. She didn't know how Drake could stand living a life like this.

That flicker of unease that had woken her increased and she tried to figure out what it was. Something was wrong and she needed to fix it.

The bedroom was dimly lit through the dark curtains and everything was washed with royal blue light. Her hair was still damp from the quick shower she'd taken and the soft sheets slid over her naked breasts as she breathed. She hadn't had the energy to dress after using the last of her strength to shower, so she'd locked the bedroom door, crawled into bed naked, and passed out.

She couldn't hear any noise, but she still felt that same disquiet itching in her mind. She pulled on the big flannel bathrobe she'd found hanging in the bathroom and quietly opened her door.

Across the hall, the door to Drake's room was open. She saw him kneeling on the floor. His chest and feet were bare and she could see that the tree covering the left side of his body had somehow changed. Even more shiny new leaves had sprung from the branches and she was sure that she could see them sway with some unseen wind. There was no sign he'd ever cut himself—not even so much as a scab. Beside him was his belt and scabbard, which she could see now that it wasn't attached to his body. In front of him lay the sword, gleaming in the dim light of his bedroom. The curtains in there were a deep crimson and they cast a bloodred glow along the naked blade.

His eyes were closed and he held himself in an almost prayerful position. Maybe he was praying. She wasn't sure. For all she knew, this was how he slept.

What she was sure of was that she'd found the source of that disquiet. It was grief tempered with acceptance and it was coming from Drake, trickling into her through the luceria around her throat. He ached with the loss of his friend, and she could feel the raw, throbbing wound it left inside him. Right now she wanted nothing more than to find a way to ease his pain.

Helen reached up and stroked the supple band, marveling at whatever magic had created it. In the mine, she'd been sure the thing had raised blisters on her throat, but she'd checked in the mirror and her skin was fine. She must have imagined the burns or exaggerated what she thought she'd felt.

She still wasn't sure how much she liked the idea of knowing he could sense her emotions through the thing, but right now she was grateful for the connection. Without it, she never would have been able to feel the depth of his grief. None of it came through in his expression and she instinctively knew he'd try to hide this part of himself from her.

She barely knew him, but the need to offer him comfort was overwhelming. He'd suffered so much over his life, she didn't want him to suffer anymore. She needed to hold him and give him the basic animal comfort of human contact. Let him know he wasn't alone.

"You're awake," he said without opening his eyes. His deep voice wrapped around her and made the air in her lungs resonate in response.

Helen felt a little shiver race through her skin. "I . . . felt you. Felt your grief."

"I'm sorry. I didn't mean to share that with you. I was trying to block you out."

She could see a subtle tension running through his limbs as if he were straining against a great weight. She couldn't see why he struggled, but she could feel his tightly held control. She wasn't sure what he was holding back, but whatever it was, it was powerful enough to make his strong body tremble.

She couldn't stand his suffering, but she wasn't sure how to help him. She wasn't even convinced he wanted her help. "Maybe you *should* share it."

"Not this, Helen. The good things, yes, but not this. I'm not very adept at blocking the connection we have yet, but I'm getting better."

She wasn't sure whether she was more worried by that news or grateful for it. "I haven't tried blocking it. Didn't know I could."

He still hadn't opened his eyes yet and she was beginning to wonder if she'd interrupted something—some ritual maybe. She was just about to excuse herself and leave him to whatever he was doing when he spoke. "You really shouldn't try to keep me out."

"So it's okay for you to do it, but not me?" She tried not to sound indignant, but couldn't help it.

"Precisely."

"Sounds a bit chauvinistic to me."

"Not chauvinistic. Practical. That link is there for a reason."

"What reason could there possibly be for a mental connection between us that only goes one way? It sounds like some kind of baby monitor and I am not a baby."

He opened his gaze and looked at her. Really looked at her. His gaze went from her head to her bare feet and back again, and by the time he was done with the journey, his golden eyes had darkened to a rich brown. "No. You're all woman, Helen. Don't think I haven't noticed."

She was not going to respond to that with anything that wouldn't embarrass her more, so she stayed silent.

Drake continued. "I'm supposed to be able to read your thoughts in battle so that I can position myself most effectively, anticipate your actions. If I don't know your mind, how will I know where you want me to go?"

"You think I'm going to be able to tell you where to go? In a battle?" What a ridiculous thought.

"Yes. Perhaps not yet, but one day you will."

"You have a lot of faith in me." And he was talking about one day, which made it sound like they would be together for a long time—long enough for her to become some military genius, apparently. They were just supposed to be together long enough to find the sword, but he seemed to imply something more . . . lasting. The idea thrilled her more than it should have.

And Drake felt that thrill. She saw it in his face—in the way his angular cheekbones rose in a satisfied smile. "No, you're the one with a lot of faith walking around covered in nothing but a flimsy scrap of fabric. Surely you know how much I want you. I haven't exactly kept it a big secret."

Suddenly, she felt part of what he'd been holding back—a hot wave of lust. It crashed into her, nearly bringing her to her knees. Instantly, her body began to heat and soften, preparing for him to take her.

Helen clamped her mouth closed over a soft cry of need.

Drake pushed to his feet, looking larger than she remembered. More powerful. Maybe it was because his chest was naked and she could easily see the heavy slabs of muscle sliding under his skin. His arms were thick and hard, especially his forearms, which had developed tightly corded muscles most men didn't have. Sword-wielding muscles.

Just seeing him gloriously bare like that made her want to feel every inch of his naked torso under her fingers.

"I heard that," said Drake. A seductive grin widened his mouth and he took a long step toward her.

Helen felt her nipples tighten against the soft flannel and a gentle warmth expanded low in her belly. She barely knew him, but that didn't seem to stop her body from wanting to get closer. Naked and closer.

Instead, she did the cowardly thing, took a step back and bumped into the door frame.

"Why are you running?" he asked. "I know you want this as much as I do."

"I came here to hold you. Comfort you."

He lifted his dark brows. "Is that so?"

She nodded.

"If you hold me, I won't be able to stop myself from taking more from you. I'll strip us both naked and make us both forget why we're here. That's the kind of comfort I want, Helen."

And she wanted that, too. As insane as it was. "I don't know you." But she wanted to. So much.

"You know more about me than nearly any person alive. You've seen inside my head and you can feel what I feel. Do I hold any malice toward you?"

He had a point. "No."

He took another step, which brought him right in front of her. She could smell the shampoo he'd used and see the shine of his freshly shaven jaw. He rubbed the back of his fingers over her cheek in an unbearably gentle caress. "So soft," he purred. "I love how soft you are. Makes me want to touch more of you. Taste you."

Helen shivered and couldn't stop herself from leaning into his caress. It felt too good not to. It made her hungry for more of his touches, but still she held back, refusing to let go the way she knew he wanted her to. The way she wanted to. She'd just meant to offer comfort, to ease his grief with her presence. Nothing more. She could not get intimate with a man she'd known less than twenty-four hours.

Could she?

What an insidiously tempting question. It got caught up in her brain, cycling through on a loop over and over.

"Do you think I want to hurt you?" he asked in a deep, silken tone. It glided over her senses, rumbling inside her, becoming part of her.

He opened his mind to her, letting her feel what he did. Another heady blast of lust slammed into her through their link, making Helen moan and clench her thighs together. He'd done it on purpose. She felt that, too. He wanted her to know how much he wanted her. As if the erection straining the front of his faded jeans wasn't enough proof.

"Well?" he asked, letting his fingertips trail lightly over her mouth. "Do you think I want to hurt you?"

"Never." She knew it on an instinctive, bone-deep level. Not only would he not hurt her, but he'd kill anyone who tried. She'd seen that, too—a brief glimpse of an honor-bound knight who'd given his vow.

"Then what else do you need to know, love? What else can I tell you or show you to get you to trust me? Open up to me?"

His hand continued its downward path over her jawline until his palm was open against her throat. She could feel how close his ring was to her necklace. Both parts of the luceria vibrated with the need to join together.

"I trust you," she managed to say. It was true. She did. She hadn't known him for a full day, but she trusted him as she had no other person. He'd risked his life for hers. He'd protected Miss Mabel. He'd made sure her elderly friends were fed when she wasn't there to do it herself. That was enough proof for her that he was a good man.

"Then why did you back away? I can feel that you want me."

She wanted him all right. More than she'd ever wanted any man in her life. That alone was a frightening thought.

"You don't have to worry," he told her in that darkly sinful voice. "I'll take good care of you."

He forced a mental image through the luceria, giving

her no choice but to see it. She saw herself spread out naked on the bed, covered in a fine sheen of sweat. Her legs were splayed obscenely, his big hands holding her thighs wide. His dark head moved between them and she could almost feel his mouth on her, his tongue hot between her slick folds.

A wave of dizzying lust washed over her and she reached out to steady herself. Her palms pressed flat against his chest, the only stability in her spinning world.

Every leaf on his tattoo quivered at the contact of skin on skin and Drake sucked in a harsh breath. "If you keep touching me, I'm not going to give you a choice any longer."

Yes. That was what she wanted. No choices. No decisions. No responsibilities. Only pleasure from a man who knew how to give it—enough pleasure to wash away all of the bad things in her life for just a little while. No death or blood or suffering. No fire. Just pleasure.

"Your wish is my command." He shifted his hand so that ring and necklace finally connected, locking on to each other like magnets.

A sizzling stream of electricity zinged through her, making her back arch. Images slammed into her, one after another—a rapid-fire collage of all the things he wanted to do to her. Things she'd never considered, things she'd never even thought possible—kinky, wild things that left her quivering with a mixture of excitement and apprehension. It was too much. He wanted too much from her—things that would burn her alive.

Before she could voice her worry, his mouth covered hers in a breath-stealing kiss and she no longer cared if he wanted too much. She wanted to be the one to give it to him. The only one.

She welcomed his tongue into her mouth, welcomed the slippery advance and retreat that forced her to think of what was to come. His hand still circled her throat and she knew he could feel each desperate moan of need she made, each frantic heartbeat pounding under his palm.

The belt on her robe was no more than a fleeting nuisance. One quick tug and the tie opened for him. He pulled away from her mouth and held her by the throat against the door frame as he parted the robe and looked at her body. His hold was careful, but unbreakable, and she could do nothing to stop him from looking his fill.

Normally, under such close scrutiny, she would have thought about all her problem areas and all the physical flaws that were too many to name. But this was far from normal. His hot stare, the way his nostrils flared, and the deep stain of lust painted high on his cheeks were enough to drive any self-doubt from her mind. He looked at her like she was the sexiest thing he'd ever seen, like he'd die if he had to look away.

"So beautiful," he growled out in a voice that had her toes curling into the carpet. "I can hardly wait to see you come."

A whimper fell from her lips.

He held her still while he lowered his mouth to her breast. The very tip of his tongue reached out and flicked across her hardened nipple.

Helen gasped and her body arched toward him.

"Just like that, love. Show me what you like."

She did. She used his example and pushed an image through their link, showing him what she wanted.

Drake groaned, making an almost animalistic sound of need. "Whatever you want, Helen. Anything you want."

The damp heat of his mouth latched on to her, drawing her nipple deep into his mouth. Lightning streaked through her nerves, making her womb clench and her body grow slick.

His right hand slipped under the loose robe and cupped her bottom. His fingers gripped her possessively, shaping her flesh to his liking. Helen felt unsteady and weak and clutched at his thick wrist to balance herself. She wanted a bed under her and Drake on top of her with his beautifully naked chest rubbing over hers.

Her world spun and when the vertigo settled, she was right where she wanted to be on the big bed. Drake was poised above her, keeping his weight from crushing her. His face was drawn tight with lust—a hungry, predatory look that made her feel vulnerable and safe all at the same time. She couldn't figure out how he did it, nor did she care to spend precious seconds worrying about it. Not when she was finally free to get what she wanted.

She pressed her hands to his chest, closed her eyes, and let them slide around, drinking in the feel of him. Smooth skin over hard muscle. A light dusting of hair. The cooling sweat of thinly held self-control.

He was holding back for her. Keeping himself in check so he didn't scare her. She sensed it in the rigid lines of his body, felt it flowing through the connection between them. It was sweet, but not at all what she wanted. She didn't want his restraint. She wanted all of him. Raw and potent and hot enough to scorch her soul.

One thick thigh pressed between her legs, and she lifted her hips, rubbing herself against the soft denim over hard muscle.

Drake hissed and came down heavily on top of her, taking her mouth in a fierce kiss. He forced her lips open and speared his tongue inside. His hand slid under her bottom and he helped her find her pace as she rode his leg. The friction of the denim against her clitoris made her body tighten and her nerves sizzle. She'd never been so close to orgasm so fast before in her life.

She tried to slow down, but Drake had other ideas. His mouth trailed hot, wet kisses over her jaw and down her neck. He paused to toy with the luceria a moment before moving down. He nipped at her collarbone, leaving stinging little bites in his wake, each one making Helen flinch and thrust her mound harder against his thigh.

"Come on, love," he whispered over her skin. "Give me what I want."

His lips found her breast and she arched to try to make him go where she wanted him to. She wanted him to draw her nipple back into his mouth, knowing that added sensation would send her over the edge. His tongue swirled over the soft underside of her breast, leaving a cooling path along her heated skin. She tried to move again, but he evaded her and let out a dark, teasing chuckle.

Helen wasn't above fighting dirty to get what she wanted. She slid her hands down between them until she could feel the bulging length of his erection under her fingers. The slightest brush made him suck in a breath and go rigid. She liked that response so much, she did it again, only this time, she pressed more firmly. His deep groan was her reward and it reverberated inside her, making her shiver with satisfaction.

Drake let more of his weight press down on her. Not only did it trap her wayward hands; it also rubbed her just right. His mouth closed over her nipple, sucking her deep and hard. She couldn't stop herself from crashing apart. She didn't even try.

Her orgasm ripped through her in waves of bright

sensation. Every muscle tensed in response to the powerful demands of her body. She existed only inside the pleasure and nothing else could penetrate it. There was nothing here but light and heat and glowing, searing joy.

As the pleasure receded, she went limp and Drake pulled away slowly, giving her soft, warm sweeps of his tongue over her skin. She was too boneless to do anything but let him do as he pleased, her mind too foggy to even consider doing otherwise.

"That was lovely," he told her. She could feel his breath sweeping out over her stomach, which still twitched with little aftershocks of her orgasm. "I think I'd like to see it again."

Oh no. Not so soon. She was too sensitive and worn out from her climax to even begin to consider another one.

And then she felt his tongue flutter over the too sensitive flesh between her thighs and knew she'd been wrong. It wasn't too soon. Not for what Drake was doing to her. Her body met that fleeting touch with hunger. Ravenous need.

"Mmm. That's right, love."

His breath along her thighs excited her and made her hips twist. Drake pinned them, holding them tightly in his big hands. "You're going to hold still while I taste you."

She didn't want to hold still. She wanted to touch him, and she knew she shouldn't let him boss her around like that, but in the next instant, his tongue was slick and hot against her and she couldn't think of anything but how good it felt. He could do whatever he wanted as long as he kept doing that.

*   *   *

Drake wasn't going to last much longer. Not with Helen making all those needy little mewling sounds. She was driving him crazy with her noise. Her taste. He'd always enjoyed pleasuring women with his mouth, but with Helen, it was beyond enjoyment—it was perfection.

His tongue kept going back to tease the birthmark high on her inner thigh—the deep red ring that identified her as a Theronai. Every time he licked it, she sucked in a startled breath as if the pleasure shocked her. Her reaction drove him wild.

His ring had long since grown hot from the stress he was putting on their link, keeping close tabs on her pleasure. She was mindless with it now, desperate for whatever he wanted to do to her.

And he wanted to do so many things.

He'd shown her only a few of them. The more tame things he thought she could handle. His baser needs he kept to himself, saving those for when he'd staked a permanent claim on her.

And he would. There was no choice about that part now. He couldn't possibly let her go knowing how perfectly she suited him. How much she needed what only he could give her and vice versa.

Drake's erection throbbed painfully. He needed to be inside her—needed to drive deep until there was no space left anywhere between them. He'd already slid inside her mind. It was time for her body to follow suit.

She was slippery and hot under his tongue, making it easy to slide his finger inside her tight sheath. She gasped at that small penetration and her hands curled into fists in the bedspread. The sexy moan she gave him made him shake with need, but he held on. Just a moment longer was all she needed to be ready for him.

He pushed two fingers inside her, testing her, stretching her. She was slick and perfect, relaxed enough from her climax that he was sure he wouldn't hurt her.

Drake shucked his jeans and was back over her before she'd had time to wonder where he'd gone. Her chest and face were rosy with desire, her eyes were closed in enjoyment, and she was splayed wantonly, all womanly curves and soft skin. He'd never get enough of the sight of her, so beautiful and glowing and made just for him. He was convinced of that now. She'd been made to tempt him and please him and drive him insane with lust. And he loved every second of it.

Her eyes fluttered open and he could see golden shards of passion shining in them. She gave him a slow, sexy smile and a second later he was blinded by bubbling wave of desire. Hers. It mingled with his own ragged need, sharpening the edges until he could no longer stand it.

For a moment, Drake couldn't drag in a breath. He'd never felt anything like it before and he wasn't sure he was going to survive. Not unless he could get inside her. Right. Now.

He took her mouth in a kiss meant to distract her, captivate her. He wasn't sure how gentle he could be any longer and part of him didn't even care. She was his for the taking, open and ready. So he took. He pressed his erection against her opening and slid the blunt tip inside.

Helen gasped and stiffened and he could feel her shock at the invasion. Drake should have stopped, pulled back, and let her become accustomed to him, but he couldn't. Not now. The frenzied need to be part of her pounded through his body. He was shaking with the force of it, unable to stop himself from pressing onward, sliding deeper, making her take more of him.

Helen let out a ragged groan. Whether it was from pleasure or pain, Drake couldn't tell. His mind was driven senseless by the feel of her slippery heat closing around him inch by slow inch. There was enough scraps of honor left in him to clear a path along the lust-filled connection between them and force through a command for her to relax. Soften. Let him inside.

Drake felt it happen. Both her mind and body opened up to him with willing acceptance. He didn't wait to take advantage of it. He pulled out of her body a mere inch and slid back inside in a slow, powerful stroke that seated him to the hilt.

Helen sighed into his mouth while Drake shook with the feeling of her gripping his erection.

He found enough sanity to ask, "You okay?"

She gave him a relaxed, almost sleepy look. No pain or discomfort. Thank God. "Only if you move."

Drake needed no further encouragement. He moved. Hard, deep thrusts that made her breasts jiggle enticingly and her breath rush from her body. Her fingers fisted in his hair and forced his mouth down to her breasts.

He loved it that she wasn't shy about showing him what she wanted. He loved the way she moaned when he suckled her nipples hard and the sexy gasps she gave him when he used his teeth.

Drake knew he wasn't going to be able to hold out much longer, but he wanted her to come with him. He wanted to feel the silken contractions of her body as he exploded. He wanted to hear her desperate cries of completion ringing in his ears while he spilled himself inside her.

Her fingernails dug into his back and she arched her hips up to meet his hungry thrusts. Every time he sank deep, she let out a desperate cry, each one louder than the last. He timed the suckling of his mouth with the pounding of his hips, feeling them both inch closer to the edge of release.

His hand circled her throat and his ring latched on to the necklace with an unbreakable grip. The connection between them flared and widened, and he could suddenly feel what it was like for her to take him into her body. He could feel the way his erection stretched her, how the angle of his thrusts hit just the right spots deep inside her. He could feel the searing current of heat that flowed through her womb every time his mouth tugged at her nipple. It was incredible.

Her sensations piled on top of his own until they were too much to bear. His balls pulled up tight against his body just as the first contraction rippled through her belly. He felt her orgasm hit a moment before his own. He buried himself inside her and let out a ragged growl while his seed pumped in hard spurts, filling her. She tightened around him with each one, milking him, making the sensation more intense than he'd ever felt before. Feelings, emotions, need, and satisfaction. He could feel everything at once. His body and hers, his orgasm and hers, his mind and hers. It clogged his brain with pleasure until he couldn't take any more.

He must have passed out for a second, which wasn't exactly the most manly thing he could have done. He just didn't give a shit. His whole body was pulsing and thrumming with electric joy—a shimmering pleasure that was part of both of them. He just let himself float in it. Let himself soak it in. He could feel Helen doing the same thing, only she was having trouble breathing. He was crushing her.

Drake rolled over until she was atop him. She was limp and sated and stayed right where he put her. She rose and fell with his uneven breathing, her head a warm weight just above his heart.

A poignant sense of satisfaction wriggled inside him and he simply couldn't tell if it was Helen's or his or a combination of both. But he liked it. He wasn't typically a sentimental man, especially not after mind-blowing sex, but he made an exception now. What they'd shared hadn't been just sex. It hadn't even been making love. It was beyond anything he'd ever known. For a few seconds, they'd shared space and feelings and emotions. They'd been so deeply a part of each other that he couldn't tell where he stopped and she began.

Some of that had been disconcerting, but even with that, the experience had been incredible. Life changing.

Drake finally knew what Angus meant when he'd said that he and Gilda were truly one. They weren't physically the same person, but if what they experienced was anything like what he and Helen had just felt, it was like sharing a soul.

He'd loved it. Wanted to do it again, but he could already feel Helen's pleasure fading and her brain kicking in. She'd felt what he had and although she'd loved it at the time, she wasn't loving it now.

She shut herself off from him, blocking him out.

He tightened his hold on her. "What we just shared changes things between us. I won't let you keep me out."

"I'm not giving you any choice," she said. "I need some time alone to think. My head's already crowded enough without you poking around in there, too."

"It didn't take you long to figure out how to shut me out."

"I'm a fast learner," she replied.

Drake sighed. Nothing was ever easy when it came to women.

Chapter 15

Helen was too tired to be freaking out. She didn't have the energy for it. Especially not after sex like that. It had been cataclysmic for her—rocking her world and cracking her foundation until she no longer felt as though she was on solid ground.

She'd felt things *through* Drake. Seen through his perceptions. She finally saw what he did when he looked at her—smooth, soft skin, gentle curves, long, shapely legs. It had been bizarre seeing herself, but not feeling the way she was supposed to about her body. It had turned her on and that was truly disturbing. At least it was now. At the time, she'd loved it—reveled in the way she could make Drake sweat with the need to push inside her. She'd never been so turned on in her life. So satisfied.

Until she sensed Drake's plans to keep her. Permanently. What a frightening thought that was. Not because she didn't think she could grow to love him, because she knew she could. In fact, part of her had already fallen for him. How could she not love him just a little when she could see what a noble, caring man he was? What he'd sacrificed to protect humanity? That he never once thought about what he should get in return for his efforts?

No, what frightened her was the fact that if she let

him get too close, when she died, that closeness would only make him suffer, and he'd already suffered so much. She didn't want that for him. She didn't want him to love her and have to watch her die the way he had Thomas—the way he had with the countless other faces she'd seen in his mind. It wasn't fair for her to do that to him no matter how much the idea of being loved by a man like Drake thrilled her. She wouldn't let herself be that selfish no matter how tempting it was.

She had a responsibility to Drake to keep her distance. She wouldn't call what they'd shared a mistake—it was too beautiful for that—but she couldn't let it happen again. That kind of intimacy was too dangerous to her resolve to protect him.

"Stop it." His voice rumbled in her ear, which was pressed firmly against his chest.

Helen pushed herself up, feeling the heated skin cool on contact with the air. "Stop what?"

One big hand cupped her head and pulled her back down while the other stroked down her back in a soothing caress. "You're keeping me out. I don't like it."

She didn't have the strength to fight his hold, so she let herself enjoy the feeling of being in his arms, of lying against his muscular chest. It might be the last time she ever got to have this feeling of being safe and sated. "I'm feeling a little vulnerable right now."

"Join the club. That was . . . incredible."

Oh, baby. It had been a lot more than that, but she wasn't going to puff up his ego by telling him. It was already going to be hard enough resisting him now that she knew what it was like. She wasn't going to give him any more ammunition. "And messy." Which reminded her. "We didn't use protection. I can't believe I didn't even think about it."

A little spurt of fear made her stiffen at the realization. She couldn't let herself get pregnant. She couldn't take another life with her when she died.

"It's okay," he told her, holding her in place so she couldn't pull away from him. "I can't make you sick, nor can I give you a child."

"How can you know that?"

"We're sterile. None of the Theronai have had children for over two hundred years." His voice was tight, almost angry, but his hands were gentle over her back.

She let herself relax against him again, trying to sort through the meaning in those few words. "That makes you more than two hundred years old?"

"Yeah. It does."

Okay, that was a little freaky, but then that was par for the course when it came to Drake. Everything that she'd witnessed since last night had veered over into freaky territory. "Tell me about what it's like."

"To be this old?"

"No, to live a life like yours. All the monsters. Carrying a sword. Living with magic. It's all so . . . strange."

She felt him shrug under her cheek. His muscles flowed with smooth strength and although she was too worn out to do anything about it, she appreciated his body and the way it made her hum inside just being near him.

"I was born into the Sentinel community. My parents were bonded Theronai. I've grown up fighting the Synestryn all my life, so I don't know any other way."

"If your parents were Theronai and had you, then what makes you think the Theronai can't have children?"

"We've run tests. All our men are infertile. We've never been a very prolific people, so it's hard to pinpoint when or how it happened. The Sanguinar theorize it's something the Synestryn did to us without our knowledge—some kind of poison, maybe."

That was a horrible thought. She couldn't imagine being violated in such a way and couldn't help but try to give him comfort.

She stroked his chest and felt the luceria warm. Until she'd felt the heat, she hadn't realized she'd been trying to reach out to him like that, trying to comfort him that way as well. Using the link was becoming more natural to her. She was going to have to be careful about that, because it was such an intimate connection—something she'd never shared with anyone else before.

Helen needed to put some distance between them. She needed some privacy and a chance to gather her thoughts. Her world was upside down and she needed some space to right it. "I'm going to go clean up."

Drake slowly released her as if begrudging her the freedom. He let out a regretful sigh. "We need to get moving again, anyway. I want to be home before sundown."

"When the monsters come out," she reminded herself. She sat up and brushed her tangled hair away from her face.

"That, and the fact that I want to get you some help with your vision. I know you think it's real—that you're going to burn to death—but I can't believe that. I don't want you to believe it, either. As long as you think you're going to die, you're going to hold me at arm's length and that's not nearly close enough for me."

Helen saw a possessive light flare in his eyes, reminding her of all the things that he'd shown her he wanted to do to her—all the wickedly wonderful things he had in store for her. A heavy heat pulsed low in her belly and her nipples tightened. She had to remind herself to pull in her next breath. "It's not?" she managed to squeak out.

"I have plans for you, Helen, and most of them involve us being very close and very naked for a long, long time. It's best for both of us if you just get used to the idea."

"I'm not sure I can get used to some of those ideas of yours."

The smile he gave her was pure, lethal sin. "You'll love every one of them. I'll make sure of it."

Helen slept on the way to Drake's home. She woke when the van slowed as it neared what she could only think of as a fortress. A thick, stone wall surrounded more acres than she could see. All the trees near the wall had been cleared away, leaving the sheer surface of granite sparkling in the setting sunlight. The wall had to be fifteen feet high, and along its top were coils of razor wire and thick metal spikes that looked just as sharp. The only way in that she could see was a huge iron gate.

Drake pulled up to that gate and pressed his hand against a lighted panel. At least three camera lenses trained on them.

"ID," spoke a deep voice from a speaker mounted by the panel.

"It's Drake, dickhead. Open up."

"You're not alone."

"Jealous, Nicholas?"

"Absolutely. I'll let Joseph know you're here."

The giant gate rolled open more swiftly than Helen would have thought possible for its size. Drake drove through, and the thing was closing again before his bumper had cleared the opening.

She wasn't sure whether that kind of attention to

detail regarding security made her feel better or much, much worse.

"We're safe here," Drake told her, sparing her a quick glance.

Helen didn't let herself look into his eyes. Ever since she'd gotten out of his bed, he'd been watching her as if gauging her emotions. She'd kept a tight clamp on the pipeline between them and she could tell it was starting to irritate him.

Too bad. He was going to have to learn to deal with it. At least until they found Kevin's sword. Or until she died. Whichever came first.

Helen looked out the window. The land here was wild and overgrown in places and painstakingly manicured in others. Ancient, towering trees shaded everything, protecting the area from the hot summer sun.

Between the trees, she could see glimpses of a large building. Like the wall, it was made of shimmering stone that reflected the pinks and oranges of the sunset. It was several stories tall, and although it was much larger than any plantation home she'd ever seen, it had the same kind of elegantly simple architecture.

As they got nearer, she could see that the building in front was only part of the mammoth structure. Behind it were twin wings shooting from the back, and each of those had two wings jutting out from it as well.

"What is this place?"

"My home. We call it Dabyr. It's also home to nearly five hundred Sentinels and humans."

"It's huge."

"It has to be. Otherwise we'd kill each other." He sounded serious. "See the north wing?"

She nodded, knowing which way north was only because the sun was setting behind them.

"That's where the Theronai live. My suite is the third one from the end."

He drove into a separate building—a garage big enough to hold at least a couple of hundred cars. He pulled into an empty, numbered slot and killed the engine.

"Whatever happens here, it's important that you know I'm on your side." His voice was sober.

"That sounds a little ominous."

"Not everyone is going to be happy that I found you. Our men are dying, Helen. Some of them will see you as a sign of hope that there are other women out there like you, but not all. Some of them will see only what they cannot have. It's important that you don't wander around alone. It's . . . painful to be a male Theronai with no way to release all that power. Not everyone can control their impulses when faced with so much pain."

"Are you saying they'd try to hurt me?"

"No. They'd try to take you for themselves, but in doing that, they would hurt you. Stay close to me. Or Angus."

"Who's Angus?"

"Gilda's husband. The only other bonded Theronai here. He has eyes only for Gilda, so you'll be safe with him."

She did not like the sound of any of this. "How long do we have to stay here?"

"Long enough to find out what your vision is trying to tell you and to pick up the next lead on Kevin's sword."

And to hang Thomas's sword in the Hall of the Fallen. She heard his thought echo in her head, laced with a deep, aching grief he couldn't hide.

She no longer cared that she was trying to keep her distance. She couldn't let him suffer through his pain alone.

She unbuckled her seat belt and crawled into his lap, heedless of how poorly she fit behind the wheel. Drake needed comfort, damn it, and she was going to give it to him.

He held her in silence while she petted his chest, giving him what little support she could. He'd locked his mind up tight again, but she could feel him struggling with his grief in other ways. He was rigid and holding her in an almost desperate embrace as if he couldn't stand the thought of letting her go. Ever.

For one crazy moment, Helen wanted that more than she'd ever wanted anything else in her life. She was falling for him too fast, too hard. His quiet suffering was killing her. She knew he was strong enough to survive, but she didn't want him merely surviving. She wanted him to be happy. She wanted him to be loved. She wanted him to have all the things out of life that he was protecting for others. Family, safety, peace.

Drake gave her a hard squeeze and she could feel him pulling his control back around him like a cloak. His body relaxed, he sucked in a deep breath, and let it out in a sigh of acceptance. "They're waiting for us. We should get moving."

"Who's waiting?"

"You'll see. Come on."

He guided her into an underground tunnel that led to the mammoth building he lived in. They went down a hallway that opened into a giant room. A glass ceiling fifty feet overhead let in the light from sunset and cast a pinkish glow over everything. Tall green plants sat in clusters here and there, thriving under the bountiful sunshine the room would have during the day.

Most of the room was a dining area with a mishmash of well-used tables and chairs. Each table was decorated

with a cheerful yellow-and-white-checked tablecloth
and a small vase of fresh flowers. A few people sat at
the tables sipping coffee or reading books, looking as
comfortable as they would have been in their own private home. The rest of the room was for entertainment.
There was a pool table and four high-tech TVs, each
surrounded by an arrangement of a couple of couches
and several comfortable-looking chairs. Two groups of
kids played video games, disdaining the furniture so
they could sit closer to the TVs. Three women lounged,
enjoying quiet conversation while they kept watch over
the kids.

"I thought you said you can't have kids," she said.

"Those are human children. There are many human
families living here and some kids who have been orphaned by the Synestryn."

"You mean there are a lot of humans who know
about you? I thought it was a big secret. You said Miss
Mabel couldn't even know about you, that it was dangerous for her."

"It is. Which is why many of these people are here.
Not everyone can have their memories effectively
erased. Their only choice is to live here or take their
chances outside."

"No wonder you need such a big place."

Drake's mouth flattened in frustration. "We'd need
a much bigger one if people weren't so stubborn. Most
people choose to take their chances."

"What happens to them?"

"They die." His tone was so bleak and angry it
shocked her. "Sometimes we're lucky enough to save
the children once the parents are slaughtered, but not
nearly often enough."

Helen couldn't imagine what that must be like—to

warn people of the danger and have them ignore it. To have that happen over and over and be powerless to do anything but clean up the pieces, which in this case were orphaned children.

She laced her fingers through his and felt the answering hum of his ring against her skin. "I'm sorry, Drake. You have so much horror in your life. I don't know how you stand it."

He shrugged, but it was too stiff to look casual. "It's why I was created. We have a job to do and wallowing in self-pity isn't going to get it done. Besides, we do save some of them," he said, his eyes warm as he watched the children play, "and that makes the hard parts a lot easier to bear."

A heavy glass door leading to a courtyard swung open, letting in the scent of freshly mowed grass and dwindling sunshine. Zach entered the room, shirtless and gleaming with sweat. He had a tree tattoo like Drake's on his dark chest and the few remaining leaves fluttered angrily on his brown skin. He headed straight for Helen with a grim, hard set to his wide jaw. His pale green eyes were fixed on her and bright with rage.

She felt Drake tense and he took a protective step in front of her. His hand settled on the hilt of his sword, and although she couldn't see it before, now that he was touching it, she noticed a wavering gleam of metal flickering in and out of sight.

Helen really hoped he wouldn't need to draw it. She remembered all too well what he was capable of with that weapon.

"Where is she?" growled Zach in an almost animalistic sound.

Helen took an involuntary step backward in the face of his powerful anger. Her mind went blank and all she could think to say was "Who?"

"Lexi. Where is she hiding?"

Lexi? Helen had been so wrapped up in her own problems she'd forgotten that Lexi had been involved in this mess, too. Then the import of his words set in and she felt a little better. Zach didn't know where Lexi was. She'd escaped before she'd seen any of the monsters, so her mind was safe. "I don't know."

Zach's mouth twisted into a snarl. "You're lying. Tell me where she is. Now."

Helen saw the people in the giant room turn to stare at them and she wanted to hide in a hole. Or maybe not. That's where the monsters lived.

"She's not lying," said Drake in a low, calming voice. He held up his left hand, showing Zach the ring that was swirling with bright, fiery reds and oranges. "I'd know if she was."

Zach's eyes homed in on the ring and went wide in shock. "You claimed her? She's . . . How is this possible?"

"I don't know, but I have a feeling Logan is working on finding out." Drake's voice was tight with anger when he mentioned Logan's name, though Helen had no idea why. He had saved Drake, after all.

Zach looked from Helen to the ring and back again. The dark lines of his face melted from anger into a desperate sort of hope. "I've got to find Lexi. Please help me." He was begging and she could tell by the thickness of his voice that he was not a man used to begging for anything.

Helen ached for him, for the pain she knew he suffered, for the frustration that tightened his big body. "I wish I could, but I can't. We were friends, but she never told me much about herself. I got the feeling that she was running from someone."

Zach reached for her arm, but Drake intercepted him

and held his thick wrist in a tight grip. "No touching," he said.

Zach gave a rigid nod and pulled his hand back. "What made you think she was running?"

Helen tried to pinpoint her reasons. "She was hyper-vigilant. She kept track of her surroundings, which is one of the things that made her such a great waitress. And . . ." Helen trailed off, feeling she was somehow betraying her friend.

"And what?" demanded Zach.

Drake turned to her and cupped her shoulder in his big hand. Warmth sank into her skin and she couldn't help but lean her head to the side, hoping he'd move that heat up to her throat. Every time his ring neared the band around her neck, she felt their need to connect. It was strange feeling the magnetic pull of an inanimate object, almost as if the things could have desires of their own.

"If you know something, you need to tell us. I swear to you Zach would never hurt Lexi."

"I know that," she said. "But I also know that Lexi is a private person. Whatever problems she has, she'll want to deal with them on her own."

"She may not be able to," said Drake.

Zach's eyes pleaded with her. "She's just a tiny thing, Helen. Don't leave her out there alone. I need to find her."

"She may be tiny, but she's hardly helpless."

"If the Synestryn are after her, she will be."

Helen hadn't thought about it that way. Maybe they were right. Maybe Lexi did need to be found. She pulled in a breath. "She lived in her car. If she ran away, she'd have everything she needed to keep running."

"Son of a bitch," grated Zach.

Several youngsters grinned and the adults watching them scowled at Zach.

"Sorry," he muttered sheepishly.

Drake asked, "Can you think of any place she might go? Did she have family? Did she ever mention a particular town?"

"No. She never talked about herself. Even when I asked. For a while I thought she was running away from an abusive husband, but then I got to know her."

"And that changed your mind?" asked Zach, giving her all of his weighty attention. It was more than a little intimidating to be the focus of so much determination.

"Lexi wouldn't have run away from a man who hit her. She would have either thrown his ass in jail or hit back."

"No kidding." Zach rubbed his arm where the stab wound Lexi had given him was nearly healed. Helen wondered whether Logan had a chance to patch him up as well. It seemed too soon for the mark to have faded to new, whole skin.

"Do you think she's in danger?" Helen asked Drake. She prayed not. She didn't want any more of her friends getting hurt. Poor Miss Mabel was already one too many.

Drake set down the duffel he was carrying and pulled her against him in a gentle embrace. She didn't fight it even though she knew she should. Relying on him for comfort brought them one step closer together. It brought her one step closer to falling for him.

"I need to find her, Helen. I need her."

Drake's head shot up too fast for her not to notice. "Need her how?"

Zach's pale eyes slid to the side. "I need to touch her. Be near her. I don't get it, but that doesn't seem to matter. I *need* her."

"I know exactly how you feel." Each word was slow and precise. "That's how I felt when I saw Helen. It can't be a coincidence."

"What can't be?" asked Helen, confused.

"I want to believe, but if you're wrong, I'm not sure I could take it," said Zach.

"You have to find out," replied Drake.

"Find out what?" asked Helen.

"If Lexi is like you. Like us."

Zach ran a wide hand over his face. "Man, don't even say it. You'll jinx it."

The side of Drake's mouth lifted in a half smile. "Are you superstitious now?"

"If it works, hell yes." Zach looked at Helen. "You've got to help me find her."

"I don't know how. I wish I did. I don't like the idea of her running around out there on her own."

Zach pressed a hand to his chest as if it hurt. "Neither do I."

"Maybe Nicholas can help."

"He hasn't been able to so far. I was counting on Helen knowing something more."

Helen felt a twinge of guilt that she couldn't help, and a whole pile of concern for Zach. He looked wildly desperate and a little sick to his stomach. "I'm sorry. I wish I did."

"If you think of anything else, even something small, will you tell me?"

"I promise."

A gentle pressure surged around her. She'd felt it before when she'd given her word. It was strange.

"You've got to quit doing that," warned Drake. "You're going to get yourself in trouble making so many vows."

"I didn't hear you complain when you were at the receiving end," she reminded him.

"Yeah, well, there are a lot of things that you can do with me that I don't want you doing with the other men." A delightfully wicked light warmed his eyes, and Helen felt her body soften in response.

She was going to need to build up some serious barriers if she was ever to have a chance at keeping her distance. One look like that from him and she was ready to find a nice, quiet spot and get naked with him for a few hours.

"I'd like that," he told her in that dark voice that melted her insides.

Drake ran a finger over her cheek and across her bottom lip. Helen's eyes shut against her will, and her tongue reached out to touch him.

A man she didn't recognize walked up to them and cleared his throat. "They're waiting for her."

Drake sighed heavily. "Right. The ceremony."

Helen's stomach tightened in a sudden rush of anxiety. "What ceremony? No one said anything to me about a ceremony."

She was dressed in a pair of borrowed sweatpants and a sloppy T-shirt. Not exactly ceremonial attire.

"It won't take long," Drake assured her. "The Theronai want to meet you and welcome you into our family."

Well, that didn't sound too bad. In fact, it sounded kinda nice.

Chapter 16

It was not nice at all. This ceremony was a disturbing combination of half-naked men, blood, and guilt.

"I'm going to kill you for this," whispered Helen under her breath to Drake.

. He merely smiled, looking proud that he had the chance to display her in front of his makeshift family.

Yet another shirtless, tree-tattooed man came to the front of the room where she stood next to Drake. He drew his sword, knelt at her feet, and sliced open his chest, vowing, "My life for yours," in a reverent tone.

There were over a dozen Theronai here and each one of them went through this same process. Each time they uttered those words, she felt them weighing down upon her. Each man's promise to give his life in defense of hers was not an idle one.

Thomas had proven that beyond a shadow of a doubt. These men would die to save her and she hated it. She wanted to scream at them to stop being stupid. Her life was nearly over and not worth saving. Even if she wasn't fated to die soon, she still would have hated their violent promise. They were much stronger than she was. Braver. More capable of fighting off the Synestryn. The world needed them a lot more than it needed her.

Drake leaned over and whispered in her ear, "You're more valuable than you realize. I'm going to prove that to you."

Yeah, right after he taught pigs to fly.

Another man stepped forward. He was leaner than Drake, but still beautifully muscled. He had dark hair and bright green eyes that glittered with intelligence. As with most of the men here, only a few leaves clung to his tree—his lifemark, Drake had called it.

Unlike the other men, he smiled at her. "Thank you for choosing to join us," he said.

"Choosing?" Helen gave him a blank look. She hadn't been given any choice about being at this ceremony, but she wasn't about to tell him that.

The man frowned, addressing Drake. "You forced her?"

Drake tensed and Helen could feel a single throbbing pulse of anger push into her before he shut down the connection. "The final decision to take my luceria was hers."

"And she knew what that meant? Both to her and to you?"

Drake's jaw bunched and he remained silent.

"What is he talking about, Drake?"

The man turned to her and his eyes slid down to the luceria. She noticed a lot of the men looking there and wasn't sure how to feel about it. She was used to men staring at her breasts, but these men seemed more interested in her necklace. She was trying not to be insulted.

"Did Drake explain to you what wearing the luceria means? Not just to him, but to all of us?"

"Uh. Kind of."

She could hear Drake's teeth grinding together.

"Did he tell you what will happen to him if you ever take it off?"

Helen's head snapped around in time for her to catch Drake's furious blush. He was beyond angry, all the way to pissed. "Enough!" he barked. "It is not your place, Paul."

"The hell it's not. Someone has to tell her what's going on. She should have known before she made the commitment."

"There wasn't time."

"There's always time to allow someone free will. You violated her," said Paul.

Helen didn't feel violated. Afraid? Sure. Confused? Absolutely. But not violated. "I really don't think this is the time or place to be having this discussion," she told them. "There are still three more men waiting to bleed and I'd really like to get this over with."

Paul looked back to her and bowed his head. "Of course, my lady."

Lady? Where had that come from?

Before she could ask, Paul drew his sword, knelt, and gave her his oath to die for her. Of all the promises she'd been given today, his was the weightiest. She had no idea why that was.

Then he held up his hand to her. The ring on his left hand vibrated visibly and began swirling with more red than any other color.

"I could claim her, too, Drake. Remember that when you tell her the rest of the truth. She may decide to choose a man who would never lie to her."

"I never lied to Helen," snarled Drake.

"You didn't give her the whole truth. It's the same thing."

Helen was swiftly getting creeped out. She grabbed Drake's arm. "What is he talking about?"

Drake looked down at her with something nearing

fear in his golden brown eyes. "I promise I'll tell you everything, but now is not the time."

Paul gave Drake a sneering smile. "No. I'm sure you don't think so."

"Leave us," ordered Drake.

Paul looked at Helen with those kind eyes of his and she felt a small, strange tug. "I'll leave, but I won't go far. All you have to do is call my name and I'll hear you, Helen. I'll hear you and I'll come for you."

Paul hurried from the room while he could still walk. Once outside in the hallway—out of sight—he leaned against the wall for support and pressed the heel of his hand against his chest. Sweat broke out over his skin and his knees no longer wanted to hold his weight. Pain pounded against his ribs with every beat of his heart until even breathing was difficult.

Helen could have been his. She could have saved *him*. But Drake had found her first.

After lifetimes of pain and loneliness, his people had found a woman who could end his suffering and she'd chosen another man.

Not that Drake had given her much choice, apparently. Then again, it was hard to blame Drake for his actions when part of Paul wanted to charge back in to the ceremony and cut Drake down where he stood. Then Helen would be free to join *him*. End *his* pain.

A sharp, stabbing sensation in his chest drove the breath from his body. He fell to one knee and looked down at his still-bare chest, half expecting to see a blade sticking out of his ribs. Instead, he watched as a leaf fell from his lifemark and landed in the ever-growing pile at the base of his tree.

His soul was dying. He was running out of time.

"I can help," came a deep voice from a shadowed doorway across the hall.

Paul looked up and found Logan lurking not ten feet away. The Sanguinar's silvery blue eyes glowed with predatory hunger and Paul's hand strayed to his sword. He'd been avoiding Logan for days, ever since Sibyl—who saw visions of the future—had told him that he should accept the Sanguinar's offer when it came. He didn't want anything Logan had to offer. He didn't trust any of the Sanguinar, especially Logan. As far as he was concerned, the Sanguinar would sell out every one of the Theronai if it suited them.

Logan held up his hands in surrender. "No need for violence. You look a bit under the weather. I merely meant to offer you my assistance."

As weak as he was, Paul found the strength to sneer at the bloodsucker. Logan's kind were growing more desperate each day and although many Sentinels were convinced that a race so beautiful and charming would never harm them, Paul wasn't fooled. The Sanguinar were as dangerous as they were cunning. The peace their people enjoyed now would not be a lasting one. "I don't need anything from you, leech."

Logan didn't even flinch at the insult; then again, he'd heard it before. "Are you sure?" His eyes slid to Paul's lifemark and back. "It would appear otherwise. If my guess is right, then the brief contact you've had with Helen is likely going to speed up the rate at which your lifemark is shedding its leaves. By my count, you've got six left. That doesn't leave you much time."

A spike of panic made Paul's stomach turn. What if he was right? Rumors said that Logan had actually looked into Helen's mind. What had he seen there? Was she as beautiful inside as she was out? Did she truly care for Drake or did Paul have a chance? For the first time in his life, Paul envied one of the Sanguinar. "As gifted a healer as you may be, not even you can change that."

"No. But I may be able to help all the same."

"How?"

"I'm a bloodhunter."

Paul pushed himself to his feet, trying to hide his shock. Although everyone knew the Sanguinar had bloodhunters among their ranks—men who tracked down bloodlines by scent alone—no one knew who they were. It was a carefully guarded secret.

"So? Why should I care?"

"Because I drank Helen's blood."

That admission pissed Paul off and had him reaching for his sword. He didn't want anyone touching Helen's blood. She was too precious.

Paul shoved Logan against the wall and put the edge of his blade against the Sanguinar's throat. "Never do that again."

Logan just smiled as if Paul were a child doing something cute. "You should thank me, Theronai. Now that I've tasted her blood, if there are any more women out there related to her, I can find them."

Hope flared bright inside Paul, making him go still as he tried to fully absorb the import of Logan's words. "You'd help me search for another like Helen? A woman who could be mine?"

"Yes."

Was this some kind of trick? Paul searched for signs of a trap, but his excitement was distracting. The lure of his own lady was a potent one. "Even if we found another female Theronai, it wouldn't guarantee she would be able to join with me."

"No, but if Helen was compatible with you and your power, then it stands to reason that another woman of her bloodline might be as well."

"No one seems to know where she came from. Do we even know if there are others out there like her?"

Logan's voice dropped to a dark, seductive tone. "No, but wouldn't you prefer it be you who finds out first rather than one of the other men?"

All of his brothers would be looking for women of their own. There was no question about that. The only thing keeping Paul from planning to do that very same thing was Helen. He wanted to stay near her. Just in case she needed him.

Paul shoved himself away from Logan and sheathed his sword. He had to think—figure out why the Sanguinar wanted to help him.

"You'd never do something for nothing. What's in this for you?"

Logan shrugged as if preparing to ask for no more than a trifle. "My people are starving. I am starving. I ask only for your blood—as much as you can safely give whenever I have need."

"A blood oath? That kind of bond would give you too much power over me. You'd be able to compel me to do things I otherwise wouldn't."

"True, but I'm not some kind of monster. I don't have any intention of using you in nefarious ways. And don't forget that once your lifemark is bare and your soul withers, you won't need anyone to force you to do things which you now find ... distasteful. You'll do whatever feels good. We've both seen it before."

And it was often ugly. Men who were once noble and selfless turned into something unrecognizable. They were reckless with the lives of others, interested only in their own desires and willing to do whatever it took to get what they wanted. No matter who it hurt.

Paul wanted to believe that he was stronger than those men, but he knew that was a lie. He would become what many of his brothers had if he allowed himself to live that long.

Logan's eyes flared with a bright, hungry light. "It's a fair trade, Theronai. I save your life by helping you find your lady, and in return, you save mine." His eyes moved deliberately to Paul's lifemark. "From the looks of it, if I fail to help you, our blood oath will be a short-lived one."

Logan had a point.

"What do you have to lose?" asked Logan.

Not much.

It would be hard to walk away from Helen, but she was bound to Drake, and he hadn't lied to her when he told her he'd hear her call for him. He knew he would.

But what if she never called?

His hand rubbed over his lifemark. Logan was right. He could feel it—his leaves withering away. He was running out of time more quickly than before. Helen had inadvertently sped his soul's death by her mere presence.

What choice did Paul have? He was surviving on hope and Logan offered him a rich source. All he had to do was bleed a little. No big deal. Happened all the time to a man who fought the Synestryn.

"Fine," said Paul. "I'll accept your bargain if you add in a stipulation that if we find my lady, you promise not to do anything that would endanger her safety. Our blood oath cannot prevent me from doing my duties."

"Of course," agreed Logan. His smile was a bright flash of white teeth that revealed sharp twin fangs. "I would never think of harming one of our women."

"You took Helen's blood."

"Does she look ill? Injured?"

"No."

"That's because she isn't. Even if you do subscribe to the notion that I'm only out for blood, you must realize that it does me no good to harm those from whom I feed. I tire of your people's dislike for our existence. It is no more my fault that I must drink blood than it is yours that you must have an outlet for your power. We are as we were created to be, no matter how much we wish it to be otherwise."

Paul felt a guilty flush rise up the back of his neck. "I know it's not your fault that you need to feed. That doesn't mean I want to be the one feeding you."

Logan waved an elegant hand as if dismissing it. "Do we have a deal, Theronai? Your blood in exchange for my aid and no action of mine harms your lady?"

"It's a deal." Paul braced himself for the weight of his vow, but it settled gently around him, becoming part of him easily. He had no idea whether Logan had felt the same thing, but if he did, it hadn't surprised him.

"When do we leave?" asked Paul.

Logan gave him a victorious smile that showed his fangs. "As soon as I've fed."

Drake wanted to kill Paul. It was only the fact that Paul was right that stayed his hand.

He could feel Helen's concerned silence as they wound their way through the halls. He'd left Thomas's sword with Nicholas in the hopes that he would be able to use the blood on it to find a new trail to Kevin's sword.

The trail to Helen's freedom from him.

Drake suffered a spurt of desperation and gripped her hand tighter. He couldn't stop touching her, not even long enough to get back to his suite. He needed to know she was still by his side. That she hadn't chosen to leave him for Paul. Yet.

The fucking bastard.

He had no right to put his nose into Drake and Helen's business. No matter how much Drake had failed her by keeping her in the dark.

"You've got to tell me what's going on, Drake." Her voice was strong but he could feel the ripple of unease lurking inside her, trickling through their link.

Drake unlocked his door and led her inside. His suite was like most of the others in this wing. The living room was big and the rest of it was small. Down a short hall, there were two bedrooms with private bathrooms. Along the interior wall was an efficient, miniature kitchen barely big enough for two to eat in comfortably, but Drake rarely used it. He preferred taking his meals in the common area with all the others when he was at home.

The living room had two-story windows facing east, and a sliding glass door leading out onto his patio. All the glass was specially treated with a reflective coating so that he could have Sanguinar visit when the sun was up if necessary. During the day, the view of the lake was lovely, but right now he couldn't see much past the part of the lawn lit with security lights unless he used his night vision. It was completely dark inside his suite, so he flipped on some lights to make Helen more comfortable. She could see in the dark, too, if she wanted, but now didn't seem like a great time to remind her.

"Would you like something to eat?" he asked her.

"Yes. I'm starved. I'd also like some answers."

Answers. He had plenty, just none he wanted to give her.

Drake didn't have much in his fridge, so he decided to call the Gerai on duty in the main kitchen.

"Kitchen," answered a young woman on the other end of the line. He didn't recognize her voice.

"I'd like two meals sent up, please."

"Yes, sir. We have grilled chicken and steak left from dinner. Which would you like?"

"One of each is fine. Thanks."

"Room number?"

"One-oh-four."

"It'll be just a few minutes, sir."

"Thank you."

Helen was watching him as he hung up the phone. "You're avoiding me. That makes me nervous."

"I'm not avoiding you. I just think some things are better handled on a full stomach."

Helen stared at him for a long moment and he had to fight the urge to cross the space and pull her into his arms. He could distract her with his hands, his mouth. He could take her back to his bedroom and drive away the thoughts of anything beyond the heat of their joined bodies. He could love her slowly and make her forget all about the questions he saw lurking in her eyes.

Of course, when it was over, the questions would still be there and the longer he waited to answer them, the more betrayed she would feel. He couldn't stand that thought.

So he stayed on his side of the room and watched her as she wandered around, looking at his collection of books and baubles. She picked up a particularly beautiful dagger that had been given to him by a Russian prince decades before she was born. Her slim fingers wandered delicately over the jeweled hilt and Drake had to clench his teeth to keep himself from begging her to touch him like that.

Cool air pooled around his ankles and he realized he was still holding the refrigerator door open in search of cold drinks.

With a silent curse, he ripped his eyes away from Helen and pulled out two cans of cola. By the time he filled glasses with ice and cola and set them on the table, a knock sounded on his door.

He opened it to a young woman he didn't know. She had curly black hair that fell in disarray around her sweet, cherubic face. She smiled, which made her round cheeks rounder, and lifted the tray of food. "Good evening, sir."

"You're new here. What's your name?"

"Grace, sir."

Drake felt Helen's body near his. The ring on his hand hummed, demanding he touch her, but he held back. If he started touching her, he wouldn't stop until their food was cold and the chasm of secrets between them grew too large to cross. He had to keep his focus and protect her, even if that meant protecting her from himself.

He offered Grace a smile he was sure didn't touch his eyes. "I'm Drake Asher and this is my lady, Helen Day."

Grace's eyes went wide at the mention of Helen being a lady. "I thought the Gray Lady was the only one here."

Drake took the tray from her. As soon as his hand moved toward her, she flinched, but covered her reaction quickly.

"I only found Helen yesterday," he said, watching as she backed out of arm's reach.

Grace blushed, took a small step back, and looked

down at the tiled entryway. "Sorry, sir. I always ask too many questions. Please forgive me."

Drake looked at her ring again. It was bright and shiny without a hint of scratches or tarnish. She might be Gerai, but she hadn't been for long.

He made his voice gentle. "There's nothing to forgive, Grace. We're all a little shocked by Helen's arrival."

Grace nodded, but didn't look up. Instead, she scurried away in the manner of someone looking for a place to hide.

"Is she okay?" asked Helen.

"I suppose. A little timid, maybe, but she's new here. She'll get used to us after she's been here awhile." He kicked the door shut with his foot and set the tray of food on the kitchen table.

"Did you see the bruises?"

Drake felt a cold stillness settle over his body—the kind he got right before he killed. "No. I didn't."

"Her arms and the back of her thighs were covered with them. They had mostly faded, so they weren't new."

"Shit. No wonder she flinched. Go ahead and start eating. I've got to make a phone call."

Helen nodded and Drake went into his bedroom and shut the door. He did not want her to hear the conversation he was going to have with Joseph about whether the person who had done that to Grace had been punished or if Drake was going to have that pleasure himself.

Helen could feel nothing coming from Drake in his bedroom. He'd clamped down hard on their link and nothing was getting through. Not that she needed much help figuring out how angry he'd been when she told him about Grace's bruises. It was clear on his face. She was pretty sure he was going to need a good dentist after grinding his teeth together like that.

She was halfway through her meal when he came out of the bedroom. He looked more relaxed, but there was still that slow-simmering anger about him that made her pity whoever he decided to aim it at.

He sat down and dug into his food with mechanical efficiency.

"Everything okay?" she asked.

"Fine."

"Do you want to talk about it?"

He eyed her plate. "It's not good dinner conversation. Maybe another time."

Helen didn't push him. She wasn't sure she really wanted to know who—or what—had made those bruises, anyway. She was a pretty good guesser and none of her guesses were pleasant ones. "She makes a mean steak," offered Helen, hoping to lighten his mood.

Drake paused in the middle of chewing a bite, as if he had to stop and think about tasting the food rather than just consuming it. "Yeah. It is good."

"So is the rest of it." Helen didn't know what Drake liked, so she put a little bit of everything on a plate for both him and herself. "And there's chocolate cake."

Drake nodded, but his gaze was far off. Distracted.

Helen finished eating and sat back in her chair, sipping her soda. "I'm ready when you are."

"I know." He wiped his mouth on a napkin and stood. The burned patch on the back of his hand had nearly healed, and it had only been a few hours. She was about to question him about it when he said, "I've stalled long enough. Come on." He held out his wide, callused hand and Helen couldn't stop herself from taking it. She didn't even try.

Drake led her to the plush couch and sat beside her. He angled his body toward hers and didn't let go of her hand. "I need to know you will try to understand why I didn't tell you all of this earlier."

Helen frowned at him in confusion. "What do you mean?"

"I mean, I should have told you everything before I bound you to me. But I didn't. I was too desperate. In too much pain. I needed you at any cost and now is the time I start paying up."

"You think I'm going to be mad?"

"I know you're going to be mad. I can handle that. I don't want you to feel hurt. Used."

All she felt right now was dread. She really wasn't entirely sure she wanted to know what was going on. "Why don't you just tell me everything and I'll decide how to feel about it?"

Drake sighed heavily and it made his knit shirt stretch tight over muscles Helen could never forget. Now she was the one feeling distracted.

"You know that you have to stay with me until we find Kevin's sword, right?"

"Yes."

He'd been looking into her eyes, but now his slid guiltily to the carpet. "Do you also realize that if we never find it, you'll never be free of me?"

"Until I die," she reminded him. Maybe that would be a bigger deal for other women, but Helen knew her days were numbered. As long as she did something good with them, she was content.

"Which you think will be soon. No wonder you weren't more freaked out by that part." His hand slid over her hair in a comforting caress. "Don't worry. I've requested that Sibyl see you. If anyone can figure out what your vision really means, it will be her."

She had no idea who Sibyl was, but it didn't really matter. If it would make him feel better to see the woman, she would. "Drake, I don't want to die, but I've learned that it's better not to get your hopes up about this kind of thing. Acceptance is easier."

"I won't accept that you are going to die. I just found you. Why would I find you now only to lose you? It doesn't make any sense."

"The fact that I have this vision at all doesn't make any sense. It's not exactly normal. My mother tried to convince me it was a gift—a way for me to remember that every day is precious. When I was young, I used to think she was nuts, but now I realize that she was right. Every day is a gift."

His eyes blazed gold with determination. "I will not lose you."

She wasn't going to get anywhere with him at this rate. "Just tell me the rest, Drake. Tell me why Paul was so freaked out."

It took him a few seconds to relax his body and loosen the death grip he had on her hand. As if realizing that he'd been holding her too tight, he massaged her hand in apology. "We're at war against the Synestryn. We have been for millennia. We're losing ground every day and if something doesn't change, we're going to fail."

That didn't sound good. "What happens if you fail?"

"The Synestryn will turn the earth into a collection of giant cattle pens and use humans for food while they begin battling their way into another world called Athanasia."

"Athanasia? You need to slow down. The Synestryn want to eat us?"

"Yes. Mostly, they just want the blooded humans—those who are descendants of Athanasians—to fuel their magic, but normal humans are as good a source of food as any."

That was too gross to dwell on. "What does that mean? Blooded?"

Drake scrubbed a hand over his face in frustration. "You should have been learning all this from the time you were a baby. There's too much to cover."

"Just give me the highlights."

"Basically, the Sentinels—of which there are several races, including us Theronai—were created to protect another world called Athanasia. Earth is the only place with a gateway into that world, and the Synestryn want to get there. They are willing to do anything to get there."

"Why?"

"Because the beings who live there are ancient and powerful. Their blood is like liquid magic. If the Synestryn can get there, they will become unstoppable."

"Which would be bad."

"Extremely."

"So where does the blooded thing come in?"

"Thousands of years ago, some of the Athanasians intermingled with humans and had children. Those children had children and so on, and now the traces of ancient blood in them are minute, but they are there. That's what we mean when we say blooded. Only those humans who descend from one of the Athanasians are blooded."

"Why do the Synestryn want that blood?"

"That ancient blood is the source of their magic. The Synestryn need it to survive."

It all sounded a little too far-fetched to be true, but then again, most of what she'd seen in the past day supported something a little far-fetched. "Okay, so the Synestryn want the blooded humans because it's the only available source of magic for them. I get that. How do I play into this? Do you think I'm one of those blooded humans?"

"I know you are. In fact, the only way you could have enough ancient blood in you to bond with me is by some freak accident of genetics, or if, like me, both your parents were Theronai, which is doubtful. Even more doubtful is that you might be a direct descendant of one of the ancients."

Helen's world tilted askew and her skin grew cold as the puzzle pieces clicked together in her head. Her father had been a one-night stand. Helen's mother had never seen him again. "My father might have been some kind of alien?"

"No. Not alien. Athanasian."

"What's the difference?"

Drake looked stumped. He opened his mouth and closed it again, but nothing came out for a long moment. "Your father couldn't have been either. The Solarc got pissed off at the Sentinels, so as punishment, he shut the gate between here and there and so no one can get through, and banned all his people from leaving their world to aid us. Basically, we've been grounded."

"What's a Solarc?"

Drake waved a hand and shook his head. "The king of Athanasia. He's a megalomaniacal tyrant who controls his people with an iron fist. He refuses to aid our war against the Synestryn because he felt insulted by something my ancestors did. He's convinced the gate is sealed well enough to hold off a Synestryn attack."

"Is it?"

Drake shrugged. "Maybe. Pray we never have to find out."

Not exactly a comforting thought. "So you don't know how I got so much ancient blood in me, but I have it, and that's why you and I can have this . . . connection?"

He looked relieved that she understood. "That's right."

"I still don't see why Paul was so upset at you. It's not your fault that I'm some freak of genetics."

"That's not what Paul was talking about."

"Okay, so what was he talking about? Why was he so angry at you?" she asked.

"When you took the luceria around your neck it . . . changed you."

A chilly rush of fear made the food in her stomach ice over into a lump. "Changed me how?"

"It woke up the part of you that makes you Theronai."

That didn't sound horrible, but his expression told her that maybe it should. "What does that mean? Exactly?"

"You've lived a fairly normal life, right? Unless you count the visions? No monsters hunting you down for your blood?"

"Right."

"That was because the ancient blood in you was masked. Hidden as a means of protection. That's why the Synestryn didn't hunt you down every time you skinned your knee or whenever you got your period."

For some stupid reason, his frank discussion about something so personal made her blush. "How is it hidden?"

"It's something the Athanasians did for their new-born children to protect them—to allow them to hide in plain sight among humans. Whatever magic they used to mask the scent within the blood became a genetic trait that was passed down through the generations."

"So I inherited this survival mechanism and my ancestry was hidden. Until I met you," she guessed.

"Yes." It was a guilty whisper of sound.

"Please tell me that doesn't mean what I think it means."

"I wish I could. I'm sorry." He reached for her but she jerked away.

"Don't touch me. Tell me exactly what you've done to me."

He let his hand fall. "For the rest of your life, the Synestryn will hunt you for your blood. They will know what you are on sight and they will try to kill you. Or worse. You'll never again be able to hide in plain sight like you have been doing all your life."

Oh yeah. That was definitely what she was hoping he wouldn't say. "You turned on my 'all you can eat' sign?"

Drake nodded grimly. "And that's not all."

Helen's stomach clenched at the thought of more bad news. "I'm not sure I want to hear it."

"I'm sure you don't, but you need to."

Helen closed her eyes, bracing herself.

"For all intents and purposes, I've enlisted you in our war. You will be forced to go into battle beside me and fight the Synestryn."

"Who want to eat me."

"Yes."

She'd never heard his voice so full of self-loathing. At least he had that much of a conscience left. "You can't force me to fight."

"I won't have to. The Synestryn will do that with or

without your cooperation. If nothing else, you'll have to fight back to stay alive."

Helen suddenly felt caged. Trapped. Everything about her old life was gone. She'd no longer be able to see her friends for fear of drawing those monsters to them. Hell, she'd no longer be able to be around people, period. Anyone she was near would be at risk. Drake had stolen her life from her and given her a new one she wanted nothing to do with. She didn't want to spend what was left of her life fighting. She wanted peace and the comfort of friends and neighbors filling the days she had left.

"How could you?" she demanded in a voice that trembled with anger. "How could you take away my choices like that?"

"I was desperate."

"That's no excuse to ruin the rest of my life, short as it may be."

"Stop talking like that. I won't let you die."

"You won't be able to stop it. You're there, remember? You *watch me burn to death.*"

"I would never do that."

"I had almost started to believe you, but then you tell me all this. You've already put me in danger, why should I believe you wouldn't let me die?"

"Because of my oath. I'm bound to protect you."

"By taking away my natural protection? That doesn't make any sense."

"You're Theronai. One of us. It's your duty to fight as it is mine."

Helen threw up her hands in defeat. She wasn't going to understand his convoluted thinking and she wasn't going to waste time trying. "Is there anything else you haven't told me?"

"So many things. It will take you years to learn."

Helen didn't have years. She could feel it in her heart. Her vision was coming to pass soon. "Is there anything you haven't told me that directly affects me and my immediate future?"

He paused as if he was going to say something and then changed his mind. "I'm sorry, Helen. I should have taken more time to explain everything before I bound you, but I was in so much pain and you made it go away. After decades of agony, you made me feel good. I couldn't let you go."

What must that have been like for him? How desperate would that kind of agony make him? She'd felt only a fraction of his power when she'd put a shield around the sludge monster and she thought the pressure would kill her. He'd been living with much more than that for longer than she'd been alive. She couldn't even begin to imagine what that was like.

Drake looked away from her. She could see his frustration in the tense lines of his body—hear the way his voice shook with regret. "I can't change what I did, but give me a chance to help you understand why I did it."

"I understand perfectly. Even my vision makes sense now. You say you'd never watch me die, but the truth is that when you put this thing around my neck, you signed my death warrant yourself. I'm already dead. It's just a matter of which monster will get to me first."

"It's not like that. My job is to keep you safe."

"Like you kept Thomas safe?" She regretted the words the moment they were out of her mouth, even before she felt the slamming pain that drove into him at her snide remark.

His voice was brittle and cold. "You're right. I should have saved Thomas, but there was only one way I could have done that. I would have had to be closer to the kajmela than he was so I got killed in his stead. Neither one of us would let you die, Helen. It's time you see why."

He took her by the wrist and led her out of his suite down the hall. She thought about trying to resist him, but it wasn't a battle she could win. Let him show her what he wanted. It wouldn't matter in the end. "There's nothing you can show me that will change my mind," she said.

They passed half a dozen rooms before they came to an intersection. Drake went straight and she followed in his wake, unable to pull away from his firm grip. "Fine. If you want to keep a tight hold on your righteous anger, be my guest, but it's my duty to show you why we need you. This isn't some game."

"I should have been given a choice whether or not to become part of your world—part of your fight."

Drake never slowed and Helen refused to throw a fit. She'd look at what he had to show her and then slap him across the face for manhandling her. It wouldn't change anything, but it might make her feel better.

His voice was low, but she could hear it fine in the quiet hallway. "None of us were given a choice, but you can think that if it helps you sleep at night, because like it or not, you're a part of this war now and you're going to need all the help you can get in that department."

"Are you trying to scare me?"

He stopped in front of a pair of massive double doors. Unlike the plain hotel-style doors on the rest of the rooms they'd passed, these were each intricately carved with a tree that looked like the one covering Drake's chest. There was a subtle power carved into the wood. She could feel it heating the air around them until it shimmered. The urge to run her fingers over the smooth curves of the leaves was almost overwhelming.

When Drake spoke, she had to blink a couple of times before she was able to look away from the carvings.

"No, Helen. I'm not trying to scare you. I'm trying to show you that there are a lot of things in this world that are bigger than what you or I want. I'm sorry I took your freedom to choose this way of life, but none of the rest of us were ever given a choice. We were born into this war. I've been fighting for centuries to keep people like you safe and you're the first bit of hope any of us has found since my mother and most of the female Sentinels were slaughtered. I couldn't let you go."

He pushed the doors open and pulled her inside. The room was dimly lit, done in dark, rich tones of burgundy, mahogany, and black. Twin leather chairs sat before an intricately carved stone fireplace, and even though it was summer, a fire burned low behind glass doors.

Helen looked away from the flames before she could panic. She concentrated on the other details in an effort to slow her pounding heart. Her feet sank into the carpet. The air smelled faintly of vanilla. The room was completely silent. Not even the fire dared to crackle and disturb the reverent stillness.

The black walls were lined with swords hanging from delicately wrought silver brackets formed in the shape of intricate vines.

There were lots of swords. Dozens of them. They covered every empty bit of wall available.

"These are the swords of the men who have died fighting the Synestryn," said Drake. There was no anger in his voice now, only quiet, aching loss and respect. "Each of them gave his life so that someone else could live. None of us can use our magic effectively, and without it, we have only brute strength. It's not enough—not against an army that grows more powerful every day."

"This is the Hall of the Fallen," she said in awe. She'd heard Thomas mention it, but she never imagined anything like this. She'd pictured a few carved gravestones or maybe a bronze plate with the name of each man engraved on it. Not this dark, comfortable room where one could come and be surrounded by the swords of the dead. So many had died and she couldn't help but wonder how many of them had been people Drake loved.

Drake shook his head sadly. "No. This is a place of remembrance. A place where we can come and sit and remember those who have recently fallen." He pushed open another pair of doors opposite the ones they'd come in and motioned for her to go in. "*This* is the Hall of the Fallen."

Helen stepped inside and the echo of that footstep reverberated in her ears. The room was huge—easily fifty feet across with a glass ceiling that towered thirty feet above them. Like the other room, the walls were black and covered in swords. More hung from fine silver wire suspended from the ceiling. Hundreds of them. Maybe thousands. Some had the unmistakable band of a luceria wound around their hilts, but most did not. Most of these men had died alone.

Helen had to fight to breathe. There were too many swords to count. Too much death to face. All of these men had died fighting to save humans who didn't even know the Theronai existed.

It was too sad, too overwhelming to try to understand the kind of strength it took to live with this reminder of death always nearby. She didn't know how Drake and his friends could stand it—how they could go on when there was so little hope.

She felt the heat of Drake's body at her back and she leaned into his living warmth, needing it. He looped his arms around her waist and she didn't try to stop him. Her previous anger seemed so petty and inconsequential in the face of what his people had suffered. What they'd lost.

"This is why we need you, why I was willing to bind you to me without giving you the chance to refuse. Part of my motivation was selfish because I wanted you to stop the pain, but I also wanted to give our people hope—a reason to keep going despite the pain and grief that is with us daily. More of us die every year and no more Theronai are being born. All of us have lived with excruciating pain, trying to hold on long enough for some glimmer of hope." His mouth brushed her hair. "You have to be that hope, Helen. We can't hold out any longer without you."

Helen had spent her entire adult life trying to find a way to leave behind some legacy of good. She'd donated most of her inheritance to charities, volunteered her time, spent countless hours just being with people who needed someone to talk to. None of these were big things and she'd always wished she could do more.

Now she could. Maybe this was what her life was supposed to be dedicated to. Or maybe that desire she'd always had to serve others was something in her genes. Either way, she couldn't turn away from Drake and his people. Her people now.

Her choices were few. She could hold Drake's decisions against him and spend whatever time she had left being angry at a man she was tied to, or she could forgive him for doing what he thought was right and accept where fate had led her. In the end, staring at the proof of so many lives sacrificed, it wasn't a hard decision.

She said, "I don't have much time left." When he started to argue, she covered his mouth with her hand. "No. Just listen. I want us to find Kevin's sword."

His arms fell to his sides and he took a step back. Air cooled her back and she missed having the comfort of his warmth. "So you can be free of me."

Helen turned and looked him in the eye. She'd hurt him and she hadn't meant to. He had to know she was telling the truth. "No. I want to find Kevin's sword so it can hang here with the rest."

Relief relaxed the tension in his angular features. "Kevin's sword was swallowed by a kajmela. The only way to get it back is to kill the thing, and the only way to kill it is with fire. Magic fire."

Just hearing the word made her flinch, and her stomach burn. "Are you sure?"

"We've been fighting them for centuries. I'm sure."

Helen wasn't sure she could do it, but she had to try. Maybe this was where her vision would inevitably lead her. Her destiny. She would take the kajmela up in flames right along with her, and Kevin's sword would be recovered. Somehow that seemed better than dying for no reason at all.

She squared her shoulders and prayed for courage. "Okay. Let's go play with fire."

Chapter 17

Logan stayed in the shadows, unwilling to let Drake see him watching Helen. He would give Drake a few days to cool off before he approached Helen for more blood. He'd nearly used up the power in the blood she'd already given him. Drake's injuries had taken much of it and Project Lullaby had taken the rest. Only hours after feeding, his gut was already twisting with hunger again.

Good thing he'd had centuries to learn to live with it.

"You're right. She's a failure," said Gilda as she watched Helen struggling to call even the smallest wisp of flame to her hand.

Gilda was as beautiful as she was deadly, with long hair that flowed in rich, black waves that ended at her hips. Her skin was fair and untouched by the passing of centuries. Only a few silvery strands, the same color as her silk gown, glinted in her hair to give away her advanced age.

Helen's body shook with effort as she tried to make fire appear from thin air. Drake stood beside her on the wooden dock jutting into the lake. Logan was sure that Drake had chosen the location solely to ease Helen's fears. How could fire be a threat when so much water was literally underfoot? Drake held his hand against the nape of her neck in an effort to ease the flow of power between them. It didn't seem to be doing any good.

"I didn't say she was a failure. I said she'd never be able to call fire. That part of her is broken and can never be mended."

"You're one of the most gifted healers on the face of this planet and yet you cannot heal her."

"No. Whatever is broken inside her has been that way since before she was born. She was created with this flaw."

"Why?" demanded the Gray Lady. She didn't even stand as tall as Logan's shoulder, but he knew that her diminutive form was deceiving. The Theronai's power grew with age and Gilda was the most powerful female Sentinel left alive. Not that she had much competition.

"I don't know why," he told her honestly.

"Find out." It was not a request. "If she cannot be healed, then she will kill Drake as she did Thomas."

"She killed Thomas? Who told you such a thing?" Drake never would have told Gilda that, even if it was the truth. He would protect Helen from scrutiny as well as danger.

A touch of sadness shimmered in Gilda's black eyes. "I took the memory from Thomas's sword. I saw what happened. If she had been able to do her job, those two kajmelas would have gone up in flames within seconds. Thomas intervened to save her and it cost him his life."

"That was his choice. Helen never would have asked it of him." Logan had read that much of her character when he'd been walking her memories.

The Gray Lady whirled around and grabbed him by the front of his shirt. Her face was smooth, but Logan could see a furious, dangerous anger lurking in her too-dark eyes. She was no match for his physical strength, but Logan didn't dare struggle. Even though Logan couldn't see him, Angus would be nearby—within striking distance—and would kill Logan if he so much as mussed her hair.

"She should have killed the kajmela herself, not let it take Thomas from us," said Gilda.

Logan wouldn't fight her, but he wouldn't let Helen be blamed for something that wasn't her fault. "There was no way she could have known what to do. Her ignorance was Drake's fault. Not hers."

"Would you have me slay him for his mistake and bond her to Paul?"

"No. Of course not."

"Then what do you suggest, leech?"

Leech. Logan couldn't help the way his hands curled into fists at her insult. He clenched his teeth to keep from shouting at her. "I suggest nothing. I came here out of respect because I thought you should know what I learned. The peace between our races is fragile and I, for one, believe that it is important we foster that peace."

Gilda released his shirt and looked back at Helen as if nothing had happened between them. She offered no apology for her behavior or insult.

"She is a liability," said Gilda.

"She is a miracle. The first female Theronai born in over two hundred years. Maybe there are more like her."

"Have you learned her lineage?"

"No. Gordon is working on it. I gave him a sample of her blood and he said he can't remember tasting anything quite like it."

"If he learns anything, you will tell me immediately," ordered Gilda.

Logan said nothing. He would not promise her anything unless he was forced. Experience had taught him that uncomfortable lesson.

Fortunately, she was too wrapped up in watching Helen struggle to realize he hadn't agreed.

Logan slipped back into darkness without a sound. He had too much work to do tonight to spend any more time with the Theronai. He had his own people to worry about. For the first time in centuries, the Sanguinar had hope and Helen's blood was the key.

Drake wasn't going to let Helen push herself any harder tonight. They'd been working for over an hour and so far she hadn't managed so much as a single spark. She was killing herself trying to break through her fear of fire, and nothing good was coming of it. Her desperate frustration was killing him.

"Enough," he told her as he pulled his hand away from her neck to break the connection. His ring buzzed in irritation at the loss of the direct link, but he ignored it.

"Just a little more," she panted. Her cheeks were flushed, her eyes were bloodshot, her thin T-shirt was clinging to her curves with sweat, and her whole body vibrated with fatigue.

Drake wanted to tuck her into a nice soft bed and let her sleep for about ten hours. Right after he made her come for him again. He was dying to hear her sweet moans of release and see her body shudder from the pleasure he'd given her. He wanted to hold her in his arms while her body quieted and drifted off to sleep. He wanted that feeling of contentment that came along with knowing he'd cared for her in every way possible. Maybe it was selfish, but he wanted it anyway.

"No more," he said gently. The last thing he needed

was for her to go all stubborn on him, refusing to listen to reason. "You've already pushed yourself too far tonight. You only slept a few hours today and you need your rest before we try again."

"There isn't time," she told him. Her breathing still hadn't evened out, but she found enough energy to give him a fierce stare. "You said that if Nicholas found a lead on where that kajmela had gone, we'd need to move on it right away. You said those things relocate every night and that our only chance to find it would be to pounce as soon as we could."

"I also said that the kajmela could only be killed with fire, and you're a long way from making that happen. Wearing yourself down like this isn't helping."

"There has to be another way to kill it. Has anyone ever tried dynamite?"

"You're kidding, right?"

"No. Let's blow the thing to hell."

"That won't kill it. It would make a mess and we'd have a dozen smaller ones to fight. We have to use fire. I'm sorry, love."

"What if I can't?" she asked him in a quiet voice.

Gilda's soft voice drifted in from the darkness. "Then you are of little use to us beyond easing our warriors' pain."

Gilda, the Gray Lady, stepped out of the shadows. Her small form was draped in a long, flowing dress of dove gray silk. A few strands of silver sparkled in her jet-black hair, which was left loose around her shoulders. The wind stirred her hair, but did not muss it. Not even the wind dared anger someone as powerful as the Gray Lady.

Drake had no idea how old she was, but as far as he

knew, she and Angus were the oldest living Theronai on earth. Drake's grandparents had learned at her knee—both magic and fear.

Drake had always respected Gilda as his elder as well as a formidable ally, but he couldn't let her beat Helen down any further. "You know that's not true," he said to her in a tone as respectful as he could manage.

Gilda's dark brows arched high. "I know no such thing. Fire is among the most basic of skills. Many of the Synestryn fear it. It will kill all but a few of their kind. If she can't even master that small feat, then she would serve us best staying here and tending our wounded."

"We have dozens of Sanguinar to play nursemaid. We need Helen on the battlefield."

"Do you truly believe that?" she asked Drake. Then she turned to Helen. "Do you believe your place is in battle, child?"

Helen looked at Drake as if searching for guidance. He had none to give her, but he twined his fingers through hers, reminding her that he was on her side.

Helen gave a little shrug. "My whole world has changed in the past twenty-four hours. I don't know what my place is anymore."

Gilda nodded her head in acknowledgment, and her black eyes glittered in the dim light. "Well said. Let me give you an example of what might be expected of you and then you will be better educated and able to decide how you can best serve our cause."

Drake knew Gilda well enough to guess she was not planning an educational session for Helen's benefit. She was trying to prove her theory that Helen had no place at his side. Drake couldn't let Gilda shake Helen's tenuous confidence like that. "Don't do this, Gilda. She's not ready for this."

Gilda tilted her head as if confused when he knew she was anything but. "I thought you planned to take her into battle. Should she not see what her role shall be? Would you prefer to simply throw her in the midst of chaos and pray she learns along the way? I would have thought Thomas's death would prove to you how poorly that worked."

Drake's teeth ground together and he had to fight back a wave of grief and guilt before he could speak. "I was trying to teach her."

"And was it working?" she asked as if she already knew the answer.

Helen's fingers squeezed his. "Let her show me. I need to learn this stuff or I'll never be able to help you."

"There are easier ways to learn," he told her.

"But are there faster ways?" asked Helen.

Gilda's beautiful mouth curved into a satisfied smile. "No. There are not." She reached out a small hand to Helen in an uncharacteristically human greeting. "I am Gilda and I will teach you what you must know. Come."

Helen followed Gilda to a section of land that had been cleared down to packed dirt. Warm summer air curled around her, drying the sweat on her skin. There were no security lights here and she had to use Drake's power to allow her to see in the dark. She was already exhausted, and using even that small amount of magic was quickly taking its toll on her. She had to struggle to take each step, and if it weren't for Drake's strong arm supporting her, she wasn't sure she could have managed even that much.

As if summoned, half a dozen men arrived—all but one of whom had given Helen his oath to die for her.

That one was older than the rest, with a craggy face and a still silence about him. He stood by Gilda's side, keeping watch over her. The pale gray band around her throat matched that of the ring on his hand. There was no movement in the colors as there were in Helen's necklace, and she wondered why they were different.

Drake stood by Helen's side, helping to keep her on her feet and letting her lean against him. Her legs were weak and shaking as if she'd just finished a marathon and she didn't trust them to hold her up. But she trusted Drake and held on to him for support. He felt solid and capable and she was beginning to wonder whether he'd ever run out of strength. The hard ridges of the muscles running along his spine under her hand tempted her and she couldn't help but slide her fingers over them, enjoying the feel of him.

He leaned down close to her ear as he pointed to the craggy-faced man. "That is Angus, Gilda's partner and husband."

"Do you know what those other men are doing here?" she asked him.

Gilda reached up and touched each one on the forehead and whispered something quietly to him. Each man nodded and went to stand at the edge of the clearing as if awaiting orders.

"Gilda is going to put on a mock battle for you. She is giving those men their roles and putting a protection over each one so that her magic won't kill them."

Wow. There was so much more to all of this than she could begin to imagine. She found it fascinating, if a bit disquieting. It was odd to think that all of this had been going on under her nose her entire life and she'd never even had a clue. "Have you done this before?"

"Many times. It's how we practice without killing

each other, though I imagine Gilda will be putting on more of a show for your benefit."

"What do you mean, 'a show'?"

"She's going to try to scare you or shock you into believing you're not good enough to do what is expected of you."

"Why? I thought all of your people wanted me to help in your war. Why would she try to convince me otherwise?"

He gave her a sad smile. "Gilda has watched all of us grow up and sees us as her children. She's protective. She's worried that your inexperience will get me or one of the other men killed."

"You know she's right. If I'd known what to do to save Thomas and been able to do it, he might not have died." She'd tried not to think about it too long because she worried the guilt would crush her, but she couldn't ignore the obvious. She'd failed and now Thomas was dead.

Drake cupped her chin in his hand and made her look up at him. His expression was hard and the golden flecks in his eyes glowed with a fierce light. "That's not true, and if you think like that—dwelling on what-ifs and should-haves—you'll never be able to overcome your own insecurities. Then you truly will be a danger to those around you."

"I don't want my inability to get anyone else killed."

"We're grown men. We've been doing this a long time and know the risks. Look at those men and tell me if you think they see you as a threat or as a weakness."

Helen looked toward the line of men Gilda had finished speaking to. They were watching her with open speculation and something else she couldn't name. It wasn't exactly hope, though that was part of it. It was more wistful—if big, somber men could be called wistful. She wasn't sure what to think about it.

"Each one of them wishes he was me right now. Each one of them sees you as a sign that their lives may not have to be a constant battle against pain. You've given them hope and it's more than they've had in a long, long time." His thumb slid over her bottom lip and Helen had to stifle a shiver of longing. As tired as she was, she still wanted him to kiss her. None of this stuff could bother her when he kissed her. "A person can do incredible things if he or she has enough hope. You should remember that."

Helen knew what he meant. He wanted her to have enough confidence to overcome her vision—her fear of fire. She wanted that, too, but acceptance was so much easier. Especially when she truly believed that she was nearly out of time. It had taken her a lot of hard years to gain that acceptance and she didn't want to go back and do it all over again. She wasn't that strong.

"We're ready to begin," said Gilda from the far side of the clearing. It was about a hundred feet across and at the center was a giant boulder carved with some kind of symbols.

Angus handed her a sword that looked like it had been used hard, and she held it up for all to see. "The goal is to retrieve this practice weapon. The Theronai will guard it and try to keep it from me. Drake and Helen will remain inside the circle but will not participate. Understood?"

"Yes, my lady," said every man there in unison. Including Drake.

Helen flinched at the unexpected sound of so many deep voices. Gilda had been watching her, and a slight smile curved her mouth when she saw Helen's startled reaction.

Gilda opened her hands and the sword floated over the heads of all the men and slammed point down into the earth behind them. "Then let us begin."

Chapter 18

Suddenly, Helen was no longer so eager to see what Gilda had to show her. Based on the sly smile Gilda wore, Helen was sure she wasn't going to like it.

Drake's arm tightened around her waist and he pulled her close to his side. "Brace yourself," he whispered to her.

Helen had no idea what he meant, but a moment later Gilda lifted her hands and a giant ring of fire erupted from the earth, closing them all in.

Helen hadn't braced herself for something like *that*, and she let out a shriek of terror. The fire was only feet from her. It was easily ten feet high and roared with an almost deafening sound. A hungry sound.

"You're fine. Just breathe." She heard Drake's soothing voice in her ear, but it didn't help. Her heart was pounding and she was frozen in terror. There was nowhere she could have run, anyway; she was surrounded by fire on all sides. Hungry, growling fire that wanted to eat her alive.

She felt Drake shove his way into her mind. She didn't know how he pushed through her frantic thoughts, but he was there. She could feel his cool, comforting presence blunting the edges of her terror.

"I won't let you get hurt," he whispered directly into her thoughts. She had no choice but to listen to him and try to believe him.

He captured her face in his big hands and forced her to look in his eyes. With his hands acting as blinders and his face filling the rest of her sight, she could no longer see the fire. She could hear it, she could sense its greedy presence only feet away, but the rest of her senses were filled with Drake. She could smell his skin and it roused a memory of his body moving over hers, filling her, driving her out of her mind with pleasure.

She was confused by such an intensely positive memory in the midst of so much fear, and that confusion forced her brain back into gear.

She pulled a deep breath back into her lungs and let it out again.

"That's right. Just breathe. I've got you."

The panic receded enough that she could focus on staying calm. Her fingers were clutched tight around his wrists and she forced herself to loosen her grip. "I'm okay," she told him. It was far from the truth, but not so far that she couldn't pretend she believed it.

"Good. You're doing great, Helen." He gave her a proud smile.

It was ridiculous. She was being a complete nutcase and he was proud of her.

"I'm going to take my hands down now, okay?"

She nodded.

"The fire is still going, but it can't hurt you. Do you understand that?"

Not really, but she nodded anyway.

Slowly, Drake took his hands down and she could see fire in her peripheral vision. Her breathing sped, but she managed to keep herself together. She was going to do

this, damn it. She was not going to let this fear of fire
beat her. Especially not in front of Gilda. That's what
the woman wanted—for Helen to admit defeat before
she'd even had a chance to try.

Drake straightened so that she was staring at his
chest. She focused on the paler band of skin around his
throat where the luceria had been for years. The rest of
his skin was lightly tanned. She could see the tips of the
leafy branches of his tree peeking out from under his
open collar.

Helen didn't want to look away. Drake was a much
more appealing sight than the fire, but she had to be
tougher than that. So she was. She gritted her teeth and
turned her head so that she had no choice but to see the
wall of fire only feet behind them.

It put off no heat. That was strange and it took her
mind off the skittering pile of panic that threatened to
overwhelm her. She clamped down on that panic and
controlled it by a sheer force of will.

"Is your lady well?" asked Gilda with a hint of smug-
ness in her tone.

"Do you want me to make them stop?" Drake asked
Helen in a voice meant only for her.

"No. Let's get this over with."

Drake raised his voice and addressed Gilda. "She is
ready, Gray Lady."

Helen was about to ask him why he'd called her that
when she saw Gilda lift her arms over her head. This
time, Helen braced herself for the worst, but no more
fire spewed from the ground. Instead, on the far side
of the circle where the men guarded the sword, she
saw them start to change. The man closest to them—a
large blond man with a scarred face—shimmered, as
she'd seen Drake's sword do when he was about to

draw it. When the wavering stopped, he no longer looked human. He looked like one of those mosquito monsters.

Helen grabbed Drake's arm, ready to pull him away, but he covered her hand. "It's only an illusion of a haest. That's still really Nicholas."

Helen tried to relax in the face of that news, but couldn't. The next man in line was already doing that shimmering thing, and when he stopped he was a sludge monster. "What's that called?" she asked Drake in a pathetic squeak.

"A kajmela. She'll probably throw in a sgath or two as well. Don't worry, it's all just special effects. Gilda's showing off for you."

Helen doubted that a woman as powerful as Gilda would concern herself with showing off to anyone. Certainly not to Helen, who appeared to be afraid of her own shadow.

The next man in line turned into a furry wolf-chimpanzee mix with glowing green eyes that spooked her down to her toes. "Is that a sgath?"

Once the last man had turned into a hideous monster, Gilda lowered her hands and said to Helen, "This is what you will be expected to do, child. Judge well whether or not you are able."

Angus drew his sword, which was apparently the sign for the monsters to attack. The furry sgath charged in on all fours, heading straight for Gilda.

Angus stepped to Gilda's right side, planted his feet, and squared his shoulders with his blade raised. His sword reflected orange flames and Helen had to fight to stay calm. The flames weren't hot, so maybe they were just an illusion, too.

Helen latched on to that thought and convinced

herself to believe it. Slowly, some of the residual panic started to fade and she was able to breathe easier.

Angus's expression was serene, but his body was poised to strike. "He's going to kill them," she said.

Drake was still holding her close and his hand smoothed over her hip in a gentle caress. "Gilda's magic protects them. Don't worry. None of them will be hurt."

Three sgath leapt toward Gilda. She flicked her hand once, as if shaking water from it. The sgath slammed into an invisible barrier and bounced off.

There were four haest and they covered the distance more cautiously. They spread out, making odd clicking sounds. Two charged Angus while one more moved toward Gilda. Angus tried to angle his body to put it between the haest and Gilda, but the two things lunged at him with those long, transparent fangs and he had no choice but to defend himself. His sword swung in a deadly arc that lopped off a foot of all four fangs.

The haest gave off frantic clicking sounds, but didn't relent. They pressed him harder, lunging with their insectoid heads, keeping his sword busy parrying their attempts.

The haest nearing Gilda hit another invisible barrier and lashed out at it. Sparks spewed out from the wall as the thing advanced.

Gilda's feet slid over the ground as the haest pushed both the barrier and her back toward the ring of fire.

Helen tensed at the thought of Gilda getting burned, but Drake stroked her back, telling her with his relaxed body language that everything was fine.

Gilda smiled and a second later, spikes made of stone shot up from the ground, skewering the haest attacking her. It waved its spindly legs in the air, but it did no good. The thing was trapped on stone spikes.

She was so busy with that monster that she hadn't noticed the haest that had come up behind her.

Helen pulled in a breath to shout a warning, but it was too late. The long fangs shot toward Gilda's back. A split second before they could land, she leapt high into the air and landed in a roll twenty feet away. The haest's fangs were buried in the ground and it pulled at them in an effort to dislodge them.

Before it could free itself, another sudden growth of stone spikes erupted from the ground and impaled it.

By this time, one of the kajmela had consumed the sword in an effort to guard it and the other was flowing over the dirt toward Angus. He'd cut down one of the haest, and the other was backing up from his viciously aggressive attack.

It backed right into the kajmela, which absorbed it and grew larger.

Angus paid it no heed. He went to Gilda's side and helped her to her feet. She brushed the dust from her skirt as Angus slid his hand over the back of her neck.

The air thrummed with power. Helen could feel it surround her, feel it vibrate the stones beneath her feet. Gilda bowed her head and her long hair fell to shield her face.

The kajmelas were heading toward the pair, getting closer and closer by the second.

The air around them cooled and when Gilda lifted her head, Helen could see fire burning in her eyes. Real fire. Gilda opened her mouth and a column of flame burst from her lips. She lifted her hand toward the kajmela and glowing drops of flame fell from her fingertips and pooled on the ground.

Angus's face twisted in a pained snarl and Gilda's body shuddered an instant before a pillar of fire as thick as a tree trunk shot out of her hand and engulfed the kajmela. A horrible high-pitched hissing sound erupted from the monster, but it continued to advance, spreading fire in its wake.

Gilda slumped, but Angus wrapped an arm around her middle and eased her down to the ground. He dropped his sword and spread his bare hand on the ground.

Helen felt the earth under her feet cool.

"Now!" Angus shouted.

Gilda weakly lifted her hand and another burst of flame spewed out, hitting the second kajmela.

That hissing scream doubled and Helen covered her ears to block it out. She didn't care if none of this was real. It looked real. It sounded real.

One of the sgath had regained its feet and circled around behind Angus and Gilda.

Helen tried to remind herself that this was all just practice. An illusion meant to scare her. Well, it was working like a charm. She wanted to scream out a warning.

Drake's hand covered her mouth. "Let it happen."

As if she had any choice.

The sgath didn't charge this time, it moved stealthily, keeping out of sight of the Theronai. The kajmelas were burning, getting smaller and smaller by the second, but still advancing.

Angus pushed himself to his feet and pulled Gilda up with him. They stood back to back in the center of the flaming circle using the giant carved boulder to protect one flank. Gilda was swaying on her feet, but the look on her face was one of determination. The flames in her eyes burned brighter and tears of fire spilled down her smooth cheek.

Angus saw the sgath and readied his blade to kill it while Gilda faced the two burning kajmelas. All three monsters attacked at once. The sgath was faster and Angus sliced at it, missing.

Its eyes glowed green in triumph as it went for Gilda's unprotected flank.

As if reading Angus's mind, Gilda spun at the last second, narrowly avoiding the black claws of the sgath. It slashed three razor-sharp gashes in her long skirt.

Gilda ducked. Angus's blade sliced through where her neck would have been and embedded itself into the chest of the sgath.

The kajmelas were now close enough to reach out with oily black tentacles. One shot out for Angus, and Gilda let out a shout of fury and blasted it with a handful of fire.

Angus ripped his sword free from the defeated sgath and lifted Gilda onto the carved boulder with one arm. His hand locked around her bare ankle and Helen could feel the connection between them strengthen. That odd thrumming energy reverberated in the air with the power of the magic that flowed between them.

Gilda was fiercely beautiful standing there with her dark hair and pale skirt flowing out behind her, her eyes glowing with fire and a victorious smile on her lips. Helen had never seen anything so striking before in her life.

Gilda lifted both hands toward the kajmelas and released another fountain of flames at them. Fire flowed from her fingertips, writhing and seething as if it were alive. The kajmelas gave off more shrill hissing screams, but she did not relent. Her body shook with effort, but the fire continued, shrinking the kajmelas until only flat, greasy puddles remained.

In the center of one of those puddles was the sword. The fire tapered off and Gilda collapsed from atop the boulder. Angus caught her easily and held her close to his chest.

The circle of flame around the battleground disappeared and the illusion of monsters did as well. Men lay on the ground, bruised and groaning, but none of them were bleeding or burned. They pushed to their feet and went to Gilda's side.

Drake took Helen's hand and led her across the clearing.

Angus sat on the ground at the base of the boulder and settled Gilda in his lap. She was unconscious and pale. His left hand encircled her throat and his expression was one of deep concentration.

"What's he doing?" asked Helen.

"Reviving her. She used too much power keeping all the illusions going as well as protecting the men and fighting the battle."

Helen could only boggle at how much energy that kind of magic had to take. Helen hadn't even managed to make a spark and she was exhausted to the point of falling over. How much firepower did Gilda possess? It was a frightening thought.

"Angus is pulling more energy from the earth and feeding it into her through her luceria."

Whatever he was doing was working. Already, Gilda was stirring, opening her eyes. They were a little bloodshot, but black again, which was a huge relief to Helen. She didn't think she could look the woman in the eye if all that fire was in there.

Gilda struggled to sit up and Angus helped her. "I am well. Leave us," she said to the men gathered there.

"Yes, my lady," came the mass reply. This time, Drake didn't join in. He stayed and held Helen by his side.

It seemed strange that a bunch of big guys would take

orders from one little woman. Of course, that one little woman could probably roast any of their asses even on her worst day, but it still seemed odd.

When the men had cleared, Gilda looked at Helen expectantly.

"That was amazing," she said.

Angus grunted. He didn't look pleased. In fact, he was giving Gilda a look that promised she'd hear just how displeased he was later. "It would have been a lot more amazing if we hadn't spent the past two weeks killing Synestryn every night, keeping them at bay so our men could find Kevin's sword. You were too tired to have done this tonight." He had a rough voice to go with his rough face. Deep lines were carved around his eyes and mouth. Everything about him was hard except the color of his eyes. They were a soft sky blue that seemed so out of place she couldn't help but stare at them.

Gilda patted Angus on the knee. "It had to be done, Angus. I'm fine." She turned to Helen. "Do you see now what is expected of you?"

"There's no way I'll ever be able to do what you did. Even if I wasn't scared to death of fire, I still wouldn't have been able to wield so much power."

"Perhaps not yet, but one day you will. The question is whether or not you should try. Going into battle without fire would be like one of our warriors going in without his sword. You could do it, but it would be foolish and dangerous to everyone around you."

Helen's vision flashed in her mind. Fire surrounded her and through the wavering flames, she could see that proud half smile tilting Drake's mouth. Only, unlike Gilda, the flames were burning her—blistering her skin. They were real and they hurt like hell.

The more she got to know Drake, the closer she got to

him, the worse her vision hurt. Why would he just stand there and watch her without trying to help? Was all his selfless nobility some kind of act? Or was it something else? Maybe he was looking at her with pride because she was doing something worthy of it. Would she be willing to burn alive if it was for a good cause? If it saved the life of another? She wanted to believe she would, but in truth, she knew she was too much of a coward. Maybe she could accept some other fate if it was to save the life of another, but not that one. She'd feared it for too long. Burning alive was her worst nightmare. "I don't want to use fire," she told Gilda in a voice filled with shame. "Not ever."

Gilda nodded in grim acceptance. "Then you should stay here and serve us as the Gerai do."

"She is not a Gerai," said Drake through clenched teeth. "She is far more than that and you know it."

Gilda turned her black gaze on Drake. As lovely as she was, there was something frightening about her—some almost alien quality that demanded respect and obedience. "What I know is that I do not want to hang your sword in the Hall of the Fallen. I also know that if you take this damaged child into battle with you, that I will be doing just that."

"It's not your decision," said Drake.

"No? I could kill her right now and be done with it. I care nothing for her and I would happily see her die in your stead."

Helen didn't doubt for one second that Gilda was telling the truth.

Drake's hand went to his sword and Angus set Gilda aside and came to his feet in a movement so fast it was hard to believe it had happened. "Back off, son. Don't make me hurt you."

Drake's jaw clenched, but he released his sword and took a deep breath. Helen could feel tension vibrating in his body, feel it humming between them. That control had cost him much effort. "Don't talk like that, Gilda. You know we need her. *I* need her."

Gilda had regained her feet, but was leaning against the carved boulder for support. "We need her to give the unbound Theronai hope, and to ease your pain, but that is all. Keep her for yourself. Use her as you will, but do not risk your life to her incompetence."

"Use me?" asked Helen, unwilling to stay silent when they were talking about her like this. "No one is going to use me or keep me. For heaven's sake, you make it sound like I'm some kind of slave."

Drake gave her a hard stare. "You're no one's slave, Helen. Don't listen to her."

"Who else should she listen to if not me? There are no other female Theronai around."

"That doesn't mean you're right," Drake insisted.

Gilda sighed. "I understand the kind of feelings you have for Helen, but Logan has seen inside her mind and there is no hope for her. She is damaged. She will never be what you want her to be."

Helen wasn't sure what shocked her more, the fact that Logan had been able to pull something like that from her mind, or that he might be right.

"You haven't even given her the benefit of the doubt, but you're willing to believe a Sanguinar? Do you even know what he did to her?" demanded Drake.

Gilda glanced at Helen, who was totally lost. She knew Logan had walked around in her memories and that he'd taken some of her blood, but the way Drake said it, it sounded as if he'd violated her civil rights or something.

A pressure filled her ears, and the sounds of the night—the crickets singing and the wind through the trees—all disappeared. Helen rubbed her ears and tried to yawn to make them pop. A moment later the feeling was gone, but she'd missed whatever Gilda had said.

Whatever it was, it infuriated Drake. His face darkened with anger and his fingers dug into her hip. "Is Logan still here? I'd like to have . . . words with him."

"You should be more worried about what your lady is going to do and less about what Logan is doing."

"The Sanguinar are up to something," said Drake.

Gilda waved her hand in a weary gesture. "The Sanguinar are always up to something. It is their nature."

Angus pulled Gilda to his side. "And it is my nature to make you rest. You've given the girl food for thought. Give her time to digest it."

Digest it? More like choke it down and pray it didn't make her sick. "I promised I'd help Drake find Kevin's sword," said Helen. "I won't go back on my word."

"Foolish child," muttered Gilda. "At least speak to Sibyl before you try something so foolish."

"I've already asked for an audience with her," said Drake.

Gilda's black eyes narrowed. "Will she receive you?"

"I don't know yet. Cain said he'd tell me in the morning if she will see Helen."

"Sibyl will see her. I'll make sure of it."

"Thank you, my lady," said Drake, bowing his head formally.

"Don't thank me until after Helen has spoken with Sibyl," said Gilda.

"That's enough of that." Angus picked Gilda up into his arms. "It's bed for you, woman."

Helen watched them go, feeling her world spinning

out of control under her feet. There was so much she didn't understand. Part of that was how Gilda could be a fierce, fire-breathing warrior one minute and cuddling in Angus's arms the next. It seemed totally out of character somehow.

"You need to rest, too," said Drake.

Helen nodded. She was bone tired and ached everywhere from her earlier attempts to create magical fire. "Who is Sibyl and why do I need to see her?"

Drake hesitated as if he didn't want to tell her, but finally said, "She knows about how visions of the future work."

"How?"

"Because she has them herself."

Chapter 19

"You were awfully hard on that girl tonight," said Angus as he laid Gilda in their bed.

Gilda wasn't sure she had the strength to even pull the covers up. She'd pushed too hard tonight. In fact, she'd been pushing herself too hard for too many nights in a row. Synestryn seemed to be bubbling up everywhere lately. Something bad was coming. She could feel it in her bones.

"I had no choice," she told her husband.

Angus pulled off Gilda's shoes and slid her feet under the cool sheets. "You shouldn't have told Drake you were willing to kill her. You had to know that would only rile the boy's protective instincts."

Gilda looked at her husband, studying his movements. He was gentle as always, but there was a slight hesitation about him that she couldn't figure out. Angus never hesitated. He moved with sure, self-controlled certainty. It was what had kept them both alive for so many centuries. Maybe he felt it, too—that impending doom that seemed to throb in the air around all of the Sentinels.

"You think I was bluffing, don't you?" she asked him.

Angus's blunt fingers moved to the top button on her

gown and started working it out of its hole. He didn't look her in the eye, but instead focused on his task. "You weren't?"

"No." She kept her emotions under tight control so that none of them could slip through their link. She was used to keeping secrets from him by now. She didn't like it, but she was good at hiding the truth. She never wanted him to know what she'd done to him—what she'd done to all the Theronai. "I would rather see her die than Drake. We've lost too many lately. Thomas, Kevin, Andrew. And that's just in the past few weeks. How many more men do we have to lose before I'm allowed to be angry?"

"You're allowed to be as angry as you want, Gilda. But you're not allowed to sacrifice one person for someone you love more."

"I can't lose any more of them. Not now. Not so soon. Poor Thomas—" Her throat clamped down as she fought off the tears she could not let fall. It took her several seconds before she was sure she wouldn't cry.

Thomas's death played through her mind again. She'd pulled his last memories from his sword and forced herself to relive them over and over until they were burned into her brain. He'd been like a son to her and he'd died in excruciating pain.

Like so many of the others.

Angus's wide hand smoothed over her hair and he looked at her with so much love in his blue eyes she thought she might split open with guilt. He loved her and she'd betrayed him. She was still betraying him with her silence, day after day.

"You have to stop doing that to yourself," he gently admonished her. "None of them would want you to carry those last moments of their life."

How could she explain to him that it was the only way she knew to keep them from dying alone? She couldn't be there to protect them. She couldn't be there to ease their pain. She couldn't be there to tell them how much she loved them, how proud she was. All she could do was carry their deaths with her so that they would never again be alone.

"I'm just tired," she told him.

They both knew it was a lie, but it was one they'd grown comfortable with. One they could both live with.

Angus finished unbuttoning her gown and slid it off over her head. She'd never been able to get used to modern underclothing, so she was naked beneath the smooth silk.

She felt a throb of desire pulse through the link before Angus had time to control himself.

It never ceased to amaze her that after having the same woman for several hundred years, Angus could still get aroused by something as simple as seeing her naked. But, rather than do something about it, he pulled the smooth sheets up over her and kissed her on the forehead. "Sleep, my lady. We'll figure out what to do about Helen tomorrow."

"I'm going to force Sibyl to see her. She's the only one who will know whether or not Helen's vision is real."

Angus's hand tightened around the sheet. "Do you really think that's a good idea? Sibyl is still angry with you, and forcing her to do anything will only make things worse between the two of you."

As if they could get any worse. "Do you have a better idea?"

Angus pushed out a weary sigh. "Helen isn't ready for Sibyl. She's not even ready to face the fact that she's one of us. I don't want to push her too hard or too fast."

"Would you rather I simply kill the girl?"

"You can't do that." His voice was hard, final.

"You don't think I'm capable of killing an innocent?"

Angus gave a sad shake of his head. "No, I know exactly what you're capable of. But you still can't kill her. If you did, you'd be killing Drake as well. He's nearly bonded to her permanently."

Permanently? It couldn't be. Gilda felt a stab of fear. "No. It's much too soon for that. He should have weeks left, if not months."

"He has a few days at best."

"How do you know?"

"The colors in her luceria have nearly solidified."

"But not totally. They were still swirling tonight. I saw it myself."

"You were too tired to sense what I did. It's been so long since I've seen another bonded pair that I almost forgot what it felt like to be near them. There's a kind of harmony in the air around them."

Gilda pulled in a deep breath as she remembered that harmony from her youth and again from tonight. "You're right. It was there. How can that be? There wasn't time for them to bond permanently yet."

Angus shrugged his wide shoulders. "I'm not sure if it's because he's waited so long for her or if it's because she's already used so much of his power. In any case, they're nearly tied together. If you try to kill her, after that's happened, Drake won't survive. One way or another."

Gilda closed her eyes against a wave of panic. She couldn't save Drake unless she got Helen to cooperate. She had to do something to make that happen. All of her boys—her adopted family—were dying one by one. She'd already lost all of her biological children. Even centuries didn't ease the gnawing pain of watching a child die. She remembered her little boy's face. His smiles.

None of her babies could smile anymore.

She'd lost Thomas and Kevin and Andrew and countless others. She was *not* going to lose Drake, too.

Drake expected to find Helen asleep when he returned to his suite. She was exhausted, which was why he'd left her alone to begin with. He knew that if he stayed there and helped her into bed the way his protective instincts were clamoring at him to do, he'd end up crawling right in with her. He'd strip them both naked, cover her curvy body with his, and thrust inside her until he was buried too deep to think about anything besides the slick heat of her gripping him. Until there was no room left for fear or worry or grief—just the two of them striving for that perfect pleasure where nothing bad could touch them.

But when he let himself back into his suite and checked in on her to see whether she was sleeping soundly, he found an empty bed instead. The blankets hadn't even been rumpled.

Drake cursed and focused on their link in an effort to find her. He knew she was safe here—at least from Synestryn—but he didn't like the idea of her wandering around alone. There were too many things that could happen to her, even at the hands of those he considered allies. There were too many men here who could hurt her without trying. Too many men who needed her for things she didn't yet understand. Logan's blood oath had proven that.

Just the thought that Logan had the right to demand she give him blood whenever he wanted it made Drake want to kill him. And that violent thought made his head pound. Fucking peace bond.

It took several deep breaths before Drake was able to clear his head enough to determine where Helen had gone. He followed the subtle tug on his ring, which led him to the sliding glass doors onto the patio at the back of his suite.

He'd never done much with the slab of concrete the way some of Dabyr's residents had. He hadn't planted any pots of flowers or bought patio furniture or installed a hot tub. He rarely had time to enjoy his home, and his patio was a bleak square of cement that glowed pale in the darkness.

Helen sat at the outside edge of the patio facing the grounds. From here, she had a view of the lake where they'd worked earlier. Beside her was an empty pitcher, which, based on her soggy clothes and hair, she'd up-ended over herself. The thin cotton of her T-shirt clung to her skin and Drake's stomach tightened against a rush of desire.

She looked good in the moonlight. Softer, which he didn't think was possible. He knew just how soft she was all over, and the memory alone was nearly enough to bring him to his knees. He wanted to touch her so bad it made his hands shake and he had to take several deep breaths before he trusted himself to get closer to her.

Drake slid the glass door open and stepped outside. Helen didn't turn around. She didn't so much as twitch or acknowledge his presence in any way. She sat completely still, her legs crossed and her forearms resting on her knees, her palms facing up.

That's when he felt it—a tiny trickle of power flowing out of him so minute he hadn't sensed it before. She was trying to call fire.

Drake sat down behind her, scooting his body as close to hers as he could get without touching. It was a lovely form of torture to be so close but not nearly close enough. He could smell her skin, warm from effort and the sultry night air, and the scent of whatever laundry soap the Gerai had used to clean her clothes. Water dripped from her earlobes and hair. Her skin was beaded with moisture so that it glistened in the faint light.

She still hadn't looked at him. Her concentration was too intense. He could feel the tension of her mental effort vibrating in her delicate bones and muscles. Her body was rigid and Drake wanted to pull her into his arms and ease away the strain. He didn't like her pushing herself like this. It was too much. She needed rest, and as her Theronai, it was part of his job to see that she got whatever she needed.

Of course, part of what she needed right now was confidence that she could do the job she was designed to do. Gilda had shaken Helen's faith in herself too much tonight and this was her way of trying to reestablish some of that confidence. Drake knew that. He didn't like it, but he understood why she felt the need to push so hard.

He had only two choices. He could help her regain her confidence or stop her from hurting herself. Both her physical and emotional health were important and it was hard to justify placing one over another.

Drake wondered whether Angus ever had to deal with this kind of dilemma. It wasn't something that was covered during all those long lessons about what his duties to his lady would be. And he hadn't had any lessons for so long that he wasn't sure how much of it he remembered, anyway. Once the Synestryn had killed most of their women, the Theronai lost hope that they would ever be so lucky to find a woman like Helen.

Drake still couldn't believe his good fortune and he

knew that he had to get this right. He had to protect her and convince her to stay with him.

Helen shuddered and gasped. Her body slumped forward and Drake was left with no more choices. He had to touch her. He had to hold her and convince her to rest. She wasn't going to make any progress as tired as she was.

Drake pulled her back against his chest and she jumped at the contact before relaxing into him. "Drake," she panted. "I didn't know you were there."

Water soaked thorough his shirt, but he didn't care. It conducted the heat of his body, letting it flow into her. Her skin was chilled and he ran his hands up and down her arms in an effort to warm her.

"You were busy," he said quietly.

She leaned her head back and looked up at him. The whites of her eyes were nearly red—more bloodshot than he'd ever seen. He'd heard that this could happen if a woman tried to channel too much power, but he'd seen Gilda handle a lot of magic at one time and her eyes had never been more than a little bloodshot. Nothing like this. If he needed any proof that he was doing the right thing, this was it. Helen had pushed herself too hard.

His arms tightened around her against his will and he fought back the primal urge to shove his way into her mind, render her unconscious, and be done with it. The only thing that held him back was the sure knowledge that if he did that, he wouldn't like the results come morning.

He wanted Helen's trust, not her anger.

Her lungs were still laboring and every few seconds, she'd shiver as if fevered. Drake pressed a hand to her head. It was cool and damp.

Helen closed her eyes and let out a sigh at his touch. "You're warm."

Her soft, quiet voice sank into him, heating him further. He loved her voice. Especially when she was crying out his name in release.

His body responded to the memory with a blast of need that had him hardening so fast it hurt. He shifted Helen's body to shield her from his rampant lack of control, but he wasn't going to be able to keep his distance for long. He needed to get her dry and warm and in bed. Alone.

"I'd like you to rest," he told her in his most diplomatic tone. Of course, with his blood pounding hotly through his veins and his cock hard enough to mine for diamonds, it came out sounding more like a growling command.

"I think I almost have it," she said. "I want to try again."

"Not tonight."

"Yes, tonight. We may not have another day for me to practice."

"Then we don't. You can't push yourself any more tonight. You're going to hurt yourself."

"I'm being careful."

"You don't know how to be careful. How could you? You've never been taught."

She shook her head a little and droplets of water sprinkled down. "I can feel it—like some sort of internal warning system."

Drake had never heard of such a thing, but he was glad she had it. "You're exhausted and so am I." That last part was a lie, but he didn't feel even a twinge of guilt.

Her mouth turned down in a sympathetic frown. "I'm

sorry, Drake. I didn't even think about how hard it had to be on you for me to pull all this power from you. Why didn't you say something?"

Okay, maybe he felt a little guilty. "It's not a big deal. Let's just get dried off and get some rest. We'll try again tomorrow, okay?"

Helen nodded wearily and Drake helped her to her feet. She swayed for a moment before steadying herself. The painful-looking redness in her eyes bothered him more by the second, but he stayed calm so that he wouldn't frighten her.

Maybe he needed to call one of the Sanguinar to tend to her. He didn't like the idea of another man touching her, but he liked the idea of her suffering a lot less. "Your eyes are pretty bad. How do they feel?"

"Like they're on fire, but I'll live."

"Do you want me to call someone to heal them?" he asked.

She gave him a sickly grimace. "One of those vampires? No, thank you. I'd rather suffer."

Drake grinned. Vampires. Logan was going to hate it when she called him that, which was exactly why he didn't correct her. "Then at least let me help you with the pain."

"You can do that?"

Rather than answer her, Drake settled his hand around her throat until the two parts of the luceria connected. He felt a sudden burst of pleasure at the touch—complete and utter rightness and contentment—and had to consciously keep his grip relaxed and not curl his fingers around her neck in a heated caress. It took him a moment to focus enough to find the pain in her mind and pull it into his own.

His eyes burned as if someone had taken a blowtorch

to them. He had to blink several times before he could clear the tears that had welled up to fight the sting. After a few moments, he became used to the burning sensation and ignored it. If there was one thing he knew how to do, it was ignore pain.

"Wow, that's one heck of an aspirin," she said, smiling. "Thanks." She went up on tiptoe and pressed a chaste kiss to his mouth.

The feel of her lips on his made his whole body clench against a hot burst of lust. She hadn't intended to turn him on with that kiss; he knew that, but it didn't matter. She had anyway.

Drake's hand cradled the back of her head, while his other tightened slightly around her throat. She couldn't go anywhere, couldn't move away from him. He saw her realize it and waited for a flash of fear or disgust he expected to follow, but it never came. If anything, she relaxed slightly, accepting his decision to hold her still, waiting to see what he'd do.

She licked her lips and Drake's gaze was drawn to the motion like a moth to the flame. He knew better than to kiss her. He knew that if he did, it would let loose the last strand of control he still held. If he kissed her, he would take her, and there was a reason he wasn't supposed to do that. He couldn't think of what it was, nor did it seem to be as important as it had been a moment ago, but there was something in his head warning him of danger.

Helen swallowed and he felt her throat move beneath his hand. He stood there, frozen, trying to figure out what had been so important. Why he shouldn't carry her inside, strip her naked, and make her come over and over until she passed out. It sounded like a really good plan.

His body throbbed with hot pulses of blood that all seemed to pool in his groin. His skin heated and his hands shook with the effort it took to restrain himself from kissing her.

He dragged his eyes away from her mouth, hoping that would help him think. Her face was lovely in the dim light—her cheeks so perfectly smooth and soft. She was soft all over, especially the delicate skin along the inside of her thighs and the undersides of her breasts. He remembered exactly how she tasted there, too, and his mouth watered in response.

Helen's body shuddered again. Was she cold? Did she want him as much as he did her? He wasn't sure, so he looked into her eyes to read her.

Her eyes were nearly bloody. Suddenly, he remembered why he couldn't make love to her now. She was tired. Fragile. He had to protect her and make her rest.

"I'll rest better after you've helped me relax. After you make me come," she whispered to him.

She'd heard his thought. He'd been too distracted by her pull on him to remember to shield her. With an effort of will, he blocked her out, but he couldn't bring himself to let her go. The only places his hands were willing to move were to more intimate territory on her body, so he held still.

"Don't shut me out, Drake. You're the only anchor I have right now and I need you."

Drake felt a thrill of triumph stampede through him. She needed him. It was more than he'd ever hoped to hear her say. If she needed him, maybe she would stay with him. "Say that again," he demanded. He hated it that his voice was so rough, but he couldn't help it.

"Say what?"

"That you need me. Say it again."

A strange look crossed her face, but he couldn't read it through the bloody haze in her eyes. His own emotions were running hot, taking up all his concentration, and try as he might, he couldn't figure out what she was thinking.

"I need you, Drake. Let me in." Her words were faint, but he heard every one of them and wanted to howl in victory.

She'd asked him to let her in and he could refuse her nothing. Not now. Drake stopped trying to hide himself from her. He let her feel every bit of his lust and hope and joy. He pressed his hips against her belly and let her feel the erection he'd been protecting her from as well.

Helen's eyes fluttered shut and she let out a moan he felt vibrate under his hand. Her nipples beaded up under the wet T-shirt and her face flushed a pretty pink.

Drake was lost. Not kissing her was impossible, so he covered her parted lips with his and just gave in. His fingers tightened in her hair and he angled her head so he could feast on her mouth. Helen's hands gripped his arms and her tongue swirled around his. She was holding on tight and he could feel the effort it took for her to stay upright.

Drake picked her up and took her inside, sliding the door closed with his elbow. The cool air hit his hot skin, but it did nothing to cool the furnace raging inside him. The only thing that could do that was Helen. He needed to be inside her. Now.

He couldn't pull his mouth from hers, and by some miracle, he found his way to his room and laid her on his bed. In seconds, her loose sweatpants and panties were no more than a soggy pile on his carpet. He opened his jeans enough to free his erection, spread her legs, and thrust into her.

Helen's shock registered somewhere in the back of his mind and he froze. Sweat broke out over his ribs with the effort it took not to give in to his need to move. Something wasn't right, but he couldn't figure out what it was.

Drake opened his eyes and looked down at her. Her hair was leaving a dark water spot on his pillow. She was still wearing her shirt. Maybe that's what was wrong. He wanted her naked, but he couldn't seem to remember how to make it happen. It was taking all his focus to stay still inside her.

She reached up and touched his face. A muscle in his jaw jumped and a shiver coursed down his spine. His hips no longer listened to him and he pressed forward, pushing Helen into the mattress. Her eyes rolled back in her head and she let out a faint whimper.

He found the part of him that lived only to protect her and asked, "Am I hurting you?"

She bit her bottom lip and shook her head. "No. It's good. Just like that."

Drake needed no further incentive. He slid out of her, feeling the slick heat of her arousal gliding between them. It was perfect. She was perfect. Warm and tight and slippery. Made just for him.

He wasn't going to last long. No way could he hold out when everything about her gave him insane pleasure. He rested his weight on his elbow and cradled the nape of her neck in his hand. Both parts of the luceria met as he thrust heavily inside her again.

Helen gasped and Drake tried to look at her and see whether it was in pleasure or pain, but he couldn't see.

Fiery colors danced in his vision, blinding him, swirling in a deep mix of reds and oranges. All he could do was feel her pleasure pulsing through the link and trust that it was right. Her body was pliant beneath his, accepting his powerful movements. Her fingers slid up under his shirt and dug into the muscles of his chest. The leaves of his lifemark shivered in response to her touch, sending a tingling heat to the base of his spine.

He felt Helen's body tighten around his erection in a silken contraction at the same time he felt her pleasure swell up and flood their link. She let out a soft cry of pleasure and it sent Drake right over the edge. His orgasm exploded inside him and he buried himself as deep as he could go, wanting to be as close to Helen as possible. He poured himself into her, both mind and body, letting her feel his rioting emotions pulsing into her in time with his release.

Her sweet voice filled the room, tapering off into a breathless sigh. Drake's body was buzzing with pleasure. He knew he was too heavy on top of her, but he couldn't make his limbs work to move.

It took him several minutes to control his breathing and get his body to cooperate. When he found the strength to push himself up and look at her, Helen was already asleep.

The colors of the luceria had nearly settled into a swirl of rich, fiery reds.

The Scarlet Lady. His lady.

A bone-deep sense of satisfaction glowed inside him. He knew that when the colors stopped shifting, their bond would be complete and that could mean his death if she chose to leave him, but he didn't care. She was accepting him and even if it was only for a short time, it was more than he'd ever hoped to have before he died.

He'd fulfilled his purpose in life and found his partner. He was going to do everything in his power to see to it that they stayed together for a long, long time. Whatever Helen wanted or needed, it would be hers. He'd make her happy and show her every day how much he loved her.

Drake stilled at the thought. Loved her? Could he truly love her so soon? He cared for her and wanted her to be safe and happy, but love?

Helen had shown him her strength and kindness from the moment he met her. She protected those she cared about and had spent her life helping others. She'd sacrificed her blood to save his life and she'd given of herself freely to help him get through his grief. He'd seen inside her mind and felt her soul brush his every time both halves of the luceria connected. She was kind and generous and strong. How could he not love her?

Acknowledging his love for her freed him somehow, satisfied him in a way nothing else could. He was going to do whatever it took to keep her by his side.

Drake smoothed a tangle of dark hair away from her smooth cheek. The flush of passion in her skin had only started to fade. Bluish crescents of fatigue hung beneath her eyes. Her shirt was still damp, as was the bed beneath them.

She needed her rest and a wet bed wasn't going to be comfortable for her, so he eased himself off her body. He made quick work of cleaning her up, stripping the wet shirt from her, and wrapped her hair in a towel. He slipped her into the clean, dry guest bed, shed his clothes, and crawled in with her, making sure his sword was close at hand. She didn't even stir once, which proved just how exhausted she was.

Drake didn't need much sleep, but he couldn't keep

himself from curling around her soft body and holding her while she slept. It was a rare treat—one he hoped he would get to enjoy for many years to come.

He knew Helen thought she was going to die soon, but Drake refused to believe it. There was enough magic in the world that he'd find a way to keep her vision from coming true. Now that they were united, there was little they wouldn't be able to accomplish together. He'd keep her by his side and keep her safe and nothing would ever hurt her. He wouldn't allow it.

Drake realized he was holding Helen too tight and loosened his grip. The next few days were going to be hard on her. She was still adjusting to this new life, and seeing Sibyl wasn't easy on anyone. And Kevin's sword was still out there.

Again, the idea of letting it go unfound was compelling. Helen would be forced to stay with him forever if they never found it, and that was enough to tempt a saint. But Drake didn't want her that way—through force. He wanted her to stay with him because she cared for him.

Because she loved him, too.

Drake nearly snorted. He was getting soft. First he fell in love and now he was all sappy about the idea that Helen should love him back. It seemed a ridiculous notion that she would, but he couldn't push it aside. Even if it did mean he'd gone soft.

Chapter 20

Helen had just showered and dressed the next morning when she heard a sound that was music to her ears.

"I want to see her now or I'm calling the police," said Miss Mabel in her age-weary voice.

Helen rushed out into the living room, reached around her walker, and pulled Miss Mabel to her chest in a gentle hug. She had to fight not to grip the woman too tight in her excitement. "What are you doing here?"

Miss Mabel scooted her walker toward the couch. "Those boys brought me here," she grumbled.

"What boys?"

"Vance and Slade," answered Drake. "Seems Miss Mabel is one of those thickheaded people who can't have their memories erased. When Joseph called me about it, I told him you'd enjoy having her come live here at Dabyr with us."

He was smiling at her and Helen felt an answering swell of tenderness fill her up. He was so beautiful. And he'd brought her Miss Mabel. Her friend was safe.

Miss Mabel scowled at Drake. "Like they gave me any choice. Those two boys wouldn't listen to a word I said. I told them I wouldn't say anything, but they wouldn't listen. I wanted to take a switch to both of them."

"Maybe later," soothed Drake. "Why don't you come have breakfast with us instead? The dining room should have cleared out some by now and we can all catch up."

"That sounds wonderful," said Helen. "You can tell me all about what happened after we left the farmhouse."

Miss Mabel began her rant as they headed out the door and hadn't finished until Helen had finished her second cup of coffee. "So they told me that I can stay here so the monsters won't get me. I'm supposed to have my own room later today."

Drake took Helen's hand and settled it on his thigh. He stroked the back of it with an idle sweep of his fingers. Helen had to force herself to concentrate on what her friend was saying. "That sounds great. It's beautiful here."

Miss Mabel gave a little snort. "I suppose. It's not home, though."

Drake gave Miss Mabel an indulgent grin. "The Gerai will take care of moving all your things here, so it will help you settle in. And of course, Helen and I will help in any way we can."

Miss Mabel seemed unconvinced. "I don't like not earning my keep, and that Joseph of yours refused to take my money."

"We don't need it," said Drake. "We've lived long enough to understand the power of compound interest."

"I'd like to teach those boys, Slade and Vance, a thing or two. They don't have a single manner between them."

Drake grinned wide. "I think that's an excellent idea. We've got a few good teachers here, but we could always use another. There are a lot of human children that would benefit from your experience."

Miss Mabel's rheumy eyes lit up in a way Helen had

never seen before. "I suppose I could exchange my teaching services for room and board."

"I'll talk to Joseph about it, if you like," offered Drake.

"No, thank you. I'd rather talk to him myself. Make sure he understands how things are going to work around here."

Drake's grin widened and Helen hoped that Joseph was man enough to take on Miss Mabel.

Before she could question Miss Mabel about her plans, Gilda came to their table. "It's time," she said.

Gilda looked lovely this morning in a soft gray gown similar to the one she'd worn yesterday, but with delicate embroidery around the neckline. Her dark hair glinted with strands of silver, and her black eyes were cold as they looked down on Helen. "It's not wise to keep Sibyl waiting."

Drake wiped his mouth on a napkin and slid smoothly to his feet. Helen couldn't help but admire the way he moved, the way he was built as if he'd been made just for her pleasure. The soft fabric of his shirt clung to his muscled chest and shoulders and she could still remember how he had felt beneath her palms last night—all hard and hot and hers—striving to bring her to climax.

Drake gave her a secret smile as if he'd read her thoughts, and offered her his hand. She took it, glad to have his strength to steady her nerves.

"If you'll please excuse us, Miss Mabel," he said, bowing his head toward the older woman. "We have an appointment to keep."

Miss Mabel waved an age-spotted hand. "You kids go on. I have work to do."

Gilda led them from the dining room, moving fast enough that her long skirt billowed out behind her.

"Are you sure Sibyl will be able to help me figure out

my vision?" Helen asked Drake as they followed behind Gilda down a long corridor.

"Yes," said Drake at the same time Gilda said, "No."

Great. Helen ignored Gilda. Obviously the woman hadn't had her coffee yet this morning. She looked tired and worried and angry, and Helen's heart went out to her. If what Drake had said was true and she thought of him like a son, then it was no wonder Gilda wasn't pleased. Helen was never going to be what these people wanted. Part of her was glad because she couldn't see herself ever doing what Gilda had done last night. No freaking way.

Drake's hand slid over her back in a comforting caress. Helen let herself enjoy it, remembering all too well the kind of magic those hands wielded. With any luck at all, she'd find a few spare minutes to get Drake alone and do all the things she'd meant to do with him before she'd fallen asleep last night.

Gilda stopped at a door at the end of a long hall and Helen nearly ran into her. Drake stopped her before she could embarrass herself and Helen gave herself a mental shake. She needed to concentrate. This meeting was important.

Gilda knocked on the door and it was answered by a huge man. He was nearly six and a half feet tall, heavily muscled with thick limbs and watchful, moss green eyes. His body was marked with various small scars, and beneath the tight fabric of his left sleeve Helen could see the empty branches of his lifemark. He was another Theronai—one she had not yet met.

He bowed his head to Gilda. "Lady."

"Good morning, Cain. Is Sibyl ready?"

Cain's eyes darted to Helen, slid from her head to

her toes and back again as if sizing her up in the blink of an eye. "I regret that my duties to Sibyl prevent me from offering you my oath," he told Helen in a deep, rumbling voice.

Oath? He meant that bloody vow all the other men had given her. What did one say to something like that? "Uh, that's okay."

He bowed his head to her as he had to Gilda. "Sibyl will see you now."

Cain opened the door wide and stepped to the side to let them in. The suite was arranged the same as Drake's, but decorated differently. The living room was done in a frilly mix of lavender and pink with lace curtains and doilies everywhere. The furniture was surprisingly small except for one large recliner that was big enough for Cain's bulk, and even that was covered in a pale pink floral fabric.

Helen bet Cain just loved that.

Cain looked at Drake and Gilda. "Please wait here."

"I'm going with her," said Gilda.

"She won't see you. You know that."

A frustrated sadness tightened Gilda's mouth and made her black eyes sparkle. "Will you please ask again? For me?"

Cain let out a resigned sigh and nodded. He went back to a bedroom, disappeared behind the closed door, and returned a minute later. He didn't quite meet Gilda's gaze. "Nothing has changed, my lady. I'm sorry."

Gilda gave a tight nod and squared her shoulders. "We'll wait here," she told Helen.

A quiet kind of apprehension settled over Helen. She had no idea who Sibyl was, but she couldn't imagine anyone tough enough to make Gilda back down. That woman was made of tempered steel and concrete. Anyone who could make Gilda look chastised had to be formidable indeed.

Drake captured her face between his palms. "You'll be fine. I promise. I wouldn't let you go in there if I didn't believe that was true."

Helen found enough confidence to nod. Drake gave her a quick kiss on the mouth that managed to distract her from her worry, and she followed Cain to the bedroom. He opened the door for her, but didn't follow her in. Instead, he shut her inside, alone with Sibyl.

Sibyl's bedroom, like the living room, was all frills and ruffles and pastels. At one end of the room, beneath a lace-curtained window, was her tiny, white iron bed. At the other was a small table and chairs made from intricately carved wood. She sat in one of those chairs.

Sibyl was a little girl. No more than eight or nine years old.

"Helen," Sibyl greeted her in the high-pitched voice of a child. "Come sit with me."

Sibyl wore a ruffled dress in soft blue that perfectly matched her eyes. Her blond hair fell in long ringlets and was tied back with a matching blue ribbon. She was a beautiful child with doll-like features—large clear eyes, a small but full mouth, a pert nose, and round, smooth cheeks. Her shiny black shoes and lacy ankle socks peeked out from beneath the table.

Across from Sibyl was a doll that looked exactly like her except for the eyes and the dress. The doll wore a stark white dress and her eyes were as black and shiny as Sibyl's patent leather shoes. In front of both of them was a dainty china teacup and saucer set on a lace place mat. A third place was set—the one Sibyl had motioned for Helen to use.

Not knowing what else to do, Helen sat in the child-sized chair, feeling huge and gangly as she tried to squeeze her legs under the table.

"Tea?" asked Sibyl politely.

Helen nodded, bemused by the girl's perfect manners. Sibyl filled Helen's cup from a hand-painted teapot as well as her cup and her doll's.

"I was told you have seen a vision of your own death," said Sibyl. Her voice was childish, but her manner of speaking was anything but.

"Yes."

"May I see it?" asked Sibyl.

"Uh. How?"

Sibyl gave her a patronizing smile and reached one small hand up to Helen's temple. Her vision flashed in her head in vivid detail. She could see the curve of every lick of fire as it consumed her. She could hear its hungry roar and feel the heat of it burning her alive.

Helen gasped and her body tightened against the vision, trying to shove it away. As suddenly as it had come, it was gone again. Helen was panting and curled on the floor on her side. Sibyl stood over her with a faintly curious expression on her face. "Are you well?" she asked sweetly.

Helen felt like she was going to throw up. Her muscles were knotted and a slick, oily fear oozed around her insides, making her sick. But she wasn't about to tell the little girl that. Instead, she swallowed, pushed herself upright, and nodded. "I'll be fine."

"Liar," she admonished. "But then we all are."

Out of the corner of her eye, Helen thought she saw the doll nod in agreement. She righted the chair, shook her head to clear it, and forced herself to sit with the little girl again. The doll was still, staring off into space with glassy black eyes.

Helen looked away from the creepy doll. "You don't need to worry about me."

"Because I'm a child?" Sibyl asked.

"Yes."

"How sweet you are to pad me from life's ugliness." She said it in a tone somewhere between amused and condescending. "Just for that, I'm going to tell you what you want to know."

"Which is?"

Sibyl sipped her tea. "You want to know how to avoid your vision."

"Does that mean I can avoid it?"

"Some visions are certainties, and other as possibilities. Yours is a certain possibility."

Freaky little vague midget. Sibyl was really starting to get on Helen's nerves. "What's that supposed to mean?"

"It means that that point in your life is fixed. You cannot avoid it. If you live to that point, your vision will come to pass."

"Then how is that not certain?" asked Helen.

"You weren't listening. I said *if* you live that long it will come to pass. You may always choose otherwise."

"You mean suicide?"

Sibyl's soft blue eyes shone with sadness. "If you do not like one death, then it is your right to choose another."

What great news that was. "How much time do I have?"

"Not much. All of us are running out of time, Helen."

"What do you mean? Who's all of us?"

"The Sentinels. The human race. The kingdom of the Solarc. All of us. The Synestryn grow more powerful with each moonrise and now that they have another Sentinel blade at their disposal, it will only get worse."

"You mean Kevin's sword is going to allow the Synestryn to win?"

Sibyl frowned and was silent for a long moment as if looking at something only she could see. "It is a turning point for them. That's all I can see. What I do know is that if they have Kevin's sword, they will be able to free the souls of the creatures slain by his blade and their army will grow. The Sentinels cannot afford such a setback—the work of an entire warrior's life undone."

"Then we have to get his sword back."

Sibyl shrugged a dainty shoulder. "I do not concern myself with such things. They are the matter of warriors and I am not one. You, on the other hand, are."

"A warrior? Hardly."

"Yes. You are. Regardless of what the Gray Lady would have you believe." Sibyl's voice was as cold and hard as ice—not at all that of a child. "You're not trained, but the potential is there. If you live long enough to fulfill that potential."

Helen felt a little shiver of unease slide down her spine. Sibyl was not what she appeared to be. Not by a long shot. "Gilda said I would be useless in battle if I can't use fire. She thinks my inability will end up killing Drake."

"If you try to fight the Synestryn beside Drake without the ability to call fire, then Drake will die. About that, there is no question."

"Then Gilda was right. I can't fight."

Sibyl rolled her eyes. "You aren't listening. This is why I refuse to see people like you. You never listen."

"I'm trying, but you aren't making any sense."

Sibyl gave Helen a hard stare. "No, I'm just not telling

you what you want to hear. You want me to tell you that
everything is going to be fine and that everyone will live
and be happy and we'll sing and hold hands and no one
will ever hurt or be hungry again. That's not the way it
is. That's not the way it will ever be. The truth is much
bleaker than that and nothing I can do will ever change
it. Nothing."

Helen suddenly felt sorry for the girl. What must it
be like for her to know things she shouldn't? Helen only
had one vision and it had been hard to bear. From all
accounts, Sibyl had a lot of visions and she was only a
child. It had to be frightening and lonely for her. "I'm
sorry," said Helen, reaching out for the girl's hand.

Sibyl jerked away before Helen could touch her.
"Don't. I don't want any more of your life in my head."

That didn't sound good. "What can I do to help
you?"

"There is nothing anyone can do for me. I am as I was
created to be."

"But you're suffering."

"We all suffer, Helen. If you truly want to do something for me, then try not to be stupid. Let your love for
Drake guide your actions."

Love for Drake? She liked him. He was sexy and
caring and courageous. How could she help but like
him. But love? That was too scary to think about, so
she set the thought aside for now. She'd figure out how
she felt about him later when her emotions weren't so
scattered.

"Tell me one thing, please. If I do decide to . . . choose
my own death, does that guarantee Drake's safety?"

Sibyl shook her head, making her blond ringlets bob.
"The only guarantee we are given when we are born is
that we will die. Even for one of our kind who lives for

centuries, death is inevitable. My advice to you is to embrace your death rather than fear it. Let it come at a time and place of your choosing and give it meaning. A meaningful death is the best any of us can hope for in life."

That was the saddest thing Helen had ever heard a child say, and she had to fight to keep from pulling Sibyl into her arms to comfort her. Only the worry that it would hurt her allowed Helen to hold herself back. "If you ever want to talk, or if you ever need a friend to just listen, I can do that for you, Sibyl."

The little girl blinked as if confused. "No one has ever offered to do that for me before."

"I think the people here are all a little afraid of you."

Sibyl tilted her head to the side. "Of course they are. I know how every one of them is going to die."

That was too freaky to think about for long. "Me, too?"

"Yes."

Helen just stared at her for a moment, stunned into silence.

Sibyl casually sipped her tea. "Aren't you going to ask me how you die?"

"No. Knowing I'm going to burn alive if I don't kill myself sooner is more than enough stress, thank you."

Sibyl gave Helen a sly, almost sinister smile. "You don't know nearly as much as you think you do. Nothing in our world is what it seems."

"Does that include you?"

Sibyl ignored the question. "You should go now. Your window of opportunity is narrow."

"What's that supposed to mean?"

A frightening light flared in Sibyl's eyes. "It means go. Now. And send Drake to see me for a moment."

She might look like a child, but she was not one. No child had that much presence or force of will.

Helen stood clumsily from her chair and left the room. Right before she shut the door, she was sure she heard Sibyl's doll giggle.

Chapter 21

Nicholas intercepted Helen and Drake right outside Drake's suite. The men stepped a few feet down the corridor so Helen couldn't hear them. Their secrecy annoyed her, so she used Drake's power to eavesdrop. She channeled power to her ears, the same way she had her eyes in order to enhance her sight. When the rush of sound blasted her eardrums, she nearly gasped. She tuned the roar down until the beating of their hearts and the air moving in and out of their lungs didn't drown out their conversation.

Nicholas handed Drake that blood monitor/GPS gadget they'd used to track the Synestryn before and a small silver vial. "There's only enough blood in here for one shot, so you'll have to find the nest tonight."

Drake's jaw tightened with determination. "I'll have a chopper ready in case the nest is too far away to drive."

"I don't think it will be. All my data points to a gathering of Synestryn in a hundred-mile radius of here. I think they're closing in on us, maybe gearing up for an all-out attack on the compound."

Drake let out a low curse, but Helen heard it clearly. She could also hear the sudden angry rush of blood through his body, which was really strange. "Does Joseph know yet?"

"Yeah," said Nicholas. "He's calling in all available Theronai just in case."

"Do you want to stay here, too, or can I convince you to come with us tonight? Helen and I sure could use your help."

"I thought Gilda didn't want you taking your lady out."

"She doesn't, but we don't have much of a choice. We've got to get Kevin's sword back."

"Then let someone else go. You two stay here, safe and sound."

Drake glanced over his shoulder at Helen, who tried to look as though she wasn't listening. Apparently her ruse worked.

"I can't do that," whispered Drake.

"Why the hell not?" demanded Nicholas.

"Because Sibyl told me that if Helen doesn't find Kevin's sword, she'll die within days. I can't let that happen."

Holy crap! Helen had not wanted to hear that. A sick feeling slithered around in her belly, but it was too late to turn back now. She had to keep listening.

Nicholas ran a hand through his dark blond hair, and his scarred face darkened with anger. "Well, shit. That's just what we need. More creepy kid prophecies to muddy things up."

"Tell me about it. It's killing me trying to deal with my need to keep Helen safe and my need to do my job—our job. Things were so much simpler when I only had myself to worry about."

"Don't look for sympathy here, buddy. You found your lady. The rest of us are still suffering, so go cry to someone else."

"Sorry. I shouldn't complain." Drake rubbed a hand over the nape of his neck. "I believe Helen isn't alone. There have to be more women like her out there. Maybe even that waitress Zach is after."

"I've already started looking for Lexi and others. I'd be able to look a lot easier if I got a sample of Helen's blood to analyze."

She felt a sudden spike of outrage shoot out of Drake. "After what Logan did to her ... don't ask me for that, please."

Helen was beginning to think that whatever Logan had done when he'd used her blood to save Drake had more meaning than she knew. She was going to have to ask Drake about it as soon as they had a moment alone. As soon as enough time had passed so that he wouldn't realize she'd been listening.

"I could ask Logan, if it would make you feel better," said Nicholas. "He'd be happy to have an excuse to get more of her blood."

"Goddamn it! Don't you dare! If I see him anywhere near her I'll have to kill him." Drake winced in pain as he said the words. "I swear I will find a way, and that will destroy what little peace there is between us. We can't afford a war on three fronts. Two is bad enough."

Nicholas held out his wide, scarred hands in a placating gesture. "Chill, man. I didn't mean to push your psycho button. Jeez. It's just a little blood."

"No, it's Helen's blood. Big difference," said Drake.

"Fine. Consider the subject dropped. When will you leave?"

"In a few hours. If you want to come hunting with us, meet us at my suite after lunch, say two o'clock."

"I'll see what I can do. Joseph has me pretty busy tracking these nests, but it would be good to get out and whack on some bad guys for a while. I don't want to get rusty."

"Rusty," snorted Drake. "If you were rusty, I'd leave you behind a desk, not ask you to come help me protect my lady."

"Don't make me blush, dickhead."

Drake grinned as the men parted ways and Helen found the landscape print on the wall suddenly intriguing. Drake's hand slid along her lower back. "Let's go get some rest. It's going to be a late night."

"I'd rather practice," she told him.

"Your eyes are still red and I don't want you wearing yourself out. Tonight is the real thing."

Fear tightened her stomach. She wasn't ready.

Drake pulled her into his arms. "It's going to be fine. You and I are going to kick some Synestryn ass tonight and find Kevin's sword."

Helen slid her finger under the luceria. "And this will come off?"

Drake stiffened against her and tightened his grip. "Yes."

"What then?" she asked him.

"That's up to you."

Helen felt lost and scared. She had no idea what to do—no idea what would happen to Drake after tonight. "What happens if I don't live through this?"

"You will," he said, his tone stone hard, determined.

"But what if I don't? We both know that's a possibility."

"I'm not going to let you die," growled Drake.

"Please. Just tell me what happens if I do. I need to know you'll be safe."

Drake pulled in a deep breath that made his chest expand against her breasts. She loved the feel of his body against hers, so strong and hard and warm.

"As long as the colors in the luceria move, I'll go back to where I was before I met you—in pain. Only a few leaves left."

Helen lifted his hand and stared at the ring. She had to look hard to see any movement at all in the colors—the ring was almost completely solid red with only a hint of orange swirling around. "We're almost out of time."

"Yes." He didn't sound upset by that notion.

"What happens if I die after the colors stop?"

"You don't need to worry about that," he told her in a gentle voice.

"I'm going to worry more if I don't know."

Drake sighed. "When the luceria has chosen your final color, then the connection between us is permanent."

"What does that mean? Exactly?"

Again, his voice was low and gentle. "It means that if you die, it's almost certain I will, too."

"That's stupid!" raged Helen, pushing away from him and tugging at the necklace, which suddenly felt like a noose. "Make it stop."

Drake gathered her hands in his and kept her from trying to rip the thing off. "I can't. Neither can you. That's the way it works."

"Then you have to get it off me." She felt herself start to panic and tried to hang on to her control.

"The only way to do that is to find Kevin's sword." His brown eyes glowed with golden shards of determination. "But I need to be clear, Helen. I don't want you to take it off. Not ever."

"But I'm going to die, you fool! You saw the vision. Even Sibyl said it's going to happen." Unless Helen chose another death first.

Damn it! Now she had to act fast. Her vision was coming to pass within days, according to Sibyl. Drake was nearly out of time and she could not take him with her. She would not be the cause of his death, too.

Drake cupped her face and slid his thumb along her cheek. Helen closed her eyes against the need to lean into him for support. "Don't worry about what Sibyl said. Believe that things will work out. Trust me to protect you."

But who would protect him?

Sibyl was right. Helen's window of opportunity was narrow. She had to act now, and fighting with Drake wasn't going to make her escape easier. She needed to lull him into believing she would go along with him. Fool him into thinking she would be willing to take such a careless chance with his life.

"I trust you," she said. And she did. She trusted him to do exactly what Thomas had done and give his life to save hers. She couldn't let that happen.

Helen's time was up, but Drake's didn't have to be. She would go after Kevin's sword and free him, but it had to be tonight and she couldn't let Drake come with her. Sibyl said that going into battle together without fire would kill him. She had to find a way to keep him here. She had to find a way to give him a future.

Drake had said he believed there were other women like her out there and she had to believe it, too. She wanted to give him the chance to find one who wasn't afraid of fire—one who wasn't fated to die so young. He could still be happy and that's what she wanted for him more than anything. He'd spent his life sacrificing so that others could be happy and it was time he got a little payback.

Helen took a deep breath and forced herself to calm down. She put a tight clamp on their connection so that he wouldn't see her plans. Her path was clear. She knew exactly what she had to do.

Helen went up on her tiptoes and kissed him. His mouth opened under hers and she slid her tongue inside for a taste. Just one more taste.

Drake groaned, cupped her hips in his hands, and pulled her against him. She could feel his need for her heat the air around him. In the space of a few seconds, the kiss turned from a means of distraction to the beginning of something hungry and demanding. She loved the way he spiraled out of control with just a kiss from her. It made her feel powerful and desired. The potent combination went straight to her head and drove all the darkness away.

He grabbed her braids and tilted her head back, holding her in place while his mouth ravished hers. His slick tongue mimicked the thrust of his erection inside her, making her body liquefy and heat. This man robbed her of all sanity and made her love it. He scalded her skin with his touches and melted her bones with his kisses until there was nothing left but hunger and heat. She was burning alive with need for him and she didn't care. This was what she wanted—what she craved. He made the world go away until there was nothing left but the two of them and the pleasure he wrung from her body.

"Need to get inside," said Drake against her mouth.

Yes. Inside. Hot and hard and thick, just where she needed him to be. Helen's hands went to the button of her jeans, frantic to get them off.

"Not in the hall, love," growled Drake in a lust-roughened voice. His body shifted against hers and a moment later, the door to the suite swung wide. Drake backed her inside, half carrying her. He tossed his keys and the items Nicholas had given him on the table and looked down at her with naked passion glowing in his eyes.

Helen knew that same look was in her eyes as well. She needed this. She needed him with a ferocity that frightened her.

"I want you naked," she told him in a voice that sounded nothing like her own. It was thick and husky and the words came out in short, sharp commands.

Drake's eyes narrowed for a moment as if he was going to ask her a question, but she'd stripped her shirt and sports bra over her head, and whatever he'd been ready to ask evaporated in the heat of his gaze on her naked breasts. "So pretty."

He reached for her, but Helen stepped back. "Naked," she ordered. "Now."

Drake's jaw bunched and his cheeks darkened, but he obeyed. His sword belt came off first, invisible until it hit the floor. Then he reached back, grabbed a fistful of T-shirt, and pulled it off over his head.

Helen kicked off her shoes and slid out of her jeans and underwear while she watched Drake do the same. His eyes never left her, taking in each new swath of bare skin as it was revealed. When they were both naked, he reached for her with shaking hands.

Helen stepped out of his reach, knowing that as soon as he touched her, she'd be lost, unable to think clearly. She wanted to look at him, to take in the masculine beauty of his body and appreciate the way the light played across the muscles of his chest and arms. The way the leaves on his lifemark swayed in time with the breeze outside. The way his erection twitched in anticipation of filling her. He was beautiful and strong and hers.

Drake's hands were fisted at his sides as he waited

for her to look her fill. The tight set of his jaw and his rapid breathing told her how impatient he was and she couldn't make him wait any longer. *She* couldn't wait any longer.

Helen pressed herself against his chest, letting him feel her tightened nipples sliding over his ribs. She threaded her fingers through his dark hair and pressed wet kisses along the branches of his tattoo. Drake sucked in a breath and the leaves shivered under her lips. She could feel them move, smell the fresh scent of forest on his skin.

Drake let out a shuddering breath and his hands slid over her back. One cupped her bottom and the other cradled her head. "Give me your mouth," he said.

Helen felt the rough rumbling of his voice vibrate against her lips and it made her smile. She could feel him holding back, trying to maintain control, and she didn't want that. She wanted him to let go and give all of himself to her. She wanted nothing held back. No restraint.

A siren's smile curved her mouth as she kissed her way down his chest, over the intricate trunk of the tree, lower to where the roots fanned out over his abdomen. She knelt before him and her hands slid over the smooth flesh of his erection in a slow caress.

Drake sucked in a breath and his fingers tightened around one of her braids. He looked down at her and the golden shards in his eyes blazed with tempered lust. His body was shaking as he fought to maintain control and a fine sweat made his skin glow.

Helen held his gaze as she took him in her mouth. Drake let out a ragged sound, his eyes rolled back into his head, and his hands tightened in her hair.

The thrill of feminine power coursed through her as she saw and felt what she could do to such a strong man.

She loved him with her fingers and mouth and it brought him to his knees.

Drake was panting and his hands moved uncertainly against her hair as if he couldn't decide whether to pull her closer or push her away. She felt him gather his will, felt a hot pulse of determination flow through their link, and a moment later, she was pushed away and laid out on the soft rug on his living room floor.

His hot body came down on top of hers, pinning her legs wide. Her skin sizzled as his hand slid up her ribs to cup her breast, and with a near snarl, he nipped the skin just above her luceria. Sparks of pleasure shot along her limbs and pooled between her legs, leaving her aching and empty. She wanted him to fill her and drive the emptiness away, over and over until she could never forget the feel of him inside her.

"Not yet," he murmured against her sensitive skin.

His hand slid over her belly, leaving a trail of shivering heat in its wake. She arched into him and clawed at his hips in an effort to bring him closer, but she couldn't budge his heavy weight. His fingers found her slick and ready and he filled her with them.

Helen let out a gasp of pleasure. His fingers were thick and skilled and drove her to the edge of climax in seconds, Drake knowing exactly how she liked to be touched. She hovered there, at the edge, and somewhere in the pleasure-fogged recesses of her brain, she found the strength to hold back. "Now," she begged him.

She felt Drake's powerful body shudder and then he was surging inside her, filling her the way she wanted— the way she needed him to. Helen held on to him, pulled her legs close to her body, and let him set the pace. He knew what she needed now better than she did and he gave it to her, holding nothing back.

He loved her. She could feel his love shimmering through their link. He didn't try to hide it, didn't try to deny it. He let her see it—forced her to feel it so she would know it was real.

Helen reveled in his love, bathed herself in it until she thought she would fly apart with the force of it. Her skin tingled and her stomach tightened as the last of her control vanished. She let go, let herself shatter into tiny pieces in Drake's arms, trusting him to hold her together. He would never let anything bad happen to her.

His body clenched and she felt him tumble headlong after her into orgasm. Her body was still quivering with the tremors of her orgasm as he climaxed deep inside her, roaring out his pleasure.

Drake's weight bore down on her as he went limp atop her, but she reveled in the feel of his body on hers. She stroked his back as their breathing slowed to normal and their pulse steadied. Her hands shook, but she doubted that he noticed her weakness.

Helen smiled at the ceiling, feeling happier than she ever had before in her life. He loved her. She was the luckiest woman in the world and she couldn't prevent herself from letting some of that joy spill through their link.

Drake stiffened and she realized her mistake too late. She'd opened herself up to him and she had no way of knowing how much of her plan he'd seen.

She panicked. She had to protect him and she could only think of one way to do it. She gathered every ounce of power from him she could and willed him to sleep. If he was asleep, she could get away and find Kevin's sword and he would stay here safe and sound.

Drake's head shot up and his eyes blazed with anger. "Don't—" was all he could get out before his eyes fluttered shut and he collapsed on top of her.

The air was forced from her lungs and she had to struggle to push him to the side. He was still hard and slick inside her and Helen felt like the worst sort of bitch when she separated herself from him. They'd still been joined when she betrayed him. She only hoped that the betrayal would make it easier for him to move on with his life after she was gone.

Helen did a quick job of cleaning herself up and dressing. Within two minutes, she was out the door with the vial of blood, the Synestryn locator, and the keys to the van in hand.

Chapter 22

A heavy pounding roused Drake from a deep, dreamless sleep. He opened his bleary eyes, recognized his surroundings as his suite, but the familiarity did little to rid him of a heavy sense of confusion and fear. Something wasn't right, but he couldn't figure out what it was.

The pounding sounded again, louder this time. "Open the hell up, Drake!"

It was Nicholas's voice, followed closely by Zach's. "Move. I'll bust the damn thing down."

"I'm coming," rasped Drake. His voice was wobbly, but loud enough that they'd heard him.

He pushed himself to his feet and had to hold on to the wall for support. He felt drunk or drugged or something. He wasn't sure, but it certainly wasn't the way he should be feeling after making love with Helen.

Helen.

His breath froze in his lungs. God, no. She couldn't be gone. He had to be wrong about what he'd seen her planning to do. She couldn't be foolish enough to think she could go after Kevin's sword on her own.

He tried to reach out to her, but he couldn't feel her presence nearby. All he could feel was a desperate need to close his eyes and sleep.

A sense of urgency shoved away some of the groggi-
ness, but his movements were still clumsy. Drake ripped
the door open, uncaring that he was naked and shaking
like a newborn colt. Zach and Nicholas took in his physical condition in a quick glance and each of them took
an arm and helped him to the couch. It was a good thing,
because he wasn't sure he could have made it across the
room on his own.

"Where's Helen?" he asked them as his friends lowered him to the couch. "Tell me she couldn't get through
the gates."

Nicolas's face darkened with anger until the multi-
tude of small scars on his skin stood out in pale contrast. "I'm sorry, Drake. I was in a meeting with Joseph
when she left. One of the Gerai was covering the gate.
He knew she was a Theronai and didn't think to stop her
from leaving."

Helen was a Sentinel and the Gerai were bound to do
her will, even if it meant letting her go out there alone.
Drake should have known she'd try something like this.
He had sensed a change in her resolve, but he hadn't
stopped to think what it meant. He'd been too busy kissing her. Loving her.

Zach's dark face twisted with a furious scowl. "Fucking women running off. What the hell do they think
they're doing?"

A wave of fatigue slammed into Drake and he had to
fight to keep his eyes even halfway open. Whatever this
was, it wasn't normal, and if he didn't get rid of it, he'd
never be able to find Helen.

"I've got to find her." Drake's voice was high pitched,
panicky.

Nicholas was the voice of reason. "Calm down. You'll

be able to find her. Just clear your head and focus. Can you sense which way she went?"

Drake closed his eyes and fought the panic clawing at his insides. Helen was gone. He could feel a faint tug on his ring, but it was so slight, she had to be miles away by now.

Zach was talking on the phone to someone, but Drake wasn't listening. He couldn't seem to clear his head of this damn fatigue. His eyes were gritty and heavy and he felt as if he weighed four hundred pounds. Sweat trickled down his ribs and it took all his concentration to stay upright on the couch. "Coffee," he croaked. "And my clothes."

"Coffee won't help," came a voice from the open door of Drake's suite. Logan.

A flood of rage drove away the sleepiness at the sound of Logan's voice. "You fucking blood-sucking bastard," growled Drake. "You talked her into leaving me so you could get her blood, didn't you?" His body lurched from the couch and he nearly fell over the coffee table. Only Nicholas's strong grip kept him up.

An arrogant smile touched Logan's mouth. "On the contrary. I'd much prefer her to stay far away from harm so that I have many years to feed from her."

Drake ripped his arm away from Nicholas and took a shaky step forward. "I'm going to kill you for committing her to you like that."

"Have you forgotten you're peace-bound?"

He had, but his pounding skull reminded him.

"Besides, if you kill me, I won't be able to fix what Helen did to you," said Logan in a calm, even tone. "Would you like me to undo it so you can find her before it's too late?"

Drake wanted to pound him into the ground until only a bloody stain remained, but he controlled the urge. For now. He needed Logan to fix him so he could find Helen. "You owe her that much after stealing her blood oath."

Logan's pale eyes glittered with hunger. "I stole nothing. She offered her oath in exchange for your life. Would you do the same?"

"I would do anything for Helen," said Drake without hesitation.

A flare of victory widened Logan's eyes and he took an anxious step forward. "Say it," he demanded. "I need the words to bind you."

Drake wanted to howl in frustration, but he was too tired, too worried. He couldn't keep his eyes open for more than a few seconds and Helen needed him. Another wave of sleepiness washed over him, making him sway. Nicholas grabbed his arm to keep him from falling over.

Drake could barely lift his own arm, much less wield a sword. He was useless to Helen like this. "Fine. You can have my blood if you help me find Helen."

"The rest, Theronai. You know what I want." A greedy smile curved Logan's mouth.

Drake hated Logan and the thought of being bound to him for eternity made his stomach twist, but he had no choice. He had to protect Helen. He pulled in a deep breath and gave Logan his vow. "You may take my blood whenever you have need of it so long as no harm comes to Helen. I won't allow you to weaken me as long as she needs me."

"Fair enough," agreed Logan.

Drake fell to his knees under the weight of his vow. It cut off his air, strangling him, making him feel caged and frantic. He'd committed himself to a predator.

Logan moved forward smoothly, making no sound.

Drake was still reeling when his friends came to his aid. Nicholas helped Drake sit on the couch while Zach helped him into his jeans. At least he wouldn't have to let the Sanguinar suck his blood while he was still bare assed. Some things simply couldn't be tolerated, and that was near the top of the list.

"We don't have much time," said Zach, anger ringing in every word. "Helicopter's waiting for us."

"I won't be long," said Logan. He knelt beside Drake and lifted his wrist to his mouth.

A stab of pain and a throbbing heat swamped Drake's arm. Logan's mouth worked over the wound and Drake felt worse than before. Weaker. He couldn't keep his eyes open. Couldn't fight the need to sleep.

"Enough!" roared Zach, making Drake jerk awake.

Logan pulled his mouth away, leaving no wound behind. He pressed his hand to Drake's forehead, and a split second later, Drake felt a hot spike of energy jolt through him. Every cell of his body was humming with strength. He was wide awake, pissed as hell, and reached for Logan's throat with the intention of breaking his neck.

His hand stalled out, frozen in midair, unable to move no matter how hard he tried.

Logan gave Drake a sly grin that made him look eerily beautiful. "You can't hurt me."

"Fuck you," growled Drake. "You'd better pray Helen makes it out of this safely or you're going to see just how much I *can* hurt you."

"Temper, temper," chided Logan.

"We don't have time for this," said Zach. "Helen may be able to slip away the way Lexi did."

Zach was right and Drake shoved his desire to kill Logan from his thoughts.

Nicholas handed Drake his sword, which he belted

around his waist as he shoved his feet into his shoes. Screw socks. He was out the door, heading for the helipad with Zach and Nicholas close on his heels.

"We're coming with you," said Nicholas.

Drake nodded, feeling a flicker of relief to have his friends at his back. He was going to need all the help he could get.

Why did it have to be a cave? A mine and now a cave. Helen was beginning to develop a serious fear of close, dark spaces. Why couldn't the Synestryn enjoy a nice, open beach or maybe even lurk in an eerie forest? At least that way there wouldn't have been tons of dirt and stone over her head to come crushing down on her. That would have made this job a whole lot easier.

Helen steeled her resolve and tugged on Drake's power. It was easier now than it had been, which made her think that he must be getting closer. She'd felt the moment her sleep trick had failed and knew he was angry and coming right for her. She had a two-hour head start, and prayed that was enough.

Helen remembered Drake telling her that the Synestryn would be able to see her for what she was now, and the idea of walking into that cave, glowing like a lighthouse, didn't sit well. So she experimented with turning herself invisible—like Drake's sword. She tried making her body see-through, but that didn't work and it hurt like hell, so instead, she urged the light to flow around her, rather than bounce off her, and that seemed to work fairly well. She checked out her reflection in the rearview mirror of the van and all she saw was a wavering spot where her head was supposed to be. It looked like heat coming off pavement in the distance, but in the dark cave, it might be enough to cloak herself. She sure hoped so.

She gathered the monster locator and a tire iron out of the back of the van—just in case—and hid in the trees near the cave. The sun was going to set any minute, and she didn't want to be in the way of all those Synestryn coming out to hunt.

Plus, there might be bats in there, which was too icky to think about. Thank goodness her hair was braided so they couldn't get tangled in it. She still wasn't convinced that was a myth and she wasn't taking any chances.

She turned on the night vision and her super hearing and watched as a swarm of monsters flowed out of the cave, snarling and clicking and howling.

Helen was sure her heartbeat would give her away and she prayed that all the noise the monsters were making would cover the frightened pounding. She held her breath and imagined pushing the air so that her scent was carried away from the monsters.

A light breeze cooled the sweat on her skin.

A pair of glowing green eyes swung her way and the sgath sniffed the air as if sensing her. It cocked its furry wolf head to the side in confusion and after a moment, bounded off to follow the rest of its pack.

Helen was shaking so hard her muscles ached and she had to make a conscious effort to relax her clenched jaw.

The last monster had been gone for several minutes before she found the courage to move into the mouth of the cave. The entrance was small and she had to crouch low to get in. Her enhanced vision made it seem bright as day inside, but she could feel the oppressive darkness clinging to her skin, eating at her resolve.

Unlike the mine, there were no tunnels leading in different directions. The cave opened up into a long, narrow hole that widened into a larger chamber. It was easily a hundred feet across and twenty feet at the widest point. Dampness and a mineral smell scented the air beneath the heavy, rotting animal smell of the Synestryn. In the distance, she could hear the steady drip of water and the gurgling, wet sound of a kajmela.

Two of them, in fact. And they were headed right toward her.

Her invisibility had worked well enough on things with eyes, but the kajmelas had none. They somehow sensed her presence.

She dropped the invisibility to conserve power, then turned up her vision to X-ray level, and sure enough, inside the bigger kajmela was Kevin's sword along with some other things that looked suspiciously like human bones that she didn't want to think about. The hilt looked corroded and pitted, but the blade was pristine and wickedly sharp. Whatever stomach acid the kajmelas had, it couldn't harm the Theronai's blade.

Fire.

The word flared in her head, though whether it was her idea or Drake's, she couldn't tell. Either way, it left her terrified, sweating and shaking.

She felt Drake getting closer, felt his anger and sense of betrayal that she'd left him. She'd done it for him, and all her noble intentions would be wasted if she didn't get that sword back and release him from her before he got here.

Helen heard Sibyl's voice ring clearly in her mind. *If you try to fight the Synestryn beside Drake without the ability to call fire, then Drake will die.*

She couldn't let that happen.

The kajmelas moved forward, slowly oozing over the cave floor. Fire was the only thing that could stop them.

Helen tried to push aside her fear of fire, but it had

been her companion for so long, she couldn't remember ever living without it. It was a part of her. Irrational. Uncontrollable.

It was going to kill Drake.

She raised her hand toward the kajmela and pretended she wasn't afraid. She closed her eyes and gathered Drake's power inside herself. She remembered what she'd seen Gilda do and forced herself to mimic that frightening act of calling fire. Heat built in her chest, making it hard to breathe. She had to get rid of the heat before it killed her, so she tried to shove it out through her fingertips. She heard a sizzling sound and opened her eyes to see her fingertips blacken. The burning pain hit her then and a sob tore from her body.

She pushed harder, trying to drive the searing heat from her, but no fire came out. Not even a spark.

She heard deep male voices echoing nearby. He was here. And he was going to die if she didn't do something to stop it.

She pulled hard on Drake's power and let it fill her even more. Pressure built inside her, and the band around her throat heated under the strain of funneling so much energy. Her insides felt as if they were boiling and the skin under the luceria started to sizzle. The scent of burning flesh filled her nose, making her gag.

"Helen!" shouted Drake.

The kajmelas hesitated as they sensed new prey.

More energy filled her, stretching her, crushing her organs until the pain threatened to make her pass out. She had all the power she needed to fry those kajmelas into a greasy puddle, but she couldn't find the courage to let it out in the form of fire. Her instincts screamed at her that this was it—the moment of her vision.

Drake came into view, followed closely by other men,

but she couldn't see them clearly. Her eyes burned and felt as if they would fly out of her head from the massive pressure inside her, but she forced herself to look at Drake.

His sword was drawn, gleaming with the need for violence. His face was a mask of pain and rage and his eyes glowed with golden fury as they met hers. His body was coiled to strike, strong and solid and designed to bring her so much pleasure. Just looking at him was a joy to her.

She loved him.

There was no denying it any longer—no putting off thinking about it until things calmed down. She was out of time. She could feel the power of her love for him beating at her to act. Sibyl had said to let her love for Drake guide her, and she would. Her last act on this earth would be one of courage and sacrifice and love for Drake.

The kajmelas turned toward bigger prey and oozed out tentacles of oily sludge toward Drake.

Helen accepted her fate. She embraced it. She was going to burn to death, but she was going to take those nasty fuckers with her so they couldn't hurt anyone else.

She lifted her hand toward the monsters, ignored the clamoring fear slicing her belly, and let the fire come for her. At first, there was a pitiful sputtering of sparks from her hand and she couldn't contain a frightened yelp.

The kajmela closest to Drake struck out with more speed than she'd thought possible and her fear for him overcame her fear of fire. Power funneled down her arm, making her bones vibrate with the force of it. She let out a harsh battle cry and flames shot from her fingers, engulfing both kajmelas in a cylinder of orange and red.

A sharp hissing scream and the rank smell of burning oil and flesh filled the cave.

The kajmelas amoebic bodies pulsed and contorted as they tried to escape the fire.

Helen gave them nowhere to run. She siphoned more of Drake's power away from him, turned it into flames, and blasted the kajmelas again.

Heat scalded her fingers and neck as she forced more fire from her body. Too much. She was losing control of it now and it spread beyond her fingers. Flames danced along her arm, racing up until they engulfed her body. A ragged cry of pain was wrenched from her chest and she gritted her teeth to cut off the horrible sound. Through the flickering, wavering heat, she saw Drake struggle against his friends' grip as they held him back. He was shouting something, but she couldn't understand the words—couldn't hear over the hungry roar of the fire consuming her.

Seconds slid by in agonizing slowness. She'd lost control over the power. She couldn't stop it from streaming into her, nor could she stop herself from making all that power burn.

The sound of her screams faded into a hoarse echo of pain she couldn't silence herself. Nothing inside her worked.

The flow of energy from Drake was suddenly turned off, but the fire still burned. She tried to remember what to do to stop it, but her brain couldn't function inside so much pain.

And then Drake was there, right in front of her with Kevin's sword in hand, his chest bare and his shirt wrapped around the smoking hilt. She could see Drake's features through the flames, see the tears running down his cheeks. And he was smiling—giving her that proud

smile she had seen too many times in her life to count—
the one that signified her death.

Drake was safe. He had Kevin's sword. It was over.

Helen let the pain win. She gave up fighting it and let
the flames have her.

Chapter 23

Drake caught Helen's body as she collapsed. The dying flames licking over her body burned him, but he didn't care. He needed to hold her.

"She's going to be okay, right?" he asked Logan. Her skin was blistered in places, but he'd seen worse. Hell, he'd felt worse. And Helen had saved him with her blood.

"Let me see," said Logan. He ran his elegant hands over her body, checking for damage. Drake couldn't even bring himself to care that another man was touching her. He was too glad she'd survived.

"The burns are superficial, but she shouldn't have had any at all," said Logan. "What went wrong? Why didn't her instincts keep the fire from burning her?"

Drake smoothed singed hair back from her face. He loved her so much it made his chest ache. He nearly lost her. "She was afraid. Maybe that shorted out her self-preservation instincts."

"I didn't think she'd ever be able to call fire." Logan settled his hands over Helen's forehead for a long moment and then his eyes widened in shock. He swallowed hard, looking a little sick.

"What?" demanded Drake.

Logan's too-pretty face went pale and his hands shook. "She's, uh . . ." He trailed off, staring at Helen in shock.

Drake grabbed Logan's collar and gave him a rough shake. Punishing pain shot up his arm, but he ignored it. "She's what?"

"She's changed."

Drake felt a nauseating sense of dread fill him. Sanguinar were not easily spooked. "Changed how?"

"That vision she had . . . it was protecting her."

"From what?"

"From becoming what she was meant to be too soon—before she was ready."

"And what was she meant to be?" demanded Drake, shaking Logan again to get him to focus. And again, he ignored the zing of pain that shake cost him.

Logan shook his head. "A weapon against the Synestryn."

"All the Theronai are," said Drake, wishing Logan would make some sense.

"Not like her."

There wasn't time to dwell on that right now. "Just heal her. Take whatever blood you need and make her better."

Logan gave an uneasy nod and went to work.

Helen woke up. That alone was enough to stun her silent.

She was in Drake's bed and he was wrapped around her, holding her like he was never going to let her go. That was really nice.

Sunlight streamed in through the windows, so she'd lost at least a few hours, but she still couldn't believe she was alive. A quiet sense of joy warmed her and she felt something she hadn't had for a long, long time: hope for the future.

A future with Drake, if she was lucky.

"You're awake," he said in a low voice.

"Yeah." It came out as little more than a rough croak of sound.

Drake shifted and lifted her up so she could drink from a cup he offered. She felt weak, but nothing hurt, which was an unexpected surprise. A quick scan of her arms showed nothing but new, pink skin.

"What happened?" she asked.

"You blasted the kajmelas to hell. The fire got a little out of control, but Logan patched you up good as new."

There was an odd quality to his voice that set off warning bells in her head. She pushed herself up so she could lean back against the headboard and put enough distance between them so she could get a good look at Drake.

He looked tired, strained, but that's not what had bothered her. It was something else. Something she remembered seeing in him when they first met—a kind of unnatural tension that radiated through his body. Pain.

"Did you get hurt?" she asked.

He was wearing a long-sleeved mock turtleneck and jeans that completely hid his body. Maybe he'd been injured and didn't want her to know. She couldn't think of any other reason he'd be so heavily clothed in the middle of summer.

"I got a few burns. Logan fixed me up, too. Don't worry." He gave her a warm smile and kissed her forehead.

Helen reached out, trying to poke around in his head to figure out what was wrong, but she hit a wall. She couldn't feel a thing.

Her hand strayed to her neck, which was bare. "It came off."

"Yeah. We found the sword, remember?"

She did, in the pain-hazed recesses of her memory. He'd picked up the hot metal using his shirt. He'd been beautifully bare chested and the leaves were falling from his lifemark like snow.

Helen's eyes went back to his chest, now covered with gray cotton. That's what he was hiding. "Take off your shirt," she ordered.

He grinned and winked, but she could see the subtle lines of strain around his mouth. "You're too tired for that right now. Just lie down and rest."

She was tired, but not so much that she wouldn't fight him over this. "Take off the damn shirt and let me see."

She reached for the hem of his shirt, but his hands collected hers and held them against his hard abdomen. His face was solemn, his eyes shadowed with pain. "I look like I did before I met you."

Probably felt like he did before, too. "You're hurting."

He shrugged as if it didn't matter, but at least he hadn't lied.

She freed one hand before he could stop her and fished under his collar in search of the luceria. It was there, around his neck, slippery and warm from his body heat. Drake's hand tugged hers out and she let him, feeling a heavy sense of loss.

Helen glanced at his ring. It had returned to its original iridescent, silvery mix of too many colors to count. It didn't remember her at all, which, for some reason, hurt her feelings.

But not as much as the fact that Drake didn't want her to wear the luceria again. She'd tricked him, forced him to sleep and gone after Kevin's sword by herself, but she'd done it for his own good. Surely he had to know that. He wasn't stupid.

There was a light rap on the doorway leading into the bedroom. Sibyl was standing there, dressed in pale pink today, clutching her black-eyed doll to her chest.

"Sibyl," said Drake, in a shocked tone. "I wasn't expecting you."

"No one ever does," said the little girl. She looked right at Helen. "We have to talk."

"I'll be right outside." Drake started to get up, but Sibyl held up a dainty hand.

"Stay, Theronai."

Helen felt Drake tense, but he settled back beside her, keeping a tight hold on her hand. "What is it?"

"Helen has some questions for me and I wanted to make sure I had time to answer them before I left."

"Left?" asked Drake. "Where are you going?"

"It's not important. Helen? Your questions?"

The creepy girl was right. Helen did have some questions, she just hadn't been awake long enough to think about them, until now. "You said that if I didn't like the vision of my death, I should choose another. You also said my vision couldn't be avoided."

"And it wasn't."

"But it wasn't a vision of my death."

"No."

"Why didn't you tell me that?"

"You didn't ask. You only asked if it was real, which it obviously was. You also asked how you could avoid it, which you couldn't."

"But why didn't you just tell me that I wasn't going to die then?"

"Because if I'd told you that, you *would* have died. It was your acceptance—your willingness to sacrifice your own life for someone else—that gave you the strength to do what you had to do. I had to know you were strong enough."

"Strong enough? For what?" asked Drake.

Sibyl's arm tightened around her doll and for a moment, she looked like a frightened little girl. "Things are changing and the Gray Lady isn't able to fight off what's coming without help. The only thing strong enough to defeat the Synestryn is love and I had to know that Helen had that kind of power inside her."

"Love?" asked Drake, looking at Helen with a hopeful expression.

"You should tell him," said Sibyl. "He's insecure and needs to hear the words."

"I am not insecure," objected Drake, sounding insulted.

Sibyl rolled her blue eyes in disgust and left the room.

"So?" asked Drake with his brows raised. "Was she right?"

Sibyl was right. He was insecure about her love for him, which was so endearing she had to hold back her smile. "Yes."

"Then say it," he demanded. He turned aggressive and straddled her lap, looming over her.

Helen thought he was too cute for words and she had to put him out of his misery. "I love you, Drake."

He gave her a satisfied smile. "About damn time, too."

"What do you mean, about time? I've known you for all of three days."

He leaned closer and she could see the golden shards in his eyes lit with happiness. "A lot has happened in those three days, though."

"More than enough," she agreed.

"I don't want you to leave me. I'll let you go if that's

what you want, but I don't want you to leave me. Not ever." He whispered the words as if ashamed to say them aloud.

"I don't want to leave you, Drake."

"Because you love me?" he insisted.

Helen nodded. She had the feeling he wasn't going to give up on making her say it any time soon. And that was fine with her. "Because I love you."

"No pity, right?"

"None. How could I pity someone as big and manly as you?"

"Damn right," he said. "So, do you want to wear my luceria again?"

His casual attitude broke her heart because she knew how much it cost him. He was giving her every chance to turn him down without guilt, which only made her love him more.

"I do."

Drake gave a relieved nod and pulled off his shirt.

One solitary leaf hung from the tree and it was shriveled and dry, barely clinging to the branch. No wonder he'd been in so much pain. He was much worse off than he'd been before she met him.

Helen sucked in a breath and reached her hand out to him. "Oh, Drake."

"No pity," he growled at her. "Remember."

Helen bit her lower lip to keep it from trembling. "No pity. Just love."

Helen reached up and willed the luceria to fall off. The band slithered from around his neck and pooled in her palm. She handed it to him and he took it with shaking hands. "So, what do I promise this time?" she asked.

"That's up to you. I'll take what I can get and try not to ask for anything more. I swear it."

Helen lifted her hair. "All right, then I promise to wear the luceria and fight by your side until every last one of the Synestryn are gone."

"But that may take forever. And you're one of us. You're going to live for centuries now, so you'll be with me a really long time."

"That was kind of the point. Unless you think you'll get sick of me."

"Hell no. I love you, Helen. And it's too late to go back on your word now. You're mine." He fastened the necklace around her throat and she welcomed the slippery weight once again.

A flurry of feelings swelled inside her, but they were all good—overwhelming in their intensity, but good. Drake's love, his hope for their future, his resolve to keep her safe and by his side forever.

He groaned and pulled her to him for a kiss. Helen melted into him, amazed once again at her good fortune. Not only had she got a new life; she got to spend it with Drake. She was the world's luckiest woman.

Drake pulled away enough to smile down at her with a sexy glow lighting his brown eyes. "I'll show you lucky."

And he proceeded to do just that.

Epilogue

Canaranth tried not to display any signs of fear as he stood before his master's giant stone desk. The black surface gleamed in the flickering candlelight of the Synestryn lord's office.

His master, Zillah, steepled his pale fingers. Those hands looked almost human—only slightly longer with too-dark fingernails. Zillah's face was also very human looking. He could go out in public wearing only a hat to shadow his face and no one knew he didn't belong among the cattle.

Canaranth didn't even need the hat. As long as no one saw his eyes, they thought he was completely human. It had been handy on more than one occasion, and tonight was no exception.

"They found the Sentinel sword, sire," said Canaranth. He was proud that his voice hardly wavered at all. "It was an excellent distraction."

Zillah leaned back in his leather chair, smiling. Sharp, pointed teeth glowed in the candlelight. "The blooded child?"

"She's downstairs with the others. She's still young enough that there's time to alter her properly."

"And the Sentinels?"

"They are congregating at their compound, preparing for our attack, as you planned. None of them were guarding her home and her parents were no problem. I doubt the Sentinels even know she exists."

"We will keep it that way."

"And the sword?" asked Canaranth.

"Let them have it. The girl is worth the loss of the sword." Zillah smiled, baring more of his sharp teeth. "She will give us beautiful children."

ALSO AVAILABLE

FROM

Shannon K. Butcher

FINDING THE LOST
The Sentinel Wars

Sentinel warrior Paul has been searching for
centuries for a woman like Andra. To find her,
he strikes a bargain with a bloodhunter that
could cost him his life. Now, his desire for
Andra threatens to destroy his much-needed
control. Against her wishes, Andra agrees to
join Paul on a journey fraught with danger—
and leading directly to the Synestryn who
victimized her family eight years ago.

S0047